**Praise for #1 *New York Times* bestselling author
Linda Lael Miller**

"[Linda Lael] Miller's masterful ability to create
living, breathing characters never flags; combined
with a taut story line and vivid prose, Miller's
romance won't disappoint."
—*Publishers Weekly* on *McKettrick's Pride*
(starred review)

"Miller has found a perfect niche with charming
western romances and cowboys who will set readers'
hearts aflutter."
—*RT Book Reviews*

"Miller tugs at the heartstrings as few authors can."
—*Publishers Weekly*

**Praise for *New York Times* bestselling author
B.J. Daniels**

"[B.J.] Daniels is truly an expert at Western romantic
suspense."
—*RT Book Reviews* on *Atonement*

"After reading *Mercy*, B.J. Daniels will absolutely
move to the top of your list of must-read authors."
—*Fresh Fiction*

The daughter of a town marshal, **Linda Lael Miller** is a *New York Times* bestselling author of more than one hundred historical and contemporary novels. Linda's books have hit #1 on the *New York Times* bestseller list seven times. Raised in Northport, Washington, she now lives in Spokane, Washington. For more information on Linda and her latest releases, visit her website at lindalaelmiller.com.

New York Times and *USA TODAY* bestselling author **B.J. Daniels** lives in Montana with her husband, Parker, and three springer spaniels. When not writing, she quilts, boats and plays tennis. Contact her at bjdaniels.com, or on Facebook at facebook.com/pages/bj-daniels, or Twitter, @bjdanielsauthor.

#1 *New York Times* Bestselling Author

LINDA LAEL MILLER

SIERRA'S HOMECOMING

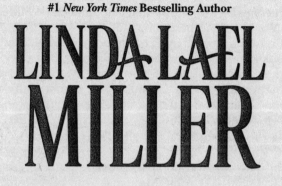

HARLEQUIN® BESTSELLING AUTHOR COLLECTION

ISBN-13: 978-0-373-01027-1

Sierra's Homecoming
Copyright © 2015 by Harlequin Books S.A.

The publisher acknowledges the copyright holders
of the individual works as follows:

Sierra's Homecoming
Copyright © 2006 by Linda Lael Miller

Montana Royalty
Copyright © 2008 by Barbara Heinlein

Recycling programs
for this product may
not exist in your area.

Printed in U.S.A.

CONTENTS

**Also available from Linda Lael Miller
and HQN Books**

SIERRA'S HOMECOMING

Linda Lael Miller

To Little Angels Everywhere

CHAPTER ONE

Present Day

"STAY IN THE CAR," Sierra McKettrick told her seven-year-old son, Liam.

He fixed her with an owlish gaze, peering through the lenses of his horn-rimmed glasses. "I want to see the graves, too," he told her, and put a mittened hand to the passenger-side door handle to make his point.

"Another time," she answered firmly. Part of her knew it was irrational to think a visit to the cemetery could provoke an asthma attack, but when it came to Liam's health, she was taking no chances.

A brief stare-down ensued, and Sierra prevailed, but barely.

"It's not fair," Liam said, yet he sounded resigned. He didn't normally give up so easily, but they'd just driven almost nonstop all the way from Florida to northern Arizona, and he was tired.

"Welcome to the real world," Sierra replied. She set the emergency brake, left the engine running with the heat on High, and got out of the ancient station wagon she'd bought on credit years before.

Standing ankle-deep in a patch of ragged snow, she took in her surroundings. Ordinary people were buried in churchyards and public cemeteries when they died, she reflected, feeling peevish. The McKettricks were a law unto themselves, living *or* dead. They weren't content with a mere plot, like other families. Oh, no. They had to have a place all their own, with a view.

And what a view it was.

Shoving her hands into the pockets of her cloth coat, which was nearly as decrepit as her car, Sierra turned to survey the Triple M Ranch, sprawling in every direction, well beyond the range of her vision. Red mesas and buttes, draped in a fine lacing of snow. Copses of majestic white oaks, growing at intervals along a wide and shining stream. Expanses of pastureland, and even the occasional cactus, a stranger to the high country, a misplaced wayfarer, there by mistake.

Like her.

A flash of resentment rose suddenly within Sierra, and a moment or two passed before she recognized the emotion for what it was: not her own opinion, but that of her late father, Hank Breslin.

When it came to the McKettricks, Sierra *had* no opinions that she could honestly claim, because she didn't know these people, except by reputation.

She'd taken their name for one reason and one reason only—because that was part of the deal. Liam needed health care, and she couldn't provide it. Eve McKettrick—Sierra's biological mother—had set up a medical trust fund for her grandson, but there were strings attached.

With the McKettricks, she heard her father say, as surely as if he were standing there beside her, *there are always strings attached.*

"Be quiet," Sierra said, out loud. She was grateful for Eve's help, and if she had to take the McKettrick name and live on the Triple M Ranch for a year to meet the conditions, so be it. It wasn't as if she had anyplace better to go.

Resolutely she approached the cemetery entrance, walked under the ornate metal archway forming the word "McKettrick" in graceful cursive.

A life-size bronze statue of a man on horseback, broad-shouldered and imposing, with a bandanna at his throat and a six-gun riding on his hip, took center stage.

Angus McKettrick, the patriarch. The founder of the Triple M, and the dynasty. Sierra knew little about him, but as she looked up into that hard, determined face, shaped by the rigors of life in the nineteenth century, she felt a kinship.

Ruthless old bastard, said the voice of Hank Breslin. *That's where McKettricks get their arrogance. From him.*

"Be quiet," Sierra repeated, thrusting her hands deeper into her coat pockets. She stood in silence for a long moment, listening to the rattle-throated hum of the station wagon's engine, the lonely cry of a nearby bird, the thrum of blood in her ears. A piney scent spiced the air.

Sierra turned, saw the marble angels marking the graves of Angus McKettrick's wives—Georgia, mother of Rafe, Kade and Jeb. Concepcion, mother of Kate.

Look for Holt and Lorelei, Eve had told her, the last time they'd spoken over the telephone. *That's our part of the family.*

Sierra caught sight of other bronze statues, smaller than Angus's but no less impressive in their detail. They were works of art, museum pieces, and if they hadn't been solidly anchored in cement, they probably would have been stolen. It said something about the Mc-

Kettrick legend, she supposed, that there had been no vandalism in this lonely, wind-blown place.

Jeb McKettrick, the youngest of the brothers, was represented by a cowboy with his six-gun drawn; his wife, Chloe, by a slender woman in pioneer dress, shading her eyes with one hand and smiling. Their children, grandchildren, great- and a few great-great-grandchildren surrounded them, their costly headstones laid out in neat rows, like the streets of a western town.

Next was Kade McKettrick, easy in his skin, wearing a six-shooter, like his brother, but with an open book in his hand. His wife, Mandy, wore trousers, a loose-fitting shirt, boots and a hat, and held a shotgun. Like Chloe, she was smiling. Judging by the number of other graves around theirs, these two had also been prolific parents.

The statue of Rafe McKettrick revealed a big, powerfully built man with a stubborn set to his jaw. His bride, Emmeline, stood close against his side; their arms were linked and she rested her head against the outside of his upper arm.

Sierra smiled. Again, their progeny was plentiful.

The last statue brought up an unexpected surge of emotion in Sierra. Here, then, was Holt, half brother to Rafe, Kade and Jeb, and to Kate. In his long trail coat, he looked both handsome and tough. A pair of very detailed ammunition belts criss-crossed his chest, and the badge pinned to his wide lapel read Texas Ranger.

Sierra stared into those bronze eyes and, once again, felt something stir deep inside her. I came from this man, she thought. We've got the same DNA.

Liam gave a jarring blast of the car horn, impatient to get to the ranch house that would be their home for the next twelve months.

Sierra waved in acknowledgment but moved on to

the statue of Lorelei. She was mounted on a mule, long, lace-trimmed skirts spilling on either side of her impossibly small waist, face shadowed, not by a sunbonnet but by a man's hat. Her spirited gaze rested lovingly on her husband, Holt.

Liam laid on the horn.

Fearing he might decide to take the wheel and drive to the ranch house on his own, Sierra turned reluctantly from the markers and followed a path littered with pine needles and the dead leaves of the six towering white oaks that shared the space, heading back to the car.

Back to her son.

"Are all the McKettricks *dead?*" Liam asked, when Sierra settled into the driver's seat and fastened the belt.

"No," Sierra answered, waiting for some stray part of herself to finish meandering among those graves, making the acquaintance of ancestors, and catch up. "*We're* McKettricks, and we're not dead. Neither is your grandmother, or Meg." She knew there were cousins, too, descended from Rafe, Kade and Jeb, but it was too big a subject to explain to a seven-year-old boy. Besides, she was still trying to square them all away in her own mind.

"I thought my name was Liam *Breslin,*" the little boy said practically.

It should have been Liam Douglas, Sierra thought, remembering her first and only lover. As always, when Liam's father, Adam, came to mind, she felt a pang, a complicated mixture of passion, sorrow and helpless fury. She and Adam had never been married, so she'd given Liam her maiden name.

"We're McKettricks now," Sierra said with a sigh. "You'll understand when you're older."

She backed the car out carefully, keenly aware of the

steep descent on all sides, and made the wide turn that would take them back on to the network of dirt roads bisecting the Triple M.

"I can understand *now*," Liam asserted, having duly pondered the matter in his solemn way. "After all, I'm *gifted*."

"You may be gifted," Sierra replied, concentrating on her driving, "but you're still seven."

"Do I get to be a cowboy and ride bucking broncs and stuff like that?"

Sierra suppressed a shudder. "No," she said.

"That bites," Liam answered, folding his arms and settling deeper into the heavy nylon coat she'd bought him on the road, when they'd reached the first of the cold-weather states. "What's the good of living on a ranch if you can't be a cowboy?"

CHAPTER TWO

THE ELDERLY STATION WAGON banged into the yard, bald
tires crunching half-thawed gravel, and came to an ob-
streperous stop. Travis Reid paused behind the horse
trailer hitched to Jesse McKettrick's mud-splattered
black truck, pushed his hat to the back of his head
with one leather-gloved finger and grinned, waiting
for something to fall off the rig. Nothing did, which
just went to prove that the age of miracles was not past.

Jesse appeared at the back of the trailer, leading
old Baldy by his halter rope. "Who's that?" he asked,
squinting in the wintry late afternoon sunshine.

Travis spared him no more than a glance. "A long-
lost relative of yours, unless I miss my guess," he said
easily.

The station wagon belched some smoke and died.
Travis figured it for a permanent condition. He looked
on with interest as a good-looking woman climbed out
from behind the wheel, looked the old car over, and gave
the driver's-side door a good kick with her right foot.

She was a McKettrick, all right. Of the female per-
suasion, too.

Jesse left Baldy standing to jump down from the bed
of the trailer and lower the ramp to the ground. "Meg's
half sister?" he asked. "The one who grew up in Mexico with her crazy, drunken father?"

"Reckon so," Travis said. He and Meg communicated

regularly, most often by email, and she'd filled him in on Sierra as far as she could. Nobody in the family knew her very well, including her mother, Eve, so the information was sparse. She had a seven-year-old son—now getting out of the car—and she'd been serving cocktails in Florida for the last few years, and that was about all Travis knew about her. As Meg's caretaker and resident horse trainer, not to mention her friend, Travis had stocked the cupboards and refrigerator, made sure the temperamental furnace was working and none of the plumbing had frozen, and started up Meg's SUV every day, just to make sure it was running.

From the looks of that station wagon, it was a good thing he'd followed the boss-lady's orders.

"You gonna help me with this horse," Jesse asked testily, "or just stand there gawking?"

Travis chuckled. "Right now," he said, "I'm all for gawking."

Sierra McKettrick was tall and slender, with short, gleaming brown hair the color of a good chestnut horse. Her eyes were huge and probably blue, though she was still a stride or two too far away for him to tell.

Jesse swore and stomped back up the ramp, making plenty of noise as he did so. Like most of the McKettricks, Jesse was used to getting his way, and while he was a known womanizer, he'd evidently dismissed Sierra out of hand. After all, she was a blood relative— no sense driving his herd into *that* canyon.

Travis took a step toward the woman and the boy, who was staring at him with his mouth open.

"Is this Meg's house?" Sierra asked.

"Yes," Travis said, putting out his hand, pulling it back to remove his work gloves, and offering it again. "Travis Reid," he told her.

"Sierra Bres—McKettrick," she replied. Her grip was firm. And her eyes were definitely blue. The kind of blue that pierces something in a man's middle. She smiled, but tentatively. Somewhere along the line, she'd learned to be sparing with her smiles. "This is my son, Liam."

"Howdy," Liam said, squaring his small shoulders.

Travis grinned. "Howdy," he replied. Meg had said the boy had health problems, but he looked pretty sound to Travis.

"That sure is an ugly horse," Liam announced, pointing towards the trailer.

Travis turned. Baldy stood spraddle-footed, midway down the ramp, a miserable gray specimen of a critter with pink eyes and liver-colored splotches all over his mangy hide.

"Sure is," Travis agreed, and glowered at Jesse for palming the animal off on him. It was like him to pull off a dramatic last-minute rescue, then leave the functional aspects of the problem to somebody else.

Jesse flashed a grin, and for a moment, Travis felt territorial, wanted to set himself between Sierra and her boy, the pair of them, and one of his oldest friends. He felt off balance, somehow, as though he'd been ambushed. What the hell was *that* all about?

"Is that a buckin' bronc?" Liam asked, venturing a step toward Baldy.

Sierra reached out quickly, caught hold of the fur-trimmed hood on the kid's coat and yanked him back. Cold sunlight glinted off the kid's glasses, making his eyes invisible.

Jesse laughed. "Back in the day," he said, "Baldy was a rodeo horse. Cowboys quivered in their boots when they drew him to ride. Now, as you can see, he's a little past his prime."

"And you would be—?" Sierra asked, with a touch of coolness to her tone. Maybe she was the one woman out of a thousand who could see Jesse McKettrick for what he was—a good-natured case of very bad news.

"Your cousin Jesse."

Sierra sized him up, took in his battered jeans, work shirt, sheepskin coat and very expensive boots. "Descended from…?"

The McKettricks talked like that. Every one of them could trace their lineage back to old Angus, by a variety of paths, and while there would be hell to pay if anybody riled them as a bunch, they mostly kept to their own branch of the family tree.

"Jeb," Jesse said.

Sierra nodded.

Liam's attention remained fixed on the horse. "Can I ride him?"

"Sure," Jesse replied.

"No way," said Sierra, at exactly the same moment.

Travis felt sorry for the kid, and it must have shown in his face, because Sierra's gaze narrowed on him.

"We've had a long trip," she said. "I guess we'll just go inside."

"Make yourselves at home," Travis said, gesturing toward the house. "Don't worry about your bags. Jesse and I'll carry them in for you."

She considered, probably wondering if she'd be obligated in any way if she agreed, then nodded. Catching Liam by the hood of his coat again, she got him turned from the horse and hustled him toward the front door.

"Too bad we're kin," Jesse said, following Sierra with his eyes.

"Too bad," Travis agreed mildly, though privately he didn't believe it was such a bad thing at all.

THE HOUSE WAS a long, sprawling structure, with two stories and a wraparound porch. Sierra's most immediate impression was of substance and practicality, rather than elegance, and she felt a subtle interior shift, as if she'd been a long time lost in a strange, winding street, thick with fog, and suddenly found herself standing at her own front door.

"Those guys are *real cowboys*," Liam said, once they were inside.

Sierra nodded distractedly, taking in the pegged wood floors, gleaming with the patina of venerable age, the double doors and steep staircase on the right, the high ceilings, the antique grandfather clock ticking ponderously beside the door. She peeked into a spacious living room, probably called a parlor when the house was new, and admired the enormous natural-rock fireplace, with its raised hearth and wood-nook. Worn but colorful rugs gave some relief to the otherwise uncompromisingly masculine decor of leather couches and chairs and tables of rough-hewn pine, as did the piano set in an alcove of floor-to-ceiling windows.

An odd nostalgia overtook Sierra; she'd never set foot on the Triple M before that day, let alone entered the home of Holt and Lorelei McKettrick, but she might have, if her dad hadn't snatched her the day Eve filed for divorce, and carried her off to San Miguel de Allende to share his expatriate lifestyle. She might have spent summers here, as Meg had, picking blackberries, wading in mountain streams, riding horses. Instead, she'd run barefoot through the streets of San Miguel, with no more memory of her mother than a faint scent

of expensive perfume, sometimes encountered among
the waves of tourists who frequented the markets, shops
and restaurants of her home town.

Liam tugged at the sleeve of her coat. "Mom?"

She snapped out of her reverie, looked down at him,
and smiled. "You hungry, bud?"

Liam nodded solemnly, but brightened when the
door bumped open and Travis came in, lugging two
suitcases.

Travis cleared his throat, as though embarrassed.
"Plenty of grub in the kitchen," he said. "Shall I put
this stuff upstairs?"

"Yes," Sierra said. "Thanks." At least that way she'd
know which rooms were hers and Liam's without having to ask. She might have been concerned, sharing
the place with Travis, but Meg had told her he lived in
a trailer out by the barn. What Meg hadn't mentioned
was that her resident caretaker was in his early thirties,
not his sixties, as Sierra had imagined, and too attractive for comfort, with his lean frame, blue-green eyes
and dark-blond hair in need of a trim.

She blushed as these thoughts filled her mind, and
shuffled Liam quickly toward the kitchen.

It was a large room, with the same plank floors she'd
seen in the front of the house and modern appliances,
strangely juxtaposed with the black, chrome-trimmed
wood cookstove occupying the far-left-hand corner. The
table was long and rustic, with benches on either side
and a chair at each end.

"Tables like that are a tradition with the Mc-
Kettricks," a male voice said from just behind her.

Sierra jumped, startled, and turned to see Jesse in
the doorway.

"Sorry," he said. He was handsome, Sierra thought.

His coloring was similar to Travis's, and so was his build, and yet the two men didn't resemble each other at all.

"No problem," Sierra said.

Liam wrenched open the refrigerator. "Bologna!" he yelled triumphantly.

"Whoopee," Sierra replied, with a dryness that was lost on her son. "If there's bologna, there must be white bread, too."

"Jesse!" Travis's voice, from the direction of the front door. "Get out here and give me a hand!"

Jesse grinned, nodded affably to Sierra and vanished.

Sierra took off her coat, hung it from a peg next to the back door, and gestured for Liam to remove his, too. He complied, then went straight back to the bologna. He found a loaf of bread in a colorful polka-dot bag and started to build a sandwich.

Watching him, Sierra felt a faint brush of sorrow against the back of her heart. Liam was good at doing things on his own; he'd had a lot of practice, with her working the night shift at the club and sleeping days. Old Mrs. Davis from the apartment across the hall had been a conscientious babysitter, but hardly a mother figure.

She put coffee on to brew, once Liam was settled on a bench at the table. He'd chosen the side against the wall, so he could watch her moving about the kitchen.

"Cool place," he observed, between bites, "but it's haunted."

Sierra took a can of soup from a shelf, opened it and dumped the contents into a saucepan, placing it on the modern gas stove before answering. Liam was an imaginative child, often saying surprising things. Rather than responding instantly, Sierra usually tried to let a couple of beats pass before she answered.

"What makes you say that?"

"Don't know," Liam said, chewing. They'd had a drive-through breakfast, but that had been hours ago, and he was obviously starving.

Another jab of guilt struck Sierra, keener than the one before. "Come on," she prodded. "You must have had a reason." Of course he'd had a reason, she thought. They'd just been to a graveyard, so it was natural that death would be on his mind. She should have waited, made the pilgrimage on her own, instead of dragging Liam along.

Liam looked thoughtful. "The air sort of…buzzes," he said. "Can I make another sandwich?"

"Only if you promise to have some of this soup first."

"Deal," Liam said.

An old china cabinet stood against a far wall, near the cookstove, and Sierra approached it, even though she didn't intend to use any of the dishes inside. Priceless antiques, every one.

Her family had eaten off those dishes. Generations of them.

Her gaze caught on a teapot, sturdy looking and, at the same time, exquisite. Spellbound, she opened the glass doors of the cabinet and reached inside to touch the piece, ever so lightly, with just the tips of her fingers.

"Soup's boiling over," Liam said mildly.

Sierra gasped, turned on her heel and rushed back to the modern stove to push the saucepan off the flame.

"Mom," Liam interjected.

"What?"

"Chill out. It's only soup."

The inside door swung open, and Travis stuck his

head in. "Stuff's upstairs," he said. "Anything else you need?"

Sierra stared at him for a long moment, as though he'd spoken in an alien language. "Uh, no," she said finally. "Thanks." Pause. "Would you like some lunch?"

"No, thanks," he said. "Gotta see to that damn horse."

With that, he ducked out again.

"How come I can't ride the horse?" Liam asked.

Sierra sighed, setting a bowl of soup in front of him. "Because you don't know how."

Liam's sigh echoed her own, and if they'd been talking about anything but the endangerment of life and limb, it would have been funny.

"How am I supposed to *learn* how if you won't let me try? You're being overprotective. You could scar my psyche. I might develop psychological problems."

"There are times," Sierra confessed, sitting down across from him with her own bowl of soup, "when I wish you weren't quite so smart."

Liam waggled his eyebrows at her. "I got it from you."

"Yeah right," Sierra said. Liam had her eyes, her thick, fine hair, and her dogged persistence, but his remarkable IQ came from his father.

Don't think about Adam, she told herself.

Travis Reid sidled into her mind.

Even worse.

Liam consumed his soup, along with a second sandwich, and went off to explore the rest of the house while Sierra lingered thoughtfully over her coffee.

The telephone rang.

Sierra got up to fetch the cordless receiver and pressed Talk with her thumb. "Hello?"

"You're there!" Meg trilled.

Sierra noticed that she'd left the china cabinet doors open and went in that direction, intending to close them. "Yes," she said. Meg had been kind to her, in a long-distance sort of way, but Sierra had only been two when she'd last seen her half sister, and that made them strangers.

"How do you like it? The ranch house, I mean?"

"I haven't seen much of it," Sierra answered. "Liam and I just got here, and then we had lunch…." Her hand went, of its own accord, to the teapot, and she imagined she felt just the faintest charge when she touched it. "Lots of antiques around here," she said, thinking aloud.

"Don't be afraid to use them," Meg replied. "Family tradition."

Sierra withdrew her hand from the teapot, shut the doors. "Family tradition?"

"McKettrick rules," Meg said, with a smile in her voice. "Things are meant to be used, no matter how old they are."

Sierra frowned, uneasy. "But if they get broken—"

"They get broken," Meg finished for her. "Have you met Travis yet?"

"Yes," Sierra said. "And he's not at all what I expected."

Meg laughed. "What did you expect?"

"Some gimpy old guy, I guess," Sierra admitted, warming to the friendliness in her sister's voice. "You said he took care of the place and lived in a trailer by the barn, so I thought—" She broke off, feeling foolish.

"He's cute and he's single," Meg said.

"Even the teapot?" Sierra mused.

"Huh?"

Sierra put a hand to her forehead. Sighed. "Sorry. I guess I missed a segue there. There's a teapot in the china cabinet in the kitchen—I was just wondering if I could—"

"I know the one," Meg answered, with a soft fondness in her voice. "It was Lorelei's. She got it for a wedding present."

Lorelei. The matriarch of the family. Sierra took a step backward.

"*Use* it," Meg said, as if she'd seen Sierra's reflexive retreat.

Sierra shook her head. "I couldn't. I had no idea it was that old. If I dropped it—"

"Sierra," Meg said, "it's not china. It's cast iron, with an enamel overlay."

"Oh."

"Kind of like the McKettrick women, Mom always says." Meg went on. "Smooth on the outside, tough as iron on the inside."

Mom. Sierra closed her eyes against all the conflicting emotions the word brought up in her, but it didn't help.

"We'll give you time to settle in," Meg said gently, when Sierra was too choked up to speak. "Then Mom and I will probably pop in for a visit. If that's okay with you, of course."

Both Meg and Eve lived in San Antonio, Texas, where they helped run McKettrickCo, a multinational corporation with interests in everything from software to communication satellites, so they wouldn't be "popping in" without a little notice.

Sierra swallowed hard. "It's your house," she said.

"And yours," Meg pointed out, very quietly.

After that, Meg made Sierra promise to call if she needed anything. They said goodbye, and the call ended.

Sierra went back to the china cabinet for the teapot.

Liam clattered down the back stairs. "I *told* you this place was haunted!" he crowed, his small face shining with delight.

The teapot was heavy—definitely cast iron—but Sierra was careful as she set it on the counter, just the same. "What on earth are you talking about?"

"I just saw a kid," Liam announced. "Upstairs, in my room!"

"You're imagining things."

Liam shook his head. "I *saw* him!"

Sierra approached her son, laid her hand to his forehead. "No fever," she mused, worried.

"Mom," Liam protested, pulling back. "I'm not sick—and I'm not delusional, either."

Delusional. How many seven-year-olds used that word? Sierra sighed and cupped Liam's eager face in both hands. "Listen. It's fine to have imaginary friends, but—"

"He's *not* imaginary."

"Okay," Sierra responded, with another sigh. It was possible, she supposed, that a neighbor child had wandered in before they arrived, but that seemed unlikely, given that the only other houses on the ranch were miles away. "Let's investigate."

Together they climbed the back stairs, and Sierra got her first look at the upper story. The corridor was wide, with the same serviceable board floors. The light fixtures, though old-fashioned, were electric, but most of the light came from the large arched window at the far end of the hallway. Six doors stood open, an indication that Liam had visited each room in turn after leaving the kitchen the first time.

He led her into the middle one, on the left side.

No one was there.

Sierra let out her breath, admiring the room. It was spacious, perfect quarters for a boy. Two bay windows overlooked the barn area, where Baldy, the singularly unattractive horse, stood stalwartly in the middle of the corral, looking as though he intended to break loose at any second and do some serious bucking. Travis was beside Baldy, stroking the animal's neck as he eased the halter off over its head.

A quivery sensation tickled the pit of Sierra's stomach.

"Mom," Liam said. "He was here. He had on short pants and funny shoes and suspenders."

Sierra turned to look at her son, feeling fretful again. Liam stood near the other window, examining an antique telescope, balanced atop a shining brass tripod. "I believe you," she said.

"You don't," Liam argued, jutting out his chin. "You're *humoring* me."

Sierra sat down on the side of the bed positioned between the windows. Like the dressers, it was scarred with age, but made of sturdy wood. The headboard was simply but intricately carved, and a faded quilt provided color. "Maybe I am, a little," she admitted, because there was no fooling Liam. He had an uncanny knack for seeing through anything but the stark truth. "I don't know what to think, that's all."

"Don't you believe in ghosts?"

I don't believe in much of anything, Sierra thought sadly. "I believe in you," she said, patting the mattress beside her. "Come and sit down."

Reluctantly, he sat. Stiffened when she slipped an arm around his shoulders. "If you think I'm going to take a nap," he said, "you're dead wrong."

The word *dead* tiptoed up Sierra's spine to dance

lightly at her nape. "Everything's going to be all right, you know," she said gently.

"I like this room," Liam confided, and the hopeful uncertainty in his manner made Sierra's heart ache. They'd always lived in apartments or cheap motel rooms. Had Liam been secretly yearning to call a house like this one home? To settle down somewhere and live like a normal kid?

"Me, too," Sierra said. "It has friendly vibes."

"Is that supposed to be like a closet?" Liam asked, indicating the huge pine armoire taking up most of one wall.

Sierra nodded. "It's called a wardrobe."

"Maybe it's like the one in that story. Maybe the back of it opens into another world. There could be a lion and a witch in there." From the smile on Liam's face, the concept intrigued rather than troubled him.

She ruffled his hair. "Maybe," she agreed.

His attention shifted back to the telescope. "I wish I could look through that and see Andromeda," he said. "Did you know that the whole galaxy is on a collision course with the Milky Way? All hell's going to break loose when it gets here, too."

Sierra shuddered at the thought. Most parents worried that their kids played too many video games. With Liam, the concern was the Discovery and Science Channels, not to mention programs like *Nova*. He thought about things like Earth losing its magnetic field and had nightmares about creatures swimming in dark oceans under the ice covering one of Jupiter's moons. Or was it Saturn?

"Don't get excited, Mom," he said, with an understanding smile. "It's going to be something like five billion years before it happens."

"Before what happens?" Sierra asked, blinking.

"The *collision*," he said tolerantly.

"Right," Sierra said.

Liam yawned. "Maybe I *will* take a nap." He studied her. "Just don't get the idea it's going to be a regular thing."

She mussed his hair again, kissed the top of his head. "I'm clear on that," she said, standing and reaching for the crocheted afghan lying neatly folded at the foot of the bed.

Liam kicked off his shoes and stretched out on top of the blue chenille bedspread, yawning again. He set his glasses on the night stand with care.

She covered him, resisted the temptation to kiss his forehead, and headed for the door. When she looked back from the threshold, Liam was already asleep.

1919

HANNAH MCKETTRICK HEARD her son's laughter before she rode around the side of the house, toward the barn, a week's worth of mail bulging in the saddlebags draped across the mule's neck. The snow was deep, with a hard crust, and the January wind was brisk.

Her jaw tightened when she saw her boy out in the cold, wearing a thin jacket and no hat. He and Doss, her brother-in-law, were building what appeared to be a snow fort, their breath making white plumes in the frigid air.

Something in Hannah gave a painful wrench at the sight of Doss; his resemblance to Gabe, his brother and her late husband, invariably startled her, even though they lived under the same roof and she should have been used to him by then.

She nudged the mule with the heels of her boots, but Seesaw-Two didn't pick up his pace. He just plodded along.

"What are you doing out here?" Hannah called.

Both Tobias and Doss fell silent, turning to gaze guiltily in her direction.

The breath plumes dissipated.

Tobias set his feet and pushed back his narrow shoulders. He was only eight, but since Gabe's coffin had arrived by train one warm day last summer, draped in an American flag and with Doss for an escort, her boy had taken on the mien of a man.

"We're just making a fort, Ma," he said.

Hannah blinked back sudden, stinging tears. A soldier, Gabe had died of influenza in an army infirmary, without ever seeing the battleground. Tobias thought in military terms, and Doss encouraged him, a fact Hannah did not appreciate.

"It's cold out here," she said. "You'll catch your death."

Doss shifted, pushed his battered hat to the back of his head. His face hardened, like the ice on the pond back of the orchard where the fruit trees stood, bare-limbed and stoic, waiting for spring.

"Go inside," Hannah told her son.

Tobias hesitated, then obeyed.

Doss remained, watching her.

The kitchen door slammed eloquently.

"You've got no business putting thoughts like that in his head," Doss said, in a quiet voice. He took old Seesaw's reins and held him while she dismounted, careful to keep her woolen skirts from riding up.

"That's a fine bit of hypocrisy, coming from you," Hannah replied. "Tobias had pneumonia last fall. We nearly lost him. He's fragile, and you know it, and as soon as

I turn my back, you have him outside, building a snow fort!"

Doss reached for the saddlebags, and so did Hannah. There was a brief tug-of-war before she let go. "He's a kid," Doss said. "If you had your way, he'd never do anything but look through that telescope and play checkers!"

Hannah felt as warm as if she were standing close to a hot stove, instead of Doss McKettrick. Their breaths melded between them. "I fully intend to have my way," she said. "Tobias is my son, and I will not have you telling me how to raise him!"

Doss slapped the saddlebags over one shoulder and stepped back, his hazel eyes narrowed. "He's my nephew—my brother's boy—and I'll be damned if I'll let you turn him into a sickly little whelp hitched to your apron strings!"

Hannah stiffened. "You've said quite enough," she told him tersely.

He leaned in, so his nose was almost touching hers. "I haven't said the half of it, Mrs. McKettrick."

Hannah sidestepped him, marching for the house, but the snow came almost to her knees and made it hard to storm off in high dudgeon. Her breath trailed over her right shoulder, along with her words. "Supper's in an hour," she said, without turning around. "But maybe you'd rather eat in the bunkhouse."

Doss's chuckle riled her, just as it was no doubt meant to do. "Old Charlie's a sight easier to get along with than you are, but he can't hold a candle to you when it comes to home cooking. Anyhow, he's been gone for a month, in case you haven't noticed."

She felt a flush rise up her neck, even though she was shivering inside Gabe's old woolen work coat. His scent was fading from the fabric, and she wished she knew a way to hold on to it.

"Suit yourself," she retorted.

Tobias shoved a chunk of wood into the cookstove as she entered the house, sending sparks snapping up the gleaming black chimney before he shut the door with a clang.

"We were only building a fort," he grumbled.

Hannah was stilled by the sight of him, just as if somebody had thrown a lasso around her middle and pulled it tight. "I could make biscuits and sausage gravy," she offered quietly.

Tobias ignored the olive branch. "You rode down to the road to meet the mail wagon," he said, without meeting her eyes. "Did I get any letters?" With his hands shoved into the pockets of his trousers and his brownish-blond hair shining in the wintry sunlight flowing in through the windows, he looked the way Gabe must have, at his age.

"One from your grandpa," Hannah said. Methodically, she hung her hat on the usual peg, pulled off her knitted mittens and stuffed them into the pockets of Gabe's coat. She took that off last, always hating to part with it.

"Which grandpa?" Tobias lingered by the stove, warming his hands, still refusing to glance her way.

Hannah's family lived in Missoula, Montana, in a big house on a tree-lined residential street. She missed them sorely, and it hurt a little, knowing Tobias was hoping it was Holt who'd written to him, not her father.

"The McKettrick one," she said.

"Good," Tobias answered.

The back door opened, and Doss came in, still carrying the saddlebags. Usually he stopped outside to kick the snow off his boots so the floors wouldn't get muddy, but today he was in an obstinate mood.

Hannah went to the stove and ladled hot water out of the reservoir into a basin, so she could wash up before starting supper.

"Catch," Doss said cheerfully.

She looked back, saw the saddlebags, burdened with mail, fly through the air. Tobias caught them ably with a grin.

When was the last time he'd smiled at her that way?

The boy plundered anxiously through the bags, brought out the fat envelope postmarked San Antonio, Texas. Her in-laws, Holt and Lorelei McKettrick, owned a ranch outside that distant city, and though the Triple M was still home to them, they'd been spending a lot of time away since the beginning of the war. Hannah barely knew them, and neither did Tobias, for that matter, but they'd kept up a lively correspondence, the three of them, ever since he'd learned to read, and the letters had been arriving on a weekly basis since Gabe died.

Gabe's folks had come back for the funeral, of course, and in the intervening months Hannah had been secretly afraid. Holt and Lorelei saw their lost son in Tobias, the same as she did, and they'd offered to take him back to Texas with them when they left. She hadn't had to refuse—Tobias had done that for her, but he'd clearly been torn. A part of him had wanted to leave.

Hannah's heart had wedged itself up into her throat and stayed there until Gabe's mother and father were gone. Whenever a letter arrived, she felt anxious again.

She glanced at Doss, now shrugging out of his coat. He'd gone away to the army with Gabe, fallen sick with influenza himself, recovered and stayed on at the ranch after he brought his brother's body home for burial. Though no one had come right out and said so, Hannah knew Doss had remained on the Triple M, instead of joining the folks in Texas, mainly to look after Tobias.

Maybe the McKettricks thought she'd hightail it home to Montana, once she got over the shock of losing Gabe, and they'd lose track of the boy.

Now Tobias stood poring over the letter, devouring every word with his eyes, getting to the last page and starting all over again at the beginning.

Deliberately Hannah diverted her attention, and that was when she saw the teapot, sitting on the counter. She looked toward the china cabinet, across the room. She hadn't touched the piece, knowing it was special to Lorelei, and she couldn't credit that Doss or Tobias would have taken it from its place, either. They'd been playing in the snow while she was gone to fetch the mail, not throwing a tea party.

"Did one of you get this out?" she asked casually, getting a good grip on the pot before carrying it back to the cabinet. It was made of metal, but the pretty enamel coating could have been chipped, and Hannah wasn't about to take the risk.

Tobias barely glanced her way before shaking his head. He was still intent on the letter from Texas.

Doss looked more closely, his gaze rising curiously from the teapot to Hannah's face. "Nope," he said at last, and busied himself emptying the contents of the coffeepot down the sink before pumping in water for a fresh batch.

Hannah closed the doors of the china cabinet, frowning.

"Odd," she said, very softly.

CHAPTER THREE

Present Day

SIERRA DESCENDED THE REAR STAIRCASE into the kitchen, being extra quiet so she wouldn't wake Liam up. He hadn't had an asthma attack in almost a month, but he needed his rest.

Intending to brew herself some tea and spend a few quiet minutes restoring her equilibrium, she chose a mug from one of the cupboards, located a box of orange pekoe, and reached for the heirloom teapot.

It was gone.

She glanced toward the china cabinet and saw Lorelei's teapot sitting behind the glass.

Jesse or Travis must have come inside while she was upstairs, she reasoned, and put it away.

But that seemed unlikely. Men, especially cowboys, didn't usually fuss with teapots, did they? Not that she knew that much about men in general or cowboys in particular.

She'd seen Travis earlier, from Liam's bedroom window, working with the horse, and she was sure he hadn't been back in the house after carrying in the bags.

"Jesse?" she called softly, half-afraid he might jump out at her from somewhere.

No answer.

She moved to the front of the house, peered between

the lace curtains in the parlor. Jesse's truck was gone, leaving deep tracks in the patchy mud and snow, rapidly filling with gossamer white flakes.

Bemused, Sierra returned to the kitchen, grabbed her coat and went out the back door, shoving her hands into her pockets and ducking her head against the thickening snowfall and the icy wind that accompanied it. Nothing in her life had prepared her for high-country weather; she'd been raised in Mexico, moved to San Diego after her father died and spent the last several years living in Florida. She supposed it would be a while before she adjusted to the change in climate, but if there was one thing she'd learned to do, on the long journey from then to now, it was adapt.

The doors of the big, weathered-board barn stood open, and Sierra stepped inside, shivering. It was warmer there, but she could still see her breath.

"Mr. Reid?"

"Travis" came the taciturn answer from a nearby stall. "I don't answer to much of anything else."

Sierra crossed the sawdust floor and saw Travis on the other side of the door, grooming poor old Baldy with long, gentle strokes of a brush. He gave her a sidelong glance and grinned slightly.

"Settling in okay?" he asked.

"I guess," she said, leaning on the stall door to watch him work. There was something soothing about the way he attended to that horse, almost as though he were touching her own skin....

Perish the thought.

He straightened. A quiver went through Baldy's body. "Something wrong?" Travis asked.

"No," Sierra said quickly, attempting a smile. "I was just wondering..."

"What?" Travis went back to brushing again, though he was still watching Sierra, and the horse gave a contented little snort of pleasure.

Suddenly the whole subject of the teapot seemed silly. How could she ask if he or Jesse had moved it? And, so what if they had? Jesse was a McKettrick, born and raised, and the things in that house were as much a part of his heritage as hers. Travis was clearly a trusted family friend—if not more.

Sierra found that possibility unaccountably disturbing. Meg had said he was single and free, but she obviously trusted Travis implicitly, which might mean there was a deeper level to their relationship.

"I was just wondering...if you ever drink tea," Sierra hedged lamely.

Travis chuckled. "Not often, unless it's the electric variety," he replied, and though he was smiling, the expression in his eyes was one of puzzlement. He was probably asking himself what kind of nut case Meg and Eve had saddled him with. "Are you inviting me?"

Sierra blushed, even more self-conscious than before. "Well...yes. Yes, I guess so."

"I'd rather have coffee," Travis said, "if that's all right with you."

"I'll put a pot on," Sierra answered, foolishly relieved. She should have walked away, but she seemed fixed to the spot, as though someone had smeared the soles of her shoes with superglue.

Travis finished brushing down the horse, ran a gloved hand along the animal's neck and waited politely for Sierra to move, so he could open the stall door and step out.

"What's really going on here, Ms. McKettrick?" he asked, when they were facing each other in the wide aisle, Baldy's stall door securely latched. Along the aisle, other horses nickered, probably wanting Travis's attention for themselves.

"Sierra," she said. She tried to sound friendly, but it was forced.

"Sierra, then. Somehow I don't think you came out here to ask me to a tea party or a coffee klatch."

She huffed out a breath and pushed her hands deeper into her coat pockets. "Okay," she admitted. "I wanted to know if you or Jesse had been inside the house since you brought the baggage in."

"No," Travis answered readily.

"It would certainly be all right if you had, of course—"

Travis took a light grip on Sierra's elbow and steered her toward the barn doors. He closed and fastened them once they were outside.

"Jesse got in his truck and left, first thing," he said. "I've been with Baldy for the last half an hour. Why?"

Sierra wished she'd never begun this conversation. Never left the warmth of the kitchen for the cold and the questions in Travis's eyes. She'd done both those things, though, and now she would have to explain. "I took a teapot out of the china cabinet," she said, "and set it on the counter. I went up to Liam's room, to help him settle in for a nap, and when I came downstairs—"

A startling grin broke over Travis's features like a flash of summer sunlight over a crystal-clear pond. "What?" he prompted. He moved to Sierra's other side, shielding her from the bitter wind, increasing his pace, and therefore hers, as they approached the house.

"It was in the cabinet again. I would swear I put it on the counter."

"Weird," Travis said, kicking the snow off his boots at the base of the back steps.

Sierra stepped inside, shivering, took off her coat and hung it up.

Travis followed, closed the door, pulled off his gloves and stuffed them into the pockets of his coat before hanging it beside Sierra's, along with his hat. "Must have been Liam," he said.

"He's asleep," Sierra replied. The coffee she'd made earlier was still hot, so she filled two mugs, casting an uneasy glance toward the china cabinet as she did so. Liam couldn't have gotten downstairs without her seeing him, and even if he had, he wouldn't have been able to reach the high shelf in the china closet without dragging a chair over. She would have heard the scraping sound and, anyway, Liam being Liam, he wouldn't have put the chair back where he found it. There would have been evidence.

Travis accepted the cup Sierra offered with a nod of thanks, took a sip. "You must have put it away yourself, then," he said reasonably. "And then forgotten."

Sierra sat down in the chair closest to the wood-burning cookstove, suddenly yearning for a fire, while Travis made himself comfortable nearby, on the bench facing the wall.

"I know I didn't," she said, biting her lower lip.

Travis concentrated on his coffee for some moments before turning his gaze back to her face. "It's a strange house," he said.

Sierra blinked.

Cool place, Liam had said, right after they arrived, *but it's haunted.*

"What do you mean, 'It's a strange house'?" she

asked. She made no attempt to keep the skepticism out of her voice.

"Meg's going to kill me for this," Travis said.

"I beg your pardon?"

"She doesn't want you scared off."

Sierra frowned, waiting.

"It's a good place," Travis said, taking the homey kitchen in with a fond glance. Clearly, he'd spent a lot of time there. "Odd things happen sometimes, though."

Sierra heard Liam's voice again. *I saw a kid, upstairs in my room.*

She shook off the memory. "Impossible," she muttered.

"If you say so," Travis replied affably.

"What *kind* of 'odd things' happen in this house?"

Travis smiled, and Sierra had the sense that she was being handled, skillfully managed, in the same way as the horse. "Once in a while, you'll hear the piano playing by itself. Or you walk into a room, and you get the feeling you passed somebody on the threshold, even though you're alone."

Sierra shivered again, but this time it had nothing to do with the icy January weather. The kitchen was snug and warm, even without the cookstove lit. "I would appreciate it," she said, "if you wouldn't talk that kind of nonsense in front of Liam. He's…impressionable."

Travis raised an eyebrow.

Suddenly, strangely, Sierra wanted to tell him what Liam had said about seeing another little boy in his room, but she couldn't quite bring herself to do it. She wouldn't have Travis Reid—or anybody else, for that matter—thinking Liam was…different. He got enough of that from other kids, being so smart, and his asthma set him apart, too.

"I must have moved the teapot myself," Sierra said, at last, "and forgotten. Just as you said."

Travis looked unconvinced. "Right," he agreed.

1919

TOBIAS CARRIED THE letter to the table, where Doss sat comfortably in the chair everyone thought of as Holt's. "They bought three hundred head of cattle," the boy told his uncle excitedly, handing over the sheaf of pages. "Drove them all the way from Mexico to San Antonio, too."

Doss smiled. "Is that right?" he mused. His hazel eyes warmed in the light of a kerosene lantern as he read. The place had electricity now, but Hannah tried to save on it where she could. The last bill had come to over a dollar, for a mere two months of service, and she'd been horrified at the expense.

Standing at the stove, she turned back to her work, stood a little straighter, punched down the biscuit dough with sharp jabs of the wooden spoon. Apparently, it hadn't occurred to Tobias that she might like to see that infernal letter. She was a McKettrick, too, after all, if only by marriage.

"I guess Ma and Pa liked that buffalo you carved for them," Doss observed, when he'd finished and set the pages aside. Hannah just happened to see, since she'd had to pass right by that end of the table to fetch a pound of ground sausage from the icebox. "Says here it was the best Christmas present they ever got."

Tobias nodded, beaming with pride. He'd worked all fall on that buffalo, even in his sick bed, whittling it from a chunk of firewood Doss had cut for him special. "I reckon I'll make them a bear for next year," he said. Not a word about carving something for her parents, Hannah noted, even though they'd sent him a bicycle and a toy fire engine back in December. The McKettricks, of course, had arranged for a spotted pony to be brought up from the main ranch house on Christmas morning, all decked out in a brand-new saddle and bridle, and though Tobias had dutifully written his Montana grandparents to thank them for their gifts, he'd never played with the engine. Just set it on a shelf in his room and forgotten all about it. The bicycle wouldn't be much use before spring, that was true, but he'd shown no more interest in it once the pony had arrived.

"Wash your hands for supper, Tobias McKettrick," Hannah said.

"Supper isn't ready," he protested.

"Do as your mother says," Doss told him quietly.

He obeyed immediately, which should have pleased Hannah, but it didn't.

Doss, meanwhile, opened the saddle bags, took out the usual assortment of letters, periodicals and small parcels, which Hannah had already looked through before the mail wagon rounded the bend in the road. She'd been both disappointed and relieved when there was nothing with her name on it. Once, in the last part of October, when the fiery leaves of the oak trees were falling in puddles around their trunks like the folds of a discarded garment, she'd gotten a letter from Gabe. He'd been dead almost four months by then, and her heart had fairly stopped at the sight of his handwriting on that envelope.

For a brief, dizzying moment, she'd thought there'd been a mistake. That Gabe hadn't died of the influenza at all, but some stranger instead. Mix-ups like that happened during and after a war, and she hadn't seen the body, since the coffin was nailed shut.

She'd stood there beside the road, with that letter in her hand, weeping and trembling so hard that a good quarter of an hour must have passed before she broke the seal and took out the thick fold of vellum pages inside. She'd come to her practical senses by then, but seeing the date at the top of the first page still made her bellow aloud to the empty countryside: March 17, 1918.

Gabe had still been well when he wrote that letter. He'd been looking forward to coming home. It was about time they added to their family, he'd said, and got cattle running on their part of the Triple M again.

She'd dropped to her knees, right there on the hard-packed dirt, too stricken to stand. The mule had wandered home, and presently Doss had come looking for her. Found her still clutching that letter to her chest, her throat so raw with sorrow that she couldn't speak.

He'd lifted her into his arms, Doss had, without saying a word. Set her on his horse, swung up behind her and taken her home.

"Hannah?"

She blinked, came back to the kitchen and the biscuit batter, the package of sausage in her hands.

Doss was standing beside her, smelling of snow and pine trees and man. He touched her arm.

"Are you all right?" he asked.

She swallowed, nodded.

It was a lie, of course. Hannah hadn't been all right since the day Gabe went away to war. Like as not, she would never be all right again.

"You sit down," Doss said. "I'll attend to supper."

She sat, because the strength had gone out of her knees, and looked around blankly. "Where's Tobias?"

Doss washed his hands, opened the sausage packet,

and dumped the contents into the big cast iron skillet waiting on the stove. "Upstairs," he answered.

Tobias had left the room without her knowing?

"Oh," she said, unnerved. Was she losing her mind? Had her sorrow pushed her not only to absent-minded distraction, but beyond the boundaries of ordinary sanity as well?

She considered the mysterious movement of her mother-in-law's teapot.

Adeptly, Doss rolled out the biscuit dough, cut it into circles with the rim of a glass. Lorelei McKettrick had taught her boys to cook, sew on their own buttons and make up their beds in the morning. You could say that for her, and a lot of other things, too.

Doss poured Hannah a mug of coffee, brought it to her. Started to rest a hand on her shoulder, then thought better of it and pulled back. "I know it's hard," he said.

Hannah couldn't look at him. Her eyes burned with tears she didn't want him to see, though she reckoned he knew they were there anyhow. "There are days," she said, in a whisper, "when I don't think I can go another step. But I have to, because of Tobias."

Doss crouched next to Hannah's chair, took both her hands in his own and looked up into her face. "There's been a hundred times," he said, "when I wished it was me in that grave up there on the hill, instead of Gabe. I'd give anything to take his place, so he could be here with you and the boy."

A sense of loss cut into Hannah's spirit like the blade of a new ax, swung hard. "You mustn't think things like that," she said, when she caught her breath. She pulled her hands free, laid them on either side of his earnest, handsome face, then quickly withdrew them. "You mustn't, Doss. It isn't right."

Just then Tobias clattered down the back stairs.

Doss flushed and got to his feet.

Hannah turned away, pretended to have an interest in the mail, most of which was for Holt and Lorelei, and would have to be forwarded to San Antonio.

"What's the matter, Ma?" Tobias spoke worriedly into the awkward silence. "Don't you feel good?"

She'd hoped the boy hadn't seen Doss sitting on his haunches beside her chair, but obviously he had.

"I'm fine," she said briskly. "I just had a splinter in my finger, that's all. I got it putting wood in the fire, and Doss took it out for me."

Tobias looked from her to his uncle and back again.

"Is that why you're making supper?" he asked Doss.

Doss hesitated. Like Gabe, he'd been raised to abhor any kind of lie, even an innocent one, designed to soothe a boy who'd lost his father and feared, in the depths of his dreams, losing his mother, too.

"I'm making supper," he said evenly, "because I can."

Hannah closed her eyes, opened them again.

"Set the table, please," Doss told Tobias.

Tobias hurried to the cabinet for plates and silverware.

Hannah met Doss's gaze across the dimly lit room.

A charge seemed to pass between them, like before, when Hannah had come back from getting the mail and found Tobias outside, in the teeth of a high-country winter, building a snow fort.

"It's too damn dark in this house," Doss said. He walked to the middle of the room, reached up, and pulled the beaded metal cord on the overhead light. The bare bulb glowed so brightly it made Hannah blink, but she didn't object.

Something in Doss's face prevented her from it.

Present Day

TRAVIS HAD LONG since finished his coffee and left the house by the time Liam got up from his nap and came downstairs, tousle-haired and puffy-eyed from sleep.

"That boy was in my room again," he said. "He was sitting at the desk, writing a letter. Can I watch TV? There's a nice setup in that room next to the front door. A computer, too, with a big, flat-screen monitor."

Sierra knew about the fancy electronics, since she'd explored the house after Travis left. "You can watch TV for an hour," she said. "Hands off the computer, though. It doesn't belong to us."

Liam's shoulders slumped slightly. "I *know* how to use a computer, Mom," he said. "We had them at school."

Between rent, food and medical bills, Sierra had never been able to scrape together the money for a PC of their own. She'd used the one in the office of the bar she worked in, back in Florida. That was how Meg had first contacted her. "We'll get one," she said, "as soon as I find another job."

"My mailbox is probably full," Liam replied, unappeased. "All the kids in the Geek Program were going to write to me."

Sierra, in the midst of putting a package of frozen chicken breasts into the microwave to thaw, felt as though she'd been poked with a sharp stick. "Don't call it the Geek Program, please," she said.

Liam shrugged one shoulder. "Everybody else does."

"Go watch TV."

He went.

A rap sounded at the back door, and Sierra peered

through the glass, since it was dark out, to see Travis standing on the back porch.

"Come in," she called, and headed for the sink to wash her hands.

Travis entered, carrying a fragrant bag of take-out food in one hand. The collar of his coat was raised against the cold, his hat brim pulled low over his eyes.

"Fried chicken," he said, lifting the bag as evidence.

Sierra paused, shut off the faucet, dried her hands. The timer on the microwave dinged. "I was about to cook," she said.

Travis grinned. "Good thing I got to you in time," he answered. "If you're anything like your sister, you shouldn't be allowed to get near a stove."

If you're anything like your sister.

The words saddened Sierra, settled bleak and heavy over her heart. She didn't know whether she was like her sister or not; until Meg had emailed her a smiling picture a few weeks ago, she wouldn't have recognized her on the street.

"Did I say something wrong?" Travis asked.

"No," Sierra said quickly. "It was—thoughtful of you to bring the chicken."

Liam must have heard Travis's voice, because he came pounding into the room, all smiles.

"Hey, Travis," he said.

"Hey, cowpoke," Travis replied.

"The computer's making a dinging noise," Liam reported.

Travis smiled, set the bag of chicken on the counter but made no move to take off his hat and coat. "Meg's got it set to do that, so she'll remember to check her email when she's here," he said.

"Mom won't let me log on," Liam told him.

Travis glanced at Sierra, turned to Liam again. "Rules are rules, cowpoke," he said.

"Rules bite," Liam said.

"Ninety-five percent of the time," Travis agreed.

Liam recovered quickly. "Are you going to stay and eat with us?"

Travis shook his head. "I'd like that a lot, but I'm expected somewhere else for supper," he answered.

Liam looked sorely disappointed.

Sierra wondered where that "somewhere else" was, and with whom Travis would be sharing a meal, and was irritated with herself. It was none of her business, and besides, she didn't care what he did or who he did it with anyway. Not the least little bit.

"Maybe another time," Travis said.

Liam sighed and retreated to the study and his allotted hour of television.

"You shouldn't have," Sierra said, indicating their supper with a nod.

"It's your first night here," Travis answered, opening the door to leave. "Seemed like the neighborly thing to do."

"Thank you," Sierra said, but he'd already closed the door between them.

TRAVIS STARTED UP his truck, just in case Sierra was listening for the engine, drove it around behind the barn and parked. After stopping to check on Baldy and the three other horses in his care, he shrugged down into the collar of his coat and slogged to his trailer.

The quarters were close, smaller than the closet off his master bedroom at home in Flagstaff, but he didn't need much space. He had a bed, kitchen facilities, a bathroom and a place for his laptop. It was enough.

More than Brody was ever going to have.

He took off his hat and coat and tossed them on to the built-in, padded bench that passed for a couch. He tried not to think about Brody, and in the daytime, he stayed busy enough to succeed. At night, it was another matter. There just wasn't enough to do after dark, especially out here in the boonies, once he'd nuked a frozen dinner and watched the news.

He thought about Sierra and the boy, in there in the big house, eating the chicken and fixings he'd picked up in the deli at the one and only supermarket in Indian Rock. He'd never intended to join them, since they'd just arrived and were settling in, but he could picture himself sitting down at that long table in the kitchen, just the same.

He rooted through his refrigerator, something he had to crouch to do, and chose between Salisbury steak, Salisbury steak and Salisbury steak.

While the sectioned plastic plate was whirling round and round in the lilliputian microwave that came with the trailer, he made coffee and remembered his last visit from Rance McKettrick. Widowed, Rance lived alone in the house *his* legendary ancestor, Rafe, had built for his wife, Emmeline, and their children, back in the 1880s. He had two daughters, whom he largely ignored.

"This place is just a fancy coffin," Rance had observed, in his blunt way, when he'd stepped into the trailer. "Brody's the one that's dead, Trav, not you."

Travis rubbed his eyes with a thumb and forefinger. Brody was dead, all right. No getting around that. Seventeen, with everything to live for, and he'd blown himself up in the back room of a slum house in Phoenix, making meth.

He looked into the window over the sink, saw his own reflection.

Turned away.

His cell phone rang, and he considered letting voice mail pick up, but couldn't make himself do it. If he'd answered the night Brody called…

He fished the thing out, snapped it open and said, "Reid."

"Whatever happened to 'hello'?" Meg asked.

The bell on the microwave rang, and Travis reached in to retrieve his supper, burned his hand and cursed.

She laughed. "Better and better."

"I'm not in the mood for banter, Meg," he replied, turning on the water with his free hand and then switching to shove his scorched fingers into the flow.

"You never are," she said.

"The horses are fine."

"I know. You would have called me if they weren't."

"Then what do you want?"

"My, my, we *are* testy tonight. I called, you big grouch, to ask about my sister and my nephew. Are they okay? How do they look? Sierra is so private, she's almost standoffish."

"You can say that again."

"Thank you, but in the interest of brevity, I won't."

"Since when do you give a damn about brevity?" Travis inquired, but he was grinning by then.

Once again Meg laughed. Once again Travis wished he'd been able to fall in love with her. They'd tried, the two of them, to get something going, on more than one occasion. Meg wanted a baby, and he wanted not to be alone, so it made sense. The trouble was, it hadn't worked.

There was no chemistry.

There was no passion.

They were never going to be anything more than what they were—the best of friends. He was mostly resigned to that, but in lonely moments, he ached for things to be different.

"Tell me about my sister," Meg insisted.

"She's pretty," Travis said. *Real* pretty, added a voice in his mind. "She's proud, and overprotective as hell of the kid."

"Liam has asthma," Meg said quietly. "According to Sierra, he nearly died of it a couple of times."

Travis forgot his burned fingers, his Salisbury steak and his private sorrow. *"What?"*

Meg let out a long breath. "That's the only reason Sierra's willing to have anything to do with Mom and me. Mom put her on the company health plan and arranged for Liam to see a specialist in Flagstaff on a regular basis. In return, Sierra had to agree to spend a year on the ranch."

Travis stood still, absorbing it all. "Why here?" he asked. "Why not with you and Eve in San Antonio?"

"Mom and I would love that," Meg said, "but Sierra needs...distance. Time to get used to us."

"Time to get used to two McKettrick women. So we're talking, say, the year 2050, give or take a decade?"

"Very funny. Sierra *is* a McKettrick woman, remember? She's up to the challenge."

"She is definitely a McKettrick," Travis agreed ruefully. And very definitely a woman. "How did you find her?"

"Mom tracked her and Hank down when Sierra was little," Meg answered.

Travis dropped on to the edge of his bed, which was unmade. The sheets were getting musty, and every night, the pizza crumbs rubbed his hide raw. One of these days he was going to haul off and change them.

"'Tracked her down'?"

"Yes," Meg said, with a sigh. "I guess I didn't tell you about that part."

"I guess you didn't." Travis had known about the kidnapping, how Sierra's father had taken off with her the day the divorce papers were served, and that the two of them had ended up in Mexico. "Eve knew, and she still didn't lift a finger to get her own daughter back?"

"Mom had her reasons," Meg answered, withdrawing a little.

"Oh, well, then," Travis retorted, "that clears everything up. What *reason* could she possibly have?"

"It's not my place to say, Trav," Meg told him sadly. "Mom and Sierra have to work it all through first, and it might be a while before Sierra's ready to listen."

Travis sighed, shoved a hand through his hair. "You're right," he conceded.

Meg brightened again, but there was a brittleness about her that revealed more than she probably wanted Travis to know, close as they were. "So," she said, "what would you say Mom's chances are? Of reconnecting with Sierra, I mean?"

"The truth?"

"The truth," Meg said, without enthusiasm.

"Zero to zip. Sierra's been pleasant enough to me, but she's as stubborn as any McKettrick that ever drew breath, and that's saying something."

"Gee, thanks."

"You said you wanted the truth."

"How can you be so sure Mom won't be able to get through to her?"

"It's just a hunch," Travis said.

Meg was quiet. Travis was famous for his hunches. Too bad he hadn't paid attention to the one that said his little brother was in big trouble, and that Travis ought to drop everything and look for Brody until he found him.

"Look, maybe I'm wrong," he added.

"What's your real impression of Sierra, Travis?"

He took his time answering. "She's independent to a fault. She's built a wall around herself and the kid, and she's not about to let anybody get too close. She's jumpy, too. If it wasn't for Liam, and the fact that she probably doesn't have two nickels to rub together, she definitely wouldn't be on the Triple M."

"Damn," Meg said. "We knew she was poor, but—"

"Her car gave out in the driveway as soon as she pulled in. I took a peek under the hood, and believe me, the best mechanic on the planet couldn't resurrect that heap."

"She can drive my SUV."

"That might take some convincing on your part. This is not a woman who wants to be obliged. It's probably all she can do not to grab the kid and hop on the next bus to nowhere."

"This is depressing," Meg said.

Travis got up off the bed, peeled back the plastic covering his dinner, and poked warily at the faux meat with the tip of one finger. Talk about depressing.

"Hey," he said. "Look on the bright side. She's here, isn't she? She's on the Triple M. It's a start."

"Take care of her, Travis."

"As if she'd go along with that."

"Do it for me."

"Oh, please."

Meg paused, took aim and scored a bull's-eye. "Then do it for Liam."

CHAPTER FOUR

1919

Doss left the house after supper, ostensibly to look in on the livestock one last time before heading upstairs to bed, leaving the dishwashing to Tobias and Hannah. He stood still in the dooryard, raising the collar of his coat against the wicked cold. Stars speckled the dark, wintry sky.

In those moments he missed Gabe with a piercing intensity that might have bent him double, if he wasn't McKettrick proud. That was what his mother called the quality, anyhow. In the privacy of his own mind, Doss named it stubbornness.

Thinking of his ma made his pa come to mind, too. He missed them almost as sorely as he did Gabe. His uncles, Rafe and Kade and Jeb, along with their wives, were all down south, around Phoenix, where the weather was more hospitable to their aging bones. Their sons, to a man, were still in the army, even though the war was over, waiting to be mustered out. Their daughters had all married, every one of them keeping the McKettrick name, and lived in places as far-flung as Boston, New York and San Francisco.

There was hardly a McKettrick left on the place, save himself and Hannah and Tobias. It deepened Doss's loneliness, knowing that. He wished everybody would just come back home, where they belonged, but it would have been easier to herd wild barn cats than that bunch.

Doss looked back toward the house. Saw the lantern glowing at the kitchen window. Smiled.

The moment he'd gone outside, Hannah must have switched off the bulb. She worried about running short of things, he'd noticed, even though she'd come from a prosperous family, and certainly married into one.

His throat tightened. He knew she'd been different before he brought Gabe home in a pine box, but then, they all had. Gabe's going left a hole in the fabric of what it meant to be a McKettrick, and not a tidy one, stitched at the edges. Rather, it was a jagged tear, and judging by the raw newness of his own grief, Doss had little hope of it ever mending.

Time heals, his mother had told him after they'd laid Gabe in the ground up there on the hill, with his Grandpa Angus and those that had passed after him, but she'd had tears in her eyes as she said it. As for his pa, well, he'd stood a long time by the grave. Stood there until Rafe and Kade and Jeb brought him away.

Doss thrust out a sigh, remembering. "Gabe," he said, under his breath, "Hannah says it's wrong of me, but I still wish it had been me instead of you."

He'd have given anything for an answer, but wherever Gabe was, he was busy doing other things. Maybe they had fishing holes up there in the sky, or cattle to round up and drive to market.

"Take care of Hannah and my boy," Gabe had told him, in that army infirmary, when they both knew there would be no turning the illness around. "Promise me, Doss."

Doss had swallowed hard and made that promise, but it was a hard one to keep. Hannah didn't seem to want taking care of, and every morning when Doss woke up, he was afraid this would be the day she'd decide to go back to her own people, up in Montana, and stay gone for good.

The back door opened, startling Doss out of his musings. He hesitated for a moment, then tramped in the direction of the barn, trying to look like a man bent on a purpose.

Hannah caught up, bundled into a shawl and carrying a lighted lantern in one hand.

"I think I'm going mad," she blurted out.

Doss stopped, looked down at her in puzzled concern. "It's the grief, Hannah," he told her gruffly. "It will pass."

"You don't believe that any more than I do," Hannah challenged, catching up with herself. The snow was deep and getting deeper, and the wind bit straight through to the marrow.

Doss moved to the windward side, to be a buffer for her. "I've got to believe it," he said. "Feeling this bad forever doesn't bear thinking about."

"I put the teapot away," Hannah said, her breath coming in puffs of white. "I know I put it away. But I must have gotten it out again, without knowing or remembering, and that scares me, Doss. That really scares me."

They reached the barn. Doss took the lantern from her and hauled open one of the big doors one-handed. It wasn't easy, since the snow had drifted, even in the short time since he'd left off feeding and watering the horses and the milk cow and that cussed mule Seesaw. The critter was a son of Doss's mother's mule, who'd borne the same name, and he was a son of something else, too.

"Maybe you're a mite forgetful these days," Doss said,

once he'd gotten her inside, out of the cold. The familiar smells and sounds of the darkened barn were a solace to him—he came there often, even when he didn't have work to do, which was seldom. On a ranch, there was always work to do—wood to chop, harnesses to mend, animals to look after. "That doesn't mean you're not sane, Hannah."

Don't say it, he pleaded silently. Don't say you might as well take Tobias and head for Montana.

It was a selfish thought, Doss knew. In Montana, Hannah could live a city life again. No riding a mule five miles to fetch the mail. No breaking the ice on the water troughs on winter mornings, so the cattle and horses could drink. No feeding chickens and dressing like a man.

If Hannah left the Triple M, Doss didn't know what he'd do. First and foremost, he'd have to break his promise to Gabe, by default if not directly, but there was more to it than that. A lot more.

"There's something else, too," Hannah confided.

To keep himself busy, Doss went from stall to stall, looking in on sleepy horses, each one confounded and blinking in the light of his lantern. He was giving Hannah space, enough distance to get out whatever it was she wanted to say.

"What?" he asked, when she didn't speak again right away.

"Tobias. He just told me—he told me—"

Doss looked back, saw Hannah standing in the moonlit doorway, rimmed in silver, with one hand pressed to her mouth.

He went back to her. Set the lantern aside and took her by the shoulders. "What did he tell you, Hannah?"

"Doss, he's seeing things."

He tensed on the inside. Would have shoved a hand through his hair in agitation if he hadn't been wearing a hat and his ears weren't bound to freeze if he took it off. "What kind of things?"

"A boy." She took hold of his arm, and her grip was strong for such a small woman. It did curious things to him, feeling her fingers on him, even through the combined thickness of his coat and shirt. "Doss, Tobias says he saw a boy in his room."

Doss looked around. There was nothing but bleak, frozen land for miles around. "That's impossible," he said.

"You've got to talk to him."

"Oh, I'll talk to him, all right." Doss started for the house, so fixed on getting to Tobias that he forgot all about keeping Hannah sheltered from the wind. She had to lift her skirts to keep pace with him.

Present Day

"TELL ME ABOUT the boy you saw in your room," Sierra said, when they'd eaten their fill of fried chicken, macaroni salad, mashed potatoes with gravy, and corn on the cob.

Liam's gaze was clear as he regarded her from his side of the long table. "He's a ghost," he replied, and waited, visibly expecting the statement to be refuted.

"Maybe an imaginary playmate?" Sierra ventured. Liam was a lonely little boy; their lifestyle had seen to that. After her father had died, drunk himself to death in a back-street cantina in San Miguel, the two of them had wandered like gypsies. San Diego. North Carolina, Georgia, and finally Florida.

"There's nothing imaginary about him," Liam said

staunchly. "He wears funny clothes, like those kids on those old-time shows on TV. He's a *ghost,* Mom. Face it."

"Liam—"

"You never believe anything I tell you!"

"I believe *everything* you tell me," Sierra insisted evenly. "But you've got to admit, this is a stretch." Again she thought of the teapot. Again she pushed the recollection aside.

"I never lie, Mom."

She moved to pat his hand, but he pulled back. The set of his jaw was stubborn, and his gaze drilled into her, full of challenge. She tried again. "I know you don't lie, Liam. But you're in a strange new place and you miss your friends and—"

"And you won't even let me see if they sent me emails!" he cried.

Sierra sighed, rested her elbows on the tabletop and rubbed her temples with the fingertips of both hands. "Okay," she relented. "You can log on to the internet. Just be careful, because that computer is expensive, and we can't afford to replace it."

Suddenly Liam's face was alight. "I won't break it," he promised, with exuberance.

Sierra wondered if he'd just scammed her, if the whole boy-in-the-bedroom thing was a trick to get what he wanted.

In the next instant she was ashamed. Liam was direct to a fault. He *believed* he'd seen another child in his empty bedroom. She'd call his new doctor in Flagstaff in the morning, talk to the woman, see what a qualified professional made of the whole thing. She offered a silent prayer that her car would start, too, because the doctor was going to want to see Liam, pronto.

Meanwhile, Liam got to his feet and scrambled out of the room.

Sierra cleared away the supper mess, then followed him, as casually as she could, to the room at the front of the house.

He was already online.

"Just what I thought!" he crowed. "My mailbox is *bulging*."

The TV was still on, a narrator dolefully describing the effects of a second ice age, due any minute. Run for the hills. Sierra shut it off.

"Hey," Liam objected. "I was listening to that."

Sierra approached the computer. "You're only seven," she said. "You shouldn't be worrying about the fate of the planet."

"Somebody's got to," Liam replied, without looking at her. "*Your* generation is doing a lousy job." He was staring, as if mesmerized, into the computer screen. Its bluish-gray light flickered on the lenses of his glasses, making his eyes disappear. "Look! The whole Geek Group wrote to me!"

"I asked you not to—"

"Okay," Liam sighed, without looking at her. "The brilliant children in the gifted program are engaging in communication."

"That's better," Sierra said, sparing a smile.

"You've got a few emails waiting yourself," Liam announced. He was already replying to the cybermissives, his small fingers ranging deftly over the keyboard. He'd skipped the hunt-and-peck method entirely, as had all the other kids in his class. Using a computer came naturally to Liam, almost as if he'd been born knowing how, and she knew this was a common phenomenon, which gave her some comfort.

"I'll read them later," Sierra answered. She didn't have that many friends, so most of her messages were probably sales pitches of the penis-enlargement variety. How had she gotten on that kind of list? It wasn't as if she visited porn sites or ordered battery-operated boyfriends online.

"They get to watch a real rocket launch!" Liam cried, without a trace of envy. *"Wow!"*

"Wow indeed," Sierra said, looking around the room. According to Meg, it had originally been a study. Old books lined the walls on sturdy shelves, and there was a natural rock fireplace, too, with a fire already laid.

Sierra found a match on the mantelpiece, struck it and lit the blaze.

A chime sounded from the computer.

"Aunt Meg just IM'd you," Liam said.

Where had he gotten this "Aunt Meg" thing? He'd never even met the woman in person, let alone established a relationship with her. "'IM'd'?" she asked.

"Instant Messaged," Liam translated. "Guess you'd better check it out. Just make it quick, because I've still got a *pile* of mail to answer."

Smiling again, Sierra took the chair Liam so reluctantly surrendered and read the message from Meg.

Travis tells me your car died. Use my SUV. The keys are in the sugar bowl beside the teapot.

Sierra's pride kicked in. Thanks, she replied, at a fraction of Liam's typing speed, but I probably won't need it. My car is just… She paused. Her car was just what? Old? tired, she finished, inspired.

The SUV won't run when I come back if somebody doesn't charge up the battery. It's been sitting too long, Meg responded quickly. She must have been as fast with a keyboard as Liam.

Is Travis going to report on everything I do? Sierra wrote. She made so many mistakes, she had to retype the message before hitting Send, and that galled her.

Yes, Meg wrote. Because I plan to nag every last detail out of him.

Sierra sighed. It won't be that interesting, she answered, taking her time so she wouldn't have to revise. She was out of practice, and if she hoped to land anything better than a waitressing job in Indian Rock, she'd better polish her computer skills.

Meg sent a smiley face, followed by, Good night, Sis. (I've always wanted to say that.)

Sierra bit her lower lip. Good night, she tapped out, and rose from the chair with a glance at the clock on the mantel above the now-snapping fire.

Why had she lit it? She was exhausted, and now she would either have to throw water on the flames or wait until they died down. The first method, of course, would make a terrible mess, so that was out.

"Hurry up and finish what you're doing," she told Liam, who had plopped in the chair again the moment Sierra got out of it. "Half an hour till bedtime."

"I had a *nap*," Liam reminded her, typing simultaneously.

"Finish," Sierra repeated. With that, she left the study, climbed the stairs and went into Liam's room to get his favorite pajamas from one of the suitcases. She meant to put them in the clothes dryer for a few minutes, warm them up.

Something drew her to the window, though. She looked down, saw that the lights were on in Travis's trailer and his truck was parked nearby. Evidently, he hadn't stayed long in town, or wherever he'd gone.

Why did it please her so much, knowing that?

1919

HANNAH STOOD IN the doorway of Tobias's room, watching her boy sleep. He looked so peaceful, lying there, but she knew he had bad dreams sometimes. Just the night before, in the wee small hours, he'd crawled into bed beside her, snuggled as close as his little-boy pride would allow, and whispered earnestly that she oughtn't die anytime soon.

She'd been so choked up, she could barely speak.

Now she wanted to wake him, hold him tight in her arms, protect him from whatever it was in his mind that made him see little boys that weren't there.

He was lonely, that was all. He needed to be around other children. Way out here, he went to a one-room school, when it wasn't closed on account of snow, with only seven other pupils, all of whom were older than he was.

Maybe she should take him home to Montana. He had cousins there. They'd live in town, too, where there were shops and a library and even a moving-picture theater. He could ride his bicycle, come spring, and play baseball with other boys.

Hannah's throat ached. Gabe had wanted his son raised here, on the Triple M. Wanted him to grow up the way he had, rough-and-tumble, riding horses, rounding up stray cattle, part of the land. Of course, Gabe hadn't expected to die young—he'd meant to come home, so he and Hannah could fill that big house with children. Tobias would have had plenty of company then.

A tear slipped down Hannah's cheek, and she swatted it away. Straightened her spine.

Gabe was gone, and there weren't going to be any more children.

She heard Doss climbing the stairs, and wanted to move out of the doorway. He thought she was too fussy, always hovering over Tobias. Always trying to protect him.

How could a man understand what it meant to bear and nurture a child?

Hannah closed her eyes and stayed where she was.

Doss stopped behind her, uncertain. She could feel that, along with the heat and sturdy substance of his body.

"Leave the child to sleep, Hannah," he said quietly.

She nodded, closed Tobias's door gently and turned to face Doss there in the darkened hallway. He carried a book under one arm and an unlit lantern in his other hand.

"It's because he's lonesome," she said.

Doss clearly knew she was referring to Tobias's hallucination. "Kids make up playmates," he told her. "And being lonesome is a part of life. It's a valley a person has to go through, not something to run away from."

No McKettrick ever ran from anything. Doss didn't have to say it, and neither did she. But she wasn't a McKettrick, not by blood. Oh, she still wrote the word, whenever she had to sign something, but she'd stopped owning the name the day they put Gabe in the ground.

She wasn't sure why. He'd been so proud of it, like all the rest of them were.

"Do you ever wish you could live someplace else?" Hannah heard herself say.

"No," Doss said, so quickly and with such gravity that

Hannah almost believed he'd been reading her mind. "I belong right here."

"But the others—your uncles and cousins—they didn't stay...."

"Ask any one of them where home is," Doss answered, "and they'll tell you it's the Triple M."

Hannah started to speak, then held her tongue. Nodded. "Good night, Doss," she said.

He inclined his head and went on to his own room, shut himself away.

Hannah stood alone in the dark for a long time.

She'd been so happy on the Triple M when Gabe was alive, and even after he'd gone into the army, because she'd never once doubted that he'd return. Come walking up the path with a duffel bag over one shoulder, whistling. She'd rehearsed that day a thousand times in her mind—pictured herself running to meet him, throwing herself into his arms.

It was never going to happen.

Without him, she might as well have been alone on the barren landscape of the moon.

Her eyes filled.

She walked slowly to the end of the hall, into the room where Gabe had brought her on their wedding night. He'd been conceived and born in the big bed there, just as Tobias had. As so many other babes would have been, if only Gabe had lived.

Hannah didn't undress after she closed the door behind her. She didn't let her hair down and brush it, like usual, or wash her face at the basin on the bureau.

Instead, she sat down in Lorelei's rocking chair and waited. Just waited.

For what, she did not know.

Present Day

AFTER LIAM HAD gone to bed, Sierra went back downstairs to the computer and scanned her email. When she spotted Allie Douglas-Fletcher's return address, she wished she'd waited until morning. She was always stronger in the mornings.

Allie was Adam's twin sister. Liam's aunt. After Adam was murdered, while on assignment in South America, Allie had been inconsolable, and she'd developed an unhealthy fixation for her brother's child.

After taking a deep breath and releasing it slowly, Sierra opened the message. Typically, there was no preamble. Allie got right to the point.

The guest house is ready for you and Liam. You know Adam would want his son to grow up right here in San Diego, Sierra. Tim and I can give Liam everything—a real home, a family, an education, the very best medical care. We're willing to make a place for you, too, obviously. If you won't come home, at least tell us you arrived safely in Arizona.

Sierra sat, wooden, staring at the stark plea on the screen. Although Allie and Adam had been raised in relative poverty, both of them had done well in life. Adam had been a photojournalist for a major magazine; he and Sierra had met when he did a piece on San Miguel.

Allie ran her own fund-raising firm, and her husband was a neurosurgeon. They had everything—except what they wanted most. Children.

You can't have Liam, Sierra cried, in the silence of her heart. *He's mine.*

She flexed her fingers, sighed, and hit Reply. Allie

was a good person, just as Adam had been, for all that he'd told Sierra a lie that shook the foundations of the universe. Adam's sister sincerely believed she and the doctor could do a better job of raising Liam than Sierra could, and maybe they were right. They had money. They had social status.

Tears burned in Sierra's eyes.

Liam is well. We're safe on the Triple M, and for the time being, we're staying put.

It was all she could bring herself to say.

She hit Send and logged off the computer.

The fire was still flourishing on the hearth. She got up, crossed the room, pushed the screen aside to jab at the burning wood with a poker. It only made the flames burn more vigorously.

She kicked off her shoes, curled up in the big leather chair and pulled a knitted afghan around her to wait for the fire to die down.

The old clock on the mantel tick-tocked, the sound loud and steady and almost hypnotic.

Sierra yawned. Closed her eyes. Opened them again.

She thought about turning the TV back on, just for the sound of human voices, but dismissed the idea. She was so tired, she was going to need all her energy just to go upstairs and tumble into bed. There was none to spare for fiddling with the television set.

Again, she closed her eyes.

Again, she opened them.

She wondered if the lights were still on in Travis's trailer.

Closed her eyes.

Was dragged down into a heavy, fitful sleep.

She knew right away that she was dreaming, and yet it was so real.

She heard the clock ticking.

She felt the warmth of the fire.

But she was standing in the ranch house kitchen, and it was different, in subtle ways, from the room she knew.

She was different.

Her eyes were shut, and yet she could see clearly.

A bare light bulb dangled overhead, giving off a dim but determined glow.

She looked down at herself, the dream-Sierra, and felt a wrench of surprise.

She was wearing a long woolen skirt. Her hands were smaller—chapped and work worn—someone else's hands.

"I'm dreaming," she insisted to herself, but it didn't help.

She stared around the kitchen. The teapot sat on the counter.

"Now what's that doing there?" asked this other Sierra. "I know I put it away. I know for sure I did."

Sierra struggled to wake up. It was too intense, this dream. She was in some other woman's body, not her own. It was sinewy and strong, this body. She felt the heartbeat, the breath going in and out. Felt the weight of long hair, pinned to the back of her head in a loose chignon.

"Wake up," she said.

But she couldn't.

She stood very still, staring at the teapot.

Emotions stormed within her, a loneliness so wretched and sharp that she thought she'd burst from the inside and shatter. Longing for a man who'd gone away and was never coming home, an unspeakable sorrow. Love for a child, so profound that it might have been mourning.

And something else. A forbidden wanting that had nothing to do with the man who'd left her.

Sierra woke herself then, by force of will, only to find her face wet with another woman's tears.

She must have been asleep for a while, she realized. The flames on the hearth had become embers. The room was chilly.

She shivered, tugged the afghan tighter around her, and got out of the chair. She went to the window, looked out. Travis's trailer was dark.

"It was just a dream," she told herself out loud.

So why was her heart breaking?

She made her way into the kitchen, navigating the dark hallway as best she could, since she didn't know where the light switches were. When she reached her destination, she walked to the middle of the room, where she'd stood in the dream, and suppressed an urge to reach up for the metal-beaded cord she knew wasn't there.

What she needed, she decided, was a good cup of tea.

She found a switch beside the back door and flipped it.

Reality returned in a comforting spill of light.

She found an electric kettle, filled it at the sink and plugged it in to boil. Earlier she'd been too weary to get out of that chair in the study and turn on the TV. Now she knew it would be pointless to try to sleep.

Might as well do this up right, she thought.

She went to the china cabinet, got the teapot out, set it on the table. Added tea leaves and located a little strainer in one of the drawers. The kettle boiled.

She was sitting quietly, sipping tea and watching fat

snowflakes drift past the porch light outside the back door, when Liam came down the back stairway in his pajamas. Blinking, he rubbed his eyes.

"Is it morning?" he asked.

"No," Sierra said gently. "Go back to bed."

"Can I have some tea?"

"No, again," Sierra answered, but she didn't protest when Liam took a seat on the bench, close to her chair. "But if there's cocoa, I'll make you some."

"There is," Liam said. He looked incredibly young, and so very vulnerable, without his glasses. "I saw it in the pantry. It's the instant kind."

With a smile, Sierra got out of the chair, walked into the pantry and brought out the cocoa, along with a bag of semihard marshmallows. Thanks to Travis's preparations for their arrival, there was milk in the refrigerator and, using the microwave, she had Liam's hot chocolate ready in no time.

"I like it here," he told her. "It's better than any place we've ever lived."

Sierra's heart squeezed. "You really think so? Why?"

Liam took a sip of hot chocolate and acquired a liquid mustache. One small shoulder rose and fell in a characteristic shrug. "It feels like a real home," he said. "Lots of people have lived here. And they were all McKettricks, like us."

Sierra was stung, but she hid it behind another smile. "Wherever we live," she said carefully, "is a real home, because we're together."

Liam's expression was benignly skeptical, even tolerant. "We never had so much room before. We never had a barn with horses in it. And we never had *ghosts*." He whispered the last word, and gave a little shiver of pure joy.

Sierra was looking for a way to approach the ghost subject again when the faint, delicate sound of piano music reached her ears.

CHAPTER FIVE

"Do you hear that?" she asked Liam.

His brow furrowed as he shifted on the bench and took another sip of his cocoa. "Hear what?"

The tune continued, flowing softly, forlornly, from the front room.

"Nothing," Sierra lied.

Liam peered at her, perplexed and suspicious.

"Finish your chocolate," she prompted. "It's late."

The music stopped, and she felt relief and a paradoxical sorrow, reminiscent of the all-too-vivid dream she'd had earlier while dozing in the big chair in the study.

"What was it, Mom?" Liam pressed.

"I thought I heard a piano," she admitted, because she knew her son wouldn't let the subject drop until she told him the truth.

Liam smiled, pleased. "This house is so cool," he said. "I told the Geek—the kids—that it's haunted. Aunt Allie, too."

Sierra, in the process of lifting her cup to her mouth, set it down again, shakily. "When did you talk to Allie?" she asked.

"She sent me an email," he replied, "and I answered."

"Great," Sierra said.

"Would my dad really want me to grow up in San Diego?" Liam asked seriously. The idea had, of course, come from Allie. While Sierra wasn't without sympathy for the woman, she felt violated. Allie had no business trying to entice Liam behind her back.

"Your dad would want you to grow up with me," Sierra said firmly, and she knew that was true, for all that Adam had betrayed her.

"Aunt Allie says my cousins would like me," Liam confided.

Liam's "cousins" were actually half sisters, but Sierra wasn't ready to spring that on him, and she hoped Allie wouldn't do it, either. Although Adam had told Sierra he was divorced when they met, and she'd fallen immediately and helplessly in love with him, she'd learned six months later, when she was carrying his child, that he was still living with his wife when he wasn't on the road. It had been Allie, earnest, meddling Allie, who traveled to San Miguel, found Sierra and told her the truth.

Sierra would never forget the family photos Allie showed her that day—snapshots of Adam with his arm around his smiling wife, Dee. The two little girls in matching dresses posed with them, their eyes wide with innocence and trust.

"Forget him, kiddo," Hank had said airily, when Sierra went to him, in tears, with the whole shameful story. "It ain't gonna fly."

She'd written Adam immediately, but her letter came back, tattered from forwarding, and no one answered at any of the telephone numbers he'd given her.

She'd given birth to Liam eight weeks later, at home, attended by Hank's long-time mistress, Magdalena. Three days after that, Hank brought her an American newspaper, tossed it into her lap without a word.

She'd paged through it slowly, possessed of a quiet, escalating dread, and come across the account of Adam

Douglas's death on page four. He'd been shot to death, according to the article, on the outskirts of Caracas, after infiltrating a drug cartel to take pictures for an exposé he'd been writing.

"Mom?" Liam snapped his fingers under Sierra's nose. "Are you hearing the music again?"

Sierra blinked. Shook her head.

"Do you think my cousins would like me?"

She reached out, her hand trembling only slightly, and ruffled his hair. "I think *anybody* would like you," she said. When he was older, she would tell him about Adam's other family, but it was still too soon. She took his empty cup, carried it to the sink. "Now, go upstairs, brush your teeth again and hit the sack."

"Aren't you going to bed?" Liam asked practically.

Sierra sighed. "Yes," she said, resigned. She didn't think she'd sleep, but she knew Liam would wonder if she stayed up all night, prowling around the house. "You go ahead. I'm just going to make sure the front door is locked."

Liam nodded and obeyed without protest.

Sierra considered marking the occasion on the calendar.

She went straight to the front room, and the piano, the moment Liam had gone upstairs. The keyboard cover was down, the bench neatly in place. She switched on a lamp and inspected the smooth, highly polished wood for fingerprints. Nothing.

She touched the cover, and her fingers left distinct smudges.

No one had touched the piano that night, unless they'd been wearing gloves.

Frowning, Sierra checked the lock on the front door. Fastened.

She inspected the windows—all locked—and even the floor. It was snowing hard, and anybody who'd come in out of that storm would have left some trace, no matter how careful they were—a puddle somewhere, a bit of mud.

Again, there was nothing.

Finally she went upstairs, found a nightgown, bathed and got ready for bed. Since Travis had left her bags in the room adjoining Liam's, she opened the connecting door a crack and crawled between sheets worn smooth by time.

She was asleep in an instant.

1919

HANNAH CLOSED THE cover over the piano keys, stacked the sheet music neatly and got to her feet. She'd played as softly as she could, pouring her sadness and her yearning into the music, and when she returned to the upstairs corridor, she saw light under Doss's door.

She paused, wondering what he'd do if she went in, took off her clothes and crawled into bed beside him.

Not that she would, of course, because she'd loved her husband and it wouldn't be fitting, but there were times when her very soul ached within her, she wanted so badly to be touched and held, and this was one of them.

She swallowed, mortified by her own wanton thoughts.

Doss would send her away angrily.

He'd remind her that she was his brother's widow—if he ever spoke to her again at all.

For all that, she took a single, silent step toward the door.

"Ma?"

Tobias spoke from behind her. She hadn't heard him get out of bed, come to the threshold of his room.

Thanking heaven she was still fully dressed, she turned to face him.

"What is it?" she asked gently. "Did you have another bad dream?"

Tobias shook his head. His gaze slipped past Hannah to Doss's door, then back to her face, solemn and worried. "I wish I had a pa," he said.

Hannah's heart seized. She approached, pulled the boy close, and he allowed it. During the day, he would have balked. "So do I," she replied, bending to kiss the top of his head. "I wish your pa was here. Wish it so much it hurts."

Tobias pulled back, looked up at her. "But Pa's dead," he said. "Maybe you and Doss could get hitched. Then he wouldn't be my uncle anymore, would he? He'd be my pa."

"Tobias," Hannah said very softly, praying Doss hadn't overheard somehow. "That wouldn't be right."

"Why not?" Tobias asked.

She crouched, looked up into her son's face. One day, he'd be handsome and square-jawed, like the rest of the McKettrick men. For now he was still a little boy, his features childishly innocent. "I was your pa's wife. I'll love him for the rest of my days."

"That might be a long time," Tobias said, with a measure of dubiousness, as well as hope. He dropped his voice to a whisper. "I don't want Doss to marry somebody else, Ma," he said. "All the women in Indian Rock are sweet on him, and one of these days he might take a notion to get himself a wife."

"Tobias," Hannah reasoned, "you must put this foolishness out of your head. If Doss chooses to take a bride,

that's certainly his right. But it won't be me he marries.
It's too hard to explain right now, but Doss was your
pa's brother. I couldn't—"

"You'd marry some man in Montana, though,
wouldn't you?" Tobias demanded, suddenly angry, and
this time, he made no effort to keep his voice down.
"Some stranger who wears a suit to work!"

"Tobias!"

"I won't go to Montana, do you hear me? I won't
leave the Triple M unless Doss goes, too!"

Hannah reddened with embarrassment and anger—
Doss had surely heard—and rose to her full height. "Tobias McKettrick," she said sternly, "you go to bed this
instant, and don't you ever talk to me like that again!"

Tobias's chin jutted out, in the McKettrick way, and
his eyes flashed. "You go anyplace you want to," he told
her, turning on one bare heel to flee into his room, "but
I'm not going with you!" With that, he slammed the
door in her face.

Hannah took a step toward it, even reached for the
knob.

But in the end she couldn't face her son.

"Hannah."

Doss.

She stiffened but didn't turn. Doss would see too
much if she did. Guess too much.

He caught hold of her arm, brought her gently
around.

She whispered his name, despondent.

He took her hand, led her to the opposite end of the
hall, opened the last door on the right, the one where
she kept her sewing machine.

"What are you—?"

Doss stepped over the threshold first, turned, and

drew her in behind him. Reached around her to shut the door.

She leaned against the panel. It was hard at her back. "Doss," she said.

He cupped her face in his hands, bent his head, and kissed her, full on the mouth.

A sweet shock went through her. She knew she ought to break away, knew he wouldn't force himself on her if she uttered the slightest protest, but she couldn't say a word. Her body came alive as he pressed himself against her. His weight was hard and warm and blessedly real.

Doss reached behind her head, pulled the pins from her hair, let it fall around her shoulders, to her waist. He groaned, buried his face in it, burrowed through to take her earlobe between his lips and nibble on it.

Hannah gasped with guilty pleasure. Her knees went weak, and Doss held her upright with the lower part of his body.

She moaned softly.

"We can't," she whispered.

"We'd damn well better," Doss answered, "before we both go crazy."

"What if Tobias…?"

Doss leaned back, opened the buttons on her bodice, put his hands inside, under her camisole, to take the weight of her breasts. Chafed the nipples lightly with the sides of his thumbs.

"He won't hear," he said.

He bent to find a nipple, take it into his mouth. Suckled in the same nibbling, teasing way he'd tasted her earlobe.

Hannah plunged her fingers into his hair, groaned and tilted her head back, already surrendering. Already lost.

She tried to bring Gabe's face to her mind, hoping

the image would give her the strength to stop—stop—before it was too late, but it wouldn't come.

Doss made free with her breasts, tonguing them until she was in a frenzy.

She sank against the door, barely able to breathe.

And then he knelt.

Hannah trembled. Even though the room was cold, perspiration broke out all over her body. She made a slight whimpering sound when Doss lifted her skirts, went under them and pulled down her drawers.

She felt him part her private place with his fingers, felt his tongue touch her, like fire. Sobbed his name, under her breath.

He took her full in his mouth, hungrily.

Her hips moved frantically, seeking him, and her knees buckled.

He braced her securely against the door, put her legs over his shoulders, first one, and then the other, and through all that, he drew on her.

She writhed against him, one hand pressed to her mouth so that the guttural cries pounding at the back of her throat wouldn't get out.

He suckled.

She felt a surge of heat, radiating from her center into every part of her, then stiffened in a spasm of release so violent that she was afraid she would splinter into pieces.

"Doss," she pleaded, because she knew it was going to happen again, and again.

And it did.

When it was over, he ducked out from under the hem of her skirt and held her as she sagged, spent, to her knees. They were facing each other, her breasts bared to him, her body still quivering with an ebbing tide of passion.

"We can stop here," he said quietly.

She shook her head. They'd gone past the place of turning back.

Doss opened his trousers, reached under her skirt and petticoat to take hold of her hips. Lifted her onto him.

She slid along his length, letting him fill her, exalting in the size and heat and slick hardness of him. She gave a loud moan, and he covered her mouth with his, kissed her senseless, even as he raised and lowered her, raised and lowered her. The friction was slow and exquisite. Hannah dug her fingers into his shoulders and rode him shamelessly until satisfaction overtook her again, convulsed her, like some giant fist, and didn't let go until she was limp with exhaustion.

Only when she wept with relief did Doss finish. She felt him erupt inside her, swallowed his groans as he gave himself up to her.

He brushed away her tears with his thumbs, still inside her, and looked deep into her eyes. "It's all right, Hannah," he said gruffly. "Please, don't cry."

He didn't understand.

She wasn't weeping for shame, though that would surely come, but for the most poignant of joys.

"No," she said softly. She plunged her fingers into his hair, kissed him boldly, fervently. "It's not that. I feel…"

He was growing hard within her again.

"Oh," she groaned.

He played with her nipples. And got harder still.

"Doss," she gasped. "Doss—"

Present Day

SIERRA AWAKENED WITH a start, sounding from the depths of a dream so erotic that she'd been on the verge of climax. The light dazzled her, and the muffled silence seemed to fill not only her bedroom, but the world beyond it.

She lay still for a long time, recovering. Listening to her own quick, shallow breathing. Waiting for her heartbeat to slow down.

Liam peeked through the doorway linking her room to his.

"Mom?"

"Come in," Sierra said.

He bounded across the threshold. "It snowed!" he whooped, heading straight for the window. "I mean, it *really* snowed!"

Sierra smiled, sat up in bed and put her feet on the floor.

A jolt of cold went through her.

"It's *freezing* in here!"

Liam turned from the window to grin at her. "Travis says the furnace is out."

"Travis?"

"He's downstairs," Liam said. "He'll get it going."

A dusty-smelling whoosh rose from the nearest heat vent, as if to illustrate the point.

"What's he doing here?" Sierra asked, scrambling through her suitcases for a bathrobe. All she had was a thin nylon thing, and when she saw it, she knew it would be worse than nothing, so she pulled the quilt off the bed and wrapped herself in that instead.

"Don't be a grump," Liam replied. "Travis is doing us a *favor,* Mom. We'd probably be icicles by now if it wasn't for him. Did you know that old stove downstairs *works?* Travis built a fire in it, and he put the coffee on, too. He said to tell you it will be ready in a couple of minutes and we're snowed in."

"Snowed in?"

"Keep up, Mom," Liam chirped. "There was a *blizzard* last night. That's why Travis came to make sure we were all right. I heard him knock, and I let him in."

Sierra joined Liam at the window and drew in her breath.

The whiteness of all that snow practically blinded her, but it was beautiful, too, in an apocalyptic way. She'd never seen anything like it before and, for a long moment, she was spellbound. Then her sensible side kicked in.

"Thank God the power didn't go out," she said, easing a little closer to the vent, which was spewing deliciously warm air.

"It *did*," Liam informed her happily. "Travis got the generator started right away. We don't have lights or anything, but he said the furnace is all that matters."

She frowned. "How could he have made coffee?"

"On the *cookstove*, Mom," Liam said, with a roll of his eyes.

For the first time Sierra noticed that Liam was fully dressed.

He headed for the door. "I'd better go help Travis bring in the wood," he said. "Get some *clothes* on, will you?"

Five minutes later Sierra joined Travis and Liam in the kitchen, which was blessedly warm. Her jeans would do well enough, but she'd had to raid Meg's room for socks and a thick sweatshirt, because her tank tops weren't going to cut it.

"Are we *stranded* here?" she demanded, watching as Travis poured coffee from a blue enamel pot that looked like it came from a stash of camping gear.

He grinned. "Depends on how you look at it," he said. "Liam and I, we see it as an adventure."

"Some adventure," Sierra grumbled, but she took the coffee he offered and gave a grateful nod of thanks.

Travis chuckled. "Don't worry," he said. "You'll adjust."

Sierra hastened over to stand closer to the cookstove. "Does this happen often?"

"Only in winter," Travis quipped.

"Hilarious," she drawled.

Liam laughed uproariously.

"You are *enjoying* this," she accused, tousling her son's hair.

"It's *great!*" Liam cried. "Snow! Wait till the Geeks hear about this!"

"Liam," Sierra said.

He gave Travis a long-suffering look. "She hates it when I say 'geek,'" he explained.

Travis picked up his own mug of coffee, took a sip, his eyes full of laughter. Then he headed toward the door, put the cup on the counter and reclaimed his coat down from the peg.

"You're *leaving?*" Liam asked, horrified.

"Gotta see to the horses," Travis said, putting on his hat.

"Can I go with you?" Liam pleaded, and he sounded so desperately hopeful that Sierra swallowed the "no" that instantly sprang from her vocal cords.

"Your coat isn't warm enough," she said.

"Meg's got an old one around here someplace," Travis said carefully. "Hall closet, I think."

Liam dashed off to get it.

"I'll take care of him, Sierra," Travis told her quietly, when the boy was gone.

"You'd better," Sierra answered.

1919

HANNAH KNEW BY the profound silence, even before she opened her eyes, that it had been snowing all night. Lying alone in the big bed she'd shared with Gabe, she burrowed deeper into the covers and groaned.

She was sore.

She was satisfied.

She was a trollop.

A tramp.

She'd practically thrown herself at Doss the night before. She'd let him do things to her that no one else besides Gabe had ever done.

And now it was morning and she'd come to her senses and she would have to face him.

For all that, she felt strangely light, too.

Almost giddy.

Hannah pulled the covers up over her head and giggled.

Giggled.

She tried to be stern with herself.

This was serious.

Downstairs the stove lids rattled.

Doss was building a fire in the cookstove, the way he did every morning. He would put the coffee on to boil, then go out to the barn to attend to the livestock. When he got back, she'd be making breakfast, and they'd talk about how cold it was, and whether he ought to bring in extra wood from the shed, in case there was more snow on the way.

It would be an ordinary ranch morning.

Except that she'd behaved like a tart the night before.

Hannah tossed back the covers and got up. She wasn't one to avoid facing things, no matter how awk-

ward they were. She and Doss had lost their heads and
made love. That was that.

It wouldn't happen again.

They'd just go on, as if nothing had happened.

The water in the pitcher on the bureau was too cold
to wash in.

Hannah decided she would heat some for a bath,
after the breakfast dishes were done. She'd send Tobias
to the study to work at his school lessons, and Doss to
the barn.

She dressed hastily, brushed her hair and wound it
into the customary chignon at the back of her head.
Just before she opened the bedroom door to step out
into the new day, the pit of her stomach quivered. She
drew a deep breath, squared her shoulders and turned
the knob resolutely.

Doss had not left for the barn, as she'd expected. He
was still in the kitchen, and when she came down the
back stairs and froze on the bottom step, he looked at
her, reddened and looked away.

Tobias was by the back door, pulling on his heavi-
est coat. "Doss and me are fixing to ride down to the
bend and look in on the widow Jessup," he told Hannah
matter-of-factly, and he sounded like a grown man, fit to
make such decisions on his own. "Could be her pump's
frozen, and we're not sure she has enough firewood."

Out of the corner of her eye, Hannah saw Doss
watching her.

"Go out and see to the cow," Doss told Tobias. "Make
sure there's no ice on her trough."

It was an excuse to speak to her alone, Hannah knew,
and she was unnerved. She resisted an urge to touch
her hair with both hands or smooth her skirts.

Tobias banged out the back door, whistling.

"He's not strong enough to ride to the Jessups' place in this weather," Hannah said. "It's four miles if it's a stone's throw, and you'll have to cross the creek."

"Hannah," Doss said firmly, grimly. "The boy will be fine."

She felt her own color rise then, remembering all they'd done together, on the spare room floor, herself and this man. She swallowed and lifted her chin a notch, so he wouldn't think she was ashamed.

"About last night—" Doss began. He looked distraught.

Hannah waited, blushing furiously now. Wishing the floor would open, so she could fall right through to China and never be seen or heard from again.

Doss shoved a hand through his hair. "I'm sorry," he said.

Hannah hadn't expected anything except shame, but she was stung by it, just the same. "We'll just pretend—" She had to stop, clear her throat, blink a couple of times. "We'll just pretend it didn't happen."

His jaw tightened. "Hannah, it did happen, and pretending won't change that."

She intertwined her fingers, clasped them so tightly that the knuckles ached. Looked down at the floor. "What else can we do, Doss?" she asked, almost in a whisper.

"Suppose there's a child?"

Hannah hadn't once thought of that possibility, though it seemed painfully obvious in the bright, rational light of day. She drew in a sharp breath and put a hand to her throat.

How would they explain such a thing to Tobias? To the McKettricks and the people of Indian Rock?

"I'd have to go to Montana," she said, after a long time. "To my folks."

"Not with my baby growing inside you, you wouldn't," Doss replied, so sharply that Hannah's gaze shot back to his face.

"Doss, the scandal—"

"To hell with the scandal!"

Hannah reached out, pulled back Holt's chair at the table and sank into it. "Maybe I'm not. Surely just once—"

"Maybe you are," Doss insisted.

Hannah's eyes smarted. She'd wanted more children, but not like this. Not out of wedlock, and by her late husband's brother. Folks would call her a hussy, with considerable justification, and they'd make Tobias's life a plain misery, too. They'd point and whisper, and the other kids would tease.

"What are we going to do, then?" she asked.

He crossed the room, sat astraddle the long bench next to the table, so close she could feel the warmth of his body, glowing like the fresh fire blazing inside the cookstove.

His very proximity made her remember things better forgotten.

"There's only one thing we can do, Hannah. We'll get married."

She gaped at him. "Married?"

"It's the only decent thing to do."

The word decent stabbed at Hannah. She was a proud person, and she'd always lived a respectable life. Until the night before. "We don't love each other," she said, her voice small. "And anyway, I might not be—expecting."

"I'm not taking the chance," Doss told her. "As soon

as the trail clears a little, we're going into Indian Rock and get married."

"I have some say in this," Hannah pointed out.

Outside, on the back porch, Tobias thumped his boots against the step, to shake off the snow.

"Do you?" Doss asked.

CHAPTER SIX

Present Day

WHILE TRAVIS AND LIAM WERE in the barn, Sierra inspected the wood-burning stove. She found a skillet, set it on top, took bacon and eggs from the refrigerator, which was ominously dark and silent, and laid strips of the bacon in the pan. When the meat began to sizzle, she felt a little thrill of accomplishment.

She was actually *cooking* on a stove that dated from the nineteenth century. Briefly, she felt connected with all the McKettrick women who had gone before her.

When the electricity came on, with a startling revving sound, she was almost sorry. Keeping an eye on breakfast, she switched on the small countertop TV to catch the morning news.

The entire northern part of Arizona had been inundated in the blizzard, and thousands were without power. She watched as images of people skiing to work flashed across the screen.

The telephone rang, and she held the portable receiver between her shoulder and ear to answer. "Hello?"

"It's Eve," a gracious voice replied. "Is that you, Sierra?"

Sierra went utterly still. Travis and Liam tramped in from outside, laughing about something. They both fell silent at the sight of her, and neither one moved after Travis pushed the door shut.

"Hello?" Eve prompted. "Sierra, are you there?"

"I'm… I'm here," Sierra said.

Travis took off his coat and hat, crossed the room and elbowed her away from the stove. "Go," he told her, cocking a thumb toward the center of the house. "Liam and I will see to the grub."

She nodded, grateful, and hurried out of the warm kitchen. The dining room was frigid.

"Is this a bad time to talk?" Eve asked. She sounded uncertain, even a little shy.

"No—" Sierra answered hastily, finally gaining the study. She closed the door and sat in the big leather chair she'd occupied the night before, waiting for the fire to go out. Now she could see her breath, and she wished the blaze was still burning. "No, it's fine."

Eve let out a long breath. "I see on the Weather Channel that you've been hit with quite a storm up there," she said.

Sierra nodded, remembered that her mother—this woman she didn't know—couldn't see her. "Yes," she replied. "We have power again, thanks to Travis. He got the generator running right away, so the furnace would work and—"

She swallowed the rush of too-cheerful words. She'd been blathering.

"Poor Travis," Eve said.

"Poor Travis?" Sierra echoed. "Why?"

"Didn't he tell you? Didn't Meg?"

"No," Sierra said. "Nobody told me anything."

There was a long pause, then Eve sighed. "I'm probably speaking out of turn," she said, "but we've all been a little worried about Travis. He's like a member of the family, you know. His younger brother, Brody, died in an explosion a few months ago. It really threw Travis. He walked away from the company and just about everyone he knew. Meg had to talk fast to get him to come and stay on the ranch."

Sierra was very glad she'd brought the phone out of the kitchen. "I didn't know," she said.

"I've already said more than I should have," Eve told her ruefully. "And anyway, I called to see how you and Liam are doing. I know you're not used to cold weather, and when I saw the storm report, I had to call."

"We're okay," Sierra said. Had she known the woman better, she might have confided her worries about Liam—how he claimed he'd seen a ghost in his room. She still planned to call his new doctor, but driving to Flagstaff for an appointment would be out of the question, considering the state of the roads.

"I hear some hesitation in your voice," Eve said. She was treading lightly, Sierra could tell, and she would be a hard person to fool. Eve ran McKettrickCo, and hundreds of people answered to her.

Sierra gave a nervous laugh, more hysteria than amusement. "Liam claims the house is haunted," she admitted.

"Oh, that," Eve answered, and she actually sounded relieved.

"'Oh, that'?" Sierra challenged, sitting up straighter.

"They're harmless," Eve said. "The ghosts, I mean. If that's what they are."

"You know about the ghosts?"

Eve laughed. "Of course I do. I grew up in that house. But I'm not sure *ghosts* is the right word. To me, it always felt more like sharing the place than its being haunted. I got the sense that they—the other people—

were as alive as I was. That they'd have been just as surprised, had we ever come face-to-face."

Sierra's mind spun. She squeezed the bridge of her nose between a thumb and forefinger. The piano notes she'd heard the night before tinkled sadly in her memory. "You're not saying you actually *believe*—"

"I'm saying I've had experiences," Eve told her. "I've never seen anyone. Just had a strong sense of someone else being present. And, of course, there was the famous disappearing teapot."

Sierra sank against the back of the chair, both relieved and confounded. Had she told Meg about the teapot? She couldn't recall. Perhaps Travis had mentioned it—called Eve to report that her daughter was a little loony?

"Sierra?" Eve asked.

"I'm still here."

"I would get the teapot out," Eve recounted, "and leave the room to do something else. When I came back, it was in the china cabinet again. The same thing used to happen to my mother, and my grandmother, too. They thought it was Lorelei."

"How could that be?"

"Who knows?" Eve asked, patently unconcerned. "Life is mysterious."

It certainly is, Sierra thought. Little girls get separated from their mothers, and no one even comes looking for them.

"I'd like to come and see you," Eve went on, "as soon as the weather clears. Would that be all right, Sierra? If I spent a few days at the ranch? So we could talk in person?"

Sierra's heart rose into her throat and swelled there. "It's your house," she said, but she wanted to throw down the phone, snatch Liam, jump into the car and speed away before she had to face this woman.

"I won't come if you're not ready," Eve said gently.

I may never be ready, Sierra thought. "I guess I am," she murmured.

"Good," Eve replied. "Then I'll be there as soon as the jet can land. Barring another snowstorm, that should be tomorrow or the next day."

The jet? "Should we pick you up somewhere?"

"I'll have a car meet me," Eve said. "Do you need anything, Sierra?"

I could have used a mother when I was growing up. And when I had Liam and Dad acted as though nothing had changed—well, you would have come in handy then, too, Mom. "I'm fine," she answered.

"I'll call again before I leave here," Eve promised. Then, after another tentative pause and a brief goodbye, she rang off.

Sierra sat a long time in that chair, still holding the phone, and might not have moved at all if Liam hadn't come to tell her breakfast was on the table.

1919

IT WAS A COLD, seemingly endless ride to the Jessup place, and hard going all the way. More than once Doss glanced anxiously at his nephew, bundled to his eyeballs and jostling patiently alongside Doss's mount on the mule, and wished he'd listened to Hannah and left the boy at home.

More than once, he attempted to broach the subject that was uppermost in his mind—he'd been up half the night wrestling with it—but he couldn't seem to get a proper handle on the matter at all.

I mean to marry your ma.

That was the straightforward truth, a simple thing to say.

But Tobias was bound to ask why. Maybe he'd even raise an objection. He'd loved his pa, and he might just put his old uncle Doss right square in his place.

"You ever think about livin' in town?" Tobias asked, catching him by surprise.

Doss took a moment to change directions in his mind. "Sometimes," he answered, when he was sure it was what he really meant. "Especially in the wintertime."

"It's no warmer there than it is here," Tobias reasoned. Whatever he was getting at, it wasn't coming through in his tone or his manner.

"No," Doss agreed. "But there are other folks around. A man could get his mail at the post office every day, instead of waiting a week for it to come by wagon, and take a meal in a restaurant now and again. And I'll admit that library is an enticement, small as it is." He thought fondly of the books lining the study walls back at the ranch house. He'd read all of them, at one time or another, and most several times. He'd borrowed from his uncle Kade's collection, and his ma sent him a regular supply from Texas. Just the same, he couldn't get enough of the damn things.

"Ma's been talking about heading back to Montana," Tobias blurted, but he didn't look at Doss when he spoke. Just kept his eyes on the close-clipped mane of that old mule. "If she tries to make me go, I'll run away."

Doss swallowed. He knew Hannah thought about moving in with the homefolks, of course, but hearing it said out loud made him feel as if he'd not only been thrown from his horse, but stomped on, too. "Where would you go?" he asked, when he thought he could get the words out easy. He wasn't entirely successful. "If you ran off, I mean?"

Tobias turned in the saddle to look him full in the face. "I'd hide up in the hills somewhere," he said, with the conviction of innocence. "Maybe that canyon where Kade and Mandy faced down those outlaws."

Doss suppressed a smile. He'd grown up on that story himself, and to this day, he wondered how much of it was fact and how much was legend. Mandy was a sharpshooter, and she'd given Annie Oakley a run for her money, in her time. Kade had been the town marshal, with an office in Indian Rock back then, so maybe it had happened just the way his pa and uncles related it.

"Mighty cold up there," he told the boy mildly. "Just a cave for shelter, and where would you get food?"

Tobias's shoulders slumped a little, under all that wool Hannah had swaddled him in. If the kid took a spill from the mule, he'd probably bounce. "I could hunt," he said. "Pa taught me how to shoot."

"McKettricks," Doss replied, "don't run away."

Tobias scowled at him. "They don't live in Missoula, either."

Doss chuckled, in spite of the heavy feeling that had settled over his heart after he and Hannah had made love and stayed there ever since. Gabe was dead, but it still felt as if he'd betrayed him. "They live in all sorts of places," Doss said. "You know that."

"I won't go, anyhow," Tobias said.

Doss cleared his throat. "Maybe you won't have to."

That got the boy's full attention. His eyes were full of questions.

"I wonder what you'd say if I married your ma."

Tobias looked as though he'd swallowed a lantern

with the wick burning. "I'd like that," he said. "I'd like that a lot!"

Too bad Hannah wasn't as keen on the prospect as her son. "I thought you might not care for the idea," Doss confessed. "My being your pa's brother and all."

"Pa would be glad," Tobias said. "I know he would."

Secretly, Doss knew it, too. Gabe had been a practical man, and he'd have wanted all of them to get on with their lives.

Doss's eyes smarted something fierce, all of a sudden, and he had to pull his hat brim down. Look away for a few moments.

Take care of Hannah and my boy, Gabe had said. Promise me, Doss.

"Did Ma say she'd hitch up with you?" Tobias asked, frowning so that his face crinkled comically. "Last night I said she ought to, and she said it wouldn't be right."

Doss stood in the stirrups to stretch his legs. "Things can change," he said cautiously. "Even in a night."

"Do you love my ma?"

It was a hard question to answer, at least aloud. He'd loved Hannah from the day Gabe had brought her home as his bride. Loved her fiercely, hopelessly and honorably, from a proper distance. Gabe had guessed it right away, though. Waited until the two of them were alone in the barn, slapped Doss on the shoulder and said, Don't you be ashamed, little brother. It's easy to love my Hannah.

"Of course I do," Doss said. "She's family."

Tobias made a face. "I don't mean like that."

Doss's belly tightened. The boy was only eight, and he couldn't possibly know what had gone on last night in the spare room.

Could he?

"How do you mean, then?"

"Pa used to kiss Ma all the time. He used to swat her on the bustle, too, when he thought nobody was looking. It always made her laugh, and stand real close to him, with her arms around his neck."

Doss might have gripped the saddle horn with both hands, because of the pain, if he'd been riding alone. It wasn't the reminder of how much Hannah and Gabe had loved each other that seared him, though. It was the loss of his brother, the way of things then, and it all being over for good.

"I'll treat your mother right, Tobias," he said, after more hat-brim pulling and more looking away.

"You sound pretty sure she'll say yes," the boy commented.

"She already has," Doss replied.

Present Day

MORE SNOW BEGAN to fall at mid-morning and, worried that the power would go off again, and stay off this time, Sierra gathered her and Liam's dirty laundry and threw a load into the washing machine. She'd telephoned Liam's doctor in Flagstaff, from the study, while he and Travis were filling the dishwasher, but she hadn't mentioned the hallucinations. She'd heard the piano music herself, after all, and then Eve had made such experiences seem almost normal.

Sierra didn't know precisely what was happening, and she was still unsettled by Liam's claims of seeing a boy in old-time clothes, but she wasn't ready to bring up the subject with an outsider, whether that outsider had a medical degree or not.

Dr. O'Meara had reviewed Liam's records, since

they'd been expressed to her from the clinic in Florida, and she wanted to make sure he had an inhaler on hand. She'd promised to call in a prescription to the pharmacy in Indian Rock, and they'd made an appointment for the following Monday afternoon.

Now Liam was in the study, watching TV, and Travis was outside splitting wood for the stove and the fireplaces. If the power went off again, she'd need firewood for cooking. The generator kept the furnace running, along with a few of the lights, but it burned a lot of gas and there was always the possibility that it would break down or freeze up.

Travis came in with an armload just as she was starting to prepare lunch.

Watching him, Sierra thought about what Eve had said on the phone earlier. Travis's younger brother had died horribly, and very recently. He'd left his job, Travis had, and come to the ranch to live in a trailer and look after horses.

He didn't look like a man carrying a burden, but appearances were deceiving. Nobody knew that better than Sierra did.

"What kind of work did you do, before you came here?" she asked, and then wished she hadn't brought the subject up at all. Travis's face closed instantly, and his eyes went blank.

"Nothing special," he said.

She nodded. "I was a cocktail waitress," she told him, because she felt she ought to offer him something after asking what was evidently an intrusive question.

Standing there, beside the antique cookstove and the wood box, in his leather coat and cowboy hat, Travis looked as though he'd stepped through a time warp, out of an earlier century.

"I know," he said. "Meg told me."

"Of course she did." Sierra poured canned soup into a saucepan, stirred it industriously and blushed.

Travis didn't say anything more for a long time. Then, "I was a lawyer for McKettrickCo," he told her.

Sierra stole a sidelong glance at him. He looked tense, standing there holding his hat in one hand. "Impressive," she said.

"Not so much," he countered. "It's a tradition in my family, being a lawyer, I mean. At least, with everyone but my brother, Brody. He became a meth addict instead, and blew himself to kingdom-come brewing up a batch. Go figure."

Sierra turned to face Travis. Noticed that his jaw was hard and his eyes even harder. He was angry, in pain, or both.

"I'm so sorry," she said.

"Yeah," Travis replied tersely. "Me, too."

He started for the door.

"Stay for lunch?" Sierra asked.

"Another time," he answered, and then he was gone.

1919

IT WAS NEAR SUNSET when Doss and Tobias rode in from the Jessup place, and by then Hannah was fit to be tied. She'd paced for most of the afternoon, after it started to snow again, fretting over all the things that could go wrong along the way.

The horse or the mule could have gone lame or fallen through the ice crossing the creek.

There could have been an avalanche. Just last year, a whole mountainside of snow had come crashing down on to the roof of a cabin and crushed it to the ground, with a family inside.

Wolves prowled the countryside, too, bold with the desperation of their hunger. They killed cattle and sometimes people.

Doss hadn't even taken his rifle.

When Hannah heard the horses, she ran to the window, wiped the fog from the glass with her apron hem. She watched as they dismounted and led their mounts into the barn.

She'd baked pies that day to keep from going crazy, and the kitchen was redolent with the aroma. She smoothed her skirts, patted her hair and turned away so she wouldn't be caught looking if Doss or Tobias happened to glance toward the house.

Almost an hour passed before they came inside—they'd done the barn chores—and Hannah had the table set, the lamps lighted and the coffee made. She wanted to fuss over Tobias, check his ears and fingers for frostbite and his forehead for fever, but she wouldn't let herself do it.

Doss wasn't deceived by her smiling restraint, she could see that, but Tobias looked downright relieved, as though he'd expected her to pounce the minute he came through the door.

"How did you find Widow Jessup?" she asked.

"She was right where we left her last time," Doss said with a slight grin.

Hannah gave him a look.

"She was fresh out of firewood," Tobias expounded importantly, unwrapping himself, layer by layer, until he stood in just his trousers and shirt, with melted snow pooling around his feet. "It's a good thing we went down there. She'd have froze for sure."

Doss looked tired, but his eyes twinkled. "For sure," he confirmed. "She got Tobias here by the ears and kissed him all over his face, she was so grateful that he'd saved her."

Tobias let out a yelp of mortification and took a swing at Doss, who sidestepped him easily.

"Stop your roughhousing and wash up for supper," Hannah said, but it did her heart good to see it. Gabe used to come in from the barn, toss Tobias over one shoulder and carry him around the kitchen like a sack of grain. The boy had howled with laughter and pummeled Gabe's chest with his small fists in mock resistance. She'd missed the ordinary things like that more than anything except being held in Gabe's arms.

She served chicken and dumplings, in her best Blue Willow dishes, with apple pie for dessert.

Tobias ate with a fresh-air, long-ride appetite and nearly fell asleep in his chair once his stomach was filled.

Doss got up, hoisted him into his arms and carried him, head bobbing, toward the stairs.

Hannah's throat went raw, watching them go.

She poured a second cup of coffee for Doss, had it waiting when he came back a few minutes later.

"Did you put Tobias in his nightshirt and cover him with the spare quilt?" she asked, when Doss appeared at the bottom of the steps. "He mustn't take a chill—"

"I took off his shoes and threw him in like he was," Doss interrupted. That twinkle was still in his eyes, but there was a certain wariness there, too. "I made sure he was warm, so stop fretting."

Hannah had put the dishes in a basin of hot water to soak, and she lingered at the table, sipping tea brewed in Lorelei's pot.

Doss sat down in his father's chair, cupped his hands around his own mug of steaming coffee. "I spoke to Tobias about our getting married," he said bluntly. "And he's in favor of it."

Heat pounded in Hannah's cheeks, spawned by indignation and something else that she didn't dare think about. "Doss McKettrick," she whispered in reproach, "you shouldn't have done that. I'm his mother and it was my place to—"

"It's done, Hannah," Doss said. "Let it go at that."

Hannah huffed out a breath. "Don't you tell me what's done and ought to be let go," she protested. "I won't take orders from you now or after we're married."

He grinned. "Maybe you won't," he said. "But that doesn't mean I won't give them."

She laughed, surprising herself so much that she slapped a hand over her mouth to stifle the sound. That gesture, in turn, brought back recollections of the night before, when Doss had made love to her, and she'd wanted to cry out with the pleasure of it.

She blushed so hard her face burned, and this time it was Doss who laughed.

"I figure we're in for another blizzard," he said. "Might be spring before we can get to town and stand up in front of a preacher. I hope you're not looking like a watermelon smuggler before then."

Hannah opened her mouth, closed it again.

Doss's eyes danced as he took another sip of his coffee.

"That was an insufferably forward thing to say!" Hannah accused.

"You're a fine one to talk about being forward," Doss observed, and repeated back something she'd said at that very height of her passion.

"That's enough, Mr. McKettrick."

Doss set his cup down, pushed back his chair and stood. "I'm going out to the barn to look in on the stock again. Maybe you ought to come along. Make the job go faster, if you lent a hand."

Hannah squirmed on the bench.

Doss crossed the room, took his coat and hat down from the pegs by the door. "Way out there, a person could holler if they wanted to. Be nobody to hear."

Hannah did some more squirming.

"Fresh hay to lie in, too," Doss went on. "Nice and soft, and if a man were to spread a couple of horse blankets over it—"

Heat surged through Hannah, brought her to an aching simmer. She sputtered something and waved him away.

Doss chuckled, opened the door and went out, whistling merrily under his breath.

Hannah waited. If Doss McKettrick thought he was going to have his way with her—in the barn, of all places—well, he was just...

She got up, went to the stove and banked the fire with a poker.

He was just right, that was what he was.

She chose her biggest shawl, wrapped herself in it, and hurried after him.

Present Day

As soon as Sierra put supper on the table that night, the power went off again. While she scrambled for candles, Liam rushed to the nearest window.

"Travis's trailer's dark," he said. "He'll get *hypothermia* out there."

Sierra sighed. "I'll bet he comes back to see to the furnace, just like he did this morning. We'll ask him to have supper with us."

"I see him!" Liam cried gleefully. "He's coming out of the barn, with a lantern!" He raced for the door, and before Sierra could stop him, he was outside, with no coat on, galloping through the deepening snow and shouting Travis's name.

Sierra pulled on her own coat, grabbed Liam's and hurried after him.

Travis was already herding him toward the house.

"Mom made meat loaf, and she says you can have some," Liam was saying, as he tramped breathlessly along.

Sierra wrapped his coat around him, and would have scolded him, if her gaze hadn't collided unexpectedly with Travis's.

Travis shook his head.

She swallowed all that she'd been about to say and hustled her son into the house.

"I'll start the generator," Travis said.

Sierra nodded hastily and shut the door.

"Liam McKettrick," she burst out, "what were you thinking, going out in that cold without a coat?"

In the candlelight, she saw Liam's lower lip wobble. "Travis said it isn't the cowboy way. He was about to put his coat on me when you came."

"*What* isn't the 'cowboy way'?" she asked, chafing his icy hands between hers and praying he wouldn't have an asthma attack or come down with pneumonia.

"Not wearing a coat," Liam replied, downcast. "A cowboy is always prepared for any kind of weather, and he never rushes off half-cocked, without his gear."

Sierra relaxed a little, stifled a smile. "Travis is right," she said.

Liam brightened. "Do cowboys eat meat loaf?"

"I'm pretty sure they do," Sierra answered.

The furnace came on, and she silently blessed Travis Reid for being there.

He let himself into the kitchen a few minutes later. By then Sierra had set another place at the table and lit several more candles. They all sat down at the same time, and there was something so natural about their gathering that way that Sierra's throat caught.

"I hope you're hungry," she said, feeling awkward.

"I'm starved," Travis replied.

"Cowboys eat meat loaf, right?" Liam inquired.

Travis grinned. "This one does," he said.

"This one does, too," Liam announced.

Sierra laughed, but tears came to her eyes at the same time. She was glad of the relative darkness, hoping no one would notice.

"Once," Liam said, scooping a helping of meat loaf onto his plate, his gaze adoring as he focused on Travis, "I saw this show on the Science Channel. They found a cave man, in a block of ice. He was, like *fourteen thousand* years old! I betcha they could take some of his DNA and clone him if they wanted to." He stopped for a quick breath. "And he was all blue, too. That's what you'll look like, if you sleep in that trailer tonight."

"You're not a kid," Travis teased. "You're a forty-year-old wearing a pygmy suit."

"I'm *really* smart," Liam went on. "So you ought to listen to me."

Travis looked at Sierra, and their eyes caught, with an almost audible click and held.

"The generator's low on gas," Travis said. "So we

have two choices. We can get in my truck and hope there are some empty motel rooms at the Lamplight Inn, or we can build up the fire in that cookstove and camp out in the kitchen."

Liam had no trouble at all making the choice. "Camp out!" he whooped, waving his fork in the air. "Camp out!"

"You can't be serious," Sierra said to Travis.

"Oh, I'm serious, all right," he answered.

"Lamplight Inn," Sierra voted.

"Roads are bad," Travis replied. "*Real* bad."

"Once on TV, I saw a thing about these people who froze to death right in their car," Liam put in.

"Be quiet," Sierra told him.

"Happens all the time," Travis said.

Which was how the three of them ended up bundled in sleeping bags, with couch and chair cushions for a makeshift mattress, lying side by side within the warm radius of the wood-burning stove.

CHAPTER SEVEN

1919

HANNAH AND DOSS returned separately from the barn, by tacit agreement. Hannah, weak-kneed with residual pleasure and reeling with guilt, pumped water into a bucket to pour into the near-empty reservoir on the cookstove, then filled the two biggest kettles she had and set them on the stove to heat. She was adding wood to the fire when she heard Doss come in.

She blushed furiously, unable to meet his gaze, though she could feel it burning into her flesh, right through the clothes he'd sweet-talked her out of just an hour before, laying her down in the soft, surprisingly warm hay in an empty stall, kissing and caressing and nibbling at her until she'd begged him to take her.

Begged him.

She'd carried on something awful while he was at it, too.

"Look at me, Hannah," he said.

She glared at Doss, marched past him into the pantry and dragged out the big wash tub stored there under a high shelf. She set it in front of the stove with an eloquent clang.

"Hannah," Doss repeated.

"Go upstairs," she told him, flustered. "Leave me to my bath."

"You can't wash away what we did," he said.

She whirled on him that time, hands on her hips, fiery with temper. "Get out," she ordered, keeping her voice down in case Tobias was still awake or even listening at the top of the stairs. "I need my privacy."

Doss raised both hands to shoulder height, palms out, but his words were juxtaposed to the gesture. "If we're going to talk about what you need, Hannah, it's not a bath. It's a lot more of what we just did in the barn."

"Tobias might hear you!" Hannah whispered, outraged. If the broom hadn't been on the back porch, she'd have grabbed it up and whacked him silly with it.

"He wouldn't know what we were talking about even if he did," Doss argued mildly, lowering his hands. He approached, plucked a piece of straw from Hannah's hair and tickled her under the chin with it.

She felt as though she'd been electrified, and slapped his hand away.

He laughed, a low, masculine sound, leaned in and nibbled at her lower lip. "Good night, Hannah," he said.

A hot shiver of renewed need went through her. How could that be? He'd satisfied her that night, and the one before. Both times he'd taken her to heights she hadn't even reached with Gabe.

The difference was, she'd been Gabe's wife, in the eyes of God and man, and she'd loved him. She not only wasn't married to Doss, she didn't love him. She just wanted him, that was all, and the realization galled her.

"You've turned me into a hussy," she said.

Doss chuckled, shook his head. "If you say so, Hannah," he answered, "it must be true."

With that, he kissed her forehead, turned and left the kitchen.

She listened to the sound of his boot heels on the

stairs, heard his progress along the second-floor hall-way, even knew when he opened Tobias's door to look in on the boy before retiring to his own room. Only when she'd heard his door close did Hannah let out her breath.

When the water in the kettles was scalding hot, Hannah poured it into the tub, sneaked upstairs for a towel, a bar of soap and a nightgown. By the time she'd put out all the lanterns in the kitchen and stripped off her clothes, her bathwater had cooled to a temperature that made her sigh when she stepped into it.

She soaked for a few minutes, and then scrubbed with a vengeance.

It turned out that Doss had been right.

She tried but she couldn't wash away the things he'd made her feel.

A tear slipped down her cheek as she dried herself off, then donned her nightgown. She dragged the tub to the back door and on to the step, drained it over one side and dashed back in, covered with gooseflesh from the chill.

"I'm sorry, Gabe," she said, very quietly, huddling by the stove. "I'm sorry."

Present Day

TRAVIS WAS BUILDING up the fire when Sierra opened her eyes the next morning. "Stay in your sleeping bag," he told her. "It's colder than a meat locker in here."

Liam, lying between them throughout the night, was still asleep, but his breathing was a shallow rattle. Sierra sat bolt-upright, watchful, holding her own breath. Not feeling the external chill at all, except as a vague biting sensation.

Liam opened his eyes, blinked. "Mom," he said. "I can't—"

Breathe, Sierra finished the sentence for him, re-played it in her mind.

Mom, I can't breathe.

She bounded out of the sleeping bag, scrambled for her purse, which was lying on the counter and rum-maged for Liam's inhaler.

He began to wheeze, and when Sierra turned to rush back to him, she saw a look of panic in his eyes.

"Take it easy, Liam," she said, as she handed him the inhaler.

He grasped it in both hands, all too familiar with the routine, and pressed the tube to his mouth and nose.

Travis watched grimly.

Sierra dropped on to her knees next to her boy, put an arm loosely around his shoulders. *Let it work,* she prayed silently. *Please let it work!*

Liam lowered the inhaler and stared apologetically up into Sierra's eyes. He could barely get enough wind to speak. He was, in essence, choking. "It's—I think it's broken, Mom—"

"I'll warm up the truck," Travis said, and banged out of the house.

Desperate, Sierra took the inhaler, shook it and shoved it back into Liam's hands. It *wasn't* empty—she wouldn't have taken a chance like that—but it must have been clogged or somehow defective. "Try again," she urged, barely avoiding panic herself.

Outside, Travis's truck roared audibly to life. He gunned the motor a couple of times.

Liam struggled to take in the medication, but the in-haler simply wasn't working.

Travis returned, picked Liam up in his arms, sleeping bag and all, and headed for the door again. Sierra, frightened as she was, had to hurry to catch up, snatching her coat from the peg and her purse from the counter on the way out.

The snow had stopped, but there must have been two feet of it on the ground. Travis shifted the truck into four-wheel drive and the tires grabbed for purchase, finally caught.

"Take it easy, buddy," he told Liam, who was on Sierra's lap, the seat belt fastened around both of them. "Take it real easy."

Liam nodded solemnly. He was drawing in shallow gasps of air now, but not enough. *Not enough.* His lips were turning blue.

Sierra held him tight, but not too tight. Rested her chin on top of his head and prayed.

The roads hadn't been plowed—in fact, except for sloping drifts on either side, Sierra wouldn't have known where they were. Still, the truck rolled over them as easily as if they were bare.

What if we'd been alone, Liam and me? Sierra thought frantically. Her old station wagon, a snow-covered hulk in the driveway in front of the house, probably wouldn't have started, and even if it had by some miracle, the chances were good that they'd have ended up in the ditch somewhere along the way to safety.

"It's going to be okay," she heard Travis say, and she'd thought he was talking to Liam. When she glanced at him, though, she knew he'd meant the words for her.

She kept her voice even. "Is there a hospital in Indian Rock?" She and Liam had passed through the town the day they arrived, but she didn't remember seeing anything but houses, a diner or two, a drugstore, several bars and a gas station. She'd been too busy trying to follow the hand-drawn map Meg had scanned and sent to her by email—the McKettricks' private cemetery was marked with an X, and the ranch house an uneven square with lines for a roof.

"A clinic," Travis said. He looked down at Liam again, then turned his gaze back to the road. The set of his jaw was hard, and he pulled his cell phone from the pocket of his coat and handed it to Sierra.

She dialed 411 and asked to be connected.

When a voice answered, Sierra explained the situation as calmly as she could, keeping it low-key for Liam's sake. They'd been through at least a dozen similar episodes during his short life, and it never got easier. Each time, Sierra was hysterical, though she didn't dare let that show. Liam was taking his cues from her. If she lost it, he would, too, and the results could be disastrous.

The clinic receptionist seemed blessedly unruffled. "We'll be ready when you get here," she said.

Sierra thanked the woman and ended the call, set the phone on the seat.

By the time they arrived at the town's only medical facility, Liam was struggling to remain conscious. Travis pulled up in front, gave the horn a hard blast and was around to Sierra's side with the door open before she managed to get the seat belt unbuckled.

Two medical assistants, accompanied by a gray-haired doctor, met them with a gurney. Liam was whisked away. Sierra tried to follow, but Travis and one of the nurses stopped her.

Her first instinct was to fight.

"My son needs me!" She'd meant it for a scream, but it came out as more of a whimper.

"We'll need your name and that of the patient," a

clerk informed her, advancing with a clipboard. "And of course there's the matter of insurance—"

Travis glared the woman into retreat. "Her *name,*" he said, "is McKettrick."

"Oh," the clerk said, and ducked behind her desk.

Sierra needed something, anything, to do, or she was going to rip apart every room in that place until she found Liam, gathered him into her arms. "My purse," she said. "I must have left it in the truck—"

"I'll get it," Travis said, but first he steered her toward a chair in the waiting area and sat her down.

Tears of frustration and stark terror filled her eyes. What was happening to Liam? Was he breathing? Were they forcing the hated tube down into his bronchial passage even at that moment?

Travis cupped her face between his hands, for just a moment, and his palms felt cold and rough from ranch work.

The sensation triggered something in Sierra, but she was too distraught to know what it was.

"I'll be right back," he promised.

And he was.

Sierra snatched her bag from his hands, scrabbled through it to find her wallet. Found the insurance card Eve had sent by express the same day Sierra agreed to take the McKettrick name and spend a year on the Triple M, with Liam. She might have kissed that card, if Travis hadn't been watching.

The clerk nodded a little nervously when Sierra walked up to the desk and asked for the papers she needed to fill out.

Patient's Name. Well, that was easy enough. She scrawled Liam Bres—crossed out the last part, and wrote McKettrick instead.

Address? She had to consult Travis on that one. Everybody in Indian Rock knew where the Triple M was, she was sure, but the people in the insurance company's claims office might not.

Occupation? Child.

Damn it, Liam was a little boy, hardly more than a baby. Things like this shouldn't happen to him.

Sierra printed her own name, as guarantor. She bit her lip when asked about her job. Unemployed? She couldn't write that.

Travis, watching, took the clipboard and pen from her and inserted, Damn good mother.

The tears came again.

Travis got up, with the forms and the clipboard and the insurance card, inscribed with the magical name and carried them over to the waiting clerk.

He was halfway back to Sierra when the doctor reappeared.

"Hello, Travis," he said, but his gaze was on Sierra's face, and she couldn't read it, for all the practice she'd had.

"I'm Sierra McKettrick," she said. The name still felt like a garment that didn't quite fit, but if it would help Liam in any way, she would use it every chance she got. "My son—"

"He'll be fine," the doctor said kindly. His eyes were a faded blue, his features craggy and weathered. "Just the same, I think we ought to send him up to Flagstaff to the hospital, at least overnight. For observation, you understand. And because they've got a reliable power source up there."

"Is he awake?" Sierra asked anxiously.

"Partially sedated," replied the doctor, exchanging glances with Travis. "We had to perform an intubation."

Sierra knew how Liam hated tubes, and how frightened he probably was, sedated or not. "I have to see him," she said, prepared for an argument.

"Of course" was the immediate and very gentle answer.

Sierra felt Travis's hand close around hers. She clung, instead of pulling away, as she would have done with any other virtual stranger.

A few minutes later they were standing on either side of Liam's bed in one of the treatment rooms. His eyes widened with recognition when he saw Sierra, and he pointed, with one small finger, to the mouthpiece of his oxygen tube.

She nodded, blinking hard and trying to smile. Took his hand.

"You have to spend the night in the hospital in Flagstaff," she told him, "but don't be scared, okay? Because I'm going with you."

Liam relaxed visibly. Turned his eyes to Travis. Sierra's heart twisted at the hope she saw in her little boy's face.

"Me, too," Travis said hoarsely.

Liam nodded and drifted off to sleep.

The doctor had ordered an ambulance, and Sierra rode with Liam, while Travis followed in the truck.

There was more paperwork to do in Flagstaff, but Sierra was calmer now. She sat in a chair next to Liam's bed and filled in the lines.

Travis entered with two cups of vending-machine coffee, just as she was finishing.

"Thank you," Sierra said, and she wasn't just talking about the coffee.

"Wranglers like Liam and me," he replied, watching the boy with a kind of fretful affection, "we stick together when the going gets tough."

She accepted the paper cup Travis offered and set the ubiquitous clipboard aside to take a sip. Travis drew up a second chair.

"Does this happen a lot?" he asked, after a long and remarkably easy silence.

Sierra shook her head. "No, thank God. I don't know what we would have done without you, Travis."

"You would have coped," he said. "Like you've been doing for a long time, if my guess is any good. Where's Liam's dad, Sierra?"

She swallowed hard, glanced at the boy to make sure he was sleeping. "He died a few days before Liam was born," she answered.

"You've been alone all this time?"

"No," Sierra said, stiffening a little on the inside, where it didn't show. Or, at least, she *hoped* it didn't. "I had Liam."

"You know that isn't what I meant," Travis said.

Sierra looked away, made herself look back. "I didn't want to—complicate things. By getting involved with someone, I mean. Liam and I have been just fine on our own."

Travis merely nodded, and drank more of his coffee.

"Don't you have to go back to the ranch and feed the horses or something?" Sierra asked.

"Eventually," Travis answered with a sigh. He glanced around the room again and gave the slightest shudder.

Sierra remembered his younger brother. The wounds must be raw. "I guess you probably hate hospitals," she said. "Because of—" the name came back to her in Eve's telephone voice "—Brody."

Travis shook his head. His eyes were bleak. "If he'd gotten this far—to a hospital, I mean—it would have meant there was hope."

Sierra moved to touch Travis's hand, but just before she made contact, his cell phone rang. He pulled it from the pocket of his western shirt. "Travis Reid."

He listened. Raised his eyebrows. "Hello, Eve. I wouldn't have thought even *your* pilot could land in this kind of weather."

Sierra tensed.

Eve said something, and Travis responded. "I'll let Sierra explain," he said, and held out the phone to her.

Sierra swallowed, took it. "Hello, Eve," she said.

"Where are you?" her mother asked. "I'm at the ranch. It looks as if you've been sleeping in the kitchen—"

"We're in Flagstaff, in a hospital," Sierra told her. Only then did she realize that she and Travis were both wearing the clothes they'd slept in. That she hadn't combed her hair or even brushed her teeth.

All of a sudden she felt incredibly grubby.

Eve drew in an audible breath. "Oh, my *God*—Liam?"

"He had a pretty bad asthma attack," Sierra confirmed. "He's on a breathing machine, and he has to stay until tomorrow, but he's okay, Eve."

"I'll be up there as soon as I can. Which hospital?"

"Hold on," Sierra said. "There's really no need for you to come all this way, especially when the roads are so bad. I'm pretty sure we'll be home tomorrow—"

"Pretty sure?" Eve challenged.

"Well, he'll need his medication adjusted, and the inflammation in his bronchial tubes will have to go down."

"This sounds serious, Sierra. I think I should come. I could be there—"

"Please," Sierra interrupted. "Don't."

A thoughtful silence followed. "All right, then," Eve said finally, with a good grace Sierra truly appreciated. "I'll just settle in here and wait. The furnace is running and the lights are on. Tell Travis not to rush back—I can certainly feed the horses."

Sierra could only nod, so Travis took the phone back.

Evidently, a barrage of orders followed from Eve's end.

Travis grinned throughout. "Yes, ma'am," he said. "I will."

He ended the call.

"You will what?" Sierra inquired.

"Take care of you and Liam," Travis answered.

1919

THAT MORNING THE WORLD looked as though it had been carved from a huge block of pure white ice. Hannah marveled at the beauty of it, staring through the kitchen window, even as she longed with bittersweet poignancy for spring. For things to stir under the snowbound earth, to put out roots and break through the surface, green and growing.

"Ma?"

She turned, troubled by something she heard in Tobias's voice. He stood at the base of the stairs, still wearing his nightshirt and barefoot.

"I don't feel good," he said.

Hannah set aside her coffee with exaggerated care, even took time to wipe her hands on her apron before she approached him. Touched his forehead with the back of her hand.

"You're burning up," she whispered, stricken.

Doss, who had been rereading last week's newspaper at the table, his barn work done, slowly scraped back his chair.

"Shall I fetch the doc?" he asked.

Hannah turned, looked at him over one shoulder, and nodded. If you hadn't insisted on taking him with you to the widow Jessup's place, she thought—

But she would go no further.

This was not the time to place blame.

"You get back into bed," she told Tobias, briskly efficient and purely terrified. The bout of pneumonia that had nearly killed him during the fall had started like this. "I'll make you a mustard plaster to draw out the congestion, and your uncle Doss will go to town for Dr. Willaby. You'll be right as rain in no time at all."

Tobias looked doubtful. His face was flushed, and his nightshirt was soaked with perspiration, even though the kitchen was a little on the chilly side. The boy seemed dazed, almost as though he were walking in his sleep, and Hannah wondered if he'd taken in a word she'd said.

"I'll be back as soon as I can," Doss promised, already pulling on his coat and reaching for his hat. "There's whisky left from Christmas. It's in the pantry, behind that cracker tin," he added, pausing before opening the door. "Make him a hot drink with some honey. Pa used to brew up that concoction for us when we took sick, and it always helped."

Doss and Gabe, along with their adopted older brother, John Henry, had never suffered a serious illness in their lives, if you didn't count John Henry's deafness. What did they know about tending the sick?

Hannah nodded again, her mouth tight. She'd lost three sisters in childhood, two to diphtheria and one to scarlet fever; only she and her younger brother, David, had survived.

She was used to nursing the afflicted.

Doss hesitated a few moments on the threshold, as though there was something he wanted to say but couldn't put into words, then went out.

"You change into a dry nightshirt," Hannah told Tobias. His sheets were probably sweat-soaked, too, so she added, "And get into our bed."

Our bed.

Meaning Gabe's and hers.

And soon, after they were married, Doss would be sleeping in that bed, in Gabe's place.

She could not, would not, consider the implications of that.

Not now. Maybe not ever.

She was like the ranch woman she'd once read about in a Montana newspaper, making her way from the house to the barn and back in a blinding blizzard, with only a frozen rope to hold on to. If she let go, she'd be lost.

She had to attend to Tobias. That was her rope, and she'd follow it, hand over hand, thought over thought.

Hannah retrieved an old flannel shirt from the rag bag and cut two matching pieces, approximately twelve inches square. These would serve to protect Tobias's skin from the heat of the poultice, but like as not, he would still have blisters. She kept a mixture on hand for just such occasions, in a big jar with a wire seal. She dumped a big dollop of the stuff on to one of the bits of flannel, spread it like butter, and put the second cloth on top, her nose twitching at the pungent odors of mustard seed, pounded to a pulp, and camphor.

When she got upstairs, she found Tobias huddled in the middle of her bed, and his eyes grew big with recollection when he saw what she was carrying in her hands.

"No," he protested, but weakly. "No mustard plaster." He'd begun to shiver, and his teeth were chattering.

"Don't fuss, Tobias," Hannah said. "Your grandfather swears by them."

Tobias groaned. "My Montana grandfather," he replied. "My grandpa Holt wouldn't let anybody put one of those things on him!"

"Is that a fact?" Hannah asked mildly. "Well, next time you write to the almighty Holt McKettrick, you ask. I'll bet he'll say he wouldn't be without one when he's under the weather."

Tobias made a rude sound, blowing through his lips, but he rolled on to his back and allowed Hannah to open the top buttons of his nightshirt and put the poultice in place.

"Grandpa Holt," he said, bearing the affliction stalwartly, "would probably make me a whisky drink, just like he did for Pa and Uncle Doss."

Hannah sighed. Privately she thought there was a good deal of the roughneck in the McKettrick men, and while she wouldn't call any of them a drunk, they used liquor as a remedy for just about every ill, from snakebite to the grippe. They'd swabbed it on old Seesaw's gashes, when he tangled with a sow bear, and rubbed it into the gums of teething babies.

"What you're going to have, Tobias McKettrick, is oatmeal."

He made a face. "This burns," he complained, pointing to the mustard plaster.

Hannah bent and kissed his forehead. He didn't pull
away, like he'd taken to doing of late, and she found that
both reassuring and worrisome.

She glanced at the window, saw a scallop of icicles
dangling from the eave. It might be many hours—even
tomorrow—before Doss got back from Indian Rock
with Dr. Willaby. The wait would be agony, but there
was nothing to do but endure.

When Tobias closed his eyes and slept, Hannah left
the room, descended the stairs and went into the pantry
again. She moved the cracker tin aside, looked up at the
bottle of whisky hidden behind it, gave a disdainful sniff,
and took a canned chicken off the shelf instead. It was
a treasure, that chicken—she'd been saving it for some
celebration, so she wouldn't have to kill one of her laying hens—but it would make a fine, nourishing soup.

After gathering onions, rice and some of her spices—
which she cherished as much as preserved meat, given
how costly they were—Hannah commenced to make
soup.

She was surprised when, only an hour after he'd ridden out, Doss returned with another man she recognized as one of the ranch hands down at Rafe's place.
She frowned, watching from the window as Doss dismounted and left the newcomer to lead both horses
inside.

That was odd. Doss hadn't been to Indian Rock yet;
he couldn't have covered the distance in such a short
time. Why would he ask someone to put up his horse?

Puzzled, impatient and a little angry, Hannah was
waiting at the door when Doss came in.

"Bundle the boy up warm," he said, without any preamble at all. "Willie's going to stay here and look after the horses and the place. Once I've hitched the draft horses to the sleigh, we'll go overland to Indian Rock."

Hannah stared at him, confounded. "You're suggesting that we take Tobias all the way to Indian Rock?"

"I'm not 'suggesting' anything, Hannah," Doss interposed. "I met Seth Baker down by the main house, when I was about to cross the stream, and he hailed me, wanted to know where I was headed. I told him I was off to fetch Doc Willaby, because Tobias was feeling poorly. Seth said Willaby was down with the gout, but his nephew happened to be there, and he's a doctor, too. He's looking after the doc's practice, in town, so he wouldn't be inclined to come all the way out here."

Hannah's throat clenched, and she put a hand to it. "A ride like that could be the end of Tobias," she said.

Doss shook his head. "We can't just sit here," he countered, grim-jawed. "Get the boy ready or I'll do it myself."

"May I remind you that Tobias is my son?"

"He's a McKettrick," Doss replied flatly, as though that were the end of it—and for him, it probably was.

CHAPTER EIGHT

Present Day

TRAVIS WAITED UNTIL Sierra had drifted off into a fitful sleep in her chair next to Liam's hospital bed. Then he got a blanket from a nurse, covered Sierra with it and left.

A few minutes later, he was behind the wheel of his truck.

The roads were sheer ice, and the sky looked gray, burdened with fresh snow. After consulting the GPS panel on his dashboard, he found the nearest Wal-Mart, parked as close to the store as he could and went inside.

Shopping was something Travis endured, and this was no exception. He took a cart and wheeled it around, choosing the things Sierra and Liam would need if this hitch in Flagstaff turned out to be longer than expected. He'd spent the night at his own place, a few miles from the hospital, showered and changed there.

When he got back from his expedition—a January Santa Claus burdened down with bulging blue plastic bags—he made his way to Liam's room.

Sierra was awake, blinking and befuddled, and so was Liam. A huge teddy bear, holding a helium balloon in one paw, sat on the bedside table. The writing on the balloon said Get Well Soon in big red letters.

"Eve?" Travis asked, indicating the bear with a nod of his head.

Sierra took in the bags he was carrying. "Eve," she confirmed. "What have you got there?"

Travis grinned, though he felt tired all of a sudden, as though ten cups of coffee wouldn't keep him awake. Maybe it was the warmth of the hospital, after being out in the cold.

"A little something for everybody," he said.

Liam was sitting up, and the breathing tube had been removed. His words came out as a sore-throated croak, but he smiled just the same, and Travis felt a pinch deep inside. The kid was so small and so brave. "Even me?"

"Especially you," Travis said. He handed the boy one of the bags, watched as he pulled out a portable DVD player, still in its box, and the episodes of *Nova* he'd picked up to go with it.

"Wow," Liam said, his voice so raw that it made Travis's throat ache in sympathy. "I've always wanted one of these."

Sierra looked worried. "It's way too expensive," she said. "We can't accept it."

Liam hugged the box close against his little chest, obstinately possessive. Everything about him said, I'm not giving this up.

Travis ignored Sierra's statement and tossed her another of the bags, this one fat and light. "Take a shower," he told her. "You look like somebody who just went through a harrowing medical emergency."

She opened her mouth, closed it again. Peeked inside the bag. He'd bought her yoga pants and a hoodie, guessing at the sizes, along with toothpaste, a brush, soap and a comb.

She swallowed visibly. "Thanks."

He nodded.

While Sierra was in Liam's bathroom, showering, Travis helped the boy get the DVD player out of the box, plugged in and running.

"Mom might not let me keep it," Liam said sadly.

"I'm betting she will," Travis assured him.

Liam was engrossed in an episode about killer bees when Sierra came out of the bathroom, looking scrubbed and cautiously hopeful in her dark-blue sweats. Her hair was still wet from washing, and the comb had left distinct ridges, which Travis found peculiarly poignant.

Complex emotions fell into line after that one, striking him with the impact of a runaway boxcar, but he didn't dare explore any of them right away. He'd need to be alone to do that, in his truck or with a horse. For now, he was too close to Sierra to think straight.

She glanced at Liam, softened noticeably as she saw how much he was enjoying Travis's gift. His small hands clasped the machine on either side, as though he feared someone would wrench it away.

Something similar to Travis's thoughts must have gone through her mind, because he saw a change in her face. It was a sort of resignation, and it made him want to take her in his arms—though he wasn't about to do that.

"I could use something to eat," he said.

"Me, too," Sierra admitted. She tapped Liam on the shoulder, and he barely looked away from the screen, where bees were swarming. Music from the speakers portended certain disaster. "You'll be all right here alone for a while, if Travis and I go down to the cafeteria?"

The boy nodded distractedly, refocused his eyes on the bees.

Sierra smiled with a tiny, forlorn twitch of her lips.

They were well away from Liam's room, and waiting for an elevator, when she finally spoke.

"I'm grateful for what you did for Liam and me," she said, "but you shouldn't have given him something that cost so much."

"I won't miss the money, Sierra," Travis responded. "He's been through a lot, and he needed something else to think about besides breathing tubes, medical tests and shots."

She gave a brief, almost clipped nod.

That McKettrick pride, Travis thought. It was something to behold.

The elevator came, and the doors opened with a cheerful chiming sound. They stepped inside, and Travis pushed the button for the lower level. Hospital cafeterias always seemed to be in the bowels of the building, like the morgues.

Downstairs, they went through the grub line with trays, and chose the least offensive-looking items from the stock array of greasy green beans, mock meat loaf, brown gravy and the like.

Sierra chose a corner table, and they sat down, facing each other. She looked like a freshly showered angel from some celestial soccer team in the athletic clothes he'd provided, and Travis wondered if she had any idea how beautiful she was.

"I'm surprised Eve hasn't shown up," he said, to get the conversation started.

Sierra's cheeks pinkened a little, and she avoided his gaze. Poked at the faux meat loaf with a water-spotted fork.

"I don't know what I'm going to say to her," she said. "Beyond 'thank you,' I mean."

"How about, 'hello'?" Travis joked.

Sierra didn't look amused. Just nervous, like a rat cornered by a barn cat.

He reached across the table, closed his hand briefly over hers. "Look, Sierra, this doesn't have to be hard. Eve will probably do most of the talking, at least in the beginning, and she'll feed you your lines."

She smiled again. Another tentative flicker, there and gone.

They ate in silence for a while.

"It's not as if I hate her," Sierra said, out of the blue. "Eve, I mean."

Travis waited, knowing they were on uneven ground. Sierra was as skittish as a spring fawn, and he didn't want to speak at the wrong time and send her bolting for the emotional underbrush.

"I don't know her," Sierra went on. "My own mother. I saw her picture on the McKettrickCo website, but she told me it didn't look a thing like her."

Still, Travis waited.

"What's she like?" Sierra asked, almost plaintively. "Really?"

"Eve is a beautiful woman," Travis said. *Like you,* he added silently. "She's smart, and when it comes to negotiating a business deal, she's as tough as they come. She's remarkable, Sierra. Give her a chance."

Sierra's lower lip wobbled, ever so slightly. Her blue, blue eyes were limpid with feelings Travis could only guess at. He wanted to dive into them, like a swimmer, and explore the vast inner landscape he sensed within her.

"You know what happened, don't you?" she asked,

very softly. "Back when my mother and father were divorced."

"Some of it," Travis said, cautious, like a man touching a tender bruise.

"Dad took me to Mexico when I was two," she said, "right after someone from Eve's lawyer's office served the papers."

Travis nodded. "Meg told me that much."

"As little as I was, I remembered what she smelled like, what it felt like when she held me, the sound of her voice." A spasm of pain flinched in Sierra's eyes. "No matter how I tried, I could never recall her face. Dad made sure there weren't any pictures, and—"

He ached for her. The soupy mashed potatoes went pulpy in his mouth, and they went down like so much barbed wire when he swallowed. "What kind of man would—"

He caught himself.

None of your business, Trav.

To his surprise she smiled again, and warmth rose in her eyes. "Dad was never a model father, more like a buddy. But he took good care of me. I grew up with the kind of freedom most kids never know—running the streets of San Miguel in my bare feet. I knew all the vendors in the marketplace, and writers and artists gathered at our *casita* almost every night. Dad's mistress, Magdalena, home-schooled me. I attracted stray dogs wherever I went, and Dad always let me keep them."

"Not a traumatic childhood," Travis observed, still careful.

She shook her head. "Not at all. But I missed my mother desperately, just the same. For a while, I thought she'd come for me. That one day a car would pull up in front of the *casita*, and there she'd be, smiling, with her arms open. Then when there was no sign of her, and no letters came—well, I decided she must be dead. It was only after I got old enough to surf the internet that I found her."

"You didn't call or write?"

"It was a shock, realizing she was alive—that if I could find her, she could have found me. And she didn't. With the resources she must have had—"

Travis felt a sting of anger on Sierra's behalf. Pushed away his tray. "I used to work for Eve," he said. "And I've known her for most of my life. I can't imagine why she wouldn't have gone in with an army, once she knew where you were."

Sierra bit her lower lip again, so hard Travis almost expected it to bleed. Her eyes glistened with tears she was probably too proud to shed, at least for herself. She'd wept plenty for Liam, he suspected, alone and in secret. It paralyzed him when a woman cried, and yet in that moment he'd have rewritten history if he could have. He'd have been there, in the thick of Sierra's sorrows, whatever they were, to put his arms around her, promise that everything would be all right and move heaven and earth to make it so.

But the plain truth was, he hadn't been.

"I'd better get back to Liam," she said.

He nodded.

They carried their trays to the dropping-off place, went upstairs again, entered Liam's room.

He was asleep, with the DVD player still running on his lap.

Travis went to speak to one of the nurses, a woman he knew from college, and when he came back, he found Sierra stretched out beside her son, dead to the world.

He sighed, watching the pair of them.

He'd kept himself apart, even before Brody died, busy with his career. Dated lots of women and steered clear of anything heavy.

Now, without warning, the whole equation had shifted, and there was a good chance he was in big trouble.

1919

THE AIR WAS so cold it bit through the bearskin throws and Hannah's many layers of wool to her flesh. She could see her breath billowing out in front of her, blue white, like Doss's. Like Tobias's.

Her boy looked feverishly gleeful, nestled between her and Doss, as the sleigh moved over an icy trail, drawn by the big draft horses, Cain and Abel. The animals usually languished in the barn all winter; in the spring, they pulled plows in the hayfields, in the fall, harvest wagons. Summers, they grazed. They seemed spry and vigorous to Hannah, gladly surprised to be working.

Where other horses or even mules might have floundered in the deep, crusted snow, the sons of Adam, as Gabe liked to call them, pranced along as easily as they would over dry ground.

Doss held the reins in his gloved hands, hunkered down into the collar of his sheepskin-lined coat, his earlobes red under the brim of his hat. Once in a while he glanced Hannah's way, but mostly when he spared a look, it was for Tobias.

"You warm enough?" he'd asked.

And each time Tobias would nod. If his blood had been frozen in his veins, he'd have nodded, Hannah knew that, even if Doss didn't. He idolized his uncle, always had.

Would he forget Gabe entirely, once she and Doss were married?

Everything within Hannah rankled at the thought.

Why hadn't she left for Montana before it was too late?

Now she was about to tie herself, for good, to a man she lusted after but would never love.

Of course she could still go home to her folks—she knew they'd welcome her and Tobias—but suppose she was carrying Doss's child? Once her pregnancy became apparent, they'd know she'd behaved shamefully. The whole world would know.

How could she bear that?

No. She would go ahead and marry Doss, and let sharing her bed with him be her private consolation. She'd find a way to endure the rest, like his trying to give her orders all the time and maybe yearning after other women because he'd taken a wife out of honor, not choice.

She'd be his cross to bear, and he would be hers.

There was a perverse kind of justice in that.

They reached the outskirts of Indian Rock in the late afternoon, with the sun about to go down. Doss drove straight to Dr. Willaby's big house on Third Street, secured the horses and reached into the sleigh for Tobias before Hannah got herself unwrapped enough to get out of the sleigh.

Doc Willaby's daughter, Constance, met them at the door. She was a beautiful young woman, and she'd pursued Gabe right up to the day he'd put a gold band on Hannah's finger. Now, from the way she looked at Doss, she was ready to settle for his younger brother.

The thought stirred Hannah to fury, though she'd

have buttered, baked and eaten both her shoes before admitting it.

"We have need of a doctor," Doss said to Constance, holding Tobias's bundled form in both arms.

"Come in," Constance said. She had bright-auburn hair and very green eyes, and her shape, though slender, was voluptuous. What, Hannah wondered, did Doss think when he looked at her? "Papa's ill," the other woman went on, "but my cousin is here, and he'll see to the boy."

Hannah put aside whatever it was she'd felt, seeing Constance, for relief. Tobias would be looked after by a real doctor. He'd be all right now, and nothing else mattered but that.

She would darn Doss McKettrick's socks for the rest of her life. She would cook his meals and trim his hair and wash his back. She would take him water and sandwiches in summer, when he was herding cattle or working in the hayfields. She'd bite her tongue, when he galled her, which would surely be often, and let him win at cards on winter nights.

The one thing she would never do was love him— her heart would always belong to Gabe—but no one on earth, save the two of them, was ever going to know the plain, regrettable truth.

"It's a bad cold," the younger doctor said, after carefully examining Tobias in a room set aside for the purpose. He was a very slender man, almost delicate, with dark hair and sideburns. He wore a good suit and carried a gold watch, which he consulted often. He was a city dweller, Hannah reflected, used to schedules. "I'd recommend taking a room at the hotel for a few days, though, because he shouldn't be exposed to this weather."

Doss took out his wallet, like it was his place to pay
the doctor bills, and Hannah stepped in front of him.
She was Tobias's mother, and she was still responsible
for costs such as these.

"That'll be one dollar," the doctor said, glancing from
Hannah's face, which felt pink with conviction and cold,
to Doss's.

Hannah shoved the money into his hand.

"Give the boy whisky," the physician added, folding
the dollar bill and tucking it into the pocket of his fine
tailored coat. "Mixed with honey and lemon juice, if
the hotel dining room's got any such thing on hand."

Doss, to his credit, did not give Hannah a triumphant
look at this official prescription for a remedy he'd already suggested and she'd disdained, but she elbowed
him in the ribs anyway, just as if he had.

They checked into the Arizona Hotel, which, like
many of the businesses in Indian Rock, was McKettrick
owned. Rafe's mother-in-law, Becky Lewis, had run the
place for years, with the help of her daughter, Emmeline. Now it was in the hands of a manager, a Mr. Thomas
Crenshaw, hired out of Phoenix.

Doss was greeted like a visiting potentate when he
walked in, once again carrying Tobias. A clerk was dis-
patched to take the sleigh and horses to the livery stable, and they were shown, the three of them, to the best
rooms in the place.

The quarters were joined by a door in between, and
Hannah would have preferred to be across the hall
from Doss instead, but she made no comment. While
Mr. Crenshaw hadn't gone quite so far as to put them
all in the same room, it was clearly his assumption, and
probably that of the rest of Indian Rock, too, that she
and Doss were intimate. She could imagine how the

reasoning went: Doss and his brother's widow shared a house, after all, way out in the country, and heaven only knew what they were up to, with only the boy around. He'd be easy to fool, being only eight years old.

Hannah went bright red as these thoughts moved through her mind.

Doss dismissed the manager and put Tobias on the nearest bed.

"I'll go downstairs and fetch that whisky concoction," he said, when it was just the three of them.

Tobias had never stayed in a hotel and, sick as he was, he was caught up in the experience. He nestled down in the bearskins, cupped his hands behind his head and gazed smiling up at the ceiling.

"Do as you please," Hannah told Doss, removing her heavy cloak and bonnet and laying them aside.

He sighed. "While we're in town, we'd best get married," he said.

"Yes," Hannah agreed acerbically. "And let's not forget to place an order at the feed-and-grain, buy groceries, pay the light bill and renew our subscription to the newspaper."

Doss gave a ragged chuckle and shook his head. "Guess I'd better dose you up with whisky, too," he replied. "Maybe that way you'll be able to stand the honeymoon."

Hannah's temper flared, but before she could respond, Doss was out the door, closing it smartly behind him.

"I like this place," Tobias said.

"Good," Hannah answered irritably, pulling off her gloves.

"What's a honeymoon," Tobias asked, "and how come you need whisky to stand it?"

Hannah pretended she hadn't heard the question.

She'd packed hastily before leaving the house, things for Tobias and for herself, but nothing for a wedding and certainly nothing for a wedding night. If the valises had been brought upstairs, she'd have something to do, shaking out garments, hanging them in the wardrobes, but as it was, her choices were limited. She could either pace or fuss over Tobias.

She paced, because Tobias would not endure fussing.

Doss returned with their bags, followed by a woman from the kitchen carrying two steaming mugs on a tray. She set the works down on a table, accepted a gratuity from Doss, stole a boldly speculative look at Hannah and bustled out.

"Drink up," Doss said cheerfully, handing one mug to Hannah and carrying the other to Tobias, who sat up eagerly to accept it.

Hannah sniffed the whisky mixture, took a tentative sip and was surprised at how good the stuff tasted. "Where's yours?" she asked, turning to Doss.

"I'm not the one dreading tonight," he answered.

Hannah's hands trembled. She set the mug down, beckoned for Doss to follow, and swept into the adjoining room. "What do you mean, tonight?" she whispered, though of course she knew.

Doss closed the door, examined the bed from a distance and proceeded to walk over to it and press hard on the mattress several times, evidently testing the springs.

Hannah's temper surged again, but she was speechless this time.

"Good to know the bed won't creak," Doss observed.

She found her voice, but it came out as a sputter. "Doss McKettrick—"

He ran his eyes over her, which left a trail of sensation, just as surely as if he'd stripped her naked and caressed her with his hands. "The preacher will be here in an hour," he said. "He'll marry us downstairs, in the office behind the reception desk. If Tobias is well enough to attend, he can. If not, we'll tell him about it later."

Hannah was appalled. "You made arrangements like that without consulting me first?"

"I thought we'd said all there was to say."

"Maybe I wanted time to get used to the idea. Did you ever think of that?"

"Maybe you'll never get used to the idea," Doss reasoned, sitting now, on the edge of the bed he clearly intended to share with her that very night. He stood, stretched in a way that could only have been called risqué. "I'm going out for a while," he announced.

"Out where?" Hannah asked, and then hated herself for caring.

He stepped in close—too close.

She tried to retreat and found she couldn't move.

Doss hooked a finger under her chin and made her look at him. "To buy a wedding band, among other things," he said. She felt his breath on her lips, and it made them tingle. "I'll send a wire to my folks and one to yours, too, if you want."

Hannah swallowed. Shook her head. "I'll write to Mama and Papa myself, when it's over," she said.

Sad amusement moved in Doss's eyes. "Suit yourself," he said.

And then he left her standing there.

She heard him speak quietly to Tobias, then the opening and closing of a door. After a few moments she returned to the next room.

Tobias had finished his medicinal whisky, and his

eyelids were drooping. Hannah tucked the covers in around him and kissed his forehead. Whatever else was happening, he seemed to be out of danger. She clung to that blessing and tried not to dwell on her own fate.

He yawned. "Will Uncle Doss be my pa, once you and him are married?" he asked drowsily.

"No," Hannah said, her voice firm. "He'll still be your uncle." Tobias looked so disheartened that she added, "And your stepfather, of course."

"So he'll be sort of my father?"

"Sort of," Hannah agreed, relenting.

"I guess we won't be going to Montana now," Tobias mumbled, settling into his pillow.

"Maybe in the spring," Hannah said.

"You go," Tobias replied, barely awake now. "I'll stay here with Uncle Pa."

It wounded Hannah that Tobias preferred Doss's company to hers and that of her family, but the boy was ill and she wasn't going to argue with him. "Go to sleep, Tobias," she told him.

As if he'd needed her permission, the little boy lapsed into slumber.

Hannah sat watching him sleep for a long time. Then, seeing snow drift past the windows in the glow of a gas streetlamp, she stood and went to stand with her hands resting on the wide sill, looking out.

It was dark by then, and the general store, the only place in Indian Rock where a wedding band could be found, had probably been closed for an hour. All Doss would have to do was rap on the door, though, and they'd open the place to him. Same as the telegraph office, or any other establishment in town.

After all, he was a McKettrick.

A tear slipped down her cheek.

She was a bride, and she should be happier.

Instead she felt as if she was betraying Gabe's memory. Letting down her folks, too, because they'd hoped she'd come home and eventually marry a local man, though they hadn't actually come out and said that last part. Now, because she'd been foolish enough, needy enough, to lie with Doss, not once but twice, she'd have to stay on the Triple M until she died of old age.

A tear slipped down her cheek, and she wiped it away quickly with the back of one hand.

"You made your bed, Hannah McKettrick," she told her reflection in the cold, night-darkened glass of the window, "and now you'll just have to lie in it."

By the time Doss returned, she'd washed her face, taken her hair down for a vigorous brushing and pinned it back up again. She'd put on a fresh dress, a prim but practical gray wool, and pinched some color into her cheeks.

He had on a brand-new suit of clothes, as fancy as the ones the doctor's nephew wore, and he'd gotten a haircut and a shave, too.

She was strangely touched by these things.

"I'd have bought you a dress for the wedding," he told her, staring at her as though he'd never seen her before, "but I didn't know what would fit, and whether you'd think it proper to wear white."

She smiled, feeling a tender sort of sorrow. "This dress will do just fine," she said.

"You look beautiful," Doss told her.

Hannah blushed. It was nonsense, of course—she probably looked more like a schoolmarm than anything else in her stern gray frock with the black buttons coming up to her throat—but she liked hearing the words. Had almost forgotten how they sounded, with Gabe gone.

Doss took her hand, and there was an uncharacteristic shyness in the gesture that made her wonder if he was as frightened and reluctant as she was.

"You don't have to go through with this, Doss," she said.

He ran his lips lightly over her knuckles before letting her hand go. "It's the right thing to do," he answered.

She swallowed, nodded.

"I guess the preacher must be here."

Doss nodded. "Downstairs, waiting. Shall we wake Tobias?"

Hannah shook her head. "Better to let him sleep."

"I'll fetch a maid to watch over him while we're gone," Doss said.

Now it was Hannah who nodded.

He left her again, and this time she felt it as a tearing-away, sharp and prickly. He came back with a plump, older woman clad in a black uniform and an apron, and then he took Hannah's hand once more and led her out of the room, down the stairs and into the office where she would become Mrs. McKettrick, for the second time.

At least, she thought philosophically, she wouldn't have to get used to a new name.

CHAPTER NINE

Present Day

THE WEATHER HADN'T IMPROVED, Sierra noted, standing at the window of Liam's hospital room the next morning. Orderlies had wheeled in a second bed the night before, and she'd slept in a paper gown. Now she was back in the sweats Travis had bought for her, rested and restored.

Dr. O'Meara had already been in to introduce herself, check on Liam's progress and do a work-up of her own, and she'd signed the release papers, too. Sierra liked and trusted the woman, though she was younger than expected, no more than thirty-five years old, with delicate features, very long brown hair held back by a barrette and a trim figure.

Armed with a prescription, Sierra was ready to take her son and leave.

Ready to face Eve, and all the emotional spade work involved.

Or not.

Just as she turned from the window, Travis entered the room, wearing slacks and a blue pullover sweater that accentuated the color of his eyes. He'd said he owned a house in Flagstaff, and Sierra knew he'd gone there to spend the night.

There was so much she *didn't* know about his life,

and this was unsettling, although she didn't have the time or energy to pursue it at the moment.

"Travis!" Liam crowed, as though he hadn't expected to see his friend ever again. "I get to go home today!"

The word *home* caught in Sierra's heart like a fish hook. The ranch house on the Triple M was Eve's home, and it was Meg's, but it didn't belong to her and Liam. They were temporary guests, and it had troubled Sierra all along to think Liam might become attached to the place and be hurt when they left.

Travis approached the bed, grinned and ruffled Liam's hair. "That's great," he said. "According to reports, the power is back on, the pantry is bulging, and your grandmother is waiting to meet you."

Sierra felt a wrench at the reminder. So much for thinking she was prepared to deal with Eve McKettrick.

Liam inspected Travis speculatively. "You don't look like a cowboy today," he declared.

Travis laughed. "Neither do you," he countered.

"Yeah, but I *never* do," Liam said, discouraged.

"We'll have to do something about that one of these days soon."

Sierra bristled. She and Liam were committed to staying on the ranch for a year, that was the bargain. Twelve months. The time would surely pass quickly, and she didn't want her son putting down roots only to be torn from that hallowed McKettrick ground.

"Liam looks fine the way he is," she said.

Travis gave her a long, thoughtful look. "True enough," he said mildly. "My buddy Liam is one handsome cowpoke. In fact, he looks a lot like Jesse did, at his age."

Another connection to the storied McKettrick clan. Uncomfortable, Sierra averted her eyes. She'd already gathered Liam's things, but now she rearranged them busily, just for something to do.

Half an hour later, the three of them were in Travis's truck, headed back to the ranch. Liam, buckled in between Travis and Sierra, promptly fell asleep, but his hands were locked around his DVD player. Mentally Sierra clutched the new inhaler, prescribed by Dr. O'Meara, purchased at the hospital pharmacy and tucked away in her bag, just as anxiously.

She had been silent for most of the ride, gazing out at the winter landscape as it whipped past the passenger window.

Travis said little or nothing, concentrating on navigating the icy roads, but Sierra was fully aware of his presence just the same, and in a way that disturbed her. He'd been a rock since Liam's asthma attack, and she was grateful but she couldn't afford to become dependent on him, emotionally or in any other way, and she didn't want her son to, either.

Trouble was, it might be too late for Liam. He adored Travis Reid, and there was no telling what fantasies he'd cooked up in that high-powered little brain of his. He and Travis riding the range, probably. Wearing baseball mitts and playing catch. Going fishing in some pristine mountain lake.

All the things a boy did with a dad.

"Sierra?"

She didn't dare look at Travis, for fear he might see the vulnerability she was feeling. All her nerves seemed to be on the outside of her skin, and they were doing the jingle-bell rock. "What?"

"I was just wondering what you were thinking."

She couldn't tell him, of course. He'd think she was attracted to him, and she wasn't.

Much.

So she lied. "All about Eve," she said.

He chuckled at the flimsy joke, but Sierra gave him points for recognizing an obscure reference to an old movie. Maybe they had a thing or two in common after all.

"I imagine the lady's on pins and needles herself, right about now. She wants to see you and Liam more than anything, I'd guess, but it won't be easy for her."

"I don't *want* it to be easy for her," Sierra answered.

Travis hesitated only a beat or two. "Maybe she has good reasons for what she did."

Sierra's silence was eloquent.

"Give her a chance, Sierra."

She glanced at him. "I'm doing that," she said. "I drove all the way here from Florida. I agreed to stay on the Triple M for a full year."

"Would you have done it if it weren't for the insurance?"

Damn it. He *was* a lawyer. "Probably not," she admitted.

"You'd do just about anything for Liam."

"Not 'just about,'" Sierra said. "*Anything* covers it."

"What about yourself? What would you do for Sierra?"

"Are we going to talk about me in the third person?"

"Stop hedging. I understand your devotion to Liam. I'd just like to know what you'd be doing right now if you didn't have a child, especially one with medical problems."

Sierra glanced at Liam, making sure he was asleep. "Don't talk about him as though he were somehow… deficient."

"I'm not. He's a great kid, and he'll grow up to be

an exceptional man. And I'm still waiting to hear what your dreams are for yourself."

She gave a desultory little chuckle. "Nothing spectacular. I'd like to survive."

"Not much of a life. Not for you and not for Liam."

Sierra squirmed. "Maybe I've forgotten how to dream," she said.

"And that doesn't concern you?"

"Up until now, it hasn't been a factor."

"That's unfortunate. Liam will pattern his attitudes after yours. Is that what you want for him? Just survival?"

"Are you channeling some disincarnate life coach?" Sierra demanded.

Travis laughed, low and quiet. "Not me," he said.

"You're just playing the cowboy version of Dr. Phil, then?"

"Okay, Sierra," Travis conceded. "I'll back off. For now."

"What are *your* dreams, hotshot?" Sierra retorted, too nettled to let the subject alone. "You have a law degree, but you train horses and shovel out stalls for a living."

This time there was no laughter. Travis's glance was utterly serious, and the pain Sierra saw in it made her ashamed of the way she'd spoken to him.

"I guess I had that coming," he said quietly. "And here's my answer. I'd like to be able to dream again. *That's* my dream."

"I'm sorry," Sierra told him, after a few moments had passed. The man had lost his brother in a very tragic way. He was probably doing the best he could, like almost everybody else. "I didn't mean to be unkind. I was just feeling—"

"Cornered?"

"That's a good word for it."

"You must have been burned pretty badly," Travis observed. "And not just by Eve." He looked down at Liam. "Maybe by this little guy's dad?"

"Maybe," Sierra said.

After that, conversation fell by the wayside again, but Sierra did plenty of thinking.

When they arrived at the ranch, all the lights in the house seemed to be on, even though it was barely noon. A glowing tangle of color loomed in the parlor window, and Sierra squinted, sure she must be seeing things.

Travis followed her gaze and chuckled. "Uh-oh," he said. "Looks as if Christmas sneaked back in while we weren't around."

Liam's eyes popped open at the magic word. "Christmas?"

Sierra smiled, in spite of the knot of worry lying heavily in the pit of her stomach. What was Eve up to?

Travis pulled up close to the back door, and Sierra braced herself as it sprang open. There was Eve McKettrick, standing on the top step, a tall, slender woman, breathtakingly attractive in expensive slacks and a blue silk blouse.

"Is *that* my grandma?" Liam asked. "She looks like a movie star!"

She *did* look like a movie star, a young Maureen O'Hara. And Sierra was suddenly, stunningly aware that she'd seen this woman before, in San Miguel, not once, but several times. She'd been a periodic guest at one of the better B&Bs when Sierra was small, and they'd had ice cream together at a sidewalk café near the *casita*, several times.

For a moment Sierra forgot how to breathe.

The Lady. She'd always called Eve "the Lady," and she'd secretly believed she was an angel. But it had been years since she'd given the memory conscious house room.

Now it all came flooding back, in a breathtaking rush.

Travis shut off the truck and opened the door to get out. "Sierra?" he prompted, when she didn't move.

"Hello!" Liam yelled, delighted, from his place next to Sierra. "My name is Liam and I'm seven!"

Eve smiled, and her vivid green eyes glistened with emotion. "My name is Eve," she said quietly, "and I'm fifty-three. Come here and give me a hug."

Sierra finally came unstuck, opened the passenger-side door and climbed down, planting her feet in the crusty snow. Liam scrambled past her so quickly that he generated a slight breeze.

Eve leaned down to gather her grandson in her arms. She kissed the top of his head and met Sierra's gaze again as she straightened.

"I'll see to the horses," Travis said.

"Don't go," Sierra blurted, before she could stop herself.

Eve steered Liam into the kitchen, watching with interest as Travis rounded the front end of the truck and stood close to Sierra.

"You'll be all right," he told her.

She bit her lower lip, feeling like a fool. It was still all she could do not to grab one of his hands with both of hers and cling like some crazy codependent girlfriend about to be hustled out of town on the last bus of the day.

So long. It's been real.

For a few long moments she and Travis just stared into each other's eyes. He was determined; she was scared. And something *else* was happening, too, something a lot harder to define.

Finally Travis broke the impasse by turning and striding off toward the barn.

Sierra drew a deep breath and marched toward the open door of the kitchen and the woman who waited on the threshold.

"There's a surprise in the living room," Eve said to Liam, once they were all inside and she'd shut the door against the unrelenting cold.

He raced to investigate.

"You're the Lady," Sierra said, stricken.

"The Lady?" Eve echoed, but Sierra could see by the expression in her mother's eyes that it was mere rhetoric.

"The one I used to see in San Miguel."

"Yes," Eve said. "Sit down, Sierra. I'll make tea, and we'll chat."

"Wow!" Liam yelled, from the living room. "Mom, there *is* a Christmas tree in here, with *major* presents under it!"

"Oh, Lord," Sierra said, and sank on to one of the benches at the table.

"They're *all* for me!" Liam whooped.

Sierra watched her mother take Lorelei's teapot from the cabinet, spoon tea leaves into it, fill and plug in the electric kettle. "Christmas presents?" she asked.

Eve smiled a little guiltily. "I had seven years of grandmothering to make up for," she said. "Cut me a break, will you?"

Sierra would have tallied the numbers differently, but there was no point in saying so. "I thought you were an angel," she confessed. "In San Miguel, I mean."

Eve busied herself with the tea-brewing process,

stealing the occasional hungry glance at Sierra. "You've certainly grown up to be a beautiful woman," she said. Finally she stopped her puttering, clasped her hands together and practically gobbled Sierra up with her eyes. "It's…it's so wonderful to see you."

Sierra didn't answer.

Liam pounded in from the living room. "Can I open my presents?"

"If it's all right with your mother," Eve said.

Sierra sighed. "Go ahead. And calm down, please. You just got out of the hospital, remember? Overexcitement and asthma do not mix."

Liam gave a shout of delight and thundered off again, ignoring her admonition completely.

The electric kettle whistled, and Eve poured the contents into the antique teapot, and brought it to the table. She selected two cups and saucers from the priceless collection and carried those over, too. Then, at last, looking as nervous as Sierra felt, Eve sat down in the chair at the end of the table.

"How's Liam?" she asked.

"He's fine," Sierra answered. "But he's just getting over a crisis, as you know, so he's going to bed as soon as he finishes opening his presents." The bear and the balloon were in the back of Travis's truck, under the heavy plastic cover, and she imagined her mother ordering them for a grandson she'd never seen.

"So many things to say," Eve fretted, "and I haven't the first idea where to start."

Suddenly Sierra was tired. And *not* so suddenly she was overwhelmed. "Why didn't you tell me who you were—when we met in San Miguel?"

Eve poured tea, warmed beautifully manicured and bejeweled hands around a translucent china cup. "Nothing like cutting to the chase," she said, with rueful appreciation.

"Nothing like it," Sierra agreed implacably.

"If I'd told you who I was, you would have told Hank, and he might have taken you and disappeared again. It took me almost five years to find you the first time, so I wasn't about to let that happen."

Sierra absorbed her mother's words quietly. She *had* mentioned "the Lady" to her father, at least after the first encounter, but if he'd suspected anything, he'd probably dismissed the accounts as flights of a child's imagination. Besides, elegant tourists were common in San Miguel, and they were generous to local children.

"If I'd been in that situation—if it were Liam who'd been snatched away and I'd found him—I'd have taken him home with me."

Eve's eyes filled with tears, but she blinked them back. "Would you?" she challenged softly. "Even if he seemed happy and healthy, and you knew he didn't remember you? Would you simply kidnap him—tear him away from everyone and everything he knew? Without thought for any of the psychological repercussions?"

Sierra blinked. She *would* have been terrified if Eve had stolen her back from Hank, whisked her out of the country in some clandestine way. And she would have had to do exactly that, because even though Sierra's father seemed benignly disinterested most of the time, word would have gotten back to him quickly, had Eve tried to spirit her away. He would have called out the *federales,* as well as the municipal authorities, many of whom were his friends, and Eve would probably *still* be languishing in a Mexican jail.

And she'd had another daughter to consider, as well as a home and a business.

"I've been grown up for quite some time," Sierra pointed out, after long reflection. "What stopped you from contacting me after Dad died and Liam and I came to the States?"

Eve looked down into her cup.

Liam burst into the room, making both women start.

"Look, Mom!" he cried, clutching an expensive telescope in both arms, already attached to its tripod. "I'll be able to see all the way back to the Big Bang with this thing!"

"You're getting too excited," Sierra reiterated, sparing a glance for Eve before rising from her chair. "You'd better go and lie down for a while."

Liam balked, of course. He was seven, faced with unexpected largesse. "But I haven't even opened half my presents!"

"Later," Sierra said. She got up, put a hand on her son's shoulder and steered him toward the back stairs.

He protested all the way, clutching Eve's telescope in the same way he had Travis's DVD player. The stuff *she'd* given him for Christmas, all bought on sale with her tips from the bar, paled by comparison to this bounty, and even though she was glad for him, she also felt a deep slash of resentment.

"Look at it this way," she said a few minutes later, tucking him into bed in a fresh pair of pajamas, the telescope positioned in front of the window, beside the antique one that had been there when they arrived. "You've still got a lot of loot downstairs. Rest awhile, and you can tear into it again."

"Do you promise?" Liam asked suspiciously. "You won't make my grandma take it all back to the store or something?"

"When have I ever lied to you?"

"When you said there was a Santa Claus."

Sierra sighed. "Okay. Name one other time."

"You said we didn't have any family. We've got Grandma and Aunt Meg."

"I give up," Sierra said, spreading her hands. "I'm a shameless prevaricator."

Liam grinned. "If that boy comes back, I'm going to show him *my* telescope!"

A tiny chill moved down Sierra's spine. "Liam," she insisted, "there *is* no boy."

"That's what *you* think," Liam replied, and he looked damnably smug as he settled back into his pillows. "This is his room. This is his bed, and that's his old telescope."

Sierra took off the boy's shoes, tucked him under the faded quilt and sat with him until he drifted off to sleep.

And even then she didn't move, because she didn't want to go downstairs again and hear more well-rehearsed reasons why her mother had abandoned her when she was smaller than Liam.

1919

HANNAH COULDN'T HELP comparing her second wedding to her first, at least in the privacy of her mind. She and Gabe had been married in the summer, in the side yard at the main ranch house. Gabe's grandfather, Angus, had been alive then and, as head of the McKettrick clan, he'd issued a decree to that effect. There had been a big cake and a band and long improvised tables burdened with food. There had been guests and gifts and dancing.

After the celebration, Gabe had driven her to town in a surrey, and they'd stayed right here at the Arizona Hotel, caught the next day's train out of Indian Rock.

Traveled all the way to San Francisco for a honeymoon. Tobias had been conceived during that magical time, and the box of photographs commemorating the trip was one of Hannah's most treasured possessions.

Now she found herself standing in the cramped and cluttered office behind the reception desk, a widow about to become a bride. Only, this time there was no cake, no honeymoon trip to look forward to, and certainly no music and dancing.

Those things wouldn't have mattered, Hannah was certain, if she'd loved Doss and known he loved her. It wasn't the modesty of the ceremony that troubled her, but the coldly practical reasons behind it.

While the preacher droned the sacred words, with Mr. Crenshaw and one of the maids for witnesses, Hannah stole the occasional sidelong glance at her groom.

Doss looked stalwart, determined and impossibly handsome.

What will become of us? Hannah wondered, in silent and stoic despair. She'd pasted a wobbly smile on her face, because she wouldn't have the preacher gossiping afterward, saying she'd looked like a deer with one foot stuck in a railroad track, and the train about to come clackety-clacking round the bend at full throttle.

Oh, no. If she did what she really wanted to do, which was either run or break down and cry, that self-righteous old coot would spread the news from one end of the state to the other, and what a time folks would have with that.

A weeping bride.

A grimly resigned groom.

The talk wouldn't die down for years.

So Hannah endured.

She repeated her vows, when she was prompted,

and kept her chin high, her backbone straight and her eyes bone dry. The ordeal was almost over when suddenly the office door banged open and Doss's uncle Jeb strolled in. He was still handsome, though well into middle age, and he grinned as he took in the not-so-happy couple.

"Thought I'd missed it," he said.

Doss laughed, evidently pleased to set eyes on another blood-McKettrick.

The minister cleared his throat, not entirely approving of the interruption, it would seem.

"I now pronounce you man and wife," he said quickly.

"Kiss your bride," Jeb prompted, watching his nephew closely.

Hannah blushed.

Doss kissed her, and she wondered if he'd have remembered to do it at all, if his uncle hadn't provided a verbal nudge.

"No flowers?" Jeb asked, after Doss had paid the preacher and the man had gone. He looked around the office. "No guests?"

"It was a hasty decision," Doss explained.

Hannah blushed again.

"Oh," Jeb said. He shook Doss's hand, whacked him once on the shoulder and then turned to Hannah, gently kissing her cheek. "Be happy, Hannah," he whispered, close to her ear. "Gabe would want that."

Tears brimmed in Hannah's eyes, and this after she'd held up so well, made such an effort to play the happy bride. Did her true feelings show? Or was Jeb McKettrick just perceptive?

She nodded, unable to speak.

"I thought you were down in Phoenix," Doss said to

his uncle. If he'd noticed Hannah's tears, he was keeping the observation to himself.

"I came up here to take care of some business at the Cattleman's Bank," Jeb explained. "Arrived on the afternoon train. It's a long ride out to the ranch, and the meeting ran long, so I decided to spend the night here at the hotel and head back to Phoenix tomorrow. I was sitting in the dining room, taking my supper, when somebody mentioned that the two of you were shut up in here with a preacher." He glanced at Hannah again, and she saw concern flash briefly in his eyes. "I decided to invite myself to the festivities. Of course when I tell Chloe about it, she'll say I ought to learn a few manners. After all this time, my wife still hasn't given up on grinding off my rough edges."

Doss slipped an arm around Hannah's waist. "We're glad you came," he told Jeb. "Aren't we, Hannah?"

She didn't answer right away, and he had the gall to pinch her lightly under her ribs, through the fabric of her sadly practical gray dress.

"Yes," she said.

"Where's Tobias?" Jeb asked. "Chloe'll skin me if I don't bring back a detailed report. That woman likes to know everything about everybody. How much the boy's grown, how he's doing with his lessons, and all that."

"He's down with a cold," Doss said. "That's why we brought him to town. So he could see the doctor."

"And you just decided to get married while you were here?"

Doss colored up.

Hannah was stricken to silence again.

Jeb smiled. "The boy's here in the hotel, then?"

Hannah nodded, still mute.

Jeb's gaze shifted to Doss. "Why don't you go up

there and see if he's agreeable to a visit from his old Uncle Jeb?" he said.

Doss hesitated, then nodded and left the room.

"I'm going to ask Doss the same thing I'm about to ask you," Jeb said, the moment they were alone with the door closed. "What's going on here?"

Hannah swallowed painfully. "Well, it just seemed sensible for us to get married."

"Sensible?"

"Both of us living out there on the ranch, I mean. You know how folks…speculate about things like that."

"I know, all right," Jeb answered. "Chloe and I stirred up plenty of talk in our day. I guess I just figured if there'd been a wedding in the offing, the family would have heard something about it before now."

"Doss wired his folks, and I was going to write to mine—"

"You're both adults and it's your business what you do," Jeb said. "Do you love Doss, Hannah?"

She fell back on something she'd said to Tobias, out at the ranch, when he'd asked a similar question. "He's family," she replied.

"He's also a man. A young one, with his whole life ahead of him. He deserves a wife who's glad to be his wife."

Hannah lifted her chin. "A few minutes ago you told me Gabe would want this. Doss and me married, I mean. And you're probably right. So I did it as much for him as anybody."

"There's only one person you ought to please in a situation like this, Hannah, and that's yourself."

"Tobias needs Doss."

"I don't doubt that's true. Losing Gabe was hard on everybody in this family, but it was worse for you and

Tobias. The question on my mind right now is, do you need Doss, Hannah?"

Hannah needed her new husband, all right, but not in a way she was going to discuss with his uncle—or anyone else on the face of the earth, for that matter. "I'll see that he's happy, if that's what you're worried about," she said, and felt her cheeks burn again, fearing she'd revealed exactly what she'd been so determined to keep secret.

"He'll be happy," Jeb said, with such remarkable certainty that Hannah wondered if he knew something she didn't. "Will you?"

"I'll learn to be," she answered.

Jeb placed his hands on her shoulders, squeezed lightly and kissed her forehead. Then, without another word, he went out, leaving Hannah standing there alone, full of confusion and sorrow.

She was waiting in the lobby when Doss came downstairs, some minutes later, looking shy as a schoolboy. Evidently, Jeb had already spoken to him and was with Tobias now.

Doss tried to smile but fell a little short. Now that they were actually married, he apparently didn't know what to say, and neither did Hannah. They were making the best of things, both of them, and it shouldn't have been that way.

"I guess we ought to have some supper," Doss said. "Tobias has already eaten. The maid went down to the kitchen and brought him up a meal while we were—"

Hannah looked down at her feet. "You deserve somebody who loves you," she said softly, miserable with shame.

Doss put a finger under her chin and raised her head, so he could look into her eyes. "I don't know if your mind and heart love me, Hannah McKettrick," he said solemnly, with no trace of arrogance, "but your body does. And maybe it will teach the rest of you to feel the same way."

She took a gentle hold on the lapels of his new suit, bought just for the wedding. "Gabe would want this," she said. "Our being married, I mean."

Doss swallowed. "I loved my brother," he told her gravely, "but I don't want to talk about him. Not tonight."

Hannah wept inside, even though her eyes were dry. "All right," she agreed.

He led her into the dining room, and they both ordered fried chicken dinners. It was an occasion, to eat a restaurant meal, almost as unusual, in Hannah's life, as getting married. She was starved, after a long and hectic day, and yet the food tasted like sawdust from the first bite.

Jeb appeared, just as they were trying to choke down dessert. Chocolate cake, normally Hannah's favorite, with powdered sugar icing.

"Tobias," Jeb announced, "is spending the night in the room next to mine. I've already made arrangements for the maid to stay with him."

Hannah laid down her fork, relieved not to have to pretend to eat any longer. It was almost as hard as pretending to be happy, and she didn't think she could manage both.

"I guess that's all right," she allowed.

Doss looked down at his plate. He hadn't eaten much more than Hannah had, though, like her, he'd made a good show of it. Making illicit love on the ranch was one thing, she realized, and being married was quite another. Was he as nervous about the night to come as she was?

Jeb congratulated them both and left.

Their plates were cleared away.

Doss paid the bill.

And then there was nothing to do but go upstairs and get on with their wedding night.

CHAPTER TEN

TOBIAS'S BED WAS EMPTY, and his things had been removed. Hannah glanced nervously at Doss, now her husband, and put a hand to her throat.

He sighed and loosened his string tie, then unbuttoned his collar. If there had been whisky in that hotel room, Hannah was sure he would have poured himself a double and downed it in a gulp. She felt moved to touch his arm, soothe him somehow, but the urge died aborning. Instead she stood rigid upon the soles of her practical high-button shoes, and wished she'd put her foot down while there was still time, called the whole idea of getting married for the damn fool notion that it was, stopped the wedding and let the gossips say what they would.

She was miserable.

Doss was miserable.

What in the world had possessed them?

"We could get an annulment," she said shakily.

Doss's gaze sliced to her, sharp enough to leave the thick air quivering in its wake. "Oh, I'd say we were past that," he retorted coldly. "Wouldn't you?"

Hannah's cheeks burned as smartly as if they'd been chapped by the bitter wind even then rattling at the windows and seeping in as a draft. "I only meant that we haven't…well…consummated the marriage, and—"

He narrowed his eyes. "I remember it a little differently," he said.

Damn him, Hannah thought fiercely. He'd been so all-fired set on going through with the ceremony—it had been his idea to exchange vows, not hers—and now he was acting as though he'd been wooed, enticed, trapped.

"I will thank you to remember this, Doss Mc-Kettrick—I didn't seduce you. You seduced me!"

He hooked a finger in his tie and jerked at it. Took an angry step toward her and glared down into her face. "You could have said no at any time, Hannah," he reminded her, making a deliberate effort to keep his voice down. "My recollection is that you didn't. In fact, you—"

"Stop," Hannah blurted. "If you're any kind of gentleman, you won't throw that in my face! I was—we were both—lonely, Doss. We lost our heads, that's all. We could find the preacher, tell him it was a mistake, ask him to tear up the license—"

"You might as well stand in the middle of Main Street, ring a cowbell to draw a crowd, and tell the whole damn town what we did as do that!" Doss seethed. "And what's going to happen in six months or so, when your belly is out to here with my baby?"

Hannah's back teeth clamped together so hard that she had to will them apart. "What makes you so sure there is a baby?" she demanded. "Gabe and I wanted more children after Tobias, but nothing happened."

Doss opened his mouth, closed it again forcefully. Whatever he'd been about to say, he'd clearly thought better of it. All of a sudden Hannah wanted to reach down his throat and haul the words out of him like a bucket from a deep well, even though she knew she'd be just as furious to hear them spoken as she was right then, left to wonder.

For what seemed to Hannah like a very long time, the two of them just stood there, practically nose to nose, glowering at each other.

Hannah broke first, shattered against that McKettrick stubbornness the way a storm-tossed ship might shatter on a rocky shore. With a cry of sheer frustration, she turned on one heel, strode into the next room and slammed the door hard behind her.

There was no key to turn the lock, and nothing to brace under the knob to keep Doss from coming after her. So Hannah paced, arms folded, until some of her fury was spent.

Her gaze fell on her nightgown, spread by some thoughtful soul—probably the maid who had looked after Tobias while she and Doss were downstairs ruining their lives—across the foot of the bed.

Resignation settled over Hannah, heavy and cold as a wagonload of wet burlap sacks.

I might as well get this over with, she thought, trying to ignore the unbecoming shiver of excitement she felt at the prospect of being alone with Doss, bared to him, surrendering and, at the same time, conquering.

Resolutely she took off her clothes, donned the nightgown and unpinned her hair.

And waited.

Where was Doss?

She sat down on the edge of the mattress, twiddling her thumbs.

He didn't arrive.

She got up and paced.

Still no Doss.

She was damned if she'd open the door and invite him in after the way he'd acted, but the waiting was almost unbearable.

Finally Hannah sneaked across the room, bent and peered through the keyhole. Her view was limited, and while she couldn't actually see Doss, that didn't mean he wasn't there. If he'd left, she would have heard him—wouldn't she?

She paced again, briskly this time, muttering under her breath.

The room was growing cold, and not just because there was no fire to light. She marched over to the radiator, under the window, and cranked on the handle until she heard a comforting hiss. Something caught her eye, through the night-darkened glass, as she straightened, and she wiped a peephole in the steam with the sleeve of her nightgown. Squinted.

Was that Doss, standing in the spill of light flowing over the swinging doors of the Blue Garter Saloon down at the corner? His shape and stance were certainly familiar, but the clothes were wrong—or were they? Doss had worn a suit to the wedding, and this man was dressed for the open range.

Hannah stared harder, and barely noticed when the tip of her nose touched the icy glass. Then the man struck a match against the saloon wall, and lit a cheroot, and she saw his face clearly in the flare of orange light.

It was Doss, and he was looking in her direction, too. He'd seen her, watching him from the hotel room window like some woebegone heroine in a melodrama.

No. It couldn't be him.

They had a lot to settle, it was true, but this was their wedding night.

Hannah clenched her fists and turned from the window for a few moments, struggling to regain her composure as well as her dignity. By now everyone in Indian Rock knew about the hurry-up wedding, knew they ought to be honeymooning, she and Doss, even if they hadn't gotten any further than the Arizona Hotel. If Doss passed the evening in the Blue Garter Saloon, tonight of all nights—

She whirled, fumbling to pull up the sash, meaning to call out to him, though God only knew what she'd say. But before she could open the window, he turned his back on her and went right through those saloon doors. Hannah watched helplessly as they swung on their hinges and closed behind him.

Present Day

SIERRA STOOD WITH her hands on her hips, studying the January Christmas tree. The lights shimmered and the colors blurred as she took in the mountain of gifts still to be unwrapped, the wads of bright paper, the expensive loot Liam had already opened.

Sweaters. A leather coat, reminiscent of Travis's. Cowboy boots and a hat. A set of toy pistols. Why, there was more stuff there than she'd been able to give Liam in all seven years of his life, let alone for one Christmas.

Eve had done it all, of course. The decorating, anyway. She might have brought the presents with her from Texas, after sending some office minion out to ransack the high-end stores.

Did it mean she genuinely cared, Sierra wondered, or was she merely trying to buy some form of absolution?

Sierra sensed Eve's presence almost immediately, but it was a few moments before she could look her in the eye.

"The pistols might have been an error in judgment," Eve conceded quietly, poised in the doorway as though unsure whether to bolt or stay and face the music. "I should have asked."

"The whole thing is an error in judgment," Sierra responded, her insides stretched so taut that they seemed to hum. "It's too much." She turned, at last, and faced her mother. "You had no right."

"Liam is my grandson," Eve pointed out, and the very rationality of her words snapped hard around Sierra's heart, like some giant rubber band, yanked to its limits and then let go.

"You had no right!" Sierra repeated, in a furious undertone.

To her credit, Eve didn't flinch. "What are you so afraid of, Sierra? That he'll like me?"

Sierra swayed a little, suddenly light-headed. "Don't you understand? I can't give Liam things like this. I don't want him getting used to this way of life—it will be too hard on him later, when we have to leave it all behind."

"What way of life?" Eve persisted. Her attitude wasn't confrontational, but it was obvious that she intended to stand her ground. It was all so easy for her, with her money and her power. She could make grand gestures, but Sierra would be the one picking up the pieces when she and Liam made a hard—and inevitable—landing in the real world.

"The *McKettrick* way of life!" Sierra burst out. "This big house, the land, the money—"

"Sierra, you *are* a McKettrick, and so is Liam."

Sierra closed her eyes for a moment, struggling to regain her composure. "I agreed to come here for one reason and one reason only," she finally said, with hard-won moderation, "because my son needs medical attention, and I can't afford to provide it. But the agreement was for one year—*one year,* Eve—and we won't be here a single day after that condition is met!"

"And after that one year is up, you think I'm just going to forget that I have a second daughter and a grandson? Whether you're still too blasted stubborn to accept my help or not?"

"I don't *need* your help, Eve!"

"Don't you?"

Sierra shook her head, more in an effort to clear her mind than to deny Eve's meaning, found a chair and sank slowly into it. "I appreciate what you're doing," she said, after a few slow, deep breaths. "I really do. But if you expect anything beyond what we agreed to, there's a problem."

Eve moved to the fireplace, took a long match from the mantel and lit the newspaper and kindling already stacked in the grate. She waited until the flames caught, crackling merrily, then added more wood from the basket next to the hearth. "What did Hank tell you about me, Sierra?" she asked quietly, turning back to study Sierra's face. "Did he tell you I was dead? Or did he say I didn't want you?"

"He didn't have to say you didn't want me. That was perfectly obvious."

"Was it?" Eve dusted off a place on the raised hearth and sat down, folding her hands loosely in her lap. "I want to know what he told you, Sierra. After all these years, after all he took from me, I think I have the right to ask."

"He never said you didn't want me. He said you didn't want *him.*"

"Well, that was certainly true enough."

Sierra swallowed. "I guess I was five or six before I noticed that other little girls had mothers, not just fathers. I started asking a lot of questions, and I guess he got tired of it. He said there'd been an accident, that you'd been badly hurt and you'd probably have to go to heaven."

Eve lowered her head then, wiped furtively at her cheek with the back of one hand. "Who would have thought Hank Breslin would say *two* true things out of three in the same lifetime?"

Sierra slid to the edge of her chair, eager and tense at the same time.

Don't get sucked in, she heard Hank say, as clearly as if he'd been standing in the room, taking part in the conversation.

"There *was* an accident?" Sierra asked on a breath, mentally shushing her father. Just asking the question meant a part of her hadn't believed Hank, but this, like so many other things, would have to be considered later, when she was alone. And calm.

Eve nodded.

"What kind of accident?"

Eve visibly collected herself, sitting up a little straighter. Her eyes seemed focused on a past Sierra hadn't been a part of. "I was having lunch at an outdoor café in San Antonio—with my lawyer, as it happens. We'd found you after two years of searching, or at least the investigators we'd hired had, and I'd seen you with my own eyes, in San Miguel. Spoken to you. I wanted to contact Hank, work out some kind of arrangement—"

A peculiar, buzzing sensation dimmed Sierra's hearing.

"Your father had to be handled very carefully. I knew that. It would have been like Hank to take you deeper into Mexico—even into South America—if he'd gotten spooked, and he'd have been a lot more careful to disappear for good the second time."

Sierra waited, willing her head to clear, listening with everything in her. "The accident?" she prompted, very softly.

"A car jumped the curb, crashed through the stucco wall between the tables and the street. We were sitting just on the other side. My lawyer—his name was Jim Furman and he had a wife and five children—was killed instantly. I was in traction for weeks, and it took me another year and a half just to walk again."

The incident sounded like something from a soap opera, and yet Sierra knew it was true. Her stomach churned as horrific images, complete with a soundtrack of crashes and screams, flashed through her mind.

"By the time I recovered," Eve went on, after a few long moments of silence, "I knew it was too late, that I'd have to wait until you were older, when you could make choices for yourself. You were happy and healthy and very bright. You were still so young. I couldn't just waltz into your life and say, 'Hello, I'm your mother.' I was still afraid of what Hank might do, and I was struggling to rebuild my life after the accident. Meg was spending most of her time with nannies as it was, and I had to turn the company over to the board of directors because I couldn't seem to focus my mind on anything. With all that going on, how could I take you away from the only home you knew, only to turn around and leave you in the care of strangers?"

Sierra sat quietly, drawing careful, measured breaths, taking it all in. "Okay," she said, finally. "I can buy all that. But there's still a pretty big gap between then and six weeks ago, when you finally contacted me."

Eve was silent.

So I was right, Sierra thought bitterly. There's more.

"I was ashamed," Eve said.

"Ashamed?"

Silence.

"Eve?"

"After the accident," Eve went on, her voice pitched so low that Sierra had to lean forward to hear, "I took a lot of pain pills. They became less and less effective, while the pain seemed to get worse, so I started washing them down with alcohol."

Sierra's mouth dropped open. "Meg never mentioned—"

"Of course she wouldn't," Eve said. "It was my place to tell you and, besides, you don't just email something like that to somebody. What was she supposed to say? 'Oh, by the way, Mother is a pill-freak and a drunk'?"

"My God," Sierra whispered.

"I was intermittently clean and sober," Eve went on. "But I always fell off the wagon eventually. If Rance hadn't stepped in after I took control of the company again, God bless him, I probably would have run McKettrickCo into the ground."

"Rance?"

"Your cousin."

Sierra struggled to hit a lighter note, because they both needed that. "Which branch of the family tree was *he* hatched in?"

Eve smiled weakly, but with a kind of gratitude that pinched Sierra's heart in one of the tenderest places. "Rance is descended from Rafe and Emmeline," she answered. "Rafe was old Angus's son."

"It took you all this time to get your life back together?" Sierra asked tentatively, after yet another lengthy silence had run its course.

"No," Eve said. Color stained her cheeks. "No, I've been on the straight-and-narrow for ten years or so. I said it before, Sierra—I was ashamed. So much time had gone by, and I didn't know what to say. Where to start. It became a vicious cycle. The longer I put it off, the harder it was to take the risk."

"But you finally tracked me down again. What changed?"

"I didn't have to track you down. I always knew where you were." Eve sighed, and her shoulders stooped a little. "I found out about Liam's asthma, and I couldn't wait any longer." She paused, straightened her back again. "Fair is fair, Sierra. I've answered the hard questions, though I realize there will be more. Now, it's your turn. Why did you spend your life moving from place to place, serving cocktails, instead of putting down roots somewhere and making something of your life?"

Sierra considered her past and felt something sink within her. She'd taken a few night courses, here and there. She'd used her fluent Spanish with customers and volunteered, when she could, at some of Liam's schools. But she'd never had roots or any direction except "away."

"There's nothing wrong with serving cocktails," she said, trying not to sound defensive and not quite succeeding.

"Of course there isn't," Eve readily agreed. "But why didn't you go to college?"

Sierra smiled ruefully. "There are only twenty-four hours in a day, Eve. I had a child to support."

Eve nodded reflectively. And waited.

Sierra waited, too.

"That doesn't explain all the moving from place to place," Eve said at last.

"I wish I had a ready answer," Sierra said, after considerable searching. "I guess I just always had this low-grade anxiety, like I was trying to outrun something."

Eve took that in silently.

"Why did you divorce my father?" Sierra asked. She hadn't seen the question coming, but she knew it had been fermenting in the back of her mind for a long time. Whenever it arose, she pushed it down, told herself it didn't matter, but this was a time for truth, however painful it might be.

"Hank," Eve replied carefully, "was one of those men who believe they're entitled to call the shots, by virtue of possessing a penis. He quit his job a month after we were married—he sold condominiums—planning to become a golf pro at the country club. He never actually got around to applying, of course, and it would have been quite a trick to get hired anyway, since there wasn't an opening and he didn't know a nine-iron from a putter."

Sierra moistened her lips, uncomfortable.

"He was an emotional lightweight," Eve went on, quietly relentless. "But you knew that, didn't you, Sierra?"

She *had* known, but admitting it aloud was beyond her. She did manage a stiff nod, though.

"How did he earn a living?" Eve asked. "Even in Mexico, there's rent to pay, and food costs money."

Sierra blushed. Hank had tended bar at the corner cantina on occasion, and played a lot of backroom poker. The house they'd lived in belonged to Magdalena. "He just seemed to…coast," she said.

"But you had clothes, shoes. Medical care. Birthday cakes. Toys at Christmas?"

Sierra nodded. Her childhood had been marked by

two things—a vague, pervasive loneliness, and a bohe-
mian kind of freedom. At last, realization struck. "*You*
were sending him money somehow."

"I was sending *you* money, through Hank's sister,
from the day he took you away. Nell, your aunt, was
pretty clever. She always cashed the check, then wired
it to Hank, through various places—sometimes a bank,
sometimes the courtesy desk in a supermarket, sometimes a convenience store. Eventually my investigators
picked up the trail, but it wasn't so easy in those days."

Sierra flashed on a series of memories—her dad
walking away from one of the many *cambio* outlets
in San Miguel, where tourists cashed traveler's checks
and exchanged their own currency for *pesos*. She'd been
very small, but she'd seen him folding a wad of bills and
tucking it into his pocket, and she'd wondered. Now she
felt a stab of shame on his behalf, recalling his small,
secret smile.

Eve was right. Hank Breslin had felt *entitled* to that
money, and while he'd always made sure Sierra had the
necessities, he'd never been overly generous. In fact, it
had been Magdalena not Hank, who had provided ex-
tras. Sweet, plump, spice-scented Magdalena of the patient smile and manner.

Sierra's emotions must have been clearly visible in
her face. Eve rose, came over to her and laid a hand on
her shoulder. Then, without another word, she turned
and left the room.

Sierra had loved her father, for all his shortcomings,
and seeing him in this light destroyed a lot of fantasies. Even worse, she knew that Adam, Liam's father,
had been a younger version of Hank. Oh, he'd had a
career. But she'd been an amusement to him and nothing more. He'd been willing to sell her out, sell out his

own wife and daughters, for a good time. Like Hank, he'd felt entitled to whatever pleasures happened to be available, and to hell with all the people who got hurt in the process.

For a moment she hated Adam, hated Hank, hated all men.

She'd been attracted to Travis Reid.

Now she took an internal step back, and an enormous *no!* boiled up from her depths, spewing like a geyser and then freezing solid at its height.

CHAPTER ELEVEN

1919

Doss RETURNED TO THE ROOM well after midnight, smelling of cigar smoke and whisky. Hannah lay absolutely still, playing possum, watching through her lashes as he shed his hat and coat and kicked off his boots. Maybe he knew she was awake, and maybe he was fooled. She wasn't about to give herself away by speaking to him and, besides, she didn't trust herself not to tear into him like a shrew. Once the first word tumbled out of her mouth, others would follow, like a raging horde with swords and cudgels.

On the other hand, if he had the pure audacity to think, for one blessed moment, that he was going to enjoy his husbandly privileges, she'd come up out of that bed like a tigress, claws bared and slashing.

She breathed slowly, deeply and regularly, making her body soft.

Doss moved to the bureau, filled the china wash basin from the pitcher provided, and washed. She waited, in delicious dread, for him to undress, since he obviously intended to sleep in that room, in that bed, with her.

To her surprise, relief and complete annoyance, he remained fully clothed, sat down on the edge of the bed, and stretched out on top of the covers.

"I know you're not asleep," he said.

Hannah bit down hard on her lower lip. Though her eyes were shut tight, tears squeezed beneath her lids. Gabe would never have done such a thing to her, never have gone out on their wedding night to smoke and drink whisky and carouse with bad companions. Never have subjected her to such a public humiliation.

A sob shook her body. "I hate you, Doss McKettrick," she said.

He sighed, sounding resigned. If he'd apologized, if he'd put his arm around her and held her close, she would have felt better, in spite of it all, but he didn't. He kept to his own side of the bed, a weight atop the blankets, within touching distance and yet as remote from Hannah as Indian Rock was from the Eastern Seaboard.

"We'll have to make the best of things," he told her.

She rolled on to her side, with her back to him. "No, we won't," she whispered snappishly, "because as soon as Tobias is well enough, he and I are getting on the train and leaving for good."

"If it's a comfort to you," Doss replied, "then you just go ahead and think that. The truth of the matter is, you're my wife now, and as long as there's a chance you're carrying my baby, you're not going anywhere."

"I hate you," Hannah repeated.

"So you said," Doss answered, with a long-suffering sigh.

"I'll leave if I want to."

"I'll bring you back. And believe me, Hannah, I can keep up the game as long as you can."

"Then you mean to keep me prisoner." Hannah spoke into the darkness, and it seemed like a shadow, cast by her very soul, that gloom, rather than mere night, with the moon following its ancient course and the stars in their right places. It was, in that moment, as if the sun would never rise again.

"I won't lock you in the cellar, if that's what you mean," Doss told her. "I won't mistreat you or force my attentions on you, and I'll be civil as long as you are. But until I know whether you're pregnant or not, you're staying right here."

Hannah huddled deeper into the covers, feeling small, and wiped away a tear with the edge of the sheet. "I hope I'm not," she whispered. "I hope I'm not carrying your baby."

Even as she said the words, though, she knew they were the frayed and tattered weavings of a lie. She longed for another child, a girl this time, yearned to feel a life growing and stirring under her heart. She just didn't want Doss McKettrick to be the father, that was all.

She cried quietly, lying there next to Doss. Cried till her pillow was wet. She'd have bet money she wouldn't sleep a wink, but at some point she succumbed.

The next thing she knew, it was morning.

Doss's side of the bed was empty, and fat, lazy flakes of snow drifted past the window. The room was cold, but she could hear voices in the next room and the clattering of silverware against dishes. The aroma of bacon teased her nose; her stomach clenched with hunger, and then she was nauseous.

"No," she said, in a whisper, sitting bolt-upright.

Yes, her body replied. She'd had the same reaction within ten days of Tobias's conception.

Tobias appeared in the doorway, with Doss standing just behind him.

"You want some breakfast, Ma?" the boy asked. He looked slightly feverish, but stronger, too, and he was wearing a new suit of clothes—black woolen trousers, a blue-and-white-plaid flannel shirt, even suspenders.

The whole picture turned hazy, and the mention of food, let alone the smell, sent bile scalding into the back of Hannah's throat. Avoiding Doss's gaze, she gulped and shook her head.

Doss laid a hand on Tobias's shoulder and gently steered him back into the other room. He pulled the door closed, too, and the instant he did, Hannah rolled out of bed, pulled the chamber-pot out from underneath, distractedly grateful that it was clean, and threw up until she collapsed onto the hooked rug, utterly spent.

She heard the door open again, heard Doss say her name, but she couldn't respond. She just lay there, on her side, wretched and empty, as though she'd lost her soul as well as the remains of her wedding supper.

Doss knelt, gathered her in his arms, and put her back into bed, covering her gently. He fetched a basin of tepid water from the other room, along with a washcloth, and cleaned her up. When that was done, he handed her a glass, and she rinsed her mouth, then spat into the basin.

"I'll get the doctor," he said.

She shook her head. "Don't," she answered, and the word came out raspy and raw. "I just need to rest."

Doss drew up a chair, sat beside the bed, keeping a silent vigil. Hannah wished he'd go away, and at the same time she dreaded his leave-taking with the whole echoing hollowness of her being.

A maid came in, replacing the fouled chamber pot, washing out the basin, taking the pitcher away and bringing it back full. Although she cast the occasional worried glance in Hannah's direction, the woman never said a word, and when she was gone, Doss remained.

He plumped the pillows behind Hannah's back and adjusted the radiator to warm the room.

"I thought I'd bundle Tobias up," Doss ventured, at some length, "and take him down to the general store. Get him some things to play with, maybe a book to read."

Hannah was in a strange, dazed state, weak all over. "You see that he doesn't take a chill," she muttered. Common sense said Tobias ought to stay in, out of the weather, and if she'd been herself, she would have insisted on that. As things stood, she didn't have the strength, and anyway she knew the boy was desperate to get out, if only for a little while.

Doss stood, tucked the covers in around her. To look at them, Hannah thought, anybody would have thought they were a normal husband and wife, people who loved each other. "Can I bring you something back?"

"No," she said, and closed her eyes, drifting.

When she opened them again, Doss was back, with the chilly scent of fresh air surrounding him. She could hear Tobias in the next room, chatting with somebody.

"Feeling better?" Doss asked. He was holding a parcel in his hands, wrapped in brown paper and tied with string.

"Thirsty," Hannah murmured.

Doss nodded, set the package aside and brought her another glass of water, this time from the pitcher on the bureau.

She drank it down, waited, and was pathetically pleased when it didn't come right back up.

"You'd best have something to eat, if you can," Doss said.

Hannah nodded. Suddenly she was ravenous.

He left again, was gone so long that she wondered if he meant to hunt down the food, skin it, and cook it over a slow fire. Tobias wandered in, cheeks pink from the cold, eyes bright. "Uncle Jeb wants to buy me a sandwich," he told her. "Downstairs, in the restaurant. Is it all right if I go?"

Hannah smiled. "Sure it is," she said.

Tobias drew a step nearer, moving tentatively, as though approaching something fragile enough to fall over and break at the slightest touch. "Doss says you're not dying," he said.

"He's right," Hannah answered.

"Then what's the matter? You never stay in bed in the daytime."

Hannah extended her hand, and after hesitating Tobias took it. "I'm being lazy," she said, giving his fingers a squeeze.

He clung for a moment, then let go. His eyes were wide and worried. "I heard you being sick," he told her.

A door opened in the distance, and Hannah heard Doss and Jeb exchange quiet words, though she couldn't make them out. "I'll be fine by tomorrow," she promised. "You go and have that sandwich. It isn't every day you get to eat in a real restaurant."

Tobias relaxed visibly. He smiled, planted a kiss on her forehead and fled, nearly colliding with Doss in the doorway. Doss tightened his grip on the tray of food he was carrying. A teapot, with steam wisping from the spout. A bowl of something savory and fragrant.

Hannah's nose twitched, and her formerly rebellious stomach growled an audible welcome.

"Chicken and dumplings," Doss said, with a grin.

He set the tray carefully on Hannah's lap. Poured her

a cup of tea and probably would have spoon-fed her, too, if she hadn't taken charge of the situation.

"Thank you," she said, trying to square this attentive man with the one who had left her alone on their wedding night to visit the Blue Garter Saloon.

"You're welcome," he replied. He sat down to watch her eat, and his gaze strayed once or twice to the package on the nightstand, still wrapped and mysterious.

Hannah did not assume it was for her, since she'd clearly refused Doss's earlier offer to bring her something from the mercantile, but she was curious, just the same. The shape was booklike, and before she'd married Gabe, she'd read so much her mother and father used to fret that her eyes might go bad. After she became a wife, she was too busy, and when Gabe went away to war, she found she couldn't concentrate on the printed word. Letters were all she'd been able to manage then.

She ate what she could and sipped her tea, hot and sweet and pale with milk, and Doss took the tray away, set it on the bureau. Jeb and Tobias had long since gone downstairs for their midday meal, and except for the sounds of wagons passing in the street below and the faint hiss of the radiator, the room was silent.

Doss cleared his throat and shifted uncomfortably in his chair. "Hannah, about last night—"

"Stop," Hannah said quickly, and with as much force as she could manage, given her curiously fragile state. The teacup rattled in its saucer, and Doss leaned forward to take it from her, set it next to the parcel. He looked resigned, and a little impatient.

Hannah leaned back on her pillows, fighting another spate of tears. She would have sworn she'd cried them all out the night before, after Doss came back from the Blue Garter and told her he wouldn't let her go home to Montana, but here they were, burning behind her eyes, threatening to spill over.

"I figure you know what this means, your being sick like this," Doss said presently, and in a tone that said he wouldn't be silenced before he'd finished his piece. "That's the only reason I didn't bring the doctor over here, first thing."

Hannah closed her eyes. Nodded.

"I know you'd rather it was Gabe sitting here," he went on. "That he'd be the one who fathered that child, the one taking you home to the ranch, the one bringing Tobias up to be a man. But the plain fact of the matter is, it'll be me doing those things, Hannah, and you might as well make peace with that."

She didn't speak, because she couldn't. She tried to summon up Gabe's image in her mind, but it wouldn't come to her. All she saw was Doss, coming in after a night at the Blue Garter, taking off his coat and hat and boots, lying down beside her on the bed, keeping a careful distance.

He retrieved the parcel from the nightstand and laid it in her lap. She listened, despondent, as he left the room, closed the door quietly behind him.

She ought to refuse the package, throw it against the wall or into Doss's face when he came back. But some part of her wanted a gift, something frivolous and impractical, chosen purely to bring a smile to her face.

She barely remembered what it was like to smile, without thinking about it first, without deciding she ought to, because it was called for or expected.

Her hands trembled as she undid the string, wound it into a little ball to keep, turned back the brown paper, which she would carefully fold and save against some future need, to find that Doss had indeed given her a book. Her breath caught at the beauty of the green leather cover. The title, embossed in shining gold, seemed to sing beneath the tips of her fingers.

The Flowers of Western America, Native and Imported: An Illustrated Guide.

Hannah held the thick volume reverently, savoring the anticipation for a few moments before opening it to look at the title page, memorize the author's name, as well as that of the artist who'd done the original wood-cuttings and metal etchings for the pictures.

When she couldn't bear to wait another moment, Hannah turned that page, expecting to read the table of contents. Instead, there was a note, written in Doss's strong, clear handwriting.

On the occasion of our marriage, and
because I know you long for spring, and your
garden.
Doss McKettrick
January 17, 1919

An emotion Hannah could not recognize swelled in her throat, fairly cutting off her breath. She traced his name with her eyes and then with the tip of her index finger. Doss McKettrick. As if men by that name were common as thorns in a blackberry thicket, and any one of them might be her husband. As if he had to be sure she knew which one would give her a book and which had noticed how fiercely, how desperately she craved that first green stirring in the cold earth and in the bare-limbed branches of trees.

Did he know how she listened for the breaking of the ice on the pond far back in the woods behind the house? How she watched the frigid sky for the first brave birds, carrying back the merry little songs she pined for, in the secret regions of her heart, when the snow was just beginning to seep into the ground?

Hannah closed the book, held it against her chest.

Then she opened it again and carefully turned to the first illustration, a lovely colored woodcut of purple crocuses, blooming above a thin snowfall. She drank them in, surfeited herself on lilacs and climbing roses, sweet williams and peonies.

Doss had given her flowers, in the dead of winter. Just looking at the pictures, she could imagine their distinctive scents, the shape of their petals, the depth upon depth of their various colors—everything from the palest of whites to the fathomless purples and crimsons.

She gobbled them all greedily with her eyes, page after page of them, tumbled flower-drunk into sleep and dreamed of them. Dreamed of spring, of trout quickening in the creeks, of green grass and of fresh, warm breezes teasing her hair and tingling on her skin.

When she wakened, drowsy and confused, the room was lavender with twilight, and a rim of golden light edged the lower part of the door. She heard Doss and Tobias talking in the next room, knew by a series of decisive clicks that they were playing checkers. Tobias gave a shout of triumphant laughter, and the sound seemed so poignant to Hannah that tears thickened in her throat.

She got up, used the chamber pot, washed her hands at the basin. She rummaged for her flannel wrapper, pulled it on and crossed the cold wooden floor to the door.

Opened it.

Tobias and Doss both turned to look at her.

Tobias smiled, delighted.

Doss looked shy, as though they'd just met. He got up suddenly, came to her, took her arm. Escorted her to a chair.

"Don't fuss," she scolded, but it was after the fussing was through.

"I beat Uncle Doss four times!" Tobias crowed.

"Did you?" Hannah asked, deliberately widening her eyes.

Doss went over to the other bed, pulled the quilt off, made Hannah stand, wrapped her up like renderings in a sausage skin and sat her down again.

What am I to make of you, Doss McKettrick? she asked silently.

"I'll go down and order us some supper," Doss said.

"Has your uncle Jeb gone?" Hannah asked Tobias, when they were alone.

Tobias nodded, kneeling on the floor, stacking checker pieces into red and black towers that teetered on the wooden board. "He took the afternoon train back to Phoenix. Said to tell you he hoped you'd be feeling better soon."

"I wish I could have said goodbye," Hannah said, but it wasn't the complete truth. She'd not been eager to face Doss's uncle; he was half again too wise and, besides, he must have known that her new husband had spent much of their wedding night in a saloon, just to avoid her. He'd never have mentioned it, of course, but she'd have seen the knowledge in his eyes.

Would he tell his wife, Chloe, when he got home? Would she, in turn, tell Emmeline and Mandy and the other McKettrick women? Get them all feeling sorry for poor Hannah?

She'd know soon enough. Concerned letters would begin arriving, probably in the next batch of mail, full

of wary congratulations and carefully worded questions. The Aunts, as both Gabe and Doss had always referred to them, were not gossips, so she needn't fear
scandal from that quarter, but they would have plenty
of private discussions among themselves, and they'd
give Doss what for when they returned to the Triple M
in the spring, settling into their houses on all parts of
the ranch, throwing open windows and doors, planting
gardens and entertaining a steady stream of children
and grandchildren.

Hannah thought she would have welcomed even
their curiosity, if it meant the long winter was over.

"Ma?"

Hannah realized she'd let her mind wander and
turned her attention to Tobias, who was studying her
closely and clearly had something of moment to say.
"Yes, sweetheart?"

"Is Uncle Doss my pa, now that you and him are
married?"

Hannah blinked. Took in a slow breath and took her
time letting it out. "I told you before, Tobias. Doss is still
your uncle. Your father will always be—your father."

Tobias's forehead creased as he frowned. "But Pa's
dead," he said.

Hannah sighed. "Yes."

"Uncle Doss is alive."

"He certainly is."

"I want a pa. Somebody to take me fishin' and teach
me how to shoot."

"Uncles can do those things." Hannah didn't want
Tobias within a mile of a gun, but she didn't have the
strength to fight that battle just then, so she let it go.

"It isn't the same," Tobias reasoned.

"Tobias, there are some things in this life a person

has to accept. Your father is gone. Doss is your uncle, not your pa. You'll just have to make the best of that."

"The best would be if he was my pa instead of my uncle."

"Tobias."

"You said once that Uncle Doss would be my stepfather if you got married. Now, you're his wife. So if you leave off the 'step' part, that makes him my pa."

Hannah rubbed her temples with her fingertips.

Tobias beamed. Eight years old, and he could argue like a senior senator at a campaign picnic.

The door to the corridor opened, and Doss came in, followed by two maids carrying trays laden with food.

"Pa's back," Tobias said.

Hannah's gaze locked with Doss's. Something passed between them, silent and charged.

Hannah looked away first.

CHAPTER TWELVE

Present Day

"YOU NEED TIME TO ABSORB all this," Eve told Sierra the next morning at the breakfast table. Eve had made waffles for them all, and everyone had eaten with a hearty appetite. Now Liam was upstairs, dressing for his first visit to Indian Rock Elementary School—Sierra planned to register him but wasn't sure he was ready for a full day of class—and Travis had given the ranch house a wide berth ever since their return from Flagstaff the previous afternoon. "So I'm going to leave," Eve finished, gently decisive.

Sierra, who had spent a largely sleepless night, had mixed feelings about Eve's going away. On the one hand, there were so many things she wanted to know about her mother—things that had nothing to do with their long separation. What kind of books did she read? What places had she visited? Had she loved anyone before or after Hank Breslin? What made her laugh? Did she cry at sad movies, or was she a stone-realist, prone to saying, "It's only a story"?

On the other, Sierra craved solitude, to think and reflect and sort what she had learned into some kind of sensible order. She wanted to huddle up somewhere, with her arms around her knees and decide what she believed and what she didn't.

"Okay," she said.

"There is one thing I want to show you before I go," Eve said, rising from the kitchen table and crossing to the china cabinet to lean down and open one of the drawers. She brought out a large, square object, wrapped in soft blue flannel, and set it before Sierra, who had shoved her plate and coffee cup aside in the meantime and wiped her part of the tabletop clean with a checkered cloth napkin.

Sierra's heart raced a little and, at a nod from Eve, she folded back the flannel covering to reveal an old photo album.

"These are your people, Sierra," Eve said quietly. "Your ancestors. There are journals and other photographs in the attic, and they need cataloging. It would be a great favor to me if you would gather them and make sure they're properly preserved."

"I can do that," Sierra said. Her hand, resting on the album cover, trembled a little, with both anticipation and a certain reluctance to get involved. Biologically she had a connection with the faces and names between the battered leather covers of the book, but in terms of real life, she was just passing through. She couldn't afford to forget that.

Eve laid a hand on her shoulder. "Sorry about the Christmas tree," she said with a slight smile. "I was the one who put it up, and I should be the one to take it down, but the plane will be arriving in an hour, so there isn't time. The corresponding boxes are in the basement, at the bottom of the steps."

Sierra nodded a second time. Liam had finished opening his presents the night before, and the mess had been cleaned up. Putting away the tree, like sorting photos and journals, would be a bittersweet enterprise. She hadn't looked closely at the ornaments, but she supposed they were heirlooms, like so many other things in that house, each one with a meaning she could never fully understand.

So many McKettrick Christmases, and she hadn't been a part of any of them. With Hank the holiday had gone almost unnoticed, although there were always a few gifts. Sierra hadn't felt deprived at the time, because she hadn't known that other people made more of a fuss.

The McKettricks, most likely, made a lot of fuss, not just over Christmas, but other holidays, too. They'd probably kept happy secrets at Yuletide, sung carols around that haunted piano, toasted each other with eggnog poured into cut-glass cups that were older than any of them....

Enough, Sierra told herself sternly. That time is gone. You missed it. Get over wishing you hadn't.

Eve bent to kiss Sierra on top of the head, then went upstairs to the big master bedroom, to pack up her things.

Sierra cleared the table and loaded the dishwasher, but her gaze kept straying to the album. It was as though the people in the photographs, all long dead, were calling to her.

Get to know us.

We are part of you. We are part of Liam.

Sierra shook off the feeling as a nostalgic whim. She was as much a Breslin as a McKettrick, after all. She knew how to be Hank's daughter, but being Eve's was a whole new ball game. It was as though she had an entirely separate and unfamiliar identity, and that person was a stranger to her.

Liam bounded down the back stairs as she was rinsing out the coffee carafe, beaming at the prospect of starting school. He'd been thrilled to learn, through the research he and Sierra had done on Meg's computer, after last night's present-unwrapping frenzy, that there was no "Geek Program" at Indian Rock Elementary.

He wanted to be an "ordinary" kid.

Not sick.

Not gifted.

"Just regular" as he'd put it.

Sierra's heart ached with love and empathy. As a child, home taught by Magdalena, she'd yearned to go to a real school, but Hank had forbidden it.

Now she realized Hank had been hiding her, probably fearful that some visitor, expatriate parent or teacher might catch on to the fact that he'd snatched her, and look into the matter.

For a moment she indulged in a primitive anger so deep that it was visceral, causing her stomach to clench and her jaws to tighten.

"Grandma says we'd better take Meg's car into town today, because ours is a heap, not to mention a veritable eyesore," Liam reported cheerfully. "When are we going to get a new car?"

"When I win the lottery or get a job," Sierra said, deliberately relaxing her shoulders, which had immediately tensed, and taking Liam's new "cowboy" coat, as he'd dubbed it, down from the peg. While she would have objected if she'd known Eve was out buying all those gifts, let alone wrapping them and putting them under a fully decorated Christmas tree, she was glad of this one. It was made of leather and lined with sheepskin, well beyond her budget, and it would definitely keep her little boy warm.

Just then Eve came back, bundled up for winter weather herself, and carrying a small, expensive suitcase in one hand. Her coat was full length and black, elegantly cut and probably cashmere.

"We're in the process of opening a branch office of McKettrickCo in Indian Rock," she announced, evidently unabashed that she'd been eavesdropping. "Keegan is heading it up, but I'm sure there will be a place for you in the organization if you want one. You do speak Spanish, don't you?"

"Keegan," Sierra mused mildly, letting the indirect job offer slide, along with the reference to her language skills, at least for the moment. "Another McKettrick cousin?"

"Descended from Kade and Mandy," Eve confirmed, smiling slightly and nodding toward the album. "It's all in the book."

"How are you getting back to the airstrip—or wherever your jet is landing?" Sierra asked, shrugging into her coat, which looked like something from the bottom of a grungy bin at a thrift store, compared to the ones Eve and Liam were decked out in.

"Travis is taking me in his truck," Eve said, setting her suitcase down by the door, heading to the china cabinet to pluck a set of keys from a sugar bowl, taking Sierra's hand, opening it and placing them on her palm. "Use the SUV. That wreck of yours won't make it out of the driveway, if it starts at all."

Sierra hesitated a moment before closing her fingers around the keys. "Not to mention that it's a veritable eyesore," she said pointedly, but with a little smile.

"You said it," Eve replied brightly. "I didn't."

"Yes, you did," Liam countered. "Upstairs, you told me—"

Outside Travis honked the truck horn.

Eve touched her grandson's neatly groomed hair.

"Give your old granny a hug," she said. "I'll be back in a few weeks, and if the weather is good, maybe you'd like to take a ride in the company jet."

Liam let out a whoop.

Sierra didn't get a chance to protest, because Travis rapped lightly, opened the back door and took up Eve's suitcase. He gave Sierra a nod for a greeting and grinned down at Liam.

"Hey, cowpoke," he said. "Lookin' good in that new gear."

Liam preened, showing off the coat. "I wanted to wear the hat, too," he replied, "but Mom said I might lose it at school."

"The world," Travis replied, with a longer glance at Sierra, "is full of hats."

"What's that supposed to mean?" Sierra asked, feeling defensive again.

Travis sighed. A look passed between him and Eve. Then he simply turned, without answering and headed for the truck.

Eve hugged Liam, then Sierra.

Moments later she and Travis were in the truck and barreling away.

Sierra found the door leading into the garage—cleverly hidden in back of the pantry, like the architectural afterthought it surely was—and assessed her sister's shining red SUV. Liam strained to reach the button on the wall, and the garage door grumbled up on its rollers, letting in a shivery chill.

Her station wagon was parked outside, behind the SUV, and Sierra muttered as she started Meg's vehicle, after she and Liam were both buckled in, and maneuvered around the eyesore.

1919

DESPITE THE BITTER COLD, Hannah sat well away from Doss as they drove home in the sleigh two days after the wedding, Tobias cosseted between them.

She was married.

Each time her thoughts drifted in that direction, she started inwardly, surprised all over again.

She was a wife—but she certainly didn't feel like one.

Doss remained silent for the greater part of the journey, his gloved hands gripping the reins with the ease of long practice. Hannah felt his gaze on her a couple of times, but when she looked in his direction, he was always watching the snow-packed trail ahead.

By the time they reached the ranch, Hannah sorely wished she could simply crawl into bed, pull the covers up over her head and remain there until something changed.

It was an indulgence ranch women were not afforded.

Doss drew the team and sleigh up close to the house, lifted a half-sleeping Tobias from the seat and carried him in. Hannah got down on her own, bringing her valise, the flower book tucked safely inside among her dirty clothes, and followed stalwartly.

The kitchen was frigidly cold.

Doss pulled the string on the lightbulb in the middle of the room as he passed, heading for the stairs with Tobias.

Hannah rose above an inclination to turn it right back off again. She set her valise down and made for the stove. By the time Doss returned, she had a fire going and lamps lighted. She'd fetch some eggs from the spring house, she decided, provided that Willie had gathered them during their absence, and make an omelet for their supper. Perhaps she'd fry up some of the sausage she'd preserved last fall, and make biscuits and gravy, too.

"I'll see to the team," Doss said.

"Where do you suppose Willie's got to?" Hannah asked. She'd seen no sign of the hired man when they were driving in, and she feared for her chickens, along with the livestock in the barn. Like many laborers, Willie was a drifter, and might have taken it into his head to kick off the traces and take to the road anywhere along the line.

"I saw him when we came in," Doss answered, opening the door to go out again. "Out by the bunkhouse, stacking firewood."

Hannah gave a sigh of relief. In the next moment, she wanted to tell Doss to stay inside where it was warm, that she'd have the coffee ready in a few minutes, but it would have been a waste of breath. He was a rancher, born and bred, and that meant he looked after the cattle and horses first and saw to his own comforts later, when the work was done.

"Supper will be on the table in half an hour," she said, as though she were a landlady in a boarding house and he a paying guest, planning the briefest of stays. "Willie's welcome to join us, if he wants."

Doss nodded, raised his coat collar around his ears and went out.

Sometime later, he returned alone. Hannah had already fetched the eggs from the spring house, and they were scrambled, cooked and waiting on a platter in the warming oven above the stove. The kitchen was snug, and the softer light of lanterns glowed, replacing the glare of the overhead bulb.

"Willie's gone on back to the main ranch house," he said. "But he thanks you kindly for the invite to supper."

Hannah wiped her hands on her apron and took plates from the china cabinet to set the table. That was when she noticed the album lying there, as though someone had been perusing it and intended to come back and look some more later.

She stopped in her tracks.

Doss, in the act of shedding his coat and hat, followed her gaze.

"What's the matter, Hannah?" he asked, with a quiet alertness in his voice.

"The album," she said.

"What about it?" Doss asked, passing her to approach the stove. He poured himself a cup of coffee and came to stand beside her.

"Willie wouldn't have gone through our things, would he?"

Doss shook his head. "Not likely it would even have occurred to him to do that," he said. "Judging by how cold it was in here when we got home, he probably didn't set foot in the house once he'd finished off that chicken soup you made before we left."

Hannah wrung her hands, took a step toward the table and then paused. "Do you...do you ever get the feeling we're not alone in this house?" she asked, almost whispering the words.

"No," Doss said, with conviction.

"It was bad enough when the teapot kept moving. Now, the album—"

"Hannah." He touched her arm. "You sound like Tobias, going on about seeing a boy in his room."

"Maybe," Hannah ventured to speculate, almost

breathless with the effort of speaking the words aloud, "he's not imagining things. Maybe it wasn't the fever."

Doss cupped Hannah's elbow in one hand and steered her to the table, letting go only to pull back a chair. It was pure fancy, of course, but as Hannah sat down, it seemed to her that the album, fairly new and reverently cared for, was very old. The sensation lasted only a moment or so, but it was so powerful that it left her feeling weak.

"We've all been under a strain, Hannah," Doss reasoned. "One of us must have gotten the album out and forgotten about it."

She looked up into his face. "Did you?" she challenged softly.

He paused, shook his head.

"I know I didn't," she insisted.

"Tobias, then," Doss said.

"No," Hannah replied. "He was too sick."

Doss set his coffee on the table, sat astride the bench, facing her. "There's a simple explanation for this, Hannah. Somebody might have come up from one of the other places, let themselves in."

As close as the McKettricks were, they didn't go into each other's houses when no one was at home. If one of them had wanted to see the album, they'd have said so. Anyway, the aunts and uncles were all in Phoenix, their children grown and gone. The people who looked after their places wouldn't have considered snooping like this, even if they'd been interested, which seemed unlikely.

"The biscuits will burn if you don't take them out of the oven," Hannah said, staring at the album, almost expecting it to move on its own, float through the air like a spirit medium's trumpet at a séance.

Doss got up, crossed the room and rescued the biscuits. The sausage gravy was done, warming at the back of the stove, so he retrieved one of the plates Hannah had gotten out, filled it for her and brought it to the table.

"Tobias will be hungry," she said, thinking aloud.

"I'll see to him," Doss answered. "Eat."

Hannah moved the album out of the way and pulled the plate toward her, resigned to taking her supper, even though she didn't want it. Doss brought her silverware, then filled another plate for Tobias and took it downstairs.

When he returned, he dished up his own meal and joined Hannah at the table. She was still staring at her scrambled eggs, sausage gravy and biscuits.

"Eat," he repeated.

She took up a fork. "There's someone here," she said. "Someone we can't see. Someone who moves the teapot and now the album, too."

"Let's assume, for a moment, that that's true," Doss ruminated, tucking into his food with an energy Hannah envied. "What do you plan to do about it?"

Hannah swallowed a bite of tasteless food. "I don't know," she answered, but it wasn't the complete truth. An idea was already brewing in her mind.

They finished their supper.

Hannah cleared the table, put the album back in its drawer in the china cabinet, and went upstairs to look in on Tobias while Doss washed the dishes.

Her son was sitting up in bed when she entered his room, his supper half-eaten and set aside on the bedside table. "The boy's not here," he said. "I wonder if he's gone away."

Hannah frowned. "What boy?" she asked, even though she knew.

"The one I see sometimes. With the funny clothes."

Hannah stroked her boy's hair. Sat down on the edge of his bed. "Does this boy ever speak to you? Does he have a name?"

Tobias shook his head. His eyes were large in his pale face. The trip back from Indian Rock had been hard on him, and Hannah was both worried about her son and determined not to let on.

"We mostly just look at each other. I reckon he's as surprised to see me as I am to see him."

"Next time he shows up, will you tell me?"

Tobias bit his lower lip, then nodded. "You believe me?"

"Of course I do, Tobias."

"Pa said he was imaginary. When we talked about it, I mean."

Hannah sighed. "Tobias, Doss is your uncle, not your pa."

Suddenly, Tobias's eyes glistened with unshed tears. "Why won't you let him be my pa?" he asked. "He's your husband, isn't he? If you can have a husband, why can't I have a pa?"

Had Tobias been older, Hannah thought, she might have explained that Doss wasn't a real husband, that theirs was a marriage of convenience, but he was still far too young to understand.

In point of fact, she didn't entirely understand the situation herself.

"A woman can have more than one husband," she said cautiously. "A boy has only one father. And your father was Gabriel Angus McKettrick. I don't want you to forget that."

"I won't forget," Tobias said. "You can wash my mouth out with soap, if you want to, but I'm still going to call Uncle Doss my pa. I've got enough uncles—Jeb and Kade and Rafe, and John Henry, too. What I need is a pa."

Hannah was too exhausted to argue, and she knew she wouldn't win anyhow. "So long as you promise me you will never forget who your real father is," she said. "And I would appreciate it if you would include your uncle David—my brother—in that list of relations you just mentioned."

Tobias brightened and put out one small hand for a shake. "It's a deal," he agreed. "I like Uncle David. He can spit a long way."

"Go to sleep," Hannah told him with a smile, reaching to turn down the wick in the lantern next to his bed.

"I didn't wash my face or brush my teeth," he confessed, settling back on to his pillows.

"Just this once we'll pretend you did," she said.

The lamp went out.

She kissed his forehead, found it blessedly cool and tucked the covers in close around him. "Good night, Tobias," she said.

"Good night, Ma," Tobias replied with a yawn.

He was probably asleep before she reached the door.

She'd hoped Doss would have turned in by the time she went downstairs, so she wouldn't have to be alone with him in the intimacy of evening, but he was right there in the kitchen, with the bathtub set out in the middle of the floor and buckets and kettles of water heating on the stove.

"I just came down to say good night," she lied. Actually, she'd been planning to sit up awhile, pondering her plan. It wasn't much, but she was bound and determined to find out something about the strange goings-on in that house.

"You can have this bath if you want," Doss told her. "I can always take one later."

"You have it," Hannah said, even though she would have loved to soak the chill out of her bones in a tub of hot water. She wondered if he was planning to share her bed, but she'd have broken the ice on top of the horse trough and stripped bare for a dunking before asking him outright.

He simply nodded.

"Don't forget to bank the fire," she said.

He grinned. "I never do, Hannah," he reminded her.

She turned, blushing a little, and went back upstairs. Entering her room, the one she'd shared with Gabe, she exchanged her clothes for a nightgown. She took her hair down, brushed it, plaited it into a long braid, trying all the while not to imagine Doss right downstairs, naked as the day he was born, lounging in that tub in front of the stove.

Would he join her later?

He was her legal husband, and he had every right to sleep beside her. She, on the other hand, had every right to turn him away, wedding band or none.

Would she?

She honestly didn't know, and in the end, it didn't matter.

She put out her lamp, threw back the covers on her bed and stretched out, waiting and listening.

Presently she heard Doss climb the stairs, walk along the hallway and pass her room.

His door closed moments later.

Hannah told herself she was relieved, and then cried herself into a fitful sleep.

Present Day

THE ROADS HAD been plowed, and Sierra was secretly proud of the way she handled the SUV. She'd grown up in Mexico, after all, and spent the last few years in Florida, which precluded driving in snow. This was an accomplishment.

At the elementary school, she got Liam registered and watched as he rushed off to join his class before she could even suggest that he start slowly. His eagerness left her feeling a little bereft.

She shook that off. He had his inhaler. The school nurse had been apprised of his asthma. She had to let go.

She would be living on the Triple M for a year, per her agreement with Eve. Might as well drive around a bit, see what the town was like.

Thirty minutes later she'd seen it all.

The supermarket. The library. The Cattleman's Bank. Two cafés, three bars, a gas station. A dry cleaners, and the ubiquitous McDonald's. The Indian Rock Historical Society. A real estate firm. A few hundred houses, many of them old and, at the edge of town, a spanking-new office complex with the word McKettrickCo inlaid in colored stone over a gleaming set of automatic doors.

I'm sure there will be a place for you in the organization, if you want one, she heard Eve's voice say.

Slowing the car, she studied the place, imagined herself going inside, in her jeans, sweatshirt and ratty coat, her hair combed in a slap-dash method, no mirror required. Face bare of makeup. "Hi, there," she would say to her cousin Keegan, who would no doubt be less than thrilled to see her but manage a polite greeting, anyway. "My name is Sierra and, what do you know? Turns out, I'm a McKettrick, just like you. Go figure.

Oh, and by the way, my mother says you're to give me a job. Top-dollar salary and all the fringe benefits, if you don't mind."

She smiled ruefully at the thought. "Of course, all I know how to do is serve cocktails and speak Spanish," she might add. "No problem, I'm sure."

She pulled up in front of the Cattleman's Bank, patted her purse, which contained a few hundred dollars in traveler's checks, all the money she had in the world, and went in to open a checking account.

"You already have one, Ms. McKettrick," a perky young teller told her, after a few taps on her computer keyboard. The girl's eyes widened as she peered at the screen. "It's pretty substantial, too."

Sierra frowned, momentarily puzzled. "There must be some mistake. I've only been in town a few days, and I haven't—"

And then it struck her. Eve had been up to her tricks again.

The teller turned her pivoting monitor around so Sierra could read the facts for herself. The bottom line made her catch hold of the counter with both hands, lest she faint dead away.

Two million dollars?

"Of course you'll need to sign a signature card," the clerk said, still chipper. "Do you have two forms of personal identification?"

"I need to use your telephone," Sierra managed to say. The floor was still at an odd tilt, and her knuckles hurt where she gripped the edge of the counter.

The teller blinked. "You don't carry a cell phone?" she marveled, in a tone usually reserved for people who think they've been abducted by aliens and subjected to a lot of very painful and explicit medical procedures.

"No," Sierra said, trying not to hyperventilate, "I do not carry a cell phone."

"Over there," the teller said, pointing to a friendly looking nook marked off in brass letters as the Customer Comfort area.

Sierra made her way to the telephone, rummaged through her purse for Eve's cell number and dialed. The operator came on and informed her the call was long distance, and there would be charges.

"Make it collect," Sierra snapped.

One ring. Two. Eve was probably still in flight, aboard the company jet, with her phone shut off. Sierra was about to give up when, after the third ring, her mother chimed, "Eve McKettrick."

"I have a bank account with two million dollars in it!" Sierra whispered into the receiver, bent around it like someone calling a 900 number during a church service.

"Yes, dear," Eve said sweetly. "I know."

"I will not accept—"

"Your trust fund?"

Sierra sucked in her breath. Almost choked on it. "My *trust fund?*"

"Yes," Eve answered. "You also have a share in McKettrickCo, of course."

Sierra swallowed, carefully this time. "I will not take your charity."

"Tell it to your grandfather," Eve responded, unruffled. "Of course, you'll need a clairvoyant to help, because he's been dead for fifteen years."

Sierra held the receiver away from her, stared at it, jammed it to her ear again. "My grandfather left me *two million* dollars?"

"Yes," Eve said. "We kept it safely tucked away in Switzerland, so your father wouldn't get his paws on it."

Sierra closed her eyes.

"Sweetheart?" her mother asked, sounding concerned now. "Are you still there?"

"Yes," Sierra breathed. She could have walked away from all that money. She really could have—if not for Liam. "Why didn't you tell me about this, when you were at the house?"

"Because I knew you weren't ready to hear it, and I didn't want to waste precious time arguing."

Sierra swallowed. "How come you can talk on a cell phone in flight?"

Eve laughed. "Because I patch the number into the phone onboard the plane before takeoff," she answered. "I'm quite the technological whiz. Any more questions?"

"Yes. What am I supposed to do with two million dollars?"

CHAPTER THIRTEEN

1919

BY THE TIME HANNAH came downstairs, Doss had built up the fire, brewed the coffee and left for the barn, like he did every morning. She put on Gabe's old coat—there was nothing of his scent left in it now—and made a trip to the privy, then the chicken house. She was washing her hands in a basin of hot water when Doss came in from doing the chores.

"I guess I'll drive the sleigh down and look in on the widow Jessup again," he said. "This cold snap might outlast her firewood."

"You'll have a good, hot breakfast first," Hannah told him. "While I'm fixing it, why don't you get some preserves from the pantry and pack them up? Mrs. Jessup especially loves those cinnamon pears and pickled crab apples I put up for Christmas."

Doss nodded, a grin crooking one corner of his mouth in a way that made Hannah feel sweetly flustered. "How's Tobias today?"

"He's sleeping in," she said, cracking eggs into a bowl, keeping her gaze averted with some difficulty. "And don't think for a moment you're going to take him with you. It's too cold and he's worn-out from yesterday."

She'd thought Doss was in the pantry, but all of a

sudden his hands closed over her shoulders, startling her so that she stiffened.

He turned her around to face him. Looked straight into her eyes.

Her heart beat a little faster.

Was he about to kiss her?

Say something important?

She held her breath, hoping he would. Hoping he wouldn't.

"Before he went back to Phoenix, Uncle Jeb said we ought to help ourselves to some hams from the smoke-house down at Rafe and Emmeline's place," he said. "A side of bacon, too. That means I'll be gone a little longer than usual."

Hannah merely nodded.

They stood, the two of them facing each other for a long moment.

Then Doss let go of Hannah's shoulders, and she turned to whip the eggs and slice bread for toasting. He found a crate and filled it with provisions for the widow Jessup.

After he'd gone, Hannah carried a plate up to To-bias, who seemed content to stay in bed with one of his many picture books.

"I'm getting worried about that boy," Tobias told Hannah solemnly. "He ought to be back by now."

"I'm sure you'll see him again soon," Hannah said moderately. "Remember, you promised to let me know right away when you do."

He nodded, looking glum.

She kissed his forehead and went out, leaving the door open so she'd hear if he called for her. What he needed most right now was rest, and good food to build his strength. When Doss got back with the bacon and hams, she'd make up a special meal.

Downstairs Hannah tidied the kitchen, washed the dishes, dried them and put them away. When that was done, she built up the fire and went to the china cabinet to open the top drawer. The album was there, where it belonged, but a little shiver went up her spine at the sight of it, just the same.

She reached past it, found the small leather-bound remembrance book Lorelei and Holt had sent her for a Christmas present. The cover was a rich shade of blue, the pages edged in shiny gold.

She hadn't written a word in the journal, hadn't even opened it. She hadn't wanted to record her grief, hadn't wanted to make it real by writing it down in dark, formal letters.

Now she had something very different in mind. She carried the remembrance book to the table, and then went to the study for a bottle of ink and a pen. The room was chilly. She rarely went there, because it always brought back memories of Gabe, sitting at the desk, reading or pondering over a ledger.

It was especially empty that day; though, strangely, it was Doss's absence Hannah felt most keenly, not Gabe's. She collected the items she needed and hurried out again.

Back in the kitchen she found a rag to wipe the pen clean. When she was finished she opened the ink and turned to the first page.

She bit her lower lip, dipped the pen, summoned up all her resolve and began to write.

My name is Hannah McKettrick. Today's date is January 19, 1919…

Present Day

THE FIRST THING Sierra noticed when she got back to the house later that morning—with a load of groceries and a head spinning with possibilities now that she was rich—was that Travis wasn't around. The second thing was that the album Eve had brought out to show her was gone.

She'd left it on the kitchen table, and it had vanished.

She paused, holding her breath. Listening. Was there someone in the house?

No, it was empty. She didn't need to search the rooms, open closet doors, peer under beds, to know that.

Her practical side took over. She brought in the rest of the supermarket bags and put everything away. Put on a pot of coffee. Made a tuna salad sandwich and ate it.

Only when she'd rinsed the plate and put it in the dishwasher did she walk over to the china cabinet and open the top drawer, as Eve had done earlier that morning.

The album was back in its place.

Sierra frowned.

Invisible fingers played a riff on her spine, touching every vertebra.

She closed the drawer again.

She would look at the photographs later. Combine that with the job of cataloging the ones stored in the attic.

She brought the Christmas boxes up from the basement, carried them into the living room. Carefully and methodically removed and wrapped each ornament. Some were obviously expensive, others were the handiwork of generations of children.

By the time she'd put them all away and dismantled the silk tree, it was time to drive into town and pick Liam up at school. Backing the SUV out of the garage, she almost ran over Travis, who had the hood up on the station wagon and was standing to one side, fiddling with one of its parts.

He leaped out of her path, grinning.

She slammed on the brakes, buzzed down the window on the passenger side. "You scared me," she said.

Travis laughed, leaning in. "*I* scared *you?*"

"I wasn't expecting you to be standing there."

"I wasn't expecting *you* to come shooting out of the garage at sixty-five miles an hour, either."

Sierra smiled. "Do you always argue about everything?"

"Sure," he said, with an affable shrug of his impressive shoulders. "Gotta stay sharp in case I ever want to practice law again. Where are you headed in such a hurry, anyway?"

"Liam's about to get out of school for the day."

"Right," Travis said, stepping back.

"Do you want to come along?"

Now what made her say *that?* She liked Travis Reid well enough, and certainly appreciated all he'd done to help, but he also made her poignantly uncomfortable.

He must have seen her thoughts playing out in her face. "Maybe another time," he said easily. "Eve told me you were going to take down the Christmas tree. It's a big sucker, so I'll lug it back to the basement if you want."

"That would be good. The coffee's on—help yourself."

Travis grinned. Nodded. Stepped back from the side of the SUV with exaggerated haste.

As she drove away, Sierra wasn't thinking about her two-million-dollar trust fund, the vanishing teapot, the piano that played itself, teleporting photo album or even Liam.

She was thinking about the hired help.

PEERING THROUGH HIS new telescope at the night sky, Liam felt that familiar shiver in the air. He knew, even before he turned around to look, that the boy would be there.

And he was. Lying in the bed, staring at Liam.

"What's your name?" the boy asked.

For a moment, Liam couldn't believe his ears. He wasn't scared, but his throat got tight, just the same. He'd planned on telling the boy all about his first day at the new school, and a lot of other things, too, as soon as he showed up, but now the words got stuck and wouldn't come out.

"Mine's Tobias."

"I'm Liam."

"That's an odd name."

Liam straightened his back. "Well, 'Tobias' is pretty weird, too," he countered.

Tobias tossed back the covers and got out of bed. He was wearing a funny flannel nightgown, more suited to a girl than a boy. It reached clear past his knees. "What's that?" he asked, pointing to Liam's telescope.

Liam patiently explained the obvious. "Wanna look? You can see all the way to Saturn with this thing."

Tobias peered through the viewer. "It's bouncing around. And it's *blue!*"

"Yep," Liam agreed. "How come you're wearing a nightie?"

Tobias looked up. His eyes flashed, and his cheeks got red. "This," he said, "is a night*shirt*."

"Whatever," Liam said.

Tobias gave him the eyeball. "Those are mighty peculiar duds," he announced.

"Thanks a lot," Liam said, but he wasn't mad. He figured "duds" must mean clothes. "Are you a ghost?"

"No," Tobias said. "I'm a boy. What are you?"

"A boy," Liam answered.

"What are you doing in my room?"

"This is *my* room. What are *you* doing here?"

Tobias grinned, poked a finger into Liam's chest, as though testing to see if it would go right through. "My ma told me to let her know first thing if I saw you again," he said.

Liam put out his own finger and found Tobias to be as solid as he was.

"Are you going to?" he asked.

"I don't know," Tobias said. He put his eye to the viewer again. "Is that *really* Saturn, or is this one of those moving-picture contraptions?"

1919

HANNAH BLEW ON the ink until it dried. Then she wiped the pen clean, sealed the ink bottle and closed the remembrance book.

Now that she'd written in it, she felt a little foolish, but what was done was done. She took the book back to the china cabinet and placed it carefully beneath the top cover of the family album.

She was just mounting the steps to go and check on Tobias when she realized he was talking to someone. She couldn't make out the words, just the conversational tone of his voice. He spoke with an eager lilt she hadn't heard in a long time.

She stood absolutely still, straining to listen.

"Ma!" he yelled suddenly.

She bolted up the stairs, along the hallway, into his room.

She found him lying comfortably in bed, wide awake, his eyes shining with an almost feverish excitement. "I saw the boy," he said. "His name is Liam and he showed me Saturn."

"Liam," Hannah repeated stupidly, because anything else was quite beyond her.

"I said it was a strange name, Liam, I mean, and he said Tobias was a weird thing to be called, too."

Hannah opened her mouth, closed it again. Twisted the hem of her apron in both hands. Her knees felt as though they'd turned to liquid, and even though she'd asked Tobias to let her know straight away if he saw the boy again, she realized she hadn't been prepared to hear it. She wished Doss were there, even though he'd probably be a hindrance, rather than a help.

"Ma?" Tobias sounded worried, and his eyes were great in his face.

She hurried to his bed, sat down on the edge of the mattress, touched a hand to his forehead.

He squirmed away. "I'm not sick," he protested. "I saw Saturn. It's blue, and it really does have rings."

Hannah withdrew her hand, and it came to rest, fluttering, at the base of her throat.

"You don't believe me!" Tobias accused.

"I don't know what to believe," Hannah admitted softly. "But I know you're not lying, Tobias."

"I'm not seeing things, either!"

"I— It's just so strange."

Tobias subsided a little, falling back on to his pillows with a sigh. "He told me lots of stuff, Ma," he said, his voice small and uncertain.

Hannah took his hand, squeezed it. Tried to appear calm. "What 'stuff,' Tobias?" she managed, after a few slow, deep breaths.

"That Saturn has moons, just like the earth does. Only, it's got four, instead of just one. One of them is covered in ice, and it might even have an ocean underneath, full of critters with no eyes."

Hannah swallowed a slight, guttural cry of pure dismay. "What else?"

"People have boxes in their houses, and they can watch all kinds of stories on them. Folks act them out, like players on a stage."

Tears of pure panic burned in Hannah's eyes, but she blinked them back. "You must have been dreaming, Tobias," she said, fairly croaking the words, like a frog in a fable. "You fell asleep, and it only seemed real—"

"No," Tobias said flatly. "I saw Liam. I talked to him. He said it was the twenty-first century, where he lives. I told him he was full of sheep dip—that it was 1919, and I'd get the calendar to prove it. Then he said if I was eight years old in 1919, I was probably dead or in a nursing home someplace in his time." He paused. "What's a nursing home, Ma? And how could I be two places at once? A kid here, and an old man somewhere else?"

Dizzy, Hannah gathered her boy in both arms and held him so tightly that he struggled.

"Let me go, Ma," he said. "You're fair smothering me!"

With a conscious effort, Hannah broke the embrace. Let her arms fall to her sides.

"What's happening to us?" she whispered.

"I need to use the chamber pot," Tobias announced.

Hannah stood slowly, like a sleepwalker. She moved out of that room, closed the door behind her and got as far as the top of the back stairs before her legs gave out and she had to sit down.

She was still there when Doss came in, back from his travels to the smokehouse and the widow Jessup's place. As though he'd sensed her presence, he came to the foot of the steps, still in his coat and hat.

"Hannah? What's the matter? Is Tobias all right?"

"He's…yes."

Doss tossed his hat away, came up the steps, sat down next to Hannah and put an arm around her shoulders. She sagged against his side, even as she despised herself for the weakness. Turned her face into his cold-weather-and-leather-scented shoulder and wept with confusion and relief and a whole tangle of other emotions.

He held her until the worst of it had passed.

She sniffled and sat up straight. Even tried to smile. "How was the widow Jessup?" she asked.

Present Day

THAT NIGHT SIERRA invited Travis to supper. Just marched right out to his trailer, knocked on the door and, the moment he opened it, blurted, "We're having spaghetti tonight. It's Liam's favorite. It would mean a lot to him if you came and ate with us."

Travis grinned. Evidently, he'd been changing clothes, because his shirt was half-unbuttoned. "If you're trying to make up for almost running over me backing out of the garage this afternoon, it's okay," he teased. "I'm still pretty fast on my feet."

Sierra was doing her level best not to admire what she could see of his chest, which was muscular. She wondered what it would be like to slide her hands inside that shirt, feel his skin against her palms and her splayed fingers.

Then she looked up into his eyes again, saw the knowing smile there and blushed. "It's more about thanking you for taking the Christmas tree downstairs," she fibbed.

"At your service," he said with a slight drawl.

Was that a double entendre?

Don't be silly, she told herself. Of course it wasn't.

"There's wine, too," she blurted out, and then blushed again. At this rate, Travis would think she'd already had a few nips.

"Everything but music," he quipped.

Afraid to say another word, she turned and hurried back toward the house, and she distinctly heard him chuckle before he closed the trailer door.

Liam was strangely quiet at supper. He usually gobbled spaghetti, but tonight he merely nibbled. He had a perfect opportunity to talk "cowboy" with Travis, or chatter on about his first day of school; instead, he asked to be excused so he could take a bath and get to bed early. At Sierra's nod, he murmured something and fled.

"He must be sick," Sierra fretted, about to go after him.

"Let him go," Travis counseled. "He's all right."

"But—"

"He's *all right,* Sierra." He refilled her wineglass, then his own.

They finished their meal, cleared the table together, loaded the dishwasher. When Sierra would have walked away, Travis caught hold of her arm and gently stopped her. Switched on the countertop radio with his free hand.

Soft, smoky music poured into the room.

The next thing she knew, Sierra was in Travis's arms, close against that chest she'd admired earlier at the door of his trailer, and they were slow dancing.

Why didn't she pull away?

Maybe it was the wine.

"Relax," he said. His breath was warm in her hair.

She giggled, more nervous than amused. What was the matter with her? She was attracted to Travis, had been from the first, and he was clearly attracted to her. They were both adults. Why not enjoy a little slow dancing in a ranch-house kitchen?

Because slow dancing led to other things, especially when it was wine powered. She took a step back and felt the counter flush against her lower back. Travis naturally came with her, since they were holding hands and he had one arm around her waist.

Simple physics.

Then he kissed her.

Physics again—this time, not so simple.

"Yikes," she said, when their mouths parted.

He grinned. "Nobody's ever said that after I kissed them."

She felt the heat and substance of his body pressed against hers, right where it counted. If Liam hadn't been just upstairs, and likely to come back down at any moment, she might have wrapped her legs around Travis's waist and kissed him nuclear-style.

"It's going to happen, isn't it?" she heard herself whisper.

"Yep," Travis answered.

"But not tonight," Sierra said on a sigh.

"Probably not," Travis agreed, grinding his hips a little. His erection burned into her abdomen like a firebrand.

"When, then?"

He chuckled, gave her a slow, nibbling kiss. "Tomorrow morning," he said. "After you drop Liam off at school."

"Isn't that…a little…soon?"

"Not soon enough," Travis answered. He cupped a hand around her breast, and even through the fabric of her shirt and bra, her nipple hardened against the chafing motion of his thumb. "Not nearly soon enough."

After Travis had gone, Sierra felt like an idiot.

She looked in on Liam, who was sound asleep, and then took a cool shower. It didn't help.

She would come to her senses by morning, she told herself, as she stood at her bedroom window, gazing down at the lights burning in Travis's trailer.

She'd get a good night's sleep. That was all she needed.

She slept, as it happened, like the proverbial log, but she woke up thinking about Travis. About the way she'd felt when he kissed her, when he backed her up against the counter…

She made breakfast.

Took Liam to school.

Zoomed straight back to the ranch, even though she'd intended to drive around town for a while, giving herself a chance to cool down.

Instead, she was on autopilot.

But it wasn't as if she gave up easily. She raised every argument she could think of. It was *way* too soon. She didn't know Travis well enough to sleep with him.

She would regret this in the morning.

No, long *before* then.

The truth was, she'd denied herself so much, for so long, that she couldn't stand it anymore.

She didn't even bother to park the SUV in the garage. She shut it down between the house and Travis's trailer, up to the wheel wells in snow, jumped out, and double-timed it to his door.

Knocked.

Maybe he's not home, she thought desperately.

Let him be here.

Let him be in China.

His truck was parked in its usual place, next to the barn.

The trailer door creaked open.

He grinned down at her. "Hot damn," he said.

Sierra shoved her hands into her coat pockets. Wished she could dig her toes right into the ground somehow and hold out against the elemental forces that were driving her.

Travis stepped back. "Come in," he said.

So much for the toehold. She was inside in a single bound.

He leaned around her to pull the door shut.

"This is crazy," she said.

He began unbuttoning her coat. Slipped it back off her shoulders. Bent his head to taste her earlobe and brush the length of her neck with his lips.

She groaned.

"Talk some sense into me," she pleaded. "Say this is stupid and we shouldn't do it."

He laughed. "You're kidding, right?"

"It's wrong."

"Think of it as therapy."

She trembled as he tossed her coat aside. "For whom? You or me?"

He opened her blouse, undid the catch at the front of her bra, caught her breasts in his hands when they sprang free.

"Oh, I think we'll both benefit," he said.

Sierra groaned again. He sat her down on the side of his bed, crouched to pull off her snow boots, peel off her socks. Then he stood her up again, and undressed her, garment by garment. Blouse…bra…jeans…and, finally, her lacy underpants.

He suckled at her breasts, somehow managing to shed his own clothes in the process; Sierra was too dazed, and too aroused, to consider the mechanics of it.

He laid her down on the bed, gently. Eased two pillows under her bottom. Knelt between her legs.

"Oh, God," she whimpered. "You're not going to—?"

Travis kissed his way from her mouth to her neck.

"I sure am," he mumbled, before pausing to enjoy one of her breasts, then the other.

He kept moving downward, stroking the tender flesh on the insides of her thighs. He plumped up the pillows, raising her higher.

Sierra moaned.

He parted the nest of moist curls at the junction of her thighs. Breathed on her. Touched her lightly with the tip of his tongue.

She arched her back and gave a low, throaty cry of need.

"I thought so," Travis said, almost idly.

"You—thought—what?" Sierra demanded.

"That you needed this as much as I do." He took her full into his mouth.

She welcomed him with a sob and an upward thrust of her hips.

He slid his hands under her buttocks and lifted her higher still.

She was about to explode, and she fought it. It wasn't as though she had orgasms every day. She wanted this experience to *last*.

He drove her straight over the edge.

She convulsed with the power of her release—once—twice—three times.

It was over.

But it wasn't.

Before she had time to lament, he was taking her to a new level.

She came again, voluptuously, piercingly, her legs over his shoulders now. And before she could begin the breathless descent, he grasped the undersides of her knees and parted them, tongued her until she climaxed yet again. Only, this time she couldn't make a sound. She could only buckle in helpless waves of pleasure.

And still it wasn't over.

He waited until she'd opened her eyes. Until her breathing had evened out. After all of the frenzy, he waited until she nodded.

He entered her in a long, slow, deep stroke, supporting himself with his hands pressing into the narrow mattress on either side of her shoulders, gazing intently down into her face. Taking in every response.

She began the climb again. Rasped his name. Clutched at his shoulders.

He didn't increase his pace.

She pumped, growing more and more frantic as the delicious friction increased, degree by degree, toward certain meltdown.

The wave crashed over her like a tsunami, and when she stopped flailing and shouting in surrender—and only then—she saw him close his eyes. His neck corded, like a stallion's, as he threw back his head and let himself go.

His powerful body flexed, and flexed again, every muscle taut, and Sierra almost wept as she watched his control give way.

Afterward he lowered himself to lie beside her, wrapping her close in his arms. Kissed her temple, where the hair was moist with perspiration. Stroked her breasts and her belly.

She listened as his breathing slowed.

"You're not going to fall asleep, are you?" she asked.

He laughed. "No," he said. He rolled on to his back, pulling her with him, so that she lay sprawled on top of him. Caressed her back, her shoulders, her buttocks.

She nestled in. Buried her face in his neck. Popped her head up again, suddenly alarmed. "Did you use…?"

"Yes," he said.

She snuggled up again. "That was…great," she confessed, and giggled.

He shifted beneath her. She felt some fumbling.

"We can't possibly do that again," she said.

"Wanna bet?" He eased her upright, set her knees on either side of his hips.

Felt him move inside her, sleek and hard.

A violent tremor went through her, left her shuddering.

He cupped her breasts in his hands, drew her forward far enough to suck her breasts. All the while, he was raising and lowering her along his length. She took him deeper.

And then deeper still.

And then the universe dissolved into shimmering particles and rained down on them both like atoms of fire.

CHAPTER FOURTEEN

SIERRA SLEPT, SNUGGLED AGAINST TRAVIS'S SIDE, one arm draped across his chest, one shapely leg flung over his thighs.

Travis pulled the quilt up over them both, so she wouldn't get cold, and considered his situation.

He'd been to bed with a lot of women in his time.

He knew how to give and receive pleasure.

He said goodbye as easily as hello.

But this was different.

Different feeling. Different woman.

He'd been a dead man up until now, and this trailer had been his coffin.

Rance had sure been right about that.

Sierra McKettrick, who had probably expected no more from this encounter than he had—a roll in the hay, some much-needed satisfaction, a break in the monotony—had resurrected him. Probably inadvertently, but the effect was the same.

"Shit," he whispered. He'd *needed* that all-pervasive numbness and the insulation it provided. Needed *not* to feel.

Sierra had awakened everything inside him, and it hurt, to the center of his soul, like frost-bitten flesh thawing too fast.

She stirred against him, uttered a soft, hmmm sound, but didn't awaken.

He held her a little closer and thought about Brody. His little brother. Brody would never make love to a woman like Sierra. He'd never watch the moon rise over a mountain creek, the water purple in the twilight, or choke up at the sight of a ragged band of wild horses racing across a clearing for no other reason than that they had legs to run on. He'd never throw a stick for a faithful old dog to fetch, watch Fourth-of-July fireworks with a kid perched on his shoulders or eat pancakes swimming in syrup in a roadside café while hokey music played on the jukebox.

There were so many things Brody would never do.

Travis's throat went raw, and his eyes stung.

The loss yawned inside him, a black hole, an abyss.

He'd thought losing his brother would be the hardest thing he'd ever had to do, but now he knew it wasn't. Dying inside was easy—it was having the guts to *live* that was hard.

He shifted.

Sierra sighed, raised her head, looked straight into his face.

It was too much to hope, he figured, that she wouldn't notice the tear that had just trickled out of the corner of his eye to streak toward his ear.

If she saw, she had the good grace not to comment, and the depth of his gratitude for that simple blessing was downright pathetic, by his reckoning.

"What time is it?" she asked, looking anxious and womanly.

Real womanly.

He stretched, groped for his watch on the little shelf above the bed. "Twelve-thirty," he answered gruffly. He wanted to say a whole lot more, but he wasn't sure what it was. He'd have to say it all to himself first, and make sense of it, before he could tell it to anyone else.

Especially Sierra.

Not that he loved her or anything. It was too early for that.

But he sure as hell felt *something,* and he wished he didn't.

"You okay?" she asked, raising herself on to one elbow and studying his face a lot more intently than he would have liked.

"Fine," he lied.

"This doesn't have to change anything," Sierra reasoned, hurrying her words a little—pushing them along, like rambunctious cattle toward a narrow chute. Was she trying to convince him, or herself?

"Right," he said.

She pulled away, sat on the backs of her thighs, the quilt pulled up to her chin. "I'd better—get back to the house."

He nodded.

She nodded.

Neither of them moved.

"What just happened here?" Sierra asked, after a long time had passed, with the two of them just staring at each other.

Whatever had happened, it had been a lot more than the obvious. He was sure of that, if nothing else.

"I'll be damned if I know," Travis said.

"Me, neither," Sierra said. Then she bent and kissed his forehead, before scrambling out of bed.

He sat up, watched as she gathered her scattered clothes and shimmied into them. He wished he smoked, because lighting a cigarette would have given him something to do. Something to distract him from the rawness of what he felt and his frustration at not being able to wrestle it down and give it a name.

"I guess you must think I do things like this all the time," she said. Maybe he wasn't alone in being confused. The idea stirred a forlorn hope within him. "And I don't. I *don't* sleep with men I barely know, and I don't—"

He smiled. "I believe you, Sierra," he said. He did, too. Anybody who came with the kind of sensual abandon she had, on a regular basis, would be superhuman, dead of exhaustion or both.

Actually, he admired her stamina, and her uncommon passion.

And she was up, moving around, dressing. He wasn't entirely sure he could stand.

She sat on the side of the bed, keeping a careful if subtle distance, to pull on her socks and boots. "Travis?" she said without looking at him. He saw a pink glow along the edge of her cheek, and thought of a summer dawn, rimming a mountain peak.

"What?"

"It was good. What we did was good. Okay?"

He swallowed. Reached out and squeezed her hand briefly before letting it go. "Yeah," he agreed. "It was good."

She left then, and Travis felt her absence like a vacuum.

He cupped his hands behind his head, lay back and began making a list in his mind.

All the things he had to do before he left the Triple M for good.

SHE'D MADE A damn fool of herself.

Sierra let herself into the house, closed the door behind her and leaned back against it.

What had she been thinking, throwing herself at Travis that way? She'd been like a woman possessed—and a *stupid* woman, at that.

Sierra McKettrick, the sexual sophisticate.

Right.

Sierra McKettrick, who had been intimate with exactly two men in her life—one of whom had fathered her child, lied to her and left her behind, apparently without a second thought.

What if Travis hadn't been telling the truth when he said he used protection?

What if she was pregnant again?

"Get a grip," she told herself out loud. Travis had clearly had a lot of experience in these matters, unlike her. Furthermore he was a lawyer. He might not have given a damn whether *she* was protected or not, but he surely would have covered his *own* backside, if only to avoid a potential paternity suit.

She stood still, breathing like a woman in the early stages of labor, until she'd regained some semblance of composure. She had to pull herself together. In a couple of hours she'd be picking Liam up at school.

He'd want to tell her all about his class. The other kids. The teachers.

There would be supper to fix and homework to oversee.

She was a *mother,* for God's sake, not some bimbo in a soap opera, sneaking off to have prenoon monkey sex in a trailer with a virtual stranger.

She straightened.

Her own voice echoed in her mind.

It was good. What we did was good. Okay?

And it *had* been good, just not in the noble sense of the word.

Sierra went slowly upstairs, took a long, hot shower, dressed in fresh jeans and a white cotton blouse. Borrowed one of Meg's cardigans, to complete the "Mom" look.

By the time she was finished, she still had more than an hour until she had to leave for town.

Her gaze strayed to the china cabinet.

She would look at the pictures in the album. Get a frame of reference for all those McKettricks that had gone before. Try to imagine herself as one of them, a link in the biological chain.

She heard Travis's truck start up, resisted an urge to go to the window and watch him drive away. There was too much danger that she would morph into a desperate housewife, smile sweetly and wave.

Not gonna happen.

Keeping her thoughts and actions briskly businesslike, she retrieved the album, carried it to the table, sat down and lifted the cover.

A small blue book was tucked inside, its corners curled with age.

A tremor of something went through Sierra like a wash of ice water, some premonition, some subconscious awareness straining to reach the surface.

She opened the smaller volume.

Focused on the beautifully scripted lines, penned in ink that had long since faded to an antique brown.

My name is Hannah McKettrick.
I know you're here. I can sense it. You've moved the teapot, and the album in which I've placed this remembrance book.

Please don't harm my boy. His name is Tobias.
He's eight years old.
He is everything to me.

Sierra caught her breath. There was more, but her
shock was such that, for the next few moments, the re-
maining words might as well have been gibberish.

Was this woman, probably long dead, addressing her
from another century?

Impossible.

But then, it was impossible for teapots and photograph albums to move by themselves, too. It was impossible for an ordinary piano to play itself, with no
one touching the keys.

It was impossible for Liam to see a boy in his room.

Sierra swallowed, lowered her eyes to the journal
again. The words had been written so very long ago,
and yet they had the immediacy of an email.

How could this be happening?

She sucked in another breath. Read on.

I must be losing my mind. Doss says it's grief,
over Gabe's dying. I don't even know why I'm
writing this, except in the hope that you'll write
something back. It's the only way I can think of
to speak to you.

Sierra glanced at the clock. Only a few minutes had
passed since she sat down at the table, but it seemed
like so much longer.

She got out of her chair, found a pen in the junk
drawer next to the sink. This was *crazy*. She was about
to deface what might be an important family record.

And yet there was something so plaintive in Hannah's plea that she couldn't ignore it.

My name is Sierra McKettrick.I have a son, too, and his name is Liam. He's seven, and he has asthma. He's the center of my life.
You have nothing to fear from me. I'm not a ghost, just an ordinary flesh-and-blood woman.
A mother, like you.

The telephone rang, jolting Sierra out of the spell.

Conditioned to unexpected emergencies, because of Liam's illness, she hurried to answer, squinting at the caller ID.

"Indian Rock Elementary School."

The room swayed.

"This is Sierra McKettrick," she said. "Is my son all right?"

The voice on the other end of the line was blessedly calm. "Liam is just a little sick at his stomach, that's all," the woman said. "The school nurse thinks he ought to come home. He'll probably be fine in the morning."

"I'll be right there," Sierra answered, and hung up without saying goodbye.

Liam is safe, she told herself, but she felt panicky, just the same.

She deliberately closed Hannah McKettrick's journal, put it back inside the album. Placed the album inside the drawer.

Then she raced around the kitchen, frantically searching for the car keys, before remembering that she'd left them in the ignition earlier, when she'd come back from town. She'd been so focused on having an illicit tryst with Travis Reid....

She grabbed her coat, dashed out the door, jumped into the SUV.

The roads were icy, and by the time Sierra sped into Indian Rock, huge flakes of snow were tumbling from a grim gray sky. She forced herself to slow down, but when she reached the school parking lot, she almost forgot to shut off the motor in her haste to get inside, find her son.

Liam lay on a cot in the nurse's office, alarmingly pale. Someone had laid a cloth over his forehead, presumably cool, but he was all by himself.

How could these people have left him alone?

"Mom," he said. "My stomach hurts. I think I'm gonna hurl again."

She went to him. He rolled on to his side and vomited onto her shoes.

"I'm sorry!" he wailed.

She stroked his sweat-dampened hair. "It's all right, Liam. Everything is going to be all right."

He threw up again.

Sierra snatched a handful of paper towels from the wall dispenser, wet them down at the sink and washed his face.

"My coat!" he lamented. "I don't want to leave my cowboy coat—"

"Don't worry about your coat," Sierra said, wondering distractedly how she could possibly be the same woman who'd spent half the morning naked in Travis's bed.

The nurse, a tall blond woman with kindly blue eyes, stepped into the room, carrying Liam's coat and backpack. Silently she laid the things aside in a chair and came to assist in the cleanup effort.

Sierra went to get the coat.

"No!" Liam cried out, as she approached him with it. "What if I puke on it?"

"Sweetheart, it's cold outside, and we can always have it cleaned—"

The nurse caught her eye. Shook her head. "Let's just bundle Liam up in a couple of blankets. I'll help you get him to the car. This coat is important to him— *so* important that, sick as he was, he insisted I go and get it for him."

Sierra bit her lip. She and the nurse wrapped Liam in the blankets, and Sierra lifted him into her arms. He was getting so big. One day soon, she probably wouldn't be able to carry him anymore.

The main doors whooshed open when Sierra reached them.

"Oh, great," Liam moaned. "Everybody's looking. Everybody knows I *ralphed.*"

Sierra hadn't noticed the children filling the corridor. The dismissal bell must have rung, but she hadn't heard it.

"It's okay, Liam," she said.

He shook his head. "No, it *isn't!* My *mom* is carrying me out of the school in a bunch of *blankets,* like a *baby!* I'll never live this down!"

Sierra and the nurse exchanged glances.

The nurse smiled and shifted Liam's coat and backpack so she could pat his shoulder. "When you get back to school," she said, "you come to my office and I'll tell you *plenty* of stories about things that have happened in this school over the years. You're not the first person to throw up here, Liam McKettrick, and you won't be the last, either."

Liam lifted his head, apparently heartened. "Really?"

The nurse rolled her eyes expressively. "If you only *knew*," she said, in a conspiratorial tone, opening the door of the SUV on the passenger side, so Sierra could set Liam on the seat and buckle him in. "I wouldn't name names, of course, but I've seen kids do a lot worse than vomit."

Sierra shut the door, turned to face the nurse.

"Thanks," she said. Liam peered through the window, his face a greenish, bespectacled moon, his hair sticking out in spikes. "You have a unique way of comforting an embarrassed kid, but it seems to be effective."

The nurse smiled, put out her hand. "My name is Susan Yarnia," she said. "If you need anything, you call me, either here at the school or at home. My husband's name is Joe, and we're in the book."

Sierra nodded. Took the coat and backpack and put them into the rig, after ferreting for Liam's inhaler, just in case he needed it on the way home. "Do you think I should take him to the clinic?" she asked in a whisper, after she'd closed the door again.

"That's up to you, of course," Susan said. "There's been a flu bug going around, and my guess is Liam caught it. If I were you, I'd just take him home, put him to bed and make a bit of a fuss over him. See that he drinks a lot of liquids, and if you can get him to swallow a few spoonfuls of chicken soup, so much the better."

Sierra nodded, thanked the woman again and rounded the SUV to get behind the wheel.

"What if I spew in Aunt Meg's car?" Liam asked.

"I'll clean it up," Sierra answered.

"This whole thing is *mortifying*. When I tell Tobias—"

Tobias.

If Sierra hadn't been pulling out on to a slick road, she probably would have slammed on the brakes.

Please don't harm my boy, Hannah McKettrick had written, eighty-eight years ago, in her journal. *His name is Tobias. He's eight years old.*

"Who is Tobias?" Sierra asked moderately, but her palms were so wet on the steering wheel that she feared her grip wouldn't hold if she had to make a sudden turn.

"The. Boy. In. My. Room," Liam said very carefully, as though English were not even Sierra's *second* language, let alone her first. "I told you I saw him."

"Yeah," Sierra replied, her stomach clenching so hard that she wasn't sure *she* wouldn't be the next one to throw up, "but you didn't mention having a conversation with him."

Liam turned away from her, rested his forehead against the passenger-side window, probably because it was cool. "I thought you'd freak," he said. "Or send me off to some bug farm."

Sierra drove past the clinic where she and Travis had taken Liam the day of his asthma attack. It was all she could do not to pull in and demand that he be put on life support, or air-lifted to Stanford.

It's stomach flu, she insisted to herself, and kept driving by sheer force of will.

"When have I ever threatened to send you *anywhere,* let alone to a 'bug farm'?"

"There's always a first time," Liam reasoned.

"You were sick last night," Sierra realized aloud. "That's why you were so quiet at supper."

"I was quiet at supper because I figured Tobias would be there when I went upstairs."

"Were you scared?"

Liam flung her a scornful look. "No," he said. And

then his cheeks puffed out, and he made a strangling sound.

Sierra pulled to the side of the road, got out of the SUV and barely got around to open the door before he decorated her shoes again.

This is your real life, she thought pragmatically.

Not the two million dollars.

Not great sex in a cowboy's bed.

It's a seven-year-old boy, barfing on your shoes.

The reflections were strangely comforting, given the circumstances.

When Liam was through, she wiped off her boots with handfuls of snow, got back into the car and drove to the nearest gas station, where she bought him a bottle of Gatorade so he could rinse out his mouth, spit gloriously onto the pavement, and hopefully retain enough electrolytes to keep from dehydrating.

Twilight was already gathering by the time she pulled into the garage at the ranch house, having noticed, in spite of herself, that Travis was back from wherever he'd gone, and the lights were glowing golden in the windows of his trailer.

Not that it mattered.

In fact, she wasn't the least bit relieved when he walked into the garage before she could shut the door or even turn off the engine.

Liam unsnapped his seat belt and lowered his window. "I *horked* all over the schoolhouse," he told Travis gleefully. "People will probably talk about it for *years*."

"Excellent," Travis said with admiration. His eyes danced under the brim of his hat as he looked at Sierra over Liam's head, then returned his full attention to the little boy. "Need some help getting inside? One cowpoke to another?"

"Sure," Liam replied staunchly. "Not that I couldn't make it on my own or anything."

Travis chuckled. "Maybe you ought to carry *me,* then." His gaze snagged Sierra's again. "It happens that I'm feeling a little weak in the knees myself."

Sierra's face heated. She switched off the ignition.

Liam giggled, and the sound was restorative. "You're too big to carry, Travis," he said, with such affection that Sierra's throat tightened again, and she honestly thought she'd cry.

Fortunately, Travis wasn't looking at her. He gathered Liam into his arms, blankets and all, and carried him inside. Sierra followed with her son's things, scrambling to get her emotions under control.

"It's *arctic* in here," Liam said.

"You're right," Travis agreed easily. He set Liam in the chair where Sierra had sat writing in the diary of a woman who was probably buried somewhere among all those bronze statues in the family cemetery, and approached the old stove. "Nothing like a good wood fire to warm a place up."

"Drink your Gatorade," Sierra told Liam, because she felt she had to say something, and that was all that came to mind.

"Can we sleep down here again?" Liam asked. "Like we did when the blizzard came and the furnace went out?"

"No," Sierra answered, much too quickly.

Travis gave her a sidelong glance and a grin, then stuffed some crumpled newspaper and kindling into the belly of the wood stove, and lit the fire. Sierra shivered, hugging herself, while he adjusted the damper.

"Is something wrong with the furnace again?" she asked.

"Probably," Travis answered.

She was oddly grateful that he hadn't called her on asking a stupid question. But then, he wouldn't. Not in front of her son. She knew that much about Travis Reid, at least. Along with the fact that he was one hell of a lover.

Don't even think about that, Sierra scolded herself. But it was like deciding not to imagine a pink elephant skating on a pond and wearing a tutu.

"I think we should all sleep right here," Liam persisted.

Travis chuckled, more, Sierra suspected, at her discomfort than at Liam's campaign for another kitchen campout. "If a man's got a bed," Travis said, "he ought to use it."

Sierra's cheeks stung. "Was that necessary?" she whispered furiously, after approaching the wood box to grab up a few chunks of pine. If she was going to live in this house for a year, she'd better learn to work the stove.

"No," Travis whispered back, "but it was fun."

"Will you *stop?*"

Another grin. He seemed to have an infinite supply of those, and all of them were saucy. "Nope."

"What are you guys whispering about?" Liam asked suspiciously. "Are you keeping secrets?"

Travis took the wood from Sierra's hands, stuffed it into the stove. She tried to look away but she couldn't. "No secrets," he said.

Sierra bit her lower lip.

The kitchen began to warm up, but she couldn't be certain it was because of the fire in the cookstove.

Travis left them to go downstairs and attend to the furnace.

"I wish he was my dad," Liam said.

Sierra blinked back more tears. Lifted her chin. "Well, he's not, sweetie," she said gently, and with a slight quaver in her voice. "Best let it go at that, okay?"

Liam looked so sad that Sierra wanted to take him on to her lap and rock him the way she had when he was younger and a lot more amenable to motherly affection. "Okay," he agreed.

She crossed to him, ruffled his hair, which was already mussed. "Think you could eat something?" she asked. "Maybe some chicken noodle soup?"

"Yuck," he answered. "And I *still* think we should sleep in the kitchen, because it's cold and I'm sick and I might catch pneumonia or something up there in my room."

The mention of Liam's room made Sierra think of Hannah again and Tobias. She went to the china cabinet, opened the drawer, raised the cover on the photo album. The journal was still there, and she looked inside.

Hannah's words.

Her words.

Nothing more.

Did she expect an answer? More lines of faded ink, entered beneath her own ballpoint scrawl?

A tingle of anticipation went through her as she closed the journal, then the album, then the drawer, and straightened.

Yes.

Oh, yes.

She *did* expect an answer.

The furnace made that familiar whooshing sound.

Liam muttered something that might have been a swear word.

Sierra pretended not to notice.

Travis came back up the basement stairs, dusting his hands together. Another job well done.

"It's still going to be *really* cold upstairs," Liam asserted.

"You're probably right," Travis agreed.

Sierra gave him an eloquent look.

Travis was undaunted. He just grinned another insufferable, three-alarm grin. "I'll make you a bed on the floor," he said, and though he was looking at Sierra, he was talking to Liam. Hopefully. "Just until it gets warm upstairs."

Liam yelped with delighted triumph, punching the air with one fist. Then, just as quickly, he sobered. "What about you and Mom?"

"I reckon we'll just tough it out," Travis drawled. With that, he went about carrying in a couple of sofa cushions to lay on the floor, not too close to the stove but close enough for warmth.

Sierra fetched a pillow and fresh blankets.

Liam stretched out on the makeshift bed like an Egyptian king traveling by barge. Sighed happily.

"Are you staying for supper, Travis?" he asked.

"Am I invited?" Travis asked, looking at Sierra.

She sighed. "Yes," she said.

Liam let out another yippee.

Sierra made grilled cheese sandwiches and heated canned spaghetti, but by the time she served the feast, Liam was sound asleep.

Travis, seated on the bench, his sleeves still rolled up from washing in the bathroom down the hall, nodded toward him.

"If I were you," he said, "I'd start checking out law schools. That kid is probably going to be on the Supreme Court before he's thirty."

CHAPTER FIFTEEN

1919

HANNAH'S HANDS TREMBLED slightly as she raised the cover of the family album and reached for the remembrance book tucked inside. She held her breath as she opened it.

Only her own words were there, alone and stark.

She was a practical woman, and she knew she should not have expected anything else. Spirits, if there was such a thing, did not take up pens and write in remembrance books. And yet she was stricken with a profound disappointment, the likes of which she'd never experienced before. She'd suffered plenty in her life, seeing three sisters perish as a girl and, as a woman grown, losing Gabe, knowing none of the brave dreams they'd talked about with such hope and faith would ever come true.

No more stolen kisses.

No more secret laughter.

No more cattle grazing on a thousand hills.

And certainly no more babies, born squalling in their room upstairs.

Hannah told herself, I will not cry, I have cried enough. I have emptied myself of tears.

So why do they keep coming?

"Hannah?"

She started, looked up to see Doss standing at the foot of the stairs. He'd been working in the barn, the last she knew, doing the morning chores. Chopping extra wood because there was another storm coming. It bothered her that she hadn't heard him come in.

"Tobias is worse," he said.

Alarm swelled into Hannah's throat, cutting off her wind.

She started for the stairs, but when she would have passed Doss, he stopped her.

"I'm going to town for the doc," he told her.

"I'll just wrap Tobias up warm and we'll—"

Doss's grip tightened on her shoulders. Only then did she realize he hadn't merely stepped into her path, he was touching her. "No, Hannah," he said. "The boy's too sick for that."

"Suppose the doctor won't come?"

"He'll come," Doss said. "You go to Tobias. Don't let the fire go out, no matter what. I'll be back as soon as I can."

Hannah nodded, bursting to get to her son, but somehow wanting to cling to Doss, too. Tell him not to go, that they'd manage some way but he oughtn't to leave, because something truly terrible might happen if he did.

"Go to him," Doss told her, letting go of her shoulders.

She felt as though he'd been holding her up. Swayed a little to catch her balance. Then, on impulse, she stood on tiptoe and kissed him right on the mouth. "You be careful, Doss McKettrick," she said. "You come back to us, safe and sound."

He looked deeply into her eyes for a moment, as though he could see secrets she kept even from herself, then nodded and made for the door. The last Hannah saw of him, just before she dashed up the rear stairs, he was putting on his coat and hat.

Tobias lay fitful in his bed, his nightshirt soaked with perspiration, like the sheets. His teeth chattered, and his lips were blue, but his flesh burned to the touch.

Hannah could not afford to let panic prevail.

She had mothering to do, and however inadequate and fearful she felt, there was no one but her to do it.

She pushed up her sleeves, added more pins to her hair so it wouldn't tumble down and get in her way, and headed downstairs to heat water.

Heedful of Doss's warning not to let the fire die, she added wood from the generous supply he'd brought in earlier without her noticing. She pumped water into every bucket and kettle she owned, and put them on the stove to heat. Then she dragged the bathtub out of the pantry and set it in the middle of the floor.

The instructions seemed to come from somewhere inside her. She didn't plan what to do, or take the time to debate one intuition against another. It was as if some stronger, smarter, better Hannah had stepped to the fore, and pushed the timid and uncertain one aside.

This Hannah knew what to do. The regular one stood in the background, wringing her hands and counseling hysteria.

Tobias was practically delirious when Hannah roused him from his bed, an hour later when the tub was full of hot water, and half carried, half led him downstairs.

In the kitchen she stripped him and put him into the bath. Scrubbed him down, all the while talking quietly, confidently, without ever stopping to think up the words she'd say next.

"You'll be fine, Tobias. Come spring, you'll be able to ride your pony through the fields and swim in the pond. We'll get you that dog you've been wanting—you can pick him out yourself—and he can sleep right in your room, too. On the foot of your bed, if you want. You can call your uncle Doss 'Pa' from now on, and there'll be a brand-new baby in this house at harvest time—think of it, Tobias. A little brother or sister. You can choose the name—"

Tobias shuddered, chilled even in water that would be too hot to stand any other time.

Hannah dried him with towels, put him in a clean nightshirt, got him back upstairs again. Settled him into her own bed while she hastened to put fresh sheets and blankets on his.

All that morning, and all that afternoon, she tended her boy, touching a cold cloth to his forehead. Holding his hands. Telling him that his pa had gone to town for the doctor, and he needn't worry because he was going to be just fine.

They were all going to be just fine.

Tobias had occasional moments of lucidity. "Liam's sick, too," he said once. "I want to be with Liam."

Another time, he asked, "Where's Pa? Is Pa all right?"

Hannah had bitten her lower lip and reassured him gently. "Yes, sweetheart, your pa's just fine."

The day wore on, into evening.

And Doss hadn't returned.

Hannah put more wood on the fire, donned Gabe's coat and made her way out to the barn, through ever-deepening snow, to feed the livestock, because there was no one else to do it.

The wind bit through to Hannah's bones as she worked. Made them ache, then go numb.

Where was Doss?

The other Hannah, the fretful one pushed into the

background, kept calling out that question, as if from the bottom of a well.

Where…where…where?

It was completely dark by the time she'd finished, and as she left the barn, she heard the faint rumble of thunder. Rare in a snowstorm, like lightning, but Hannah had seen that, too, there in the high country of Arizona, and in Montana, as well. A staggering sense of foreboding descended upon her, and it had nothing to do with Tobias being sick.

Hannah returned to the house, switched on the kitchen bulb before even taking off Gabe's coat, thinking somehow the light might draw Doss back to her and Tobias, through the storm. Even in daylight, and even for a man as tough and as skilled as Doss, navigating the most familiar trails would be difficult in weather like that, if not impossible. In the dark, it was plain treacherous.

"Ma?" Tobias called. "Ma, are you down there?"

It heartened her, the strength she heard in his voice, but her joy was tempered by worry. Doss should have been home by then. Unless—please, God, let it be so—he'd decided to stay in town.

"Yes," she called back, as cheerfully as she could. "I'm here, and I'm about to fix you some supper."

"Come up, Ma. Right now. That boy's here."

In the process of shedding the coat she'd worn to feed the livestock and the chickens and milk the cow, Hannah let the garment drop, forgotten, to the floor. She took the stairs two at a time and burst into Tobias's room.

With no lamp burning, it was stone dark. She made out the outline of Tobias's bed and him lying there.

"He's here, Ma," Tobias said, in a delighted whisper,

as though speaking too loudly might cause his invisible friend to disappear. "Liam's here."

Hannah hurried to the bedside.

"I don't see him," she said.

Just then the sky itself seemed to part, with a great, tearing roar so horrendous Hannah put her hands to her ears. The floor trembled beneath her feet, and the windowpanes rattled. Light quivered in the room—she knew it was snow lightning, but it was otherworldly, just the same—and for one single, incredulous moment, she saw not Tobias lying in that bed, but another little boy. And she saw the woman standing on the other side of the bed, too. Staring at her. Looking every bit as surprised as Hannah herself.

Within half a heartbeat, the whole incident was over.

"Did you see them?" Tobias asked desperately, grasping at her hand. Clinging. "Ma, did you see them?"

"Yes," Hannah whispered. She dropped to her knees next to Tobias's bed, unable to stand for another instant. Tobias had said "them." He'd seen the woman, too, then, as well as the boy. "Dear God, yes."

"She was wearing trousers, Ma," Tobias marveled.

Hannah raised herself from the floor to perch tremulously on the side of Tobias's bed. Fumbled for the matches and lit the lamp on the stand.

"Tell me what else you saw, Tobias," she said. Her hands were shaking so badly that the lamp chimney rattled when she set it back in place.

"She had short hair. Brown, I think. And she saw us, Ma, just as sure as we saw her!"

Hannah nodded numbly.

"What does it mean, Ma?" Tobias asked.

"I wish I knew," Hannah said.

Present Day

SIERRA STOOD STILL at Liam's bedside, hugging herself and trembling, trying to understand what she'd just seen.

What the hell *had* she just seen?

Lightning.

A woman in an old-fashioned dress, standing on the opposite side of Liam's bed.

Hannah?

"What's wrong, Mom?" Liam asked sleepily. He'd protested a little, when she'd roused him from his slumbers in the kitchen and brought him up here to sleep in his own bed. Then he'd fallen into natural oblivion.

She couldn't catch her breath.

"Mom?" Liam prompted, sounding more awake now.

"We'll…we'll talk about it in the morning."

"Can I sleep with you?"

Sierra swallowed. Travis had gone back to his trailer several hours before. She'd sat downstairs in the study, with a low fire going, catching up on her email, checking in on Liam at regular intervals. Anything, she realized now, but open the family album and come face-to-face with a long line of McKettricks, every one of them a stranger.

The house seemed empty and, at the same time, too crowded for comfort.

"I'll sleep in here with you," she said. "How would that be?"

"Awesome," Liam said.

"Just let me change." Down the hall, she stripped to the skin, put on sweats and made for the bathroom, where she splashed her face with cool water and brushed her teeth.

Such ordinary things.

In the wake of what she'd just experienced, she wondered if anything would ever be "ordinary" again.

Liam was snoring softly when she got back to his room. She slipped into the narrow bed beside him, turned on to her side and stared into the darkness until at last she, too, fell asleep.

1919

WHILE DOC WILLABY'S nephew was getting his medical gear together, Doss took the opportunity to slip into the church down on the corner. He hadn't set foot inside it since he and Gabe had come back from the army, him sitting ramrod straight on a train seat and Gabe lying in a pine box.

He'd had no truck with God after that.

Now they had some business to discuss.

Doss opened the door, which was always unlocked, lest some wayfarer seek to pray or to find salvation, and took off his hat. He walked down front, to the plain wooden table that served as an altar, and lit one of the beeswax candles with a match from his pocket.

"I'm here to talk about Tobias," he said.

God didn't answer.

Doss shifted uncomfortably on his feet. They were so cold from the long drive into town that he couldn't feel them. Cain and Abel had been fractious on the way, and he'd had all sorts of trouble with them. Once, they'd just stopped and refused to go any farther, and then, crossing the creek, the team had made it over just fine but the sleigh had fallen through. Sunk past the runners in the frigid water.

He'd still be back there, wet to the skin and frozen

stiff as laundry left on a clothesline before a blizzard, if three of Rafe's ranch hands hadn't come along to help. They'd given him dry clothes, fetched from a nearby line shack, dosed him with whisky, hitched their lassos to the half-submerged sleigh and hauled it up on to the bank by horsepower.

He'd thanked the men kindly and sent them on their way, and then spent more precious time coaxing Cain and Abel to proceed. They'd been mightily reluctant to do that, and he'd finally had to threaten them with a switch to get them moving.

The whole day had gone like that, though the frustrations were at considerable variance, and by the time he'd pulled up in front of the doc's house, the worthless critters were so worn-out he knew they wouldn't make it back home. He'd sent to the livery stable for another rig and fresh horses.

Doss cleared his throat respectfully. "Hannah can't lose that boy," he went on. "You took Gabe, and if You don't mind my saying so, that was bad enough. I guess what I want to say is, if You've got to claim somebody else, then it ought to be me, not Tobias. He's only eight and he's got a lot of living yet to do. I don't know exactly what kind of outfit You're running up there, but if there are cattle, I'm a fair hand in a roundup. I can ride with the best of them, too. I'll make myself useful—You've got my word on that." He paused, swallowed. His face felt hot, and he knew he was acting like a damn fool, but he was desperate. "I reckon that's my side of the matter, so amen."

He blew out the candle—it wouldn't do for the church to take fire and burn to the ground—and turned to head back down the aisle.

Doc Willaby was standing just inside the door, leaning on his cane, because of that gouty foot of his, and dressed for a long, hard ride out to the Triple M.

"You ought to tell Hannah," the old man said.

"Tell her what?" Doss countered, abashed at being caught pouring out his heart like some repentant sinner at a revival.

"That you love her enough to die in place of her boy."

Doss heard a team and wagon clatter to a stop out front. "Nobody needs to know that besides God," he said, and slammed his hat back on his head. "What are you doing here, anyhow? Besides eavesdropping on a man's private conversation?"

The doc smiled. He was heavy-set, with a face like a full moon, a scruff of beard and keen little eyes that never seemed to miss much of anything. "I'm going out to your place with you. And we'd better be on our way, if that boy's as sick as you say he is."

"What about your nephew?"

"He'd never stand the trip," Doc said. "My bag's out on the step, and I'll thank you to help me up into the wagon so we can get started."

Doss felt a mixture of chagrin and relief. Doc Willaby was old as desert dirt, but he'd been tending McKettricks, and a lot of other folks, for as long as Doss could remember. His own health might be failing, but Doc knew his trade, all right.

"Come on, old man," Doss said. "And don't be fussing over hard conditions along the way. I've got neither the time nor the inclination to be coddling you."

Doc chuckled, though his eyes were serious. He slapped Doss on the shoulder. "Just like your grandfather," he said. "Tough as a boiled owl, with a heart the size of the whole state of Arizona and two others like it."

Getting the old coot into the box of the hired wagon

was like trying to hoist a cow from a tar pit, but Doss managed it. He climbed up, took the reins in one hand and tossed a coin to the livery stable boy, shivering on the sidewalk, with the other. Cain and Abel would be spending the night in warm stalls, maybe longer, with all the hay they required and some grain to boot, and, cussed as they were, Doss was glad for them.

He and the doc were almost to the ranch house when the lightning struck, loud enough to shake snow off the branches of trees, throwing the dark countryside into clear relief.

The horses screamed and shied.

The wagon slid on the icy trail and plunged on to its side.

Doss heard the doc yell, felt himself being thrown sky high.

Just before he hit the ground, it came to him that God had taken him up on the bargain he'd offered back there in Indian Rock at the church. He was about to die, but Tobias would be spared.

SOMEONE WAS POUNDING at the back door.

Hannah muttered a hasty word of reassurance to Tobias, who sat up in bed, wide-eyed, at the sound.

"That can't be Pa," he said. "He wouldn't knock. He'd just come inside—"

"Hush," Hannah told him. "You stay right there in that bed."

She hurried down the stairs and was shocked to see old Doc Willaby limping over the threshold. He looked a sight, his clothes wet and disheveled, his hair wild around his head, without his hat to contain it. His skin was gray with exertion, and he seemed nigh on to collapsing.

"There was an accident," he finally sputtered. "Down yonder, at the base of the hill. Doss is hurt."

Hannah steered the old man to a chair at the table. "Are you all right?" she asked breathlessly.

The doctor considered the question briefly, then nodded. "Don't mind about me, Hannah. It's Doss—I couldn't wake him—I had to turn the horses loose so they wouldn't kick each other to death."

She hurried into the pantry, moved the cracker tin aside and took down the bottle of Christmas whisky Doss kept there. She offered it to Doc Willaby, and he gulped down a couple of grateful swigs while she pulled on Gabe's coat and grabbed for a lantern.

"You'd better take this along, too," Doc said, and shoved the whisky bottle at her.

Hannah dropped it into her coat pocket. She didn't like leaving the old man or Tobias alone, but she had to get to Doss.

She raised her collar against the bitter wind and threw herself out the back door. Out in the barn, she tossed a halter on Seesaw and stood on a wheelbarrow to mount him. There was no time for saddles and bridles.

Holding the lamp high in one hand and clutching the halter rope with the other, Hannah rode out. She soon met two of the horses Doc had freed, and followed their trail backward, until the shape of an overturned wagon loomed in the snowy darkness.

"Doss!" she cried out. The name scraped at her throat, and she realized she must have called it over and over again, not just the once.

She found him sprawled facedown in the snow, at some distance from the wagon, and feared he'd smothered, if not broken every bone in his body. Scrambling off Seesaw's back, she plodded to where he lay, utterly still.

She knelt, setting the lantern aside, and turned him over.

"Doss," she whispered.

He didn't move.

Hannah put her cheek down close to his mouth. Felt his breath, his blessed breath, warm against her skin.

Tears of relief sprang to her eyes. She dashed them away quickly, lest they freeze in her lashes.

"Doss!" she repeated.

He opened his eyes.

"What are you doing here?" he asked, sounding befuddled.

"I've come looking for you, you damn fool," she answered.

"You're not dead, are you?"

"Of course I'm not dead," Hannah retorted, weeping freely. "And you're not either, which is God's own wonder, the way you must have been driving that wagon to get yourself into a fix like this. Can you move?"

Doss blinked. Hoisted himself on to his elbows. Felt around for his hat.

"Where's the doc?" His features tightened. "Tobias—"

"Tobias is fine," she said. "And Doc's up at the house, thawing out. It's a miracle he made it that far, with that foot of his."

A grin broke over Doss's face, and Hannah, filled with joy, could have slapped him for it. Didn't he know he'd nearly killed himself? Nearly fixed it so she'd have to bear and raise their baby all alone?

"I reckon Doc was right," Doss said. "I ought to tell you—"

"Tell me what?" Hannah fretted. "It's getting colder

out here by the minute, and the wind's picking up, too. Can you get to your feet? Poor old Seesaw's going to have to carry us both home, but I think he can manage it."

"Hannah." Doss clasped both her shoulders in his hands, gave her just the slightest shake. "I love you."

Hannah blinked, stunned. "You're talking crazy, Doss. You're out of your head—"

"I love you," he said. He got to his feet, hauling Hannah with him. Knocked the lantern over in the process so it went out. "It started the day I met you."

She stared up at him.

"I don't know how you feel about me, Hannah. It would be a grand thing if you felt the same way I do, but if you don't, maybe you can learn."

"I don't have to learn," she heard herself say. "I came out into this wretched snowstorm to find you, didn't I? After I suffered the tortures of the damned wondering what was keeping you. Of course I love you!"

He kissed her, an exultant kiss that warmed her to her toes.

"I'm going to be a real husband to you from now on," he told her. He made a stirrup of his hands, and Hannah stepped into them, landed astraddle Seesaw's broad, patient old back.

Doss swung up behind her, reached around to catch hold of the halter rope. "Let's go home," he said, close to her ear.

Hannah forgot all about the whisky in her coat pocket.

It was stone dark out, but the lights of the house were visible in the distance, even through the flurries of snow.

Anyway, Seesaw knew his way home, and he plodded patiently in that direction.

Present Day

THE WORLD WAS frozen solid when Sierra awakened the next morning, to find herself clinging to the edge of Liam's empty bed. Voices wafted up from downstairs, along with heat from the furnace and probably the wood stove, too.

She scrambled out of bed, finger combed her hair and hurried down the hallway.

Travis said something, and Liam laughed aloud. The sound affected Sierra like an injection of sunshine. Then a third voice chimed in, clearly female.

Sierra quickened her pace, her bare feet thumping on the stairs as she descended them.

Travis and Liam were seated at the table, reading the comic strips in the newspaper. A slender blond woman wearing jeans and a pink thermal shirt with the sleeves pushed up stood by the counter, sipping coffee.

"Meg?" Sierra asked. She'd seen her sister's picture, but nothing had prepared her for the living woman. Her clear skin seemed to glow, and her smile was a force of nature.

"Hello, Sierra," she said. "I hope you don't mind my showing up unannounced, but I just couldn't wait any longer, so here I am."

Travis stood, put a hand on Liam's shoulder. Without a word, the two of them left the room, probably headed for the study.

"Everything Mom said was true," Meg told Sierra quietly. "You're beautiful, and so is Liam."

Sierra couldn't speak, at least for the moment, even though her mind was full of questions, all of them clamoring to be offered at once.

"Maybe you should sit down," Meg said. "You look as though you might faint dead away."

Sierra pulled back the chair at the head of the table and sank into it. "When…when did you get here?" she asked.

"Last night," Meg answered. She poured a fresh cup of coffee, brought it to Sierra. "I hope I'm not interrupting anything."

"Interrupting anything?"

Meg's enormous blue eyes took on a mischievous glint. She swung a leg over the bench and straddled it, as several generations of McKettricks must have done before her, facing Sierra.

"Something's going on between you and Travis," Meg said. "I can feel it."

Sierra wondered if she could carry off a lie and decided not to try. She and Meg had been apart since they were small children, but they were sisters, and there was a bond. Besides, she didn't want to start off on the wrong foot.

"The question is," she said carefully, "is anything going on between *you* and Travis."

"No," Meg answered, "more's the pity. We tried to fall in love. It just didn't happen."

"I'm not talking about falling in love."

Wasn't she? Travis had rocked her universe, and much as she would have liked to believe it was only physical, she knew it was more. She'd never felt anything like that with Adam, and she *had* been in love with him, however naively. However foolishly.

Meg grinned. "You mean sex? We didn't even get that far. Every time we tried to kiss, we ended up laughing too hard to do anything else."

Sierra marveled at the crazy relief she felt.

"Too bad he's leaving," Meg said. "Now we'll have to find somebody else to look after the horses, and it won't be easy."

The bottom fell out of Sierra's stomach.

"Travis is leaving?"

Meg set her coffee cup down with a thump and reached for Sierra's hand. "Oh, my God. You didn't know?"

"I didn't know," Sierra admitted.

Damned if she'd cry.

Who needed Travis Reid, anyway?

She had Liam. She had a family and a home and a two-million-dollar trust fund.

She'd gotten along without Travis, and his lovemaking, all her life. The man was entirely superfluous.

So why did she want to lay her head down on her arms and wail with sorrow?

CHAPTER SIXTEEN

1919

COME MORNING HANNAH made her way through the still, chilly dawn to the barn. Besides their own stock, four livery horses were there, gathered at the back of the barn, helping themselves to the haystack. Remnants of harness hung from their backs.

Hannah smiled, led each one into a stall, saw that they each got a bucket of water and some grain. She was milking old Earleen, the cow, when Doss joined her, stiff and bruised but otherwise none the worse for his trials, as far as Hannah could see.

They'd shared a bed the night before, but they'd both been too exhausted, after the rigors of the day and getting Doc Willaby settled comfortably in the spare room, to make love.

"You ought to go into the house, Hannah," Doss said, sounding both confounded and stern. "This work is mine to do."

"Fine," she said, still milking. There was a rhythm in the task that settled a person's thoughts. "You can gather the eggs and get some butter from the spring house. I reckon Doc will be in the grip of a powerful hunger when he wakes up. He'll want hotcakes and some of that bacon you brought from the smokehouse."

Doss moved along the middle of the barn, limping

a little. Stopping to peer into each stall along the way. Hannah watched his progress out of the corner of her eye, smiling to herself.

"I meant what I said last night, Hannah," he said, when he finally reached her. "I love you. But if you really want to go back to your folks in Montana, I won't interfere. I know it's hard, living out here on this ranch."

Hannah's throat ached with love and hope. "It is hard, Doss McKettrick, and I wouldn't mind spending winters in town. But I'm not going to Montana unless you go, too."

He leaned against one of the beams supporting the barn roof, pondering her with an unreadable expression. "Gabe knew," he said.

She stopped milking. "Gabe knew what?"

"How I felt about you. From the very first time I saw you, I loved you. He guessed right away, without my saying a word. And do you know what he told me?"

"I can't imagine," Hannah said, very softly.

"That I oughtn't to feel bad, because you were easy to love."

Tears stung Hannah's eyes. "He was a good man."

"He was," Doss agreed gruffly, and gave a short nod. "He asked me to look after you and Tobias, before he died. Maybe he figured, even then, that you and I would end up together."

"It wouldn't surprise me," Hannah replied. Dear, dear Gabe. She'd loved him so, but he'd gone on, and he'd want her to carry on and be as happy as she could. Tobias, too.

"What I mean to say is," Doss went on, taking off his hat and turning it round and round in his hands by the brim, "I understand what he meant to you. You can say it, straight out, anytime. I won't be jealous."

Hannah stood up so fast she spooked Earleen, who kicked over the milk bucket, three-quarters of the way full now, steaming in the cold and rich with cream. She put her arms around Doss and didn't try to hide her tears.

"You're as good a man as Gabe ever was, Doss Mc-Kettrick," she said, "and I won't let you forget it."

He grinned down at her, wanly, but with that familiar spark in his eyes. "I'll build you a house in town, Hannah," he said. "We'll spend winters there, so you can see folks and Tobias can go to school without riding two miles through the snow. Would you like that?"

"Yes," Hannah said. "But I'd stay on this ranch forever, too, if it meant I could be with you."

Doss bent his head. Kissed her. His hands rested lightly on the sides of her waist, beneath the heavy fabric of Gabe's coat.

"You go inside and see to breakfast, Mrs. McKettrick. I'll finish up out here."

She swallowed, nodded. "I love you, Mr. McKettrick," she said.

His eyes danced mischievously. "Once we get Doc back to town," he replied, "I mean to bed you, good and proper."

Hannah blushed. Batted her lashes. "When is he leaving?"

Present Day

TRAVIS WAS PACKING, loading things into his truck. Even whistling as he went about it. Meg got into her car and drove off somewhere.

Sierra waited as long as she could bear to—she didn't know how she was going to explain this to Liam, who was sleeping off his flu bug—didn't know how to explain it herself.

She got out the album, for something to do, and set the remembrance book aside without opening it. Even after seeing Hannah and Tobias the night before, in Liam's room, she just didn't believe in magic anymore.

So she took a seat at the table and lifted the cover of the album.

A cracked and yellowed photograph, done in sepia, filled most of the page. Angus McKettrick, the patriarch of the family, stared calmly up at her. He'd been handsome in his youth; she could see that. Though, in the picture his thick hair was white, his stern, square-jawed face etched with lines of sorrow as well as joy. His eyes were clear, intelligent and full of stubborn humor.

It was almost as though he'd known Sierra would be looking at the photo one day, searching for some part of herself in those craggy features, and crooked up one corner of his mouth in the faintest smile, just for her.

Be strong, he seemed to say. *Be a McKettrick.*

Sierra sat for a long time, silently communing with the image.

I don't know how to "be a McKettrick." What does that mean, anyway?

Angus's answer was in his eyes. Being a McKettrick meant claiming a piece of ground to stand on and putting your roots down deep into it. Holding on, no matter what came at you. It meant loving with passion and taking the rough spots with the smooth. It meant fighting for what you wanted, letting go when that was the best thing to do.

Sierra absorbed all that and turned to the next page.

A good-looking couple posed in the front yard of the very house where Sierra sat, so many years later.

A small boy and a girl in her teens stood proudly on either side of them, and underneath someone had written the names in carefully. Holt McKettrick. Lorelei McKettrick. John Henry McKettrick. Lizzie McKettrick.

They wore the name like a badge, all of them.

After that came more pictures of Holt and Lorelei together and separately. In one, they were each holding the hand of a laughing, golden-haired toddler.

Gabriel Angus McKettrick, stated a fading caption beneath.

On the facing page, Lorelei sat proud and straight in a chair, holding an infant. Young Gabriel, older now, stood with a hand on her thigh, his ankles crossed, with the toe of one old-fashioned shoe touching the floor. Holt flanked them all, one hand resting on Lorelei's shoulder. The baby, according to the inscription, was Doss Jacob McKettrick.

Sierra continued to turn pages, and moved through the lives of Gabe and Doss along with them, or so it seemed, catching a glimpse of them on important dates. Birthdays. School. Mounted on ponies. Fishing in a pond.

Sierra felt as though she were looking not at mere photographs, but through little sepia-stained windows into another time, a time as vivid and real as her own.

She watched Gabe and Doss McKettrick grow into young men, both of them blond, both of them handsome and sturdy.

At last she came to the wedding picture. Her gaze landed on Hannah, standing proudly beside Gabe. She was wearing a lovely white dress, holding a nosegay.

Hannah.

The woman with whom, in some inexplicable way, she shared this house. The woman she had seen in Liam's bedroom the night before, caring for her own sick child even as Sierra was caring for hers.

Sierra could go no further. Not then.

She closed the album carefully.

"Mom?"

She turned, looked around to see Liam standing at the foot of the stairs, in his flannel pajamas. His hair was rumpled, his glasses were askew, and he looked desperately worried.

"Hey, buddy," she said.

"Travis is putting stuff in his truck," he told her. "Like he's going away or something."

Sierra's heart broke into two pieces. She got up, went to him. "I guess he was just here temporarily, to look after your aunt Meg's horses."

Liam blinked. A tear slipped down his cheek. "He can't go," he said plaintively. "Who'll make the furnace work? Who'll get us to the clinic if I get sick?"

"I can do those things, Liam," Sierra said. She offered a weak smile, and Liam looked skeptical. "Okay, maybe not the furnace. But I know how to get a fire going in the wood stove. And I can handle the rest, too."

Liam's lower lip wobbled. "I thought…maybe—"

Sierra hugged him, hard. She wanted to cry herself, but not in front of Liam. Not when his heart was breaking, just like hers. One of them had to be strong, and she was elected.

She was an adult.

She was a McKettrick.

Before she could think of anything to say, the back door opened and suddenly Travis was there. He looked at her briefly, but then his gaze went straight to Liam's face.

"If you came to say goodbye," Liam blurted out,

"then don't! I don't care if you're leaving—*I don't care!*" With that, he turned and fled up the stairs.

"That went well," Travis said, taking off his hat and hanging it on the peg. He didn't take his coat off, though, which meant he really *was* going away. Sierra had known that—and, at the same time, she *hadn't* known it. Not until she was faced with the reality.

"He's attached to you," she said evenly. "But he'll be all right."

Travis studied her so closely that for a moment she thought he was going to refute her words. "I know this all seems pretty sudden," he began.

Sierra kept her distance, glad she wasn't standing too close to him. "It's your life, Travis. You've done a lot to help us, and we're grateful."

Upstairs, something crashed to the floor.

Sierra closed her eyes.

"I'd better go up and talk to him," Travis said.

"No," Sierra replied. "Leave him alone. Please."

Another crash.

She found Liam's backpack, unzipped it and took out the inhaler. "I've got to get him calmed down," she said quietly. "Thanks for…everything. And goodbye."

"Sierra…"

"Goodbye, Travis."

With that, she turned and went up the stairs.

Liam had destroyed his new telescope and his DVD player. He was standing in the middle of the wreckage, trembling with the helplessness of a child in a world run by adults, his face flushed and wet with tears.

Sierra picked up his shoes, made her way to him. "Put these on, buddy," she said gently, crouching to help. "You'll cut your feet if you don't."

"Is he—" Liam gulped down a sob "—gone?"

"I think so," Sierra said.

"Why?" Liam wailed, putting a hand on her shoulder to keep from falling while he jammed one foot into a shoe, then the other. "Why does he have to go?"

Sierra sighed. "I don't know, honey," she answered.

"Make him stay!"

"I can't, Liam."

"Yes, you can! You just don't want to! You don't *want* me to have a dad!"

"Liam, that is enough." Sierra stood, handed him the inhaler. "Breathe," she ordered.

He obeyed, puffing on the inhaler between intermittent, heartbreaking sobs. "Make him stay," he pleaded.

She squired him to the bed, pulled his shoes off again, tucked him in. "Liam," she said.

Outside, the truck door slammed. The engine started up.

And suddenly Sierra was moving.

She ran down the stairs, through the kitchen, and wrenched open the back door. Coatless, shivering, she dashed across the yard toward Travis's truck.

He was backing out, but when he saw her, he stopped. Rolled down the window.

She jumped on to the running board, her fingers curved around the glass. *"Wait,"* she said, and then she felt stupid because she didn't know what to say after that.

Travis eased the door open, and she was forced to step back down on to the ground. Unbuttoning his coat as he got out, he wrapped it around her. But he didn't say anything at all. He just stood there, staring at her.

She huddled inside his coat. It smelled like him, and she wished she could keep it forever. "I thought it meant something," she finally murmured. "When we made love, I mean. I thought it *meant something*."

He cupped a gloved hand under her chin. "Believe me," he said gruffly, "it did."

"Then why are you leaving?"

"Because there didn't seem to be anything else to do. You were busy with Liam, and you'd made it pretty clear we had nothing to talk about."

"We have *plenty* to talk about, Travis Reid. I'm not some…some rodeo groupie you can just have sex with and forget!"

"You can say that again," Travis agreed, smiling a little. "Do you mind if we go inside to have this conversation? It's colder than a well-digger's ass out here, and I'm not wearing a coat."

Sierra turned on her heel and marched toward the house, and Travis followed.

She tried not to think about all the things that might mean.

Inside she gestured toward the table, took off Travis's coat and started a pot of coffee brewing, so she'd have a chance to think up something to say.

Travis stepped up behind her. Laid his hands on her shoulders.

"Sierra," he said. "Stop fiddling with the coffee-maker and talk to me."

She turned, looked up into his eyes. "It's not like I was expecting marriage or anything," she said, whispering. Liam was probably crouched at the top of the stairs by then, listening. "We're adults. We had…we're adults. But the least you could have done, after all that's gone on, was give us a little notice—"

"When Brody died," Travis said, "I died, too. I walked away from everything—my house, my job, everything. Then I met you, and when—" He paused, with a little smile, and glanced toward the stairs, evidently suspecting that Liam was there, all ears, just as she did. "When we *were adults,* I knew the game was up. I had to get it together. Start living my life again."

Sierra blinked, speechless.

He touched his mouth to hers. It wasn't a kiss, and yet it affected Sierra that way. "It's too soon to say this," he said, "but I'm going to say it anyway. Something happened to me yesterday. Something I don't understand. All I know is, I can't live another day like a dead man walking. I called Eve and asked for my old job back, and I'll be working in Indian Rock, at McKettrickCo, with Keegan. In the meantime I've got to put my house on the market and make arrangements to store my stuff. But it won't be long before I'm at your door, with every intention of winning you over for good."

"What are you saying?"

Liam came shooting down the stairs, wheeling his arms. "Get a clue, Mom! He's in love with you!"

"That's right," Travis said. He gave Liam a look of mock sternness. "I *was* planning to break it to her gradually, though."

"You're in…?" Sierra sputtered.

"Love," Travis finished for her. "Just tell me this one thing. Do I have a chance with you?"

"Give him a *chance,* Mom!" Liam cried jubilantly. "That's not too much to ask, is it? All the man wants is a chance!"

Sierra laughed, even as tears filled her eyes, blurring her vision. "Liam, hush!" she said.

"What do you say, McKettrick?" Travis asked, taking hold of her shoulders again. "Do I get a chance?"

"Yes," she said. "Oh, yes."

"If you're going to work in town," Liam enthused, tugging at Travis's shirtsleeve by then, "you might as well just move in with us!"

Travis chuckled, released Sierra to lean down and scoop Liam up in one arm. "Whoa," he said. "I'm all for *that* plan, but I think your mother needs a little more time."

"You're not leaving?" Liam asked, so hopefully that Sierra's heartbeat quickened.

"I'm not leaving," Travis confirmed. "I've got some things to do in Flagstaff, then I'll be back."

"Will you live right here, on the ranch?" Liam demanded.

"Not right away, cowpoke," Travis answered. "This whole thing is real important. I don't want to get it wrong. Understand?"

Liam nodded solemnly.

"Good," Travis said. "Now, get on back upstairs, so I can kiss your mother without you ogling us."

"I broke my DVD player," Liam confessed, suddenly crestfallen. "On purpose, too." He paused, swallowed audibly. "Are you mad?"

"You're the one who'll have to do without a DVD player," Travis said reasonably. "Why would *I* be mad?"

"I'm sorry, Travis," Liam told him.

Travis set the boy back on his feet. "Apology accepted. While we're at it, *I'm* sorry, too. I should have talked to you—your mother, too—before I packed up my stuff. I guess I was just in too much of a hurry to get things rolling."

"I forgive you," Liam said.

Travis ruffled his hair. "Beat it," he replied.

Liam scampered toward the stairs and hopped up them as though he were on a pogo stick.

"Are you sure he's sick?" Travis asked.

Sierra laughed. "Kiss me, cowpoke," she said.

1919

Doc Willaby was with them for three full days, waiting
for his bumps and bruises to heal and the weather to
clear. He played endless games of checkers with Tobias,
next to the kitchen stove, and Hannah and Doss tried
hard to pretend they were sensible people. The truth
was, they could barely keep their hands off each other.

"How come I have to move to the other end of the
hall?" Tobias asked Doss, on the morning of the third
endless day.

"You just do," Doss answered.

Early that afternoon, the sleigh came pulling into the
yard, drawn by Cain and Abel and driven by Kody Jack-
son, from the livery stable. Two outriders completed
the procession.

"Glory be," Doc said, peering out the window, along
with Hannah. "They've come to fetch me back to Indian
Rock." He looked down at Hannah and smiled wisely.
"Now you and Doss can stop acting like a couple of old
married folks and do what comes naturally."

Hannah blushed, but she couldn't help smiling in the
process. "It's been good having you here, Doc," she said,
and she meant it, too. "You saved Doss's life the other
night, coming all that way to fetch me, in the shape you
were in. I'll be grateful all my days."

He took her hand. Squeezed it. "He loves you, Hannah."

"I know," she said softly. "And I love him, too."

"That's all that counts, in the long run. Or the short
one, for that matter. We each of us get a certain num-

ber of days to spend on this earth. Only the good Lord knows how many. Spend them loving that man of yours and that fine boy, and you'll have done the right thing."

Hannah stood on tiptoe. Kissed the doctor on the cheek. "Thank you," she said.

Doss came out of the barn to greet Kody and the other men.

They all went down the hill together to set the other wagon upright, leading the team along behind them. Doss put Cain and Abel away, while Kody drove the rig up alongside the house.

Doc was outside by then, ready to go, with his medical bag clutched in one hand and his cane in the other. He turned and waved at Hannah through the window, and she waved back, watching fondly as Doss and another man helped him up into the wagon box.

When Doss didn't come back in right away, Hannah busied herself making the kitchen presentable. Tobias was upstairs, resting in his new bedroom at the front of the house. Now that he'd adjusted to the change, he liked being able to see so clear across the valley from the gabled window, but what had really swayed him was the reminder that Doss and Gabe had shared that room when they were boys.

She swept the floor and put fresh coffee on to brew and even switched on the lightbulb instead of lighting lamps, as wintry afternoon shadows darkened the room.

Still, there was no sign of Doss, so she built up the fire in the stove, opened the drawer of the china cabinet, lifted the cover of the album and took out her remembrance book.

In the three busy days since she'd seen the other woman and her boy, up there in Tobias's bedroom, she'd thought often of the journal, and kept a close eye on the teapot, too.

Nothing extraordinary happened, but inside, in a quiet part of herself, Hannah was waiting. She carried the remembrance book over to the rocking chair drawn up close to the stove and sat down. Perhaps she'd begin making regular entries in that journal.

She'd write about her and Doss, and make notes as Tobias grew toward manhood. She'd record the dates the peonies bloomed, and tuck a photograph inside, now and then. Doss had promised her they'd build a house in Indian Rock, and pass the hard high-country winters there. She would capture the dimensions of the new place in these pages, and perhaps even make sketches. One day she'd take up a pen and write that the baby had come, safe and strong and well.

She was so caught up in the prospect of all the years ahead, just waiting to be lived and then set down on paper, that a few moments passed before she realized that another hand had written beneath her own short paragraphs.

My name is Sierra McKettrick.
I have a son, too, and his name is Liam. He's seven, and he has asthma. He's the center of my life.
You have nothing to fear from me. I'm not a ghost, just an ordinary flesh-and-blood woman. A mother, like you.

Hannah stared at the words in disbelief.
Read them again, and then again.
It couldn't be.
But it was.

The woman she'd seen was a McKettrick, too, living far in the future. She had the proof right here—not that she meant to show it to just everybody. Some folks would say she'd written those words herself, of course, but Hannah knew she hadn't.

She touched the clear blue ink in wonder. It looked different, somehow, from the kind that came in a bottle.

The door opened, and Doss came in. He took off his coat and hat, hung them up neatly, like he always did.

Hannah held the remembrance book close against her chest. Should she let Doss see? Would he believe, as she did, that two different centuries had somehow managed to touch and blend, right here in this house?

Her heart fluttered in her breast.

"Hannah?" He sounded a little worried.

"Come and look at this, Doss," she said.

He came, crouched beside her chair, read the two entries in the journal, hers and Sierra's.

She watched his face, hopeful and afraid.

Doss raised his eyes to meet hers. "That," he said, "is the strangest thing I've ever run across."

"There's more," Hannah said. "I saw her, Doss. I saw this woman, and her little boy, the night of your accident."

He closed a hand over hers. "If you say so, Hannah," he told her quietly, "then I believe you."

"You do?"

He grinned. "Does that surprise you?"

"A little," she admitted. "When Tobias mentioned seeing the boy, you said it must be his imagination."

Doss handed back the book. "Life is strange," he said. "There's a mystery just about everywhere you look, when you think about it. Babies being born. Grass poking up through hard ground after a long winter. The way it makes me feel inside when you smile at me."

Hannah leaned, kissed his forehead. "Flatterer," she said.

"Is Tobias asleep?" he asked.

She blushed. "Yes."

He pulled her to her feet, set the remembrance book aside on the counter and kissed her.

"I think we've waited long enough, don't you?" he asked.

Hours later, hair askew, bundled in a wrapper, well and thoroughly loved, Hannah sneaked back downstairs. She gathered ink and a pen from the study and lit a lantern in the kitchen.

Then, smiling, she sat down to write.

Present Day

TRAVIS LAY SPRAWLED on his stomach in Sierra's bed, sound asleep. She sat up beside him, stroked his bare back once with a gentle pass of her hand. In the three days since he'd moved out of the trailer, he'd been back several times, on one pretext or another. Finally Meg had packed some of her things and some of Liam's, and the two of them had gone to stay in town with friends of hers.

"You two really need some time alone," she'd said, with a wicked grin lighting her eyes.

Sierra smiled down at Travis. So far they'd made good use of that time alone. They'd talked a lot, in between bouts of lovemaking, and they still had plenty to say to each other—maybe enough to last a lifetime.

She switched on the lamp, took Hannah's remembrance book from the bedside table, and opened it. Her eyes widened, and she drew in a breath.

Beneath her own entry, in the same stately, faded writing as before, Hannah had written:

> It's nice to know there's another woman in the house, even if I can't see or hear you, most of the time. We must be family, since your name is McKettrick. Maybe you're descended from us, from Doss and me. I told my son, Tobias, that your name is Sierra. He said that was pretty, and he'd like the new baby to be called that, too, if it's a girl...

There was more, but Sierra couldn't read it, because her eyes were blurred with tears of amazement. She bounded out of bed, not caring if she awakened Travis, and hurried downstairs, switching on lights as she went. She had the album out and was flipping through the pages at the middle when he joined her, blinking and shirtless, with his jeans misbuttoned.

"What's going on?" he asked, yawning.

Sierra's heart thumped at the base of her throat.

She forced herself to slow down, turn the pages gently. And then she found what she was looking for—an old, old photograph of two children, smiling for the camera lens. The little boy she'd seen in Liam's room, with Hannah, holding a baby wearing a long, lacy gown.

Beneath the picture, Hannah had written Tobias's name and the baby's.

Sierra Elizabeth McKettrick.

Sierra put a hand to her mouth and gasped.

Travis drew closer. "Sierra—"

"Look at this," Sierra said, stabbing at the image with one finger. "What do you see?"

Travis frowned. "An old picture of two kids."

"Look at the baby's name."

"Sierra. You must have been named for her."

"I think *she* was named for *me*," Sierra said.

"How could *she* be named for *you*?"

"Sit down," Sierra told him. She reached for Hannah's remembrance book, offered it when he was seated. "Read this."

He read. Looked up at her with wide eyes. "You don't really think—"

"That I've been communicating with a woman who lived in this house in 1919, and probably for years after that? Yes, Travis, that is *exactly* what I think!"

"But, *how?*"

"You said it yourself, when I first got here. Strange things happen in this house."

"This is beyond strange. Are you going to tell anybody else about this?"

"Mother and Meg," Sierra said. "Liam, too, when he's a little older."

He reached for her hand, wove his fingers through hers, squeezed. "And me. You told *me*, Sierra."

"Well, *yeah*."

"You must trust me."

She grinned. "You're right," she said. "I must trust you a whole lot, Travis Reid."

"Can we go back to bed now?"

She closed the album and tucked Hannah's remembrance book carefully inside. "Race you!" she cried, and dashed for the stairs.

* * * * *

Also available from B.J. Daniels

HQN Books

Unforgiven
Redemption
Forsaken
Atonement
Mercy
Wild Horses
Lone Rider

Harlequin Intrigue

Justice at Cardwell Ranch
Cardwell Ranch Trespasser
Christmas at Cardwell Ranch
Rescue at Cardwell Ranch
Wedding at Cardwell Ranch
Deliverance at Cardwell Ranch

And coming soon

Lucky Shot

MONTANA ROYALTY

B.J. Daniels

CHAPTER ONE

THE NARROW SLIT of light between the partially closed bedroom curtains drew him through the shadowed pines.

He moved stealthily, the moonless darkness heavy as a cloak. The moment he'd seen the light, realized it came from her bedroom window, the curtains not quite closed, he'd been helpless to stop himself.

He'd always liked watching people when they didn't know he was there. He saw things they didn't want seen. He knew their dirty secrets.

Their secrets became *his* dirty little secrets.

But this was different.

The woman behind the curtains was Rory Buchanan.

He began to sweat as he neared the window even though the fall night was cold here in the mountains. The narrow shaft of light from between the curtains spilled out onto the ground. Teasing glimpses of her lured him on.

As he grew closer, he stuck the wire cutters he carried into his jacket pocket. His heart beat so hard he could barely steal a breath as he slowly stepped toward the forbidden.

The window was the perfect height. He closed his left eye, his right eye focusing on the room, on the woman.

Inside the bedroom, Rory folded a pair of jeans into one of the dresser drawers and closed the drawer, turning back toward the bed and the T-shirt she'd left lying on it.

He didn't move, didn't breathe—didn't blink as she began to disrobe.

He couldn't have moved even at gunpoint as he watched her pull the band from her ponytail, letting her chestnut hair fall to her shoulders.

She sighed, rubbing her neck with both hands, eyes closed. Wide green eyes fringed in dark lashes. He watched breathlessly as she dropped her hands to unbutton her jeans and let them drop to the floor.

Next, the Western shirt. Like her other shirts and the jackets she wore, it was too large for her, hid her body.

Anticipation had him breathing too hard. He tried to rein it in, afraid she would hear him and look toward the window. It scared him what he might do if she suddenly closed the curtains then. Or worse, saw him.

One shirt button, then another and another and the shirt fell back, dropping over her shoulders to the floor at her feet. She reached down to retrieve both items of clothing and hang them on the hook by the door before turning back in his direction.

He sucked in a breath and held it to keep from crying out. Her breasts were full and practically spilling out of the pretty pink lacy bra. The way she dressed, no one could have known.

She slid one bra strap from her shoulder, then the other. He could hear her humming now, but didn't recognize the tune. She was totally distracted. He felt himself grow hard as stone as she unhooked the bra and her breasts were suddenly freed.

A moan escaped his throat. A low keening sound filled with lust and longing. He *wanted* her, had wanted her for years, would do anything to have her...

Instinctively, he took a step toward the back of the ranch house. Rory was alone. Her house miles from any others. Her door wouldn't be locked. No one locked their doors in this part of Montana.

The sound of a vehicle engine froze him to the spot. He dropped to the ground behind the shrubs at the corner of the house as headlights bobbed through the pines. The vehicle came into view, slowed and turned around in the yard. Someone lost?

He couldn't be caught here. He hesitated only a moment before he broke for the pines behind the house and ran through the woods to where he'd hidden his car.

As he slid behind the wheel, his adrenaline waned. He'd never done more than looked. Never even contemplated more than that.

But the others hadn't been Rory Buchanan.

If that pickup hadn't come down the road when it did…

The sick odor of fear and excitement filled the car. He rolled down his window, feeling weak and powerless and angry. Tonight, he could have had her—and on his terms. *But at what cost,* he thought as he reached for the key he'd left in the ignition of the patrol car, anxious to get back to Whitehorse.

He froze. The wire cutters. He didn't feel their weight in his jacket pocket. His hand flew to the opening only to find the pocket empty.

CHAPTER TWO

RORY BUCHANAN HUNKERED down in the dark beside the stables as six royal guards trooped past, all toting semi-automatic rifles.

To say she was in deep doo was an understatement. Not only was it now completely dark, but a storm had blown in. She felt the chill on the wind only moments before the first stinging drops of rain began to fall.

Shivering, she checked her watch. Earlier, she'd left her ranch with only a lightweight jacket, planning to return long before dark. The sky had been clear and blue, not a cloud in sight. But this was Montana, where it could snow—and did—in any month of the year.

According to her calculations the next set of guards wouldn't come past for another three minutes. Fortunately, most of the grooms and trainers had left the stables, but she could still hear someone inside with the horses.

Rory waited until the guards disappeared into the dark before she made a run for the woods.

She'd never done anything like this in her life and hated to think what her parents would have said had they still been alive. But Rory doubted her new neighbors would be trying to take her ranch if her father were around.

A duke and duchess or prince and princess—she didn't know or care which and wouldn't know a duke from a drug lord and doubted anyone else in Montana would either—had bought up all the ranches around hers.

An emissary for the royals had been trying to buy her ranch, putting pressure on her to sell. Clearly they were rich and powerful and had built a palace with all its trapping just miles from her ranch.

Rory had turned down the first few offers, saying her ranch wasn't for sale at any price. But the offers had kept coming, and just that morning she'd seen tracks again where someone had been snooping around her place.

The footprints in the dust definitely weren't hers, and since she hadn't had any male visitors for so long she couldn't remember...

She didn't even want to think about that.

Her mare was where she'd left her, hidden in the ponderosas. Retrieving her horse, Rory swung up into the saddle thinking maybe she would try to outrun the worst of the storm.

But she hadn't gone fifty yards when the sky above the pines splintered in a blinding flash of lightning followed in a heartbeat by a boom of thunder. From over by the stables, she thought for a moment she saw a dark figure standing in the shadows watching her.

Her horse shied and she had to rein in the mare to keep her seat and the mare from taking off for home. When Rory looked toward the stables again, the figure was gone. Had the person gone back inside to call the guards?

With a shudder of both cold and fear, she pulled down her cowboy hat to the storm and took off at a gallop, praying she hadn't been seen—and could get away.

Rain ran off the brim of her hat as she spurred her

horse, racing toward her ranch. She regretted that she hadn't even had the sense to grab a slicker earlier. It had been one of those beautiful fall Montana days, the stands of aspens glowing red-gold in the sunlight and the air smelling of the fallen leaves, while over the tops of the ponderosa pines, clouds floated in a sea of blue.

Lightning lit the western horizon ahead of her. She tightened the reins as thunder exploded so close it made the hair on her neck stand up. Glancing back, she could see the lights of Stanwood, a blur in the pouring rain, disappear. If she was being followed, she couldn't tell.

Suddenly being caught by armed foreign soldiers didn't seem as dangerous as trying to get to the ranch in this storm.

Better Safe Than Sorry had never been Rory Buchanan's motto. But in this case, trying to get home in the storm and darkness was crazier than even she was normally. Especially when there was an old line shack just up the mountain in a grove of aspens.

The fact that the line shack was on royal property gave her a little pause. But she valued her neck and her horse's more than she feared her neighbors at the moment. Not only was the line shack much closer than her ranch house, but also there was an old lean-to that would provide some shelter for her horse and get her out of the weather, as well.

She doubted the royal owners even knew the shack was there given the enormous amount of property they'd bought up around her. Just the thought forced a curse from her as she rode through the drowning rain and darkness to the shack.

Rory's head was still swimming with the excessiveness she'd seen only miles from her century-old ranch house. The new owners had built a palace that would rival Montana's capital. Behind it was a private airstrip, stables with an arena and a colony of small cottages and a dormitory that could house a small army—and apparently did given the number of armed soldiers she'd seen on the grounds.

Of course what had caught her eye were the horses. She'd watched a dozen grooms at least exercising the most beautiful horses she'd ever seen. She hated to think what even one of those horses might cost.

All that wealth and all these armed soldiers had her even more worried that her royal neighbors wouldn't stop until they forced her off her ranch. That and the fact that someone had definitely been snooping around her place.

She'd always felt safe on the ranch.

Until recently.

Another burst of lightning splintered the dark horizon. Thunder ricocheted through the pines. A blinding flash of lightning exposed the line shack in eerie two-dimensional relief. Rory braced herself for the thunderous boom that wasn't far behind. She hated storms worse than even the idea of spending a cold rainy night in a line shack. Her baby sister Brittany had disappeared on a night like this and just four years ago Rory's parents had been killed in a blizzard on their way back to the ranch. It had come right after she'd graduated from college and had left her with no family and a ranch to run alone.

Dismounting, she hurriedly unsaddled her horse, hobbling the mare under the lean-to and out of the downpour.

Soaked to the skin, she carried her saddle and blanket into the shack, stomping her feet on the tiny wooden porch to make sure any critters living inside would know she was coming and hopefully evacuate the premises.

The shack was about ten feet by twelve and smelled musty, but as she stepped in out of the rain, she was glad to see that there didn't seem to be anything else sharing the space with her.

It was warmer and drier inside, and she was thankful for both as she put down her saddle and slipped the still-dry horse blanket from under her arm to drop it on a worn spot on the floor next to the wall that appeared to have the least amount of dust.

Chilled, she had just started to strip off her soaked jean jacket when a flash of lightning shot through a crack in the chinking between several of the logs of the line shack, making her jump.

Outside, her horse whinnied as thunder rumbled across the mountaintop. She froze at the sound of an answering whinny from another horse nearby.

Drawing her wet jacket around her, she opened the door a crack and peered out.

A beautiful white horse with leopard spots stood in the trees below the shack. Rory caught the flash of silver from the expensive tack and saddle as lightning sliced through the darkened sky. The horse started, then bolted, taking off into the trees back the way Rory knew it had come.

She recognized the horse from earlier. A Knabstrup. She'd only read about the horses before she'd seen the groomers working with them at her royal neighbors'. Not surprising since the horses were originally from Germany—the Knabstrup breed having always been a symbol of the decadence of the aristocracy in Europe.

But where was the rider?

Rory swore as she turned back inside the shack to

button her jacket and grab her hat, knowing even before she stepped into the pounding rain that the rider of the horse had been thrown and was probably lying in a puddle on the ground with his fool neck broken.

As much as she disliked storms—and the kind of neighbors who'd bought up half the county to build a palace in the middle of good pasture land that they wouldn't live in for more than a few weeks a year, if that—Rory couldn't let another human die just outside her door.

The temperature had dropped at an alarming rate, signaling an early snowstorm. Anyone left out in it was sure to freeze to death before morning.

"It would serve the danged fool right," she muttered to herself as she stomped down the mountainside to where she'd seen the horse. "Who with any common sense would go out in this kind of weather?" Unless they were trespassing on their royal neighbors' property, of course.

In a flash of lightning, she spotted the man lying in an open spot between the trees, surrounded by a bed of soft brown pine needles and a thick clump of huckleberry bushes, both of which, she hoped, had broken his fall.

She heard a groan as she neared, relieved he was alive. As he tried to sit up, she saw the blood on his forehead before the rain washed it down onto the white shirt and riding britches that he wore. He saw her and tried to struggle to his feet and failed.

"Easy," she said as she dropped down next to him on the ground.

A lock of wet black hair had tumbled over his forehead. She brushed it back to check the source of the blood and found a small cut over his left eye. There was also a goose egg rising on his temple.

Neither looked fatal.

He turned his face up to her and blinked into the driving rain. His dark hair fell back and she saw the dazed look in his very dark blue eyes. His lips turned up in a ridiculous grin as those eyes locked with hers.

"A beautiful forest sprite has come to save me?"

A forest sprite?

Clearly he was either drunk or delirious. Maybe he'd hit his head harder than she thought. He had that odd accent like the others she'd seen at her royal neighbors'. As she leaned down to gaze into his eyes, lightning flashed around them and she was able to rule out a concussion.

"It is my lucky day, is it not?" From the smell of brandy on his warm breath and that goofy grin on his face, she'd say the man was tipsy.

Now that she saw he wasn't badly hurt and was apparently intoxicated, she took some satisfaction in the fact that he'd been thrown from his fancy mount and immediately felt guilty for the uncharitable thought.

Her teeth chattered as she glanced around for his horse, wanting nothing more than to get out of the cold and rain. His horse had apparently hightailed it back to its expensive heated stables. She couldn't blame it. She would have loved a heated stable herself just then.

A horse whinnied nearby, startling her. Not his horse. She'd seen the way it had bolted, and she doubted the horse had doubled back for the groom. Was it possible he hadn't been out riding alone? More than possible, she realized. One of the other grooms must have been with him.

"Hello?" she called through the rain and the thick

darkness of the pines and descending nightfall. "You've got a groom down over here."

No answer.

She looked at the groom at her feet. He was still grinning up at her. She might have found him cute and charming and this whole incident humorous under other circumstances. Or not.

Her horse whinnied from the lean-to. This time the answering whinny was farther away. If he had been riding with someone else, they had turned back toward home, leaving him to fend for himself.

She was almost tempted to do the same thing given that the man was clearly inebriated and would now have to share her shack.

"Come on," she said cursing under her breath as she bent down to help him up. "Let's get you on your feet."

Like her, he was underdressed for this type of storm, soaking wet and shivering. She had no choice. Given his condition, he would never be able to find his way back.

"Take me to your palace beautiful forest sprite," he said and attempted a bow.

"Palace, indeed," she muttered.

Unsteady on his feet he plainly wasn't going far under his own power. He slung an arm over her shoulder. As they started up the mountainside, she wondered if he had any idea of how much trouble he was in.

He was bound to get fired for taking such an expensive horse out while drunk. He'd better hope that horse made it back to the barn safely. She'd bet that animal was worth more than this groom made in a year.

Lucky for him that he would be able to sleep it off before he had to face his boss—the duke or prince or whatever. As long as the horse returned unharmed, he might be spared being returned to his country to face a firing squad.

He shifted against her. "You are too kind, fair forest sprite."

"Aren't I, though," she grumbled. Lucky for him she couldn't let him die of hypothermia or wander off a cliff in the dark.

Lightning illuminated the landscape, the line shack appearing for an instant out of the rain and darkness. She stumbled toward the structure, staggering under the man's drunken weight as thunder boomed overhead.

"I owe you a great debt," he said as she shoved open the line shack door. "How shall I ever repay you?"

CHAPTER THREE

RAIN POUNDED THE tin roof overhead as Rory closed the line shack door behind them. It was pitch-black in the small room except for the occasional flashes of lightning that shot through the holes in the chinking. Ear-splitting booms of thunder reverberated through the shack.

Teeth chattering, Rory untangled herself from the groom and eased him to the floor beside the horse blanket. He slumped against the wall, shuddering from the cold, his eyes half-closed, making her aware of his long dark lashes—and the fact that he looked as if he was about to pass out.

Thunder rumbled overhead again, and she shivered from the cold—and her aversion to storms. She could feel the damp seeping into her bones. She was going to have to get out of her wet clothes, and quickly. So was he. And they had only the one blanket.

Fortunately, the groom looked harmless enough.

"You need to take off your wet clothing," she informed him over the pounding rain.

No response. She kicked off her boots, then started to unbutton her jeans in the dark of the cabin. She heard a thump and in a flash of lightning saw the groom had fallen over onto his side. He was curled up, shaking from the cold and apparently out like a light.

"Great." She cursed and knelt down to shake him

lightly. The lashes parted, the blue behind them clearly fighting to focus on her as another shaft of light from the storm penetrated the slits between the logs. "Your clothes. They're wet," she said enunciating each syllable.

He grinned, pushed himself up and attempted to unbutton his shirt, but she saw in the flickering light from the storm that he was shivering too hard to do the job.

"Here, let me help you," she said, pushing his icecold fingers away to work at the buttons.

"I'm afraid my life is in your hands, my fair forest sprite." His eyelids drooped again, and she had to catch him to keep him upright.

"You *should* be afraid," she said, her own fingers trembling from the cold as she unbuttoned the dozens of tiny buttons on his fancy shirt.

As the storm raged over their heads, she pulled him forward to slip the fabric off one broad shoulder, then the other. His muscles rippled across his chest and stomach, a trail of dark curly hair dipping in a V to the waist of his riding britches.

She half turned away as she removed his britches. He slid down the wall to the floor, eyes fluttering open for a moment. Britches off, he drew the horse blanket to him, curled up and closed those blue eyes again.

Two seconds later he was snoring softly.

"Just like a man," she muttered as she stripped down to her underwear. She was chilled to the core and *he* had the horse blanket.

She stared down at the man for a moment. He had passed out, obviously having consumed more than his share of alcohol. Outside, the storm wasn't letting up. There was little chance it would before morning. She was stuck there, and while she didn't mind sharing what little she had—the shack and her only dry horse blanket—she was piqued by the groom.

As drunk as he was, he'd had no business riding a horse, and she intended to tell him so first thing in the morning.

In the meantime... She knelt down next to him, gave him a nudge. He didn't budge. Nor did he quit snoring. Sliding under the edge of the blanket with her back to him, she shoved him over.

"Blanket hog," she muttered.

He let out a soft, unintelligible murmur, his warm breath teasing the tender skin at the back of her neck as he snuggled against her. She started to pull away, but his body felt fairly warm and definitely very solid, even the soft sound of his snoring reassuring. At least the man was good for something.

As much as she had grumbled and complained, the truth was she didn't mind having company tonight. As she began to warm up, she almost forgot about the storm raging around them as she closed her eyes and snuggled against him, drifting off to sleep.

RORY WOKE TO the sound of her horse's whinny. Aware of being wonderfully warm, as if wrapped in a cocoon, the last thing she wanted to do was open her eyes.

Her horse whinnied again close by. Confused, since her horse should have been out by the barn some distance from her ranch house, she opened her eyes a slit.

Three things hit her at once.

She wasn't in her bed at the ranch.

There was an arm around her, a body snuggled behind her.

And she was *naked*.

Rory froze, listening to the man's soft, steady breath-

ing as the events of the previous night came back in a
rush. The storm, the shack, the groom she'd taken in
out of the goodness of her heart.

But she was absolutely certain she had been wearing
her undergarments, as skimpy as they were, when she'd
lain down next to him last night. She recalled snuggling
against him under the blanket to get warm...

She let out a silent curse as she recalled drowsily
coming, half-awake, during the night to what she'd first
thought was an erotic dream.

He stirred behind her, his warm breath tickling her
bare shoulder, his arm tightening around her, one large
hand cupping her left breast.

With a silent groan, it all came back, every pleasur-
able dreamlike moment of it, up until she'd awakened
to the shock of her life.

She wasn't in the habit of waking with a stranger in
her bed, let alone with a stranger on the floor of a shack
under a horse blanket after having wild wanton sex.

This was all Bryce's fault. After breaking off her engagement with him four years ago, she'd been gun-shy
of men. But then, who could blame her?

Blaming Bryce for this made her feel a little better. And of course there were other factors to blame:
the storm, her fear of storms, the intimacy of the dark
shack, the closeness of their near-naked bodies, the need
for warmth to survive, Bryce again and that other need
she'd ignored for obviously too long.

Not to mention trying to run the ranch single-hand-
edly. She hadn't had time to date even though she'd had
a few offers. Shoot, she'd bet everyone in the county
was laying odds that she would end up a spinster. After
all, she *was* nearly thirty.

Not that any of that was an excuse. She had her principles. And sleeping with a royal groom, whose name she didn't even know, didn't meet any of them.

As his breathing slowed again, signaling he'd fallen back into a deep sedated sleep, Rory slowly lifted his arm and slipped out from under it and the horse blanket. He stirred. She froze.

Then he rolled over, pulling the blanket with him, but not before she'd seen his naked backside.

She closed her eyes as she was assaulted with images of the two of them in the throes of lovemaking. A groan escaped her lips. She clamped a hand over her mouth, her eyes flying open, fearing she'd awakened him.

With relief, she saw that he was still sleeping soundly.

Her clothing was on a nail, where she'd hung it the night before. Her underwear was at the end of the horse blanket next to the groom's bare feet.

She gingerly extracted the lingerie and pulled it on. From the nail, she retrieved her shirt, which was almost dry, as were her socks. Her jeans and jean jacket were still cold and wet.

But she hardly noticed as she dressed and tried her best to ignore the hot flush of her skin or the slight whisker burn on certain parts of her body.

Don't think about it.

She wished it were that simple. She was appalled that she'd made love to a perfect stranger—and that she'd enjoyed it more than she should have.

Completely dressed, she stood for a moment telling herself maybe it *had* just been a dream. *Right.* She wasn't letting herself off that easily. Last night had been reckless, scandalous and…and…amazing. At least according to her limited experience.

As she turned to stare at the man curled in her horse blanket, she felt almost guilty about just leaving him there to meet his fate. When she'd found him lying in the pine needles drunk and confused, she'd thought he deserved whatever punishment his royal boss would give him for riding, in an inebriated state, such a beautiful horse.

But this morning she worried that he really might be sent home to face a firing squad. She hoped that wasn't the case, but there was nothing she could do about it. In fact, since she'd refused to sell her property to his employer, it was good that no one would ever know where the groom had spent the night—or with whom.

She was grateful that he didn't know who she was. With luck, she would never see him again since the man obviously was a bad influence on her.

It dawned on her that the only two men she'd ever slept with she now had to avoid.

Not a great track record, she told herself as she picked up her saddle, eased open the door and slipped out.

DEVLIN BARROW WOKE with the worst hangover of his life. He opened his eyes to find himself wrapped in a horse blanket.

Sitting up with a start, he looked around in confusion—and alarm. He spotted his clothing draped over nails on the log walls of what appeared to be a very small cabin. But he didn't recall hanging his clothing there any more than he could remember this place or the previous night.

The sun was up and a slight breeze blew through several cracks between the logs, chilling what he realized was his very bare skin.

"What the devil?" He rubbed his stubbled jaw and desperately tried to remember how he'd gotten there.

He had not the faintest idea. Not as to how he'd come to be there nor where he even was. Nor could he explain his massive headache or the cut over his left eye or the tender bump he felt on his temple.

Getting shakily to his feet, he retrieved his clothing and dressed. Since he'd been wearing his riding britches and boots, he could only assume he'd gone for a ride. So where was his horse? Where was *he?*

His riding britches were cold and damp to the touch. He frowned as he remembered something. He quickly searched his pockets, only to find the first empty. In the other, he discovered a slip of paper.

The note that had been slipped under his door yesterday afternoon.

The ink had run on the paper, but he could still make out the words: *I must see you. Meet me in the aspen woods a mile to the east of Stanwood tonight after dark.*

If he'd met someone in the woods last night, he couldn't remember it.

The bump on the head, the hangover from alcohol he couldn't remember drinking and the feeling that something important had happened last night made him fear that he'd been tricked into coming to this isolated spot not to receive the news he so desperately sought, but to be…what? Killed?

He stuffed the note into his shirt pocket and, fighting a wave of nausea, opened the door and stumbled out into the sunlight. To his growing concern, he saw no sign of his horse. Nor had the horse blanket he'd been wrapped in been one from Stanwood stables.

He was becoming more concerned about the consequences of finding himself in such a predicament. He licked his lips, his mouth dry and tasting of stale brandy. Another taste teased his memory.

He shook his head as if to clear away the cobwebs and shuddered at the pain. Why was it he could remember having only one drink since he must have imbibed more than that to be feeling this awful?

Common sense told him he wouldn't have gotten drunk before his meeting in the woods. So how did he explain this headache, his lack of memory?

The thick pines outside at least told him he was in Montana, but nothing looked familiar. Not that he'd been there long enough to know his way around. Yesterday had been his first day at Stanwood.

That seemed to jar a memory. He saw himself standing in the main parlor, having a brandy with several of the nobility visiting Stanwood. He'd been called up from the stables and complimented on his riding abilities. After that, he recalled nothing.

His riding abilities? How ironic since it appeared he'd not only lost his memory—but his horse, as well.

The ground, he noted, was still wet, the pine boughs dripping bejeweled drops that caught the sunlight in blinding prisms. When had it rained? He recalled being cold, then warm.

An image flirted with his memory, but didn't stick around any longer than to make him anxious. He had to get back to Stanwood.

Taking a moment, Devlin studied the angle of the sun and started walking down the mountainside, hoping to find a road or fence or someone who could tell him where he was.

As he rubbed the knot on his temple, he chastised himself for being a fool. He'd wager he'd been tricked into riding into the storm and woods last night. As terrible as he felt, he had a feeling he was lucky to be alive.

He'd gone on a fool's errand and now he would have

to pay the price. He feared it would mean his job and being sent back to his home country. He couldn't let that happen. He'd come too far, had already taken too many chances to get at the truth.

Stumbling through the woods, he headed due west. He wasn't sure how far he'd gone when he heard the thunder of hooves pounding toward him, and he looked up to see a half dozen of the royal police bearing down on him.

ALL RORY WANTED was to get back to the ranch, take a hot shower and put the storm and the groom out of her mind.

If only she could exorcize the images of the groom as easily. His lips on her skin, his strong arms around her, his hard body pressing into—

She swore as she rode out of the pines and saw the car parked in front of her ranch house.

Deputy Griffin Crowley stood against his patrol car, arms crossed over his chest, a frown on his face. He glanced at his watch as she approached, then back up at her with obvious irritation.

Rory had completely forgotten about her call to the sheriff's department yesterday morning when she'd discovered the tracks in her ranch yard. The sheriff had been unavailable. The dispatcher had promised to give someone the message though.

And here was Deputy Crowley. He'd certainly taken his sweet time getting there.

But that didn't bother her as much as the fact that she was going to have to put off the shower and dry clothing awhile longer.

"Rory," Griff said with a nod as she swung down from her saddle. He was a big man, with a head of dark blond hair and a thick mustache that curled around his thin lips. He looked like the boy next door, more boyish than handsome.

"I heard you called. The sheriff's off to some lawman's seminar in San Francisco. I got here as soon as I could. I was getting worried." He studied her openly. Almost as if he knew that she'd spent the night in the line shack with a fancy-dressed foreign groom.

She and Bryce Jones had double-dated with Griff and his girlfriend back in high school when the boys had been football stars, taking the team to state all four years. The two men had been close friends. She'd always suspected that Griff hadn't forgiven her for breaking her engagement to Bryce any more than Bryce had.

But Griff and Bryce weren't such close friends that the deputy hadn't asked her out soon after the breakup and after Bryce's leaving town. She'd turned Griff down all four times he'd asked her out since. To her relief, he'd finally quit asking.

Unfair or not, Griff reminded her of Bryce, which was the kiss of death as far as she was concerned, not to mention she couldn't forget the way Griff had tormented her when they were kids.

"Sorry. Let me put my horse up." Needing a moment, she led her horse into the barn, slipped off the saddle and tack and hung everything in the tack room.

On the ride back to the ranch, Rory had told herself that she'd put last night behind her. It was over and done. No reason to beat herself up over it. And no one had to know about her lapse in judgment. Or whatever it had been in the middle of the night during the storm. The groom had no doubt been fired by now and was probably on his way back to whatever country he'd come from.

She filled the mare's bucket with oats before turning to find Griffin standing in the doorway watching her.

"Early morning ride?" he asked.

She knew her hair was a mess as well as her clothing, and saw no reason to lie. "Got caught in that storm last night. I had to spend the night in an old line shack."

He raised an eyebrow. "I didn't know you had a line shack on your property."

"I don't. The one to the west was closer than trying to make it back to the ranch," she said avoiding his gaze.

Fortunately, he let it drop. "Well, at least that explains why I couldn't reach you when I called last night and again this morning," he said. "I was worried about you out here all alone after you called the department. That was a pretty bad storm last night. Temperature dropped quite a bit. I'm surprised you didn't freeze to death."

She'd always been a lousy poker player, every emotion showing in her face. "It wasn't bad in the line shack," she said, turning her whisker-burned face away.

Out of the corner of her eye, she saw him frown. "Isn't that line shack on the old Miller place? I thought that land was bought by—"

"That's the reason I called you," she cut in. "Someone has been hanging around the ranch. I think it's my new neighbors, that Duke—"

"Prince. He's a prince."

"Whatever." She just wanted to cut this short and get a hot shower and into some dry clothes. "He's been trying to buy my property and since I've made it clear I'm not selling—"

"You're telling me that the prince has been sneaking around your ranch? Come on, Rory, that's the craziest thing I've ever heard."

This was exactly why she hadn't wanted Griff responding to her call. "What are those people doing in Montana anyway? Do you even know? They could be infiltrating our country to attack us."

Griff shook his head as if he couldn't believe this. "A *prince and princess?*"

"How do you know that? Have you checked their identification? What do you actually know about these people?" She could see that he didn't know any more than she did. Maybe less since she doubted he'd been over there, while she had.

"Shouldn't someone try to find out exactly what these people are up to given they have soldiers over there carrying semiautomatic weapons?"

"How do you know what kind of weapons they carry?" he demanded.

She said nothing, not about to incriminate herself further.

Griff let out a long sigh. "First off, because they are royalty of course they are going to have armed guards. Second, you don't have to sell your land to them. Just ignore the offers."

"What about whoever's been on my property snooping around?" Rory saw his expression. "You're not going to do a thing, are you? Why am I not surprised?" She started to turn away from him, too angry to have this discussion with the pig-headed, son of a..."

"Hold on, now," Griff said grabbing her arm and turning her back to face him. "I'll have a look around, okay?"

She jammed her fists on her hips and said nothing.

Apparently he seemed to think it best to follow her example and stepped past her to circle the house.

She thought about going into the house and letting

him do his job, but she knew Griff. Tailing after him, she watched him wander around her ranch yard, looking bored and annoyed. He glanced back once to see if she was watching him. She was.

After a few minutes, he stopped his pretense of investigating and came back to where she was standing, her arms crossed over her chest.

"There's some tracks where someone has been hanging around, all right," he said.

"I believe I'm the one who told you that," she said, trying to contain her temper. She was cold and tired and couldn't wait for him to leave. It would be a cold day in hell before she called him out there again. Maybe when the sheriff got back…

The deputy sighed. "Look, I've been meaning to talk to you about this very thing. I don't like you living out here alone. I'm worried about you, Rory."

She shot an eyebrow upward. "Why? Since you're so sure I have nothing to worry about with my new royal neighbors…." She couldn't help the sarcasm. His concern apparently only went so far.

"Damn it, Rory, you have no business trying to run this ranch alone and this proves it. By your own admission, you got caught in that storm last night. What if you hadn't been able to get to the line shack? Or worse—what if you'd gotten bucked off your horse and hurt?"

She bristled. "I'm *fine*."

Griffin was shaking his head. "I'm not sure you can trust your judgment on this. You aren't behaving rationally, and you know it."

If he only knew. "If you're going to tell me you think I should sell the ranch—"

"You know you're doing this out of sheer stubbornness. It would be different if you had a man around—"

"I'm in no mood for this."

"I can see that you didn't get much sleep last night," he said. "Maybe this isn't the best time to bring this up."

"There is no good time if this is about me getting rid of the ranch," she said with heat although she knew others in town had speculated on the same thing—if not bet on how long before she ran the place into the ground. What Griffin and everyone else didn't seem to understand was that she loved the ranch and couldn't bear to part with it.

Just this year, she'd sold off the cattle and leased the land, telling herself it was only temporary, just until she could get the ranch back in business.

"I'm not selling." With that she turned and stomped toward the house.

"I wasn't offering to *buy* the place," Griff called after her. "I was asking you to *marry* me."

Rory stumbled to a halt, his words pelting her like stones. Slowly she turned to look back at him.

"What?" she asked, telling herself she must have heard wrong. She'd turned him down for even a date. What would make him think she would marry him?

"We should get married." He walked to her, kneading the brim of his hat in his fingers nervously as he approached. "I'd planned to ask you a lot better than this, but when you weren't around this morning... I'm asking you to marry me."

Her first indication was to laugh, but the deputy looked so serious... "Griff, I don't know what to say." That was putting it mildly.

"I know this is probably a little unexpected."

You think?

"But I've been considering it for some time," he continued, clearly nervous. "You need a man out here. You can't run the place by yourself."

She bristled at that. "Even if that were true, it's no reason to get married," she said, still stunned by his proposal.

"Hell, Rory, people get married every day with a whole lot less in common than the two of us. You and I have known each other all our lives. There shouldn't be any surprises."

Yeah, who'd want any surprises in a marriage? Or mystery? Or excitement? Or, say…love?

"Griff, I appreciate the offer, but I believe people should be in love when they get married. I don't love you." She hardly liked him after the way he used to tease and taunt her when they were kids.

"Love?" He snorted. "Like you're one of those silly romantic types."

"I beg your pardon?"

"Come on, Rory. Look at you. The way you dress. The way you act. Hell, if someone saw you out in the pasture they'd take you for a cowhand rather than a woman." He sounded angry with her.

For a moment, she was too shocked to speak. She might be a tomboy, but that didn't mean she wasn't a woman under these clothes. She had a right to romance, love, passion. A red-hot memory of last night in the shack leaped into her thoughts against her will. Talk about passion…

"You know what I mean," he said, softening his words. "You've never acted like a woman."

"If there is a compliment in there, I'm afraid I missed it," she said, fire in her eyes.

"What are you getting all riled about?" Griff demanded. "I was just saying that you could do a whole lot worse than me."

"I think you've said enough, Griff."

"I didn't mean to offend you."

"I'm not offended." She was. Not that everything he'd said wasn't the truth. Obviously, she didn't dress or act much like his idea of a woman. But under her damp dirty clothes, there was a woman's body and a beating heart.

Her thoughts flashed to the groom she'd shared her horse blanket—and a lot more—with last night. He'd found her desirable, hadn't he? True, he'd been drunk as a skunk and thought she was a forest sprite.

"Well, at least consider my offer," Griff said irritably. "I'll give you some time to think about it. But I could be the answer to your problems."

"I don't have any problems," she snapped. Except Griff right then. "You and I are *friends*." A lie. "Let's leave it at that."

"*Friends* isn't a bad place to begin a marriage."

"My answer is no," she said more forcefully.

"You are one mule-headed woman, you know that?"

"Thank you. That's the nicest thing you've said to me this morning." She turned again and headed for the house, calling over her shoulder, "Let me know about what you find out about my new neighbors."

Once inside the house, the front door locked behind her, Rory waited until Griff drove away before she stripped off her damp clothing and stepped into the shower, hopping mad. Griff had caught her off guard with his ridiculous marriage proposal. But it was his description of her that had her fuming because she feared it was too close to the truth.

She'd been so involved in saving the ranch that maybe she had forgotten how to be a woman.

Until last night.

CHAPTER FOUR

WITH DREAD, DEVLIN watched the horsemen approach. Jules Armitage, the head of royal security, rode in the lead, his back ramrod straight.

Devlin heard Armitage referred to as "Little Napoleon" behind his back. Small in stature but with an air of importance because of his long-standing position with the royal family, Jules was a man easily ridiculed.

But Devlin knew Jules Armitage was also a man to be feared. Jules had been in the service of the royal family for thirty years. His loyalties were never questioned, his harsh dealings with those under him legendary.

Devlin had seen Jules take a horse whip to one groom. Another groom had simply disappeared. The head of security had free rein here in Montana. Anything could fall under the protecting of the only daughter of the king, including murder.

Devlin could see even from a distance that the head of security was furious. It showed in the set of his shoulders, in the way he forced his horse's head up. Jules would report this incident—if he hadn't already.

This was the worst thing that could happen. Devlin couldn't be sent home now, and yet he knew the princess could do whatever she wanted with him. He was at her whim. As were the rest of those under her rule here at Stanwood.

With a wave of his hand, the head of security ordered the other riders to hold back. Jules rode on alone, bringing his horse to an abrupt halt within a few feet of Devlin.

His horse danced to one side as Jules dismounted with a curse that could have been directed at the horse—or at the groom.

Back still stiff, his reproach barely contained, Jules turned to face him. "Lord Ashford requests your presence in the stables at once," he said, voice taut with fury.

Devlin expected a tongue-lashing at the very least. This reaction was all wrong. "Lord Ashford?" he repeated, his aching head adding to his confusion.

Jules's complexion darkened. "I suggest you ride directly to the Stanwood stables. His lordship is *waiting*." The little man held out his reins with a stiff arm, and Devlin realized Jules was furious at being sent on such an errand let alone being forced to give up his horse in doing so.

While Jules could do little about Lord Ashford, he could definitely make Devlin's life hell—and his look promised as much.

Without a word, Devlin took the reins and swung up into the saddle. His head swam and he had to steady himself for a moment before he spurred the horse and took off at a gallop toward the stables.

As Stanwood came into view, Devlin thought, as he had the first time he'd seen it yesterday, it was amazing what too much wealth and self-indulgence could do when let loose.

Stanwood, a miniature of the royal palace in their homeland, rose out of the pines, a massive palace of quarried stone. One second-floor wing housed the princess and her prince, while the other wing was for royal guests.

Behind the palace were the stables, corrals and arena. Tucked back into the mountainside in the trees were a dozen small cottages that had been built for the grooms and horse trainers. Servants quarters had been erected in the opposite direction for those who saw to the princess and her entourage's daily needs as well as those of visiting nobility.

As he stepped into the stables, Devlin found Lord Nicholas Ashford, one such guest, leaning against a stall door. One glance around told him that the building was empty except for Lord Ashford. This, he knew, was no accident.

Lord Nicholas Ashford was tall, slim and immaculately groomed as any in his social stratosphere. Like the other nobles Devlin had come in contact with, Ashford had an air of privilege about him and an underlying impatience; he was easily bored. And he was a man who didn't like being kept waiting.

Nicholas frowned when he saw him. "You look like hell."

"I feel worse," Devlin said. He glanced around. Even though the stables appeared empty, he always feared that someone was close by, listening. Royal gossip was a hot commodity.

"We're alone. I cleared everyone out." Nicholas smiled. He'd never made it a secret that he enjoyed the privileges that came with wealth and power. His smile waned, though, as he studied Devlin.

"I feared something had happened when I heard your horse returned last night without you. Apparently there was cause for concern," he said, eyeing the knot on Devlin's temple. "What the devil happened?"

"It seems I was unseated from my horse."

Nicholas scoffed. "You? Not likely."

Devlin had practically grown up on the back of a horse. The last time he recalled being thrown was when he was five. "I have no memory of it."

"The head wound doesn't appear that serious," Nicholas noted.

"It's not. I fear it was the brandy I had before I left Stanwood. I suspect it was drugged." How else could he explain ending up in that cabin with the unfamiliar horse blanket and no memory of what had happened the entire night?

"Drugged, you say?" Nicholas didn't seem surprised. "There's something you might want to see."

Nicholas, he realized, had been waiting for him at the stall containing the horse Devlin had ridden out into the woods last night. The horse that had returned without him.

"Take a look at his right hind quarter," Nicholas said as Devlin opened the stall door. The mount shied away from him, eyes wild, nostrils flaring.

Devlin felt his senses go on alert. The horse hadn't behaved in this manner when he'd ridden him away from Stanwood last night. Even when the storm had come in, the horse hadn't reacted to the thunder and lightning because it had been trained to be ridden by hunters, who would be shooting while riding.

Speaking in a low soothing voice, Devlin cautiously entered the stall. The horse relaxed some as Devlin continued to gentle it with his words and slow, measured movements. Gingerly, he ran his hand the length of the animal and felt something. The gelding shied away from him again.

"Easy, boy." He found the spot Nicholas had mentioned. Something had penetrated the hide, leaving a small hole. It wasn't deep, hadn't come from a bullet.

He glanced at Nicholas, who nodded. "Shot with, if I had to guess, a pellet gun. You do recall that old pellet gun we used to get in trouble with?"

Devlin did indeed. Their friendship had been a secret. The son of a stables owner and the son of a noble. Nicholas, who'd been skinny and pale, had been sent to the stables to learn to ride. They'd been close in age, Devlin strong and fearless, Nicholas puny and timid.

The friendship had been good for both of them. Nicholas had learned to ride a horse, as well as take part in rough-and-tumble adventures with Devlin. And in turn, Devlin had learned the speech and manners of a noble.

"I think we can assume that someone knows why you're here," Nicholas said, concern in his tone.

"It would appear so." Devlin took out the note that had been slipped under his door at his cottage. "You didn't send this, then?"

Nicholas took the piece of paper, squinting in the poor light at the water-blurred writing.

"I don't recognize the handwriting, but whoever sent it either appeared to be in a hurry or purposely scrawled the note so as to remain anonymous," he said, handing it back.

"I thought it might have been from you. Or Anna," he added quietly. His mother's housemaid and friend had been an excellent horsewoman.

"Dev, I was as fond of your mother as my own, but even if you find out who murdered her, it won't bring her back and will only succeed in getting you killed, as well. I was opposed to this from the beginning, but now that someone knows why you're here..." Nicholas stopped as he must have realized he was wasting his breath.

They'd had this conversation before and always with

the same outcome. Devlin had to know not only who had murdered his mother but also why. It made no sense. His only lead was the woman who'd found his mother's body—his mother's housemaid and friend. Anna Pickering had been in the house. She would know if the rumor he'd heard was true—that a royal soldier had been seen leaving the house that night shortly before his mother's body was discovered.

It made no sense to kill a woman who owned a stable, who wasn't politically motivated and who had always catered to royalty.

"If you're right about Anna seeing the murderer that night, she won't want to see you," Nicholas said.

Devlin didn't blame the woman. She had disappeared right after the murder. Nicholas had helped Devlin trace her to the princess's new palace in Montana—and had helped Devlin get hired as a groom there.

"Do you remember who handled your drink last night?" Nicholas asked. "I'm afraid I didn't notice."

Devlin had replayed the scene in his mind. He'd been given a brandy in the main parlor of Stanwood, surrounded by the noble class.

Nicholas had instigated the whole thing as a way to get Devlin into Stanwood so he could check out the layout of the place. He'd introduced him as a master horseman, touted his skills at training horses and riders alike, himself included, and made sure everyone understood his kinship with the groom and respected it.

Of course, that wouldn't save Devlin if the princess found out what he was really up to.

"The longer you stay here, the more dangerous it will become," Nicholas said now. "Perhaps I should try to speak with this woman, Anna Pickering. You say she is a handmaid for the princess?"

"You have done enough." Nicholas had already stuck his neck out far enough just helping him get the groom job—and getting him access to Stanwood last night.

"If anyone can persuade her to meet you, it's me," Nicholas said with a grin.

"And should she tell Princess Evangeline what you have done?"

"I shall deny it, of course." Nicholas laughed. "Just as I shall deny any knowledge of your deception when you get caught."

"Of course," Devlin said, but knew better. He feared Nicholas would put himself in danger to save his friend.

That was why he had to protect Nicholas—and Anna—at all costs.

"Watch your back around Jules Armitage," Devlin warned his friend.

"Don't worry about the Little Napoleon. I can handle him."

Devlin didn't doubt it, but he'd seen how upset Jules had been. The head of security didn't like being treated like an errand boy. He wouldn't forget this slight. Nor who had caused it.

After saddling a horse for Nicholas, as if that had been why Lord Ashford had ordered him to the stables, Devlin headed for his cottage to shower and change.

Last night was still a black hole. Worse, he couldn't shake the feeling that it was imperative that he remember. There was little doubt that he'd been lured into the woods, drugged and meant to lose his horse, but for what purpose?

Had his attacker hoped the fall from the horse would kill him? Or had his attacker planned to finish him off but hadn't for some reason?

He was almost to his cottage when he had a sud-

den vision. Hot skin, silken and flushed with heat, full
rounded breasts, nipples erect and thighs as creamy
as… He stumbled in surprise.

Being drugged and thrown from his horse had done
more than left him with a raging headache. It had apparently played hell with his dreams last night.

RESTLESS AFTER CHORES, Rory stormed into the house
and went straight to her bedroom and the antique full-
length mirror that had belonged to her grandmother.

Her face was flushed from the cold morning, ten-
drils of her chestnut hair curled around her face from
where they'd escaped from her ponytail. Her Western
jacket and flannel Western shirt had been her father's.
She hadn't been able to part with either of them. The
jacket was worn and too big for her, but like the shirt,
it was soft and comfortable and one of her favorites.

Her jeans were boot-cut, slim-fit but the large shirt
and jacket she wore over them pretty much hid her figure.

She cocked her head, shoved back her Western straw
hat and studied her face in the mirror. No makeup. She'd
bought some lip gloss recently, but she didn't know
where she'd put it. As for mascara, well, she hadn't
worn any since…her high school prom? Had it really
been over ten years ago?

Rory groaned. Griff was right. She looked like a
cowhand. She'd always preferred working outside with
her father rather than being in the kitchen cooking with
her mother.

Even now, if she wasn't on a horse, then she'd just as
soon be out mending fences. Because of that, she was a
mediocre cook, could bake if forced to, and her sewing
abilities extended to reinforcing a button.

She much preferred jeans and boots to dresses and had never owned a pair of high heels. She'd borrowed a pair of her mother's for the high school prom—and had kicked them off the moment she'd gotten to the dance.

Damn Griffin Crowley. Tears smarted her eyes. She brushed angrily at them. It made it all the worse that Griff of all people was right, she thought as she stalked into the kitchen and dug out her mother's recipe book.

Damn if she wouldn't cook something.

It would keep her mind off last night and the groom who'd awakened something in her that she realized had been asleep. Or in a coma.

HEAD OF SECURITY Jules Armitage watched the small jet taxi to a stop on the airstrip behind Stanwood. Lord Charles Langston emerged from the craft.

A steady flow of guests had been arriving for several days, no doubt to attend the masquerade ball the princess had planned for this coming Saturday.

But still, it seemed odd that the royal family barrister would be invited to the ball. More than likely, Princess Evangeline had sent for him on a legal matter.

Jules knew the princess felt slighted because being born female exempted her from the throne in their home country. Nor could her husband, merely a lord before he married the princess, take the throne upon her father's death.

But Prince Broderick would be elevated to a high position within the country should the king die. That was part of the reason for the unrest in their home country. Few people wanted to see Prince Broderick Windham having anything to do with the running of their country.

It was one reason Jules suspected that the princess and her husband had been sent to Montana. While the princess had overseen the construction of Stanwood since the first shovel of dirt had been turned over, she clearly hadn't been happy about her apparent exile.

Her husband, Prince Broderick, had been in charge of buying up as many ranches as possible for their new home.

Jules questioned this entire move. While he could understand the king's reasoning, since both Princess Evangeline and Prince Broderick were definite liabilities in their homeland, Jules had to wonder, why the U.S.—let alone Montana?

If the king hoped that Montana would change his son-in-law and perhaps keep him at home long enough to produce an heir, His Royal Highness would have been sorely disappointed had he known the truth.

Jules swore as a second person stepped from the plane onto the tarmac. Lady Monique Gray, a recent widow. Black widow, that was.

What was *she* doing here? As if Jules had to ask. The princess's husband. Broderick had been anything but discreet about his scandalous affair with the woman. If the king hadn't controlled the media, it would have been all over the news. Princess Evangeline had to have heard about it, even though her father had worked so hard to keep it from her.

What the king didn't know was that his precious princess was a lot less fragile than he thought. She could squash a black widow like Lady Monique Gray—and would if given half a mind to. Lady Gray might not realize it yet, but she'd made a mistake coming here. Here in Montana, Princess Evangeline ruled like her father. If there wasn't blood shed within a fortnight, Jules would be surprised.

"Royals," he muttered under his breath, then quickly

turned to make sure no one had overheard. In Stanwood, the walls had ears and unless he wanted to lose his, he'd best watch himself. The king had personally put him in charge of the princess's safety. Not that she needed it. Instead, he would probably find himself trying to protect the others from her.

He found the whole lot of them tiresome. Especially the lords and ladies who hung around the princess like flies to spoiled meat. Lord Nicholas Ashford came to mind. Jules hated beginning the day by being sent like a messenger boy to find a missing groom.

Especially this particular groom.

Princess Evangeline had asked him to keep an eye on Devlin Barrow and make sure he had everything he needed, including a cottage of his own near the stables and the run of the place. Jules suspected she planned to take him as a lover. What other reason could she have for singling out the groom?

Jules had done as ordered, but there'd been a breach in security just before dark last evening and he'd lost track of the groom. Someone had been seen on the property, sneaking around. That had taken his attention and the next thing he'd known Devlin Barrow had disappeared, last seen riding off into the rain and darkness.

It wasn't until that morning that Jules had been informed that a horse had returned without a rider—and that not all of the hired help had been accounted for. Devlin Barrow hadn't returned.

Jules had barely gotten that news when Lord Nicholas Ashford had demanded that the head of security not only find Devlin, but bring him at once to the stables.

Given no choice, since he was subordinate to every guest of the princess's, Jules had done as ordered.

But it had stuck in his craw. Why had the groom ridden off so late last night and in a storm? And where had he spent the night after losing his horse?

If Lord Ashford hadn't ordered his favorite groom be found for his morning ride, Jules would have given the groom more than the tongue-lashing he deserved. Within reason, he thought, as he reminded himself that Devlin Barrow was to receive special treatment. Wasn't it always the troublemakers who curried the nobles' favor?

But why this particular groom?

Jules knew he should just let it go. Who cared what had happened to the groom last night? The princess hadn't found out. Better it be forgotten.

But Jules couldn't let it go. As head of security, he was going to find out not only what Devlin Barrow had been up to last night, but also why the son of a stables owner was suddenly being afforded such special treatment.

Picking up the phone, Jules called down to the stables. "Ready me a horse. No, I'll be going alone."

PRINCESS EVANGELINE Stanwood Wycliffe Windham studied herself in the full-length mirror. Behind her back, she knew people tsk-tsked about how sad it was that she'd taken after her mother's side of the family instead of her father's. The king was quite good-looking, while her mother, rest her soul, had been average.

Evangeline herself was below average. While she was average height, slim enough, blessed with her father's dark hair and dark blue eyes, her facial features would have been more attractive on a horse than a woman.

She knew she was being too critical. She had what once would have been called *handsome* features. Strong, striking bone structure. And she carried it off with a regal air that had definitely made some men turn their heads.

But then again, she was *the* princess. She knew that was why Broderick had pursued her. He'd wanted the title, the wealth, the prominence. He'd been so handsome, so charming and so attentive that she'd overlooked his less favorable qualities and married him because she thought they'd produce beautiful heirs to the throne.

Evangeline snorted and spun away from the mirror to stare out the window. "Bastard," she spat out at the thought of her philandering husband. She could overlook his infidelities and had. But his latest offense was unforgivable.

The bastard hadn't given her an heir and now he wasn't even sharing her bed. Maybe he thought he'd outlive her and have a chance to rule. Once her father was dead.

Her father. Just the thought of him made her a little ill. She knew he found her a scheming wench. He had no idea, she thought, then warned herself to tread carefully. She had taken too many liberties as it was. She'd disappointed her father too many times.

Her failure to produce a male heir, any heir at all, had angered him. He blamed her even though Lord Broderick Windham had given her little choice. Broderick, it seemed, was her punishment for her sins.

And sins, she had many. Her latest, though, was the most dangerous. She knew if she crossed her father that she risked not only being exiled from her homeland indefinitely, but also losing her freedom, possibly even her life.

Not that she didn't have everything under control.

She reminded herself how clever she'd been when Lord Nicholas Ashford had come to her with his request that she hire Devlin Barrow as a groom at her new home in Montana.

It was clear to her that while Devlin had gone into hiding and no one had been able to find him after his mother's murder, Lord Nicholas was in contact with him.

Evangeline had provided the bait—Anna Pickering—by bringing the woman to Montana on the pretense of protecting her. Everything had worked just as she'd planned it.

So far.

But Evangeline could feel time slipping through her fingers like the finest sand. It was a two-edged sword, keeping both Anna Pickering and Devlin Barrow safe while at the same time planning their destruction.

Evangeline let out an un-princesslike curse as she focused on the scene below her window.

"What is Monique doing here?" her companion Laurencia cried as she joined the princess at the window.

Evangeline spun away from the window as the Black Widow entered Stanwood.

"You don't think *Broderick* invited her, do you?" Laurencia asked, wide-eyed.

"Of course not," Evangeline snapped sarcastically. It was so like her friend to say the obvious. Who else could have invited her? Lady Monique was relentless once she set her sights on a man. And now apparently she'd set her sights on the prince. And vice versa.

This was the last straw. Evangeline had put up with her husband's philandering for the last time. The fool was going to produce a bastard who would try to overthrow the crown one day. Evangeline had to get pregnant, and soon, to put an end to the talk of her being barren.

But that would mean getting her husband into their marital bed. That, she knew, would take more than fortitude on her part, due to his complete lack of interest—and her own.

It would take a miracle.

Or something Princess Evangeline was better equipped for: deception.

"You should have Lady Monique sent from the grounds at once," Laurencia was saying. "She is only here to rub your face in her affair with your husband."

Thank you, Laurencia, Evangeline thought. That was the problem with having a stupid companion—while she could be useful, she was annoyingly clueless.

"We will welcome Monique," Evangeline said as she suddenly saw Lady Monique's arrival as a possible godsend.

"But I thought—"

"Best let me do the thinking," she told her. Laurencia had always been the perfect companion—meek and slow-witted and completely loyal. In short, Evangeline could wrap her around her little finger.

"I want you to be nice to Monique," the princess said. "She has arrived just in time for the masquerade ball. In fact, I want you to make sure she wears the costume *you* were planning to wear. I shall have the seamstress make you something more suitable."

Laurencia looked disappointed but nodded.

Evangeline smiled. Her original plan had been to use her companion to lure in Lord Prince Broderick by offering Laurencia on a silver platter. But this new plan would work much better since she had been dangling Laurencia in front of her husband for weeks and he hadn't gone for the bait.

With Monique, the Black Widow, there would be no need to dangle her. Instead, Evangeline would have to make sure Broderick was kept so busy he wouldn't have the time to catch Monique—until the night of the masquerade ball.

With everyone masked, it would be the time to spring her trap and produce an heir to the throne. Broderick, without realizing it, would do his part. Once she was pregnant with a legitimate heir...well, then she wouldn't need Broderick anymore, would she?

Montana was such a wild, isolated country. Anything could happen to a man as adventurous as Prince Broderick Windham. Most certainly a very painful death.

Evangeline glanced at her watch. "Off with you now to make sure Lady Monique is comfortable in the large suite on the east wing." Laurencia, who as always did as she was told, scampered off to do the princess's bidding.

The princess stepped to the window again, pleased with herself. A lone rider galloped across the meadow.

Jules? Riding off alone? Odd, she thought, but quickly returned her thoughts to a more important task. Tying up one last loose end.

At the sound of a knock on her suite door, Princess Evangeline glanced at her watch. The man was prompt, she thought as she opened the door to her second cousin by marriage, Lord Charles Langston, the family barrister from a noble but poor family.

"Your Royal Highness," Lord Charles said with a bow. He looked scared out of his wits. She considered that a very good sign as she ushered him into the room, closed the door and demanded to see what he'd brought her.

Holding her breath, she watched him reach into his briefcase and draw out a large manila envelope. What Charles carried was of such high security that if caught with the papers, he would have been put to death.

Her fingers shook as she took the envelope and drew out the papers, noting not only the royal seal, but the thick, pale green paper used only for important government documents in her country.

"These are the originals?" she asked.

Charles nodded.

"So it is true," she said, feeling sick to her stomach. There would be no turning back now. She put the documents back into the manila envelope, willing her fingers not to tremble at even the thought of what she'd done.

Finally, she looked to the family barrister. She feigned surprise, then anger. "Where is this bastard?"

"In your employ, your Royal Highness. He's one of your grooms."

JULES RODE TO THE SPOT where he'd encountered Devlin Barrow that morning. The day was cold and clear, the sun slicing through the tall, dense pines. Plenty of light to track Devlin's footprints in the still-wet ground.

Determined to find out where the groom had spent the night, he followed the trail, glad for last night's rain, which made tracking easier.

A hawk squawked as it circled over the treetops. Closer, a squirrel chattered at him as he worked his way through the pines.

Jules lost the tracks at one point in the thick, dried pine needles but picked them up again as he led his horse up the mountainside, surprised the groom had ridden this far from the ranch. He could make out the old county road—all that stood between the princess's property and the one ranch that was still privately owned.

The owner had refused to sell. He'd heard Evangeline discussing the problem with her husband, Prince Broderick. The Buchanan Ranch was now all that stood between the prince's holdings and the river.

The owner would *have* to sell. It was only a matter of time since the princess wanted it—and Broderick was responsible for acquiring the property for her.

Jules turned his attention back to the mountainside and the boot tracks he'd been following. As he walked through a stand of aspens, the leaves golden, he saw the small log structure ahead.

The groom's boot tracks led right up to the front door. Was it possible this was where Devlin Barrow had spent the night?

Ground-tying his horse, Jules walked toward the shack, noting the shed roof off to one side. A horse had been kept under the overhang recently. He could still smell it.

Not the groom's horse since it had returned to the stables without him. Had Devlin been thrown? That would explain his odd behavior that morning as well as the wound on his temple.

Except that Devlin Barrow was extolled as being an extraordinary horseman.

To Jules's surprise, the door to the structure wasn't locked. Cautiously he peered inside, not sure what he expected to find.

That was just it. He hadn't expected to find *anything*. It took a moment for his eyes to adjust to the darkness—and see the horse blanket lying on the shack's worn wood floor.

Frowning, he stepped in for a closer look. The horse

blanket wasn't one of Stanwood's, which were monogrammed with the royal crest.

He caught a scent in the stale air of the small room
and smiled knowingly. A man who knew about the
baser desires, Jules was familiar with the aroma of sex.

He stared down at the blanket, wondering who had
shared that blanket with the groom last night and how
he could use that knowledge to his advantage.

Obviously, the woman wasn't from the Stanwood
household or she would have been riding one of the
royal horses with the monogrammed blanket and tack.

So who was she?

He started to turn to leave when he saw something
that stopped him. Crouching down, he lifted the edge
of the horse blanket. It had appeared to be nothing more
than cheap material like most blankets used under a
Western saddle in this part of the world.

But this blanket had leather trim. It was what had
been stamped into the leather that caught his eye.
Whitehorse Days.

Jules frowned as he read the date and the words: All-
around Best Cowgirl.

He dropped the blanket back to where he'd found it
and rose. All-around Best Cowgirl. She shouldn't be
that hard to find given that he now had the event date.

If Devlin Barrow—or even the princess—thought
either of them could keep secrets from him, they were
both mistaken.

CHAPTER FIVE

"WHAT IS *THAT?*" Georgia Michaels asked as she answered the door to find her best friend standing on her step.

Rory held out the dish as an offering. "Pie. Apple. I baked it."

Georgia looked suspiciously from Rory to the pie and back but didn't take it. "You're kidding."

"No. Take the damned thing. Why is everyone giving me such a hard time about this?" Rory said, shoving the pie at her friend.

Georgia took the pie, eyeing her warily, before leading the way into the house. "Who's giving you a hard time about this pie?" she asked on the way to her warm, sunny kitchen.

"Deputy Griffin Crowley. And not about the pie," Rory said with a groan as she climbed onto a stool at the breakfast bar. "He asked me to marry him."

"Get out of here." Georgia laughed as she found a knife, cut the pie and dished them up each a slice, still eyeing the pie with suspicion.

"He called his proposal an *offer* and made it sound like a business proposition."

"*Romantic.*" Georgia took a tentative bite of the pie, her expression turning to one of surprise. "Hey, this is *good.*"

Rory cut her eyes to her. "Don't sound so shocked. I can bake. If I want to."

"Did Griff say you couldn't bake? Is that what this is about?"

"He insinuated that I wasn't a real woman."

Georgia raised an eyebrow.

"He actually made fun of me when I told him I didn't want to marry anyone I didn't love, then he pointed out that I wasn't much of a *girl*."

Her friend laughed. "I remember when you punched Joey Franklin in the mouth in third grade because he called you a girl. You can't have it both ways."

Rory had to laugh as well. "I know."

"So what did you tell him?" she asked and took another bite of the pie.

"I told him no, of course. He said he only suggested it because I need help with the ranch. I think I hurt his feelings. He got pretty angry."

Georgia kept her gaze on the pie in front of her. "You do need help out there. What are you going to do?"

"I don't know." Rory didn't have money to hire hands and the place was getting rundown without an infusion of cash. She couldn't afford to ranch. And she couldn't afford not to since ranching was her life.

"Have you given any more thought to my offer?" Georgia asked cautiously. Her friend wanted her to come into the knitting shop as a business partner even though attempts to teach Rory to knit had failed miserably.

"I'd die without the ranch," Rory said dramatically. "Or at least I'd want to. And as for selling out to royalty…" She shook her head. "I hate that they bought up so many working ranches to build some monstrosity. You know they'll tire of it and go back to wherever they came from. Or just visit here a few months a year after ruining all that range land."

"Nice to see you getting along so well with your new neighbors. Can I assume you didn't take *them* a pie?"

Rory let out a curse that made her friend laugh. "But I did meet one of the grooms from the place."

"Oh?" Georgia's head came up, eyes gleaming. She knew Rory too well.

"We both got caught in that big storm that blew through last night," Rory said, picking up her fork and poking at her piece of pie. She still hadn't taken a bite.

"And?"

Rory wished she hadn't mentioned it. But Georgia was her best friend and had been since they were knee-high to a squirrel. And Rory couldn't just bake a pie and show up on her best friend's doorstep and not confide all.

"And…we might have made love," she blurted.

"Might have? You don't *know?"*

Rory felt her face grow warm. "I'm pretty sure we did."

"It couldn't have been very memorable."

"Actually…" She looked away, her face now flaming.

"Rory!" Georgia laughed. "Does this mean you aren't joining the nunnery like everyone in town has been saying since your breakup with Bryce?"

"Not funny."

"So when are you seeing him again?"

"I'm not."

"What?" Georgia didn't even bother to hide her disappointment.

"Even if he didn't work for my royal-pain-in-the-behind neighbors, I'm pretty sure he got fired after last night." She wasn't about to admit that she'd been thinking of riding back over there that afternoon, get close enough that she could see the grooms exercising the horses to see if he was all right.

She doubted he remembered last night as out of it as he'd been. But it would be nice to know he hadn't been sent back to his country to be executed for risking one of the horses.

"You haven't touched your pie," her friend noted suspiciously again.

"I haven't been hungry all day. I feel like I'm coming down with something."

"Nothing kills my hunger," Georgia said proudly and finished her piece of pie. "Except love." Her eyes shone as she grinned at Rory. "Maybe you're in love."

"Please. I don't even know the man's name and I can assure you what happened last night wasn't love. It was more like lust. A lot like lust."

"Or fate. Apparently this royal *groom* thought you were a woman," Georgia said hiking up one eyebrow. "You should have told Griffin Crowley that!"

Rory laughed, glad she'd come to see her friend, glad she'd confided in her. Georgia always made her feel better. "Thank you. Talking about last night, well, I feel better."

"I suppose this means no more pies, then," Georgia joked.

Talking about last night, though… Rory let out a curse and jumped to her feet. "My horse blanket."

"What?" Georgia looked alarmed.

"I left my horse blanket in the line shack. The groom was still sleeping on it so I left it."

"So it's probably still there," her friend said reasonably. "Or you can replace it, right?"

"You don't understand. I just remembered. It was the horse blanket I won at Whitehorse Days in high school."

"That old thing?"

"Georgia, the date of the event, Whitehorse Days and Best All-around Cowgirl were imprinted on the leather trim."

Her friend's eyes widened. "So he'll find you. What's wrong with that?"

"I told you, he is probably on his way back to his country right now." Rory had to get the blanket back. She was sure it was still in the shack. The blanket was old and certainly not a keepsake since Rory had won her share of horse blankets over the years. But she didn't want anyone else to find it and trace it back to her.

The last thing she needed was for her royal neighbors to find out she'd been trespassing on their property.

DEVLIN HAD GOTTEN CALLED BACK to the stables to saddle more horses for the royal guests.

Hours later, he finally reached his cottage. Now, standing under the spray of the shower, he closed his eyes. His head still ached, but he felt a little stronger. He'd tried to remember who'd poured him the brandy last night. It could have been anyone, one of the servants or one of the aristocrats who'd been in the room.

He'd tried to picture where everyone had been as he'd entered. Princess Evangeline Windham had been sitting on the couch. Her husband, Prince Broderick, had been standing before the fireplace, a drink already in his hand.

Nicholas had been talking to Lady Laurencia Hurst,

a mousy-looking woman with timid brown eyes. Lord Alexis Kent had been behind Evangeline. A pretty boy, Alexis had been the lover of a variety of royal women, including Evangeline herself, at least according to Nicholas, and Nicholas did love royal gossip.

None of them had looked as if they were a crack shot with a pellet gun, but looks could be deceiving, Devlin knew only too well.

He had been introduced by Nicholas as his favorite groom from the famous Barrow Stables.

"He comes highly recommended," Nicholas had said.

"Here, here," said Prince Broderick. "Your mother trained some of our horses. A fine, talented woman." Some of King Wycliffe's horses, not the Windhams', Devlin had thought. Broderick's family had been at the low end of nobility.

"Devlin's mother is recently deceased," Nicholas had added.

"Oh?" Broderick had seemed genuinely surprised to hear that. "My condolences. Get the man a drink," he'd said to the servant at the bar.

Then Princess Evangeline had insisted Devlin have a seat in front of the fire next to her and tell her how she could improve her riding skills.

All Devlin remembered was someone thrusting a glass into his hand. As darkness had descended, he'd excused himself and hurried to the stables, anxious to reach the stand of aspens and his appointment.

Had someone left the group in the main parlor and followed him through the rain and darkness? Or was the person who'd sent him on the wild goose chase not of royal class? And the person who shot his horse, an accomplice? Perhaps a servant? Or a royal soldier?

Devlin closed his eyes and concentrated on the feel

of the hot water pelting his body. The images came in a rush, hitting him harder than the water, bombarding him with visions of a woman with green eyes, long legs and—

His eyes flew open, the images were so real he'd half expected to find the woman in his arms. Disappointment and confusion made his head swim.

He leaned against the shower wall for a moment, wondering if he was losing his mind or if it had just been the drug he'd been given. But the images were so vivid, so defined, so powerful...

How was it possible that he could remember the feel of the woman's skin beneath his fingertips, the weight of her breasts cupped in his palms, the sound of her quickened breathing if it had only been a dream?

Because it *hadn't* been a dream.

He shut off the water, his head clearing a little. What if he hadn't been alone last night?

It was the only explanation for the taunting images of this illusive green-eyed mystery woman. She was branded on his skin and still raging in his blood.

But who was she? And what had she been doing in that old cabin last night?

He'd been sent to that clearing, drugged, his horse shot and thrown from his mount to be injured. How had he ended up in the arms of a woman?

His every instinct told him that all of it—including the woman—was part of something much larger. But what? How could any of this tie in with his mother's murder thousands of miles across the sea in another country?

Even with his screaming headache, it was clear what he had to do.

Find the woman.

And get the truth out of her.

ON RETURNING TO THE RANCH, Rory stopped only long enough at the mailbox on the county road to pick up her mail.

Another official-looking letter from her royal neighbors. She cursed under her breath, then reminded herself cursing wasn't very ladylike and only proved that what Griff had said about her was true.

She cursed at the thought—and Griff—as she drove to the ranch house. She didn't bother to open the letter, knowing it was just another offer on her ranch from her new royal neighbors.

She tossed the offer into the fireplace. How many times did she have to say it? No amount of money could make her change her mind about selling her ranch.

They'd thrown serious amounts of money at her already, as if convinced she could be bought—the price just hadn't been agreed on yet. She'd written them numerous times and even called twice, both times being told she should leave a message since it was impossible for her to speak to Her Highness.

Maybe in the princess's country she could force Rory to sell, but they were in America now.

More to the point, they were in *Montana*. Montanans didn't take kindly to being pressured into anything, especially when it came to their livelihood.

In Montana people like her felt that not only did they have the right to protect their land, they were also capable of doing so. It was one reason there were more shotguns over the fireplaces in this state than in any other. There was still a little of the Old West alive and well up here, and her royal neighbors were going to find that out if they didn't leave her alone.

THE WOMAN WITH THE GREEN EYES haunted Devlin throughout the rest of the day as he worked in the stables with the other grooms. Several more guests had arrived.

But the guest who had the grooms gossiping when no nobles were around was Lady Monique Gray.

"They call her the Black Widow," one groom confided. "All her husbands die."

"Which makes her richer than the king," one said.

"Not the king," another argued. "But richer than us, that's for sure."

They all laughed.

"She just buried the last one, so you know what that means. She's here looking for her next prey."

"Maybe back to even the score with her former lover, Lord Alexis. I heard she threatened to kill him if she ever saw him again."

The servants of the court did love the drama that always surrounded royalty.

"I say the Black Widow has her eye on the Prince himself," interjected one groom.

The others exchanged nods.

"If that be the case, then I'd wager the king sent her so he could finally get Broderick out of the family," the groom said quietly, afraid of being overheard. It was one thing to speak of lords and ladies. Another to be heard disparaging the royal family.

Devlin only half listened to the gossip. He'd heard enough about Princess Evangeline that he doubted she would allow anyone to steal her husband.

He left the group to see if he could find Nicholas as he was returning from his ride.

"I'm sorry, Dev. I can't say who left the main parlor after you last night. I had to make a phone call before dinner. All I can tell you was that everyone was in the dining hall when I arrived for dinner."

"But someone could have followed me and gotten back in time to dress for dinner?" Devlin asked.

"I suppose they could have. You're that convinced it was one of the guests?"

"I'm just trying to consider all the possibilities." He thought about mentioning the green-eyed woman. She hadn't been one of the royal guests staying at Stanwood. If she was one of the servants, Nicholas wouldn't know. Maybe when Devlin had more information about her, he'd ask for Nicholas's help. But for the time being, he would keep the woman to himself.

It wasn't until later, his work done for the day, that Devlin saddled a horse on the pretext of exercising it. He planned to take a circuitous route to the cabin he'd awakened in that morning. Just in case he was being followed.

He couldn't wait to find a clue to the green-eyed woman haunting his every waking thought.

That was probably why he didn't notice someone standing in the shadows of the stables as he left.

Only one set of eyes seemed to follow his departure with interest. The dark blue eyes of Princess Evangeline.

RORY TOLD HERSELF she had no choice but to return to the line shack and retrieve her horse blanket. But this time, she felt even more nervous about trespassing—let alone getting caught.

What if the groom had told someone about her?

As she neared the line shack, Rory slowed her horse.

A magpie cawed from a pine as she dismounted in the trees several dozen yards from the shack. The sky overhead was blue and cloudless after the storm last night, the peaks lightly dusted with fresh snow.

A slight breeze stirred the heavy boughs of the pines, emitting a soft sigh, as Rory walked toward the shack, her senses on alert. She half expected to hear the sound of hooves pounding in her direction. Light and dark played in the thick stand of aspens as she glanced in the direction of the royal palace, but she saw no spotted horses, no fancy dressed grooms, nothing but sunlight and shadow.

At the shack door she hesitated, listening for any sound within before she pushed it open. The hinges groaned loudly, the door giving only a few inches, the noise making her jump. She let out an embarrassed, nervous chuckle and started to enter when she heard a familiar sound that stopped her cold.

The jingle of a bridle. She'd know that sound anywhere. Leaving the door ajar, she hurriedly stepped to the side of the shack, flattening herself against the outer wall as she heard a horse snort. The snort was followed by the sound of horse's hooves in the fallen leaves of the aspen grove on the far side of the shack.

Rory glanced toward her own horse, only partially visible through the pines, and prayed the mare didn't make a sound. Fortunately her horse seemed more interested in munching the tall grass.

The creak of leather made her freeze as she heard the rider dismount. The horse let out a shudder and pawed at the ground, taking a few steps closer to where she was hidden.

The door of the shack groaned all the way open.

Silence. Then the heavy tread of boots on the worn wooden shack floor as the rider entered the building.

Rory didn't dare breathe. What could someone be doing in there?

More footfalls on the wood floor. The line shack door groaned closed. She heard him swing up into the saddle, the leather creaking again, the sound of the horse moving, and feared for a moment he might ride in her direction and see her.

Silence.

She hadn't heard him leave. Was he just sitting there?

Unable to stand it a second longer, Rory edged to the corner of the shack and peered around it.

Her heart jumped.

It was the groom from last night.

A gasp caught in her throat.

He had her horse blanket in his hands and was studying the lettering in the leather.

She ducked back, cursing silently. To hell with the horse blanket. It was too late anyway.

With relief, she heard him ride away from her, back in the direction he'd come, back toward the royal kingdom he must still be employed by. So he hadn't gotten fired and sent back to his country.

Rory would have been relieved—if he hadn't taken her horse blanket.

Her pulse thrummed in her ears.

Was it possible he was looking for her?

Why else return to the line shack? Why else take her horse blanket with him?

He was trying to find her.

But why?

CHAPTER SIX

IT HAD COME back to him, standing in the shack over the horse blanket. The images of the green-eyed woman in the throes of lovemaking had almost dropped Devlin to his knees.

He felt confused by the images, worse by the emotions the images evoked. The woman had touched him in a way that surprised and angered him. Clearly, she'd done her job well. But to what end, other than to lure him to the woods so she could seduce him?

He ground his teeth at the thought that he'd let himself be deceived in such a manner.

Well, the woman would answer for it when he found her. And he would find her—and her accomplice. Someone at Stanwood knew the truth and he was bound and determined to find them.

Devlin rode the horse a few yards into the trees, then circled back. He'd seen the fresh tracks around the old shack. His instincts told him that whoever had been there, hadn't left. He feared that after last night, he couldn't trust his instincts.

But he'd been right about the green-eyed woman. She *did* exist. All-around Best Cowgirl. Oh, yeah, she existed all right and he had a feeling he was about to find her.

He eased through the pines until he could see the back side of the shack. Just as he'd thought, a figure moved from the shadows along the side and headed into the trees.

He frowned. It didn't appear to be a woman. Western hat pulled low, large old worn jean jacket, jeans and boots. A horse whinnied in the distance. Whoever it was had ridden there.

Just as he'd feared, his horse let out an answering whinny. He spurred his mount as he heard the pounding of horse hooves as the person took off.

Devlin caught sight of the rider racing through the pines and went after him. He loved nothing better than the chase. The wind in his face. The powerful horse beneath him. The knowledge that no one could outrun him. Not on a horse. Especially the one he was riding.

But the rider in front of him was giving him a damned good run. Devlin pushed his horse, gaining on the horse in front of him. The pines parted in a wide open meadow rimmed in aspens. Devlin drew alongside, both horses running flat out, neck and neck.

That's when he saw not only that the rider was female—but very familiar. Fear flashed in a set of beautiful green eyes. The same beautiful green eyes that had been haunting him since last night.

Reaching over, he grabbed her reins, drawing both horses up. His horse danced to a stop under him as hers bucked.

Devlin bailed off his horse, grabbed her by the waist and swung her down to the ground, surprised how well she'd managed to stay on the bucking horse.

"What are you doing?" the woman demanded. "You could have gotten us both killed!"

Her hair had come loose of the Western hat. She jerked the hat off and slammed it on her pant leg. Chestnut curls tumbled around her shoulders. Devlin remembered the feel of her hair beneath his fingertips. Remembered those eyes firing with passion in a flash of lightning. Remembered the body hidden beneath the oversized worn jean jacket she now wore.

"It's you," he said, sounding as breathless as he felt. His gaze lit on her mouth and he was struck by the memory of the taste of her. For a moment, he forgot that this woman was part of a plot against him.

"Who hired you to lure me to that shack last night and seduce me?" he demanded, towering over her as that memory came back to him.

Those green eyes flashed with fury. "*Excuse* me? You're the one who seduced *me*."

"That's not the way I remember it."

"I'm surprised you remember anything given the shape you were in," she snapped.

"I remember," he said, his gaze locking with hers. "I have flashes of you naked in my arms."

Her cheeks flamed, but she didn't break eye contact. "From that, you decided I was part of some kind of diabolical plot against you?"

He grinned. "I have to admit that part of the plot did make me wonder."

"If you remember as you say, then you'd know that I saved your life," she said with a shake of her head.

"You saved my life?" He let out a humorous laugh. "You were in on the plot to get me to that shack. Don't deny it. I found your horse blanket."

"I don't know what you're talking about, but I want my blanket back," she said reaching for it.

He stepped between her and his horse, where her horse blanket was still thrown over his saddle. They were so close he could feel her warm breath brush his cheek. "If you didn't lure me to the cabin, then how was it you just happened to be there?"

"Luck. *Good* luck for you. If I'd left you out in that storm after you got thrown from that beautiful horse you were riding, I doubt we'd be having this conversation right now. But then again, as drunk as you were, maybe the alcohol in your system would have kept you alive."

"I wasn't drunk. Someone drugged me."

She raised an eyebrow. *"Drugged?"*

He nodded, scowling at her. "And that beautiful horse I was riding? Someone shot it with a pellet gun to unseat me."

Her horrified expression surprised him because it appeared to be genuine. "Who would do such a thing?"

"Why don't *you* tell me?"

"If you think I would be involved in anything that injured a horse…" The ferocity of her words made him take a step back to study her.

"Okay," he said, finding himself at least wanting to believe her. The fall air smelled of pine and fallen aspen leaves. He breathed it in, picking up the fresh scent of the woman, as well. The last of the day's sunlight caught in her hair, turning it to spun gold.

"So you're trying to convince me that what happened wasn't planned?"

She snorted under her breath. "Not on *my* part."

The breeze rustled the aspens. A moment later, they were showered with dried leaves that danced around them like snowflakes.

He watched her shake off the leaves that caught in her hair.

"You never said what you were doing there last night, if not waiting for me." He couldn't help being suspicious.

"Actually, I suspected you were following me." She sighed again and he could see her making up her mind whether to tell him something as she settled her hat back on her head. "I was checking out the royalty and got caught in the storm."

He wouldn't have taken her for one of those people impressed by royalty.

"I knew where the line shack was so I headed for it. When I heard your horse and looked out to see you on the ground, I braved the storm to bring you into the line shack, where you hogged my horse blanket. You were so drunk—"

"Drugged."

She sighed. "Fine. Drugged. You called me a forest sprite and asked how you would ever be able to repay me for my kindness. Right before you passed out."

Her words had such a ring of truth to them... He cringed at how he'd repaid her. "If you're telling the truth—"

"Of course I'm telling the truth."

"Then someone didn't expect you to be there and take me into the line shack."

She brushed her hair back from her face as another gust scattered leaves around them. "I did hear a horse nearby and thought you might not have been riding alone, but the other mount went back the way it had come."

So there had been someone out there. Maybe the plan *had* been to finish him off if being drugged and thrown from his horse didn't do the job.

As he looked at the woman, he realized she very well may have saved his life. *If* she was telling the truth.

He pulled her to him, his mouth dropping to hers. She tasted familiar. He felt desire shoot through him as their lips touched. He'd definitely made love to this woman. The experience was burned in his soul.

The kiss brought back the memory of her warm and willing in his arms and left an ache when she pulled back to glare angrily at him.

But the kiss was impulsive and dangerous. What *had* he been thinking? That from one kiss he could tell whether she was lying or not....

"That might have worked once," she said, sounding as breathless as he felt. "But this time we're not sharing a horse blanket."

"I had to know the truth." The truth was he'd been dying to kiss her from the moment he'd pulled her down from her horse and seen it was the same woman from last night.

She cocked her head at him. "That was a *test?*" She seemed amused by that. "I guess I passed." She reached for her horse's reins. "I'd like my horse blanket now," she said, tilting her chin skyward.

"Not until you tell me your name."

She shook her head. "It's better you don't know." She swung up into the saddle.

"I can find out. All-around Best Cowgirl. White-horse Days."

She held out her hand for her blanket. "My name's Rory." She cocked an eyebrow at him.

"Devlin Barrow." He handed her the horse blanket. "You have a last name?"

They both turned at the sound of riders coming their way.

RORY SPURRED HER HORSE at the sight of the royal guards riding in their direction and took off, making a beeline

for home. All she could think about was getting away
from Devlin Barrow.

She was still shaken by her encounter with the
groom. All her bravado when she'd been caught by
him was long gone. He was even more handsome in
the daylight. The kiss had brought back last night and
the emotions he'd evoked in her, as well as the desire.

What he must think of her. Worse, what would he
think once he knew who she really was? Not that brazen
woman from the line shack, that was for sure.

Wouldn't he be surprised to find out she was the
woman who refused to sell to his employer.

She glanced back, half afraid he and the royal army
were following her. They weren't. She could see his
broad back and the way he was standing to face them.
If anything he was trying to protect her, she thought
with a stab of guilt. She'd run out on him, leaving him
to face the consequences.

But Rory assured herself that being caught with her
wouldn't have helped his case.

She realized that she believed his story about being
drugged and his poor horse shot with a pellet. Maybe
there was something to his kiss test after all.

It felt odd, trusting a complete stranger. Except it
hadn't felt like that between them. It was as if they had
shared more than a night of passion. She'd been joking
about saving his life. Kinda. But maybe she had.

Odd as it seemed, she felt as if she knew him.

She could just imagine what Georgia would have to
say about that.

Rory just hoped he was all right. Surely those soldiers wouldn't do him harm. And yet even as she
thought it, she realized that if she really did believe

him, then someone had tried to do him harm just the night before.

She shuddered at the thought. Who would want to hurt a royal groom? Or was it possible that it had something to do with her and her ranch?

Maybe Griff was right. She was seeing conspiracy plots everywhere she looked. But so was her royal groom, then.

Suddenly, all thought of the royal groom or the deputy flew out of her head as she saw where her barbed wire fence had been cut. Not just in one spot but several.

Rory drew up her horse and swung down from the saddle. There were tracks in the soft earth. Boot tracks. Man-sized.

She cursed as she picked up one end of the barbed wire and inspected the clean cut.

Vandals? Or had someone been looking for fresh beef still on the hoof?

The problem was there weren't any cattle being run in this section, so why cut fence? No fool rustler would cut the fence without first seeing cattle on the other side.

Not only that—whoever had cut the fence had apparently walked in from the road—a good half mile away.

Rustlers tended to steal cattle close to the road so they could be quickly loaded into a trailer for a fast getaway. Also, most rustlers worked in pairs. Whoever this was had been alone from what she could tell of the tracks.

This hadn't been a rustler. Nor some drunked-up kid out to destroy property because his girlfriend had dumped him.

No, this person had to have had another reason to vandalize her property.

Rory glanced back the way she'd come. She could

see part of the royal family's palatial roofline above the trees.

She shifted her gaze to the two spots where her fence had been cut. This felt more like a warning.

Whatever it was, she was going to have to call the sheriff's department again and that was something she really wasn't looking forward to.

PRINCESS EVANGELINE WATCHED her husband come into their suite. He hadn't seen her, didn't realize she'd returned.

Broderick went straight to the bedroom. She could hear him in there opening and closing drawers.

Quietly, she got up from where she'd been sitting and moved to the bedroom doorway in time to see him emptying his pockets into one of the drawers. He caught his reflection in the mirror as he closed the drawer. All his attention went to his face.

Hurriedly he wiped at a spot on his cheek, then spun toward the doorway as if sensing her there. She saw the startled, guilty look in his eyes. It was easy to recognize since she'd seen it so many times before.

"Evangeline," he said on whiskey-scented breath. "I didn't realize you were here."

"So I gathered," she said stepping deeper into the room. The scent of whiskey did little to mask the underlying sweet odor of cheap perfume. She blinked back tears, surprised that Broderick could still disappoint her.

Had she really hoped that he would quit his philandering once they were in the States? Then that would make her a bigger fool than even her husband.

"I see you're up to your old tricks, so to speak," she said, furious with herself for thinking he might be capable of change. "You always did stoop to the lowest point possible."

"My dear, my dear," Broderick said with a laugh. "Are we to resort to name calling? I think you might want to reconsider. You know what they say about mud-slinging. If you can't take wallowing in it yourself—"

"Aren't you afraid I'll grow tired of your antics and have my father terminate our marriage and throw you back into the gutter where I found you?"

He smiled. "So you admit you knew what I was when you married me. A gambler, a womanizer, a rogue. That, my dear, is what you fell in love with and that's what you get," he finished, throwing his arms wide with dramatic, drunken theatrics.

"You're drunk," she snapped.

"How else could I put up with your tedious lectures?"

She grabbed his arm as he started to turn away. "If I told my father, he'd have you killed."

Broderick laughed. "Not before I told him about you and Alexis and the others." He quirked an eyebrow. "What? You didn't think I knew? While you might be more discreet than I am, you are none the less innocent, my dear. Your exploits, like mine, are legendary. That's why we're made for each other."

"I know you're seeing someone."

"Seeing someone? What a quaint expression."

"You are supposed to be buying up land for my father," she said, growing angrier by the moment. She could just imagine the kind of woman he'd been with. It turned her stomach.

"Haven't I always done your father's and your bidding, my dear?"

"What about the Buchanan property? I assume you closed on it and were celebrating."

He scowled at her. "I'm working on it."

"So you haven't gotten anywhere with the owner."

"Rory Buchanan. Not yet."

"Have you even been over there to talk to the man?" Evangeline demanded.

"I'm taking care of it, trust me."

"I don't trust you and you've already wasted enough time." Evangeline had hoped that buying up land would keep her husband out of trouble. She should have known better.

A laugh floated up to the open window. Lady Monique Gray's flirting laugh.

"Is that who you've been with?" Evangeline demanded, wondering where the devil Laurencia had been since she had been ordered to keep the two apart at all costs.

"Monique isn't here because of me."

Evangeline didn't believe him for a moment. She rang for Laurencia but got no answer. "Did you happen to see Laurencia on your way in?"

"Laurencia?" There was contempt in his tone. "Sorry, my dear, it appears another of your schemes isn't working so well," Broderick noted with no small amount of scorn.

She shot him a murderous look before pushing past him to storm out of the room.

To DEVLIN'S RELIEF, the royal soldiers were simply riding the property as per orders by the head of security, Jules Armitage.

The lead soldier had recognized Devlin as one of the grooms and apparently the group hadn't seen Rory. Devlin had stepped out of the trees to meet them, hoping to give her a chance to get away.

And she had gotten away.

Again.

But at least now he had a first name. And the information from her horse blanket. Her quick escape had him all the more curious about her. She didn't act like a woman who had nothing to hide.

As soon as everyone cleared out of the stables, Devlin used the phone to call the town of Whitehorse. The small Western town was just down the road.

It took several calls to find out who kept records of winners from the annual Whitehorse Days rodeo. He was directed to one Miss Adele Brown.

After four rings, an elderly woman finally picked up the phone. "Hello?" She sounded ninety if a day.

"Adele Brown?"

Silence, then a weak, "Yes?"

"I recently moved to the area and I'm interested in finding out about Whitehorse Rodeo Days. In particular, I'm trying to find out about your former All-around Best Cowgirl winners. I was hoping you could help me."

"I suppose so. I could tell you weren't from around here," she said with a chuckle. "If you tell me the year, I'm sure I can tell you who won All-around Best Cowgirl."

He breathed a sigh of relief. This had proved to be easier than he'd thought. "It would have been 1997. I have her first name. Rory."

"Oh." He could almost hear her purse her lips. "I was afraid of that."

"Excuse me?"

"You weren't around so you wouldn't know about our office burning down in 1999," Adele Brown said. "It was one heck of a fire. The fire marshal suspected it was arson, and land sake's, it was. The entire county was shocked when they heard who had started the fire. Misty Justin from up by Stinky Creek. Seems she was mad because she lost. Can you believe that?"

"So what you're saying is…" He'd jumped in at the first opening.

"Everything burned up. Records and all. I can probably give it some thought, ask around and come up with a name if I put my mind to it over the next few days. But the name Rory doesn't ring any bells at the moment. Must not be from Whitehorse, and right now I've got cinnamon rolls cooking in the oven that I have to see to."

Before he could tell her that he might not have a few days, Adele hung up.

CHAPTER SEVEN

As Rory rode up to her ranch house, she spotted a large dark car waiting for her out front. Was it possible the groom had already found her?

No, she was willing to bet it was about buying her ranch. She thought of her cut fence and reined in her horse, wishing she could rein in her temper as easily.

Sliding out of the saddle, she walked her horse slowly toward the waiting car and the confrontation she knew was coming.

As a man emerged from the backseat of the car she saw from the way he was dressed that he was from the royal family next door. The dark three-piece suit was a dead giveaway. Only undertakers and lawyers wore suits in this part of Montana.

"Is Rory Buchanan available?" the man asked in that now familiar foreign accent. "I would like to speak with him on a matter of shared importance."

She smiled, amused, although it wasn't the first time someone had thought Rory was a male name. "*I'm* Rory Buchanan."

The man's gaze widened only slightly. "I see."

She figured he did as she put her hands on her hips, knowing what was coming next.

"Prince Broderick Windham," he said with a slight bow. "I have come in the name of Her Royal Highness Princess Evangeline Wycliffe Windham to make an offer on your property," he said, pulling out a long white envelope from his breast pocket beneath his coat. He held the envelope out, but she didn't move to take it.

"My ranch isn't for sale," Rory said calmly, not in the least impressed that the prince had come himself to make the offer. "I believe I've made that perfectly clear. So you can stop cutting my fence because it isn't going to make me change my mind. All it's going to do is make me madder."

The man frowned, looking confused. "I wouldn't know anything about your fence."

She almost believed him. "Right." She turned to lead her horse toward the corral.

"You might want to take a look at the offer," he said behind her.

She turned back to him. "I said no. And I mean *no*."

"We both know you'll sell eventually. It would be in your best interest to sell now," he said biting off each word.

Rory's gaze drilled the man. "That almost sounded like a threat." She caught the smell of alcohol and something sweet like perfume.

The prince sighed. "The Princess, the only daughter of King Roland Wycliffe, wants your property. We can save ourselves a lot of trouble if we settle this now. Just tell me how much you want." He pulled out a checkbook and pen and looked up at her expectantly.

Jamming her hands on her hips again, she stared at him in disbelief. "How many times am I going to have to say this? My land isn't for sale at *any* price."

"I don't think you understand—"

"Oh, I understand. But I'm not selling. Especially to your princess. I don't like the way you do business. I don't like you buying up Montana. I wouldn't sell to you if I didn't have a dime and was starving to death. And tell your Royal Highness for me that if any more of my fence gets cut I'm not going to call the sheriff. I'm going to come over there personally."

The prince smiled as he knew what a waste of time that would be for her. He slowly put the pen and checkbook away. Clearly, he didn't see her as much of a threat.

"I'm sorry you feel that way," he said smoothly, "but I can assure you Her Royal Highness had nothing to do with the cutting of your fence. Perhaps someone has played a joke on you."

"Some joke. I think you'd better leave now."

He met her gaze. "I do hate to see you make a mistake you will regret."

Her eyes narrowed at the implied threat. The second within minutes. She thought about the shotgun just inside the back door of the house. Probably not a good idea.

"If you come here again," she said not mincing her words, "it will be *your* mistake. I'll call the sheriff on you." Like that would help. Since the sheriff was out of town. With her luck, Griff would come out again.

"Good day, then," the prince said as he turned and climbed back into his big black car with the dark tinted windows. The engine revved and the driver turned the car around.

Rory watched until it left her property and tried to calm down. It took all her self control not to get back on her horse and ride over to her neighbor's and demand to see the princess herself.

But Rory was certain someone would call the sheriff's department before she got near Her Royal Highness. And knowing Griff, she'd be the one to end up behind bars.

DEVLIN HAD THE strangest feeling that someone was watching him as he hung up the stables phone after calling Adele Brown about Whitehorse Days. He'd unsaddled his horse as soon as he had returned to the stables. By now, he'd hoped to have the full name of the woman.

What he planned to do with it, he had no idea. After meeting her—and kissing her—did he still believe she had something to do with his being lured into the woods last night?

He knew he was in jeopardy the longer he stayed there. As Nicholas had said, clearly someone there knew who he was and why he'd come to Montana.

The stables seemed eerily quiet. It was late enough that no one was around. Or at least he'd thought that was true. Dust hung in the air along with the scent of horseflesh and oats.

He turned at a scurrying sound in time to see one of the house servants slipping past. Had she been eavesdropping on his conversation? Gossip was a pastime among the servants and grooms, he knew only too well. But if this information got back to the wrong person…

Devlin took off after her. The woman appeared headed for the grooms' cottages. Servants were forbidden to fraternize with the grooms and trainers, which would explain why she appeared to be sneaking along the side of the stables.

As she reached the end of the building, Devlin came around the corner, making her jump back in surprise at the sight of him.

She was much older than he'd first thought. As she raised her head, he saw her face. "Anna?" His mother's friend and housemaid.

She glanced around as if afraid of who might be

lurking in the dark. "I shouldn't have come." She took a step back, her face a mask of terror.

Nicholas had sent her, just as he'd said he would.

"I must speak with you. No one will know," Devlin assured her as he took her arm and drew her into the shadows.

"I can't be seen with you," she whispered, sounding close to tears.

"You found my mother the night she was murdered," he said, keeping his voice low and watching the shadows for any sign they weren't alone. "I have heard that the person who killed her wore the colors of the crown. Is this so?"

She gave a quick, frightened nod. Tears welled in her eyes. "Your mother was kind and good."

"Yes," Devlin agreed. That's why her murder was such a mystery. Clare Barrow had worked with nobles all her life, teaching them and their children and grandchildren to ride horses, boarding their horses, training their horses, pampering both.

She wasn't the kind of woman who made enemies. Everyone loved her. She was beautiful in so many ways.

Devlin had always wished he'd been more like her instead of like the father he'd never known. His mother had raised him alone from birth. His father, Leonard Barrow, had been killed in an accident shortly after he'd married Clare. Leonard had never even known about his wife's pregnancy.

Devlin could only assume he'd gotten his impatience, his intolerance for most of the rich and privileged and his temper from his father. All these years he'd tried to be more like his mother, but he'd failed miserably.

Maybe that was one reason he refused to take the royal government's word that his mother had been killed by a stranger, a beggar who'd been passing through town even though Devlin's mother's stolen brooch had been found on the poor man.

If a beggar had come to the door, his mother would have offered him food and shelter. But not the brooch his father had given her on their wedding night.

Devlin suspected that the brooch had been put on the poor beggar so that Clare Barrow's murder would appear solved. Add to that Anna Pickering's disappearance shortly after she discovered the body—and the rumor that a man dressed in the colors of the crown had been seen running from the house.

"I have heard that she was still alive when you found her. Did she tell you who killed her? Is that why you're so frightened? Why you left and came to the States?"

Anna shook her head.

"But you must know something. Please help me. I have to know the truth." He saw compassion fill her lined face.

"The princess," she answered in a sob-choked whisper. "She has the papers. She knows your mother's secret."

"What papers?" His mother had never kept anything from him. Or had she?

"You are not safe here and if I am seen with you…" Anna pulled away to leave.

"Where are these papers?"

Anna hesitated. He could see that she wanted to help him but she was afraid for them both. "In the locked bottom drawer of her desk in her suite. But if you try to get them, you will be killed. Please, I must go."

Devlin felt her shudder just before she broke free of him to escape and head back toward the palace.

It was all he could do not to go after her. But he

knew she was right. They must not be seen together. He had already jeopardized the woman's life by coming to Montana. If anyone had seen them talking...

Devlin leaned back against the wall of the stables, heart in his throat, and tried to make sense of what Anna had told him.

Princess Evangeline had papers that exposed some secret of his mother's? A secret that got his mother murdered.

Devlin glanced toward the palace and considered how he was going to get into a locked drawer in the princess's suite in a palace full of guards.

JULES ARMITAGE DROVE to the small western town of Whitehorse, Montana, to talk to Adele Brown that evening. For all the good it did. A fire had destroyed all the records?

"You didn't back up the results on a computer disk?" Jules demanded. He had thought his home country was backward. But then he'd never been to Montana before. "Someone else must have kept records."

Adele shook her head. "What would be the point?" She was a tiny gray-haired woman with sparkling blue eyes and dimples and the habit of smiling a lot. If her cheerfulness wasn't bad enough, the woman was completely disorganized. Her desk was covered in papers stacked so high, he could barely see her over the top.

"The point would be... Never mind." He had to bite his tongue since obviously the point would be that she would still have the records, she would be able to give him a name and he would be out of there.

"Funny, though," Adele said with a chuckle. "Wonder what it was about that year and that title."

He had to ask. "I beg your pardon?"

"You're the second person to ask about that particular winner," she said. "I can't remember the last time anyone asked. Around here, people only care about the year they or someone in their family won and they aren't likely to forget it, so…"

"I get the picture," Jules said irritably. "About this other person who was inquiring—"

"Like I told him, I'll remember who won that year. Sooner or later," Adele said optimistically.

"Did this other person give you his name?"

"Nope. I just assumed you knew each other since you both have the same accent."

Jules blinked. "Did the person leave a number for when you did remember?"

"Caller ID. I got it right here." She dug through the piles on her desk and came up with the number surprisingly fast, all things considered.

"Recognize it?" Adele asked as she copied it down for him on a scrap of paper.

"No, but apparently we're on the same mission." Jules waited until he got outside before he used his cell phone to dial the number she'd given him.

The line rang four times before a young male voice answered.

"Who is this?" Jules demanded.

Silence, then a timid, "Dunhaven."

Dunhaven? One of the grooms?

"Where have I reached?"

"Uh, the stables at Stanwood."

The stables. Jules clicked his cell phone shut and frowned. Devlin Barrow could have made the call. But why would he be searching for the owner of the horse blanket?

After what Jules had discovered in that horrible shack, wouldn't it seem likely that Devlin had known the woman in question?

RORY WAS MENTALLY kicking herself for calling the sheriff's department. She'd already mended the darned fence and after her talk with Prince Broderick Windham, she had her doubts anything would dissuade the princess. So what was the point except to have the vandalism on record?

She dialed Georgia as she waited for a deputy to come out, wanting her friend to assure her she'd done the right thing.

"A man came into the shop a little while ago asking about you," Georgia told her. "He had a European accent and he wanted to know all about you and your family."

"You didn't tell him anything?"

"Of course not. But after he left he went across the street to Janis Ames's beauty shop and you know he got an earful. He knows you're out there alone."

Rory asked what the man looked like and the car he was in. "Prince Broderick Windham."

"He was a *prince?*" Georgia cried, sounding impressed.

"Georgia!"

"It's just that I've never seen a real live prince before. Especially one that good-looking."

Rory groaned. "Hello? The man is only a prince because he married the princess and he's trying to force me off my ranch. He made it clear that the princess gets whatever she wants."

"If it makes you feel any better, I heard around town that the princess's husband is a rake." Georgia read too many Regency novels. "His noble blood is very watered down. Anyway, they can't *make* you sell. Have you told the sheriff that the man threatened you?"

"Actually, the sheriff's out of town and one of the deputies is coming up the road now. I'll talk to you later."

The minute Deputy Griffin Crowley got out of the car and Rory saw who it was, she knew this had been a mistake.

"What's this about some cut barbed wire?" he demanded.

Rory gritted her teeth. "This morning I found where my fence had been cut in two places and I just had a visit from a prince who threatened me if I don't sell."

Griff gave her a skeptical look. "Threatened what?"

"Said I was making a mistake I would regret and that the princess always gets what she wants." She saw at once that Griff wasn't going to take the threats seriously. She had to admit that they didn't sound as threatening when repeated.

"Yeah. Okay, let's go take a look at your cut fence," Griff said with little enthusiasm.

"I already fixed the fence. There were boot tracks, man-sized, in the dirt that led to that old mining road."

Griff had stopped and turned to look back at her, his gaze pinning her to the spot. "You already fixed the fence?"

"Yes, did you hear what I said about where the fence was cut? It's next to the princess's property."

The sheriff took off his Western hat and raked a hand through his hair before putting it back on his head again. "You aren't trying to tell me that this princess cut your barbed-wire fence."

"I doubt she did it herself," Rory snapped. "She has lots of people to do her dirty work. Georgia said the princess's husband, the prince, was in her shop asking about me and my ranch."

"There isn't any law against—"

"They're trying to run me off my ranch." Angry tears burned her eyes. She willed herself not to cry, but when she spoke, her voice broke. "You know this ranch has been in my family for more than a hundred years. I was born and raised here, my parents and sister are buried on the hill over there with the rest of my ancestors. This is my *home,* my *life.*" She swallowed, dangerously close to crying.

She would not be run off this ranch.

"You have any idea when the fence was cut?" he asked.

"The tracks looked fresh."

Griff kicked at a dirt clod with the toe of his boot as if avoiding her gaze.

"What?" she demanded. She and Griff went way back. And while it had been years since he'd put a frog down her shirt and rolled her in a snowdrift, she still knew him and knew this look.

He had the good grace to look uncomfortable. "Are you sure this isn't just a ruse, you know, a cry for help?"

"What?" He'd better not be saying what she thought he was saying.

"I mean is there any chance all this is just a ploy to get me to come out here?" He actually looked hopeful. "I did ask you to marry me and I thought maybe—"

"Stop!" She let out the breath she'd had trapped in her lungs, her blood pressure soaring. "If you're saying that you think I made up the story about the cut fence to get you out here—"

"I know how stubborn you are. If you changed your

mind about my proposal, you might be embarrassed to tell me."

She really could not believe this. "Griff, I called the sheriff's department because someone cut my damned fence, snooped around my place and threatened me." She had to bite her tongue to keep from telling him she'd been hoping it would be any deputy but him who responded.

"Okay." He raised both hands as if in surrender. "I'll take another look around."

She knew how much good that would do. Turning on her boot heel, she stalked to the house, slamming the front door behind her for good measure, too furious to deal with Deputy Griffin Crowley right then.

Through the window, she watched him look around the yard half-heartedly until she couldn't stand it anymore and went back outside.

He didn't seem to hear her as she approached. He was moving along the side of the house, his head down. He suddenly stopped next to her bedroom window to bend down to pick up something.

As he started to pocket whatever it was, she demanded, startling him, "What did you find?"

PRINCESS EVANGELINE HAD set her plan into motion and now she felt trepidation that this whole thing might blow up in her face.

She was taking a terrible risk. At worst, she could lose everything if her father found out what she'd been up to. At best, she could finally have the life she'd always dreamed of living.

As she stood at the window, surveying her domain, she realized, it wasn't enough. She'd built a replica of the palace back in her homeland, furnished it with the best that money could buy, indulged her every whim.

And still it wasn't enough.

Nothing seemed to satisfy this ache in her. Not food. Nor men. Nor possessions.

She told herself that once she gave birth to an heir to the throne, then she would have everything she wanted. Her father would finally see her value. And once Broderick was gone from her life, she could return home to take her place in society instead of being hidden away in this godforsaken place.

Scowling, she turned at the tentative knock on her door. "Come in," she said irritably, not surprised when Laurencia entered.

"I hope I'm not bothering you."

Sometimes Evangeline wanted to shake Laurencia until her teeth rattled in her head. The woman had no gumption, no backbone, no pride. What had ever made Evangeline think Broderick might be interested in the pathetic woman?

"Where have you been?" the princess asked impatiently. "Never mind." It was too late to do anything about Broderick and she wasn't in the mood for Laurencia's simpering.

"I just thought you'd like to know that Lady Monique sent me away, saying she needed to be alone, complaining of a headache."

Evangeline raised an eyebrow. So her husband hadn't been with Lady Monique after all. It must have been one of the servants. That would explain the cheap perfume.

"Prince Broderick left, saying he was going to buy that last piece of property as per your request."

Maybe Laurencia wasn't as big a fool as Evangeline

thought. She was keeping an eye on both the prince and Lady Monique.

"It won't be easy to keep the two apart until the ball," Evangeline said more to herself than her companion.

"It might be easier than you think. I believe that Lord Alexis's being here has dampened the fires of her lady's desire for anyone else." Laurencia smiled.

Monique and Alexis. "I thought he had cast her off?"

"Possibly it was the other way around," Laurencia said with a sly smile. "There seems to be some embers still burning there."

Evangeline couldn't help but smile. Still, though, she knew her husband. And the Black Widow. "You shall continue to keep a close eye on Lady Monique."

"Of course," Laurencia replied with a small, amused curtsey. "And Prince Broderick, as well."

DEPUTY GRIFFIN CROWLEY looked startled as he rose and turned around to face Rory. She'd seen him slip something into his pocket and now she saw his guilty expression and felt her heart take off at a gallop.

"What did you just find on the ground?" she demanded.

"Take it easy," Griff said as he slowly pulled a pair of wire cutters from his pocket.

Her pounding heart stuck in her throat. "You weren't going to tell me about finding those." It was an accusation, not a question.

"I was going to ask you if they were yours."

"You know they aren't mine. They belong to the person who cut my fence and now you've destroyed any chance of getting a clear fingerprint off them."

"This is why I wasn't going to show them to you," he said calmly. "In the first place, because of the type of

handle on these there is little chance of getting a fingerprint from them. Also they're a common type of wire
cutter sold at the local hardware store. Thirdly, even if
they were the ones used to cut your fence, there is no
proof of that. And what would be the point since you
apparently already know who cut your fence."

Rory didn't like his tone any more than she liked
his attitude. "What were you going to do with them?
Get rid of them so I wouldn't know you found them?"

"I didn't want to upset you any more than you obviously are since they don't prove anything."

"Except that someone has been snooping around my
house!" Flushed with anger, suddenly she felt herself
turn to ice as she saw where he'd found the wire cutters.
Right under her bedroom window. One of the limbs on
the bushes had been snapped off where someone had
stood next to the building.

Rory hugged herself as a shudder went through her.
Her bedroom curtains were gapped open. Just enough
that whoever had stood there could have looked through
the window...

When had the person dropped the wire cutters?
When had they been within yards of her house? Within
yards of her?

Anger warred with the cold tentacles of fear that had
wrapped around her heart.

"This is why I don't like you living out here alone,"
Griff said, pocketing the wire cutters again. "Rory, if
you would just let me—"

"What I need from you, Griff," she said biting off
each word, "is for you to stop my so-called royal neighbor from harassing me. Can you do that, Griff?" She
was scared and crying and that made her all the more
angry.

"Rory, for just once, can you stop being so strong and let someone take care of you?" He took a step toward her as if he meant to comfort her.

She stepped back. "I don't need anyone to take care of me." She wiped hastily at her tears.

"We all need someone, Rory."

"Not me." She swallowed and looked away, wishing it was true. The other night in the line shack had only made her more aware of the need deep inside her. Seeing Devlin again today, kissing him, had only made it worse.

She had missed the warmth of another person. Missed human touch. Missed the connection that went beyond mere sex. For that time in the shack during the storm, she'd been close to another person. And now she found herself aching for it again.

But those thoughts always involved dark blue eyes and a royal groom with a European accent.

Not Griff Crowley.

He stepped back, a pained look on his face.

She hadn't meant to hurt him. She pulled herself together. For weeks she'd told herself that if she could ride this out, her new royal neighbors would stop once they realized she really wasn't going to sell.

But that was before someone had taken an interest in more than her ranch. That was before Griff had found the wire cutters lying in the bushes under her bedroom window.

"You're a damned deputy sheriff. Can't you at least talk to the princess, warn her to leave me alone?"

"Rory—"

"You know who's doing this." Her voice broke. "If I'm right, this is just the beginning. When are you going to do something? When they burn down my house? Or worse?"

"Oh, for cryin' out loud, Rory," Griff snapped. "You're making too much of a couple snipped barbed wires. It was probably just kids messing around your place."

She stared at him, hearing the coldness in his voice, the anger.

"Maybe if you took all the offers on your place to the judge, he might think they constitute harassment. Without proof these people are threatening you, Rory, my hands are tied."

But hers weren't, she thought as she looked into the distance, where she could make out a portion of a royal roofline gleaming in the sun.

And it sure as the devil beat sitting around waiting for someone to save her since her life was visibly short of heroes.

DEVLIN WAS IN the stables when Lord Nicholas Ashford found him.

"Let's take a ride," Nicholas suggested. "I need help on my cantering."

Devlin quickly saddled both horses, knowing that something must have happened and that was why Nicholas was providing them with an opportunity to be alone and talk.

It was dangerous, though. As head of security, Jules Armitage would find out. He was already suspicious of Devlin.

But nothing could have stopped Devlin from taking the ride with his friend. Whatever was wrong, Nicholas thought he needed to know about it—and at once.

They rode out across the wide pasture, the tall golden

grasses swaying in the breeze in contrast to the fringe of deep dark pines in the distance. Overhead the sky arched from horizon to horizon, a blinding blue dotted with white cumulus clouds.

But it was the air that Devlin had come to appreciate in this strange country. So clear and crisp. He understood why Montana had been called God's country. It was as close to Eden as a man could get.

Unless, of course, the man was there for deceitful purposes and living in a viper's den.

"I saw Anna," Nicholas said as soon as they were out of earshot. "She told me she talked to you. The woman is petrified that she'll be found out. If she's caught, she'll break down. I thought I'd better warn you."

"I can understand her fear," Devlin said, drawing up his horse the moment they couldn't be seen from Stanwood. "I wish there was some way to get her out of Stanwood."

"Believe me, that would only draw attention to you," Nicholas said. "Someone already knows who you are and why you're here. Or at least suspects why you're here."

"Did Anna tell you what she told me?" Devlin asked.

Nicholas shot him a look. "Nobility such as myself? Not likely. She doesn't trust anyone. I'm surprised she came down to the stables. She wanted nothing to do with me. Which just shows she has good taste."

"I need to get into Stanwood proper."

"Of course. I could probably get you in for drinks again, if you're willing to get drugged again."

"Thanks, but I'll pass. No, what I need is the run of the second floor royal wing."

Nicholas looked at him as if he'd lost his mind. "Well, hell, I'll just ask Evangeline to give you your own key."

Aspen leaves rustled gently over their heads. "I have a plan."

"I was afraid you were going to say that."

"But I'll need your help."

His friend smiled. "You're determined to get us both killed, aren't you? So what do you need me to do?"

"It will be risky."

Nicholas laughed. "I would have been disappointed if it was otherwise."

"I need to get into Lady Evangeline's quarters."

Nicholas looked skeptical. "I can't even get you up on the second floor, let alone into the princess's quarters."

"Are there guards?"

"Two posted at the entrance to the royal wing. But even if there weren't guards, you'd be spotted immediately unless…"

"Unless I was wearing the same costume as someone who actually lived on the royal wing," Devlin suggested.

Nicholas smiled. "You *are* the same size as Broderick…"

"I'll just need a costume exactly like his."

His friend was nodding. "I think I can see to that since the princess has hired an in-house seamstress to make our costumes and asked for two of each in case anyone has a spill. There is nothing like royalty." He grinned.

"I assumed she would have the costumes made in-house so there was no chance of seeing anyone else in a costume like her own."

Nicholas nodded. "Ah, vanity. Anything else?"

"I might need a distraction to get upstairs."

"Now that is something I can definitely handle," he

said with a laugh. "Leave it to me." He sobered. "You do realize that if you're caught up there…"

"Don't worry. I'll wing it."

"That is what worries me."

"GRIFF IS SUCH A JACKASS," Georgia cried when Rory called her and told her what he'd said about her alleged cut fence being nothing more than an excuse to see him.

"Tell me you didn't do anything that got you arrested," her friend said. "You aren't calling for bail, are you?"

"No, but it was all I could do not to deck him." Rory walked around the ranch house with the phone to her ear, still angry and frustrated. "I might have threatened to get my shotgun and shoot him."

Georgia groaned. "You told him who you suspected?"

Rory heard the misgiving in her friend's voice. "*I* know it sounds crazy. But who else has anything to gain by cutting my fence?"

"You can't think of anyone else you've ticked off lately?" Georgia asked only half joking. "Bryce isn't back in town, is he?"

Her former fiancé? She certainly hoped not. "You know I thought Griff couldn't shock me any more after he asked me to marry him. But suggesting I cut my fence to give me an excuse to see him? Did I tell you he found a pair of wire cutters under my bedroom window?"

"Rory, that's frightening. That means whoever cut your fence—"

"Came up to my house, possibly looking in my window. Griff says it was probably just kids messing around."

"You're kidding? Well, I hope he plans to do something about it."

Rory sighed. "He says his hands are tied without evidence."

"What about the wire cutters?"

"Apparently they're a common variety that anyone could have purchased at the local hardware store."

"What about fingerprints?" Georgia asked.

Rory loved her for asking. They were both big fans of mystery novels and movies. "Griff says the handles wouldn't hold prints. He said he'd check, when I insisted. But as he pointed out, even if he found the prince's fingerprints on the wire cutters, it doesn't prove he cut my fence or that he was trying to force me to sell my ranch to him."

"But it would prove that he was on your property," Georgia said. "Oh, honey, I'm so sorry. Griff still doesn't think the answer is for you to marry him, does he?"

"He did. But, no, I think he's finally gotten the message," she said, remembering the ice she'd heard in his voice as well as the anger.

"So what are you going to do now?"

"I don't know." Rory feared the vandalism would escalate if she didn't sell to the prince and she wasn't about to call the sheriff's department again.

She would have to take care of it herself and said as much to her friend.

"Ah, I'm not sure that's a good idea, kiddo," Georgia said. "If you're right, messing with this bunch would be dangerous. Have you seen this princess who wants your property so badly?"

"Are you kidding? That place is an armed fortress."

"You aren't thinking about going over there again,

are you? I mean after what happened the first time…
Maybe you should come stay with me for a while," Georgia suggested.

"I will not be run off my own ranch."

"How did I know you were going to say that?" Georgia laughed. "Promise me you won't do anything…"

"Stupid?"

"I was going to say crazy."

"You know me so well."

"Actually… Have you checked your mail yet today?"

"Why?" Rory asked.

"I've heard some people are getting invitations to a masked ball at Stanwood on Saturday night," Georgia said.

"Believe me, I'm not invited."

"I guess not. But if you could get your hands on one of the invitations, maybe you could meet this princess and explain why you're not willing to sell your ranch. On second thought—"

"No, this is good. A masked ball? It's perfect. Meeting this princess wouldn't do any good, trust me. But Griff said if I had copies of all the offers, I might be able to prove harassment."

"Let me guess, you threw all of yours away?"

"If I could find copies, I could take them to Judge Randall…"

"Why do I not like the sound of this?" Georgia joked.

"Any ideas how I could get my hands on an invitation?" Rory asked.

She heard her friend hesitate. "If the royal couple had the invitations printed down at Harper's Print Shop here in town… Even with an invitation, you'll need a costume and I've heard that there are none to be had in the entire county at this late date, but I might be able to scare up something. As for finding your way around Stanwood, I would imagine the plans for the place are on file at Whitehorse Construction."

"The company where your sister Sara works?" Rory asked with a laugh. "I knew you'd help me," she said, feeling close to tears again. "I owe you."

She'd just have to make sure she didn't run into her groom, Devlin Barrow, on the grounds the night of the ball. Fortunately, a groom wouldn't be invited to the ball so she didn't have to worry once she got inside Stanwood.

Meanwhile, she thought, as she studied the darkening sky outside the window, she intended to lock her doors and keep the shotgun by the back door handy—just in case anyone came snooping around again.

CHAPTER EIGHT

THE NIGHT OF the Stanwood ball a huge harvest moon hung over the tops of the pines, spilling shimmering silver rays over the palace.

Millions of tiny lights glittered throughout the grounds. White carriages and the finest horses had been sent down to the parking area on the county road to collect the guests.

Princess Evangeline had sent out several hundred invitations to what she hoped would constitute Montana royalty.

"I want to share Stanwood with them for a night," she'd told Broderick when she'd announced she was hosting a masquerade ball.

He'd laughed pitifully at her. "You are so transparent, Evangeline. You know that few of them have ever seen a princess. You just want to show off."

She'd been instantly angered at his response. Probably because it was partly true. She knew rumors had been running wild about what a bitch she was because of the way she handled people during the building of Stanwood. She planned to squelch those rumors tonight. Everyone would see her at her best.

Broderick, meanwhile, would try to see Lady Monique before the ball when everyone was busy—especially his wife. But Evangeline had foreseen this. Just as she had kept her husband busy since Monique's arrival.

For her plan to work, Broderick had to be desperate for his precious Black Widow. The drug Evangeline would put in his drink later would make this ball the success she was determined it would be.

As she watched her husband dress for the event she told herself that before this night was over, he would regret everything he'd ever said or done to her. She would make sure of that.

"This ball was the best idea I've ever had," she said.

Broderick lifted an eyebrow. "Or your worse mistake yet. Worse than coming to this godforsaken place."

"We are only here because you are a contemptible, lying bastard," she said glaring at him. She couldn't have hated him more than at that moment.

"That is why you and I are so perfectly matched," he said as he slid his mask into place, brushing a kiss across her cheek as he passed her on his way to the door.

"Before you leave, would you mind helping me with this zipper?" she asked as she reached for her costume. Not the one she would don later. That costume was hidden until the appropriate time.

"Where is your precious Laurencia?" Broderick asked, sounding annoyed. "I thought she saw to these matters."

"Lady Monique asked for her help dressing," Evangeline said, turning her back to her husband so he couldn't see her face. Or her his. She wasn't sure she could constrain herself if she saw the disappointment in her husband's face that Monique was otherwise involved.

"I thought that's why we had servants," he snapped. "It's bad enough you treat Lady Laurencia like your handmaid…"

"Since when do you care how I treat Laurencia?" she demanded as she waited for him to zip her.

"Evangeline," he said softly behind her, making her heart quiver. She hadn't heard him use that tone with her since before they'd married, back when he was trying to win her over. "When will you learn?"

He zipped the costume, his fingers brushing the tender flesh at the nape of her neck. She felt herself trembling. Worse, she felt herself weaken toward him, yearning for that tender tone, that tender touch.

"I need a drink," Broderick said, pulling away again as if he feared letting himself be drawn to her. He left, slamming the door behind him.

Evangeline brushed at her tears, straightened and thought of Broderick's funeral, the condolences and sympathy she would receive after the horrendous death of her beloved husband. That day couldn't come soon enough.

It would be all the more touching since she would be carrying the heir to the throne.

RORY BUCHANAN SHIVERED as she slid from her horse. She could see Stanwood through the pines and catch snatches of melody on the light breeze.

It took her only a few minutes to change into the costume Georgia had found for her—the last costume to be had in the county.

"It's not ideal, but it will hide your hair and, hey, how often do you get to wear a dress?" Georgia said, obviously seeing more humor in this than Rory.

"You don't really think I can ride a horse in that, do you?" Rory had exclaimed.

"So you ride over, change in the woods. Trust me, no one will recognize you in this costume. That's what you wanted, right?"

Rory pulled on the black wig. She'd braided her

chestnut locks so they would be easy to push up under the wig. Taking a deep breath, she straightened her dress and slipped on the mask. Now that she was there, she couldn't help being a little anxious.

She tied her horse, promising to return soon, and headed toward the back of the palace. She'd anticipated that there might be guards, but she didn't see any. To her relief she saw that costumed guests swarmed over an outside terrace. Music spilled out from the open French doors.

Rory studied the crowd milling on the terrace, half afraid she would see Devlin. But after the last time... She hated to think what the soldiers had wanted with him.

She wished she could forget him, but how could she forget the feel of his mouth on hers or the warmth of his body pressed to hers or the way he looked at her with those oh-so-blue eyes?

Her temperature rose a few degrees at just the memory. She fanned herself as she slipped up the stairs to the terrace and was instantly swallowed up in the crowd and the excitement in the air.

Rory moved cautiously toward the doors of Stanwood, expecting someone would stop her and demand to see her invitation. She'd hoped that by coming later as she had that she could go unnoticed.

As she slipped through the door, eyes wide at just the sight of the lavish costumes, decorations, furnishings, her heart pounded. As impossible as it seemed, the place appeared larger inside than it had even from the outside. She couldn't help but feel that she'd just stepped into a fairyland, where anything could happen.

The jewels alone were blinding, not to mention the extraordinary costumes. She felt like Cinderella *before* the ball in the understated costume and ballet slippers. She'd known better than to even consider high heels.

Griffin's description of her bit into her conscience as she watched women dressed in gorgeous costumes dance with handsomely attired men in a huge ballroom.

It made her think of being in the groom's arms, that feeling she'd had of being safe, being cared for, being a woman.

She swatted the thought away, annoyed with herself. "Excuse me."

Rory froze at the sound of the voice beside her. Slowly she turned to find a waiter holding a silver tray filled with champagne glasses.

He thrust the tray toward her. "Champagne?"

She took one of the fragile stemmed glasses, concentrating on not spilling the bubbly liquid since her hands were trembling with nerves.

The stiff costume made her squirm beneath the starched fabric and the black wig was hot. She should have gone with her first instinct and come as Calamity Jane, the infamous woman outlaw.

But then, as Georgia had pointed out, everyone who knew her would have recognized her.

The ballroom was full, spilling over onto terraces from French doors that circled the massive room. She recognized people she knew drinking champagne and visiting with what had to be some of the royalty given the costumes and the weighty jewels that glittered under the crystal chandeliers.

Across the room, she spotted a wide staircase that wound up to the second floor. Near the top, she saw two guards standing at the entrance to a hallway that led to the south wing. Rory noted that the other hallway entrance had no guards.

She took a sip of the champagne, the bubbles tickling her nose, and she slipped deeper into the crowd as she debated how to get on that wing, which, according to the information Georgia had gotten for her, held not only the princess's suite, but some huge antique desk that had taken six men to carry up the stairs.

It was in that desk that Rory hoped she'd find what she was looking for.

DEVLIN BARROW MOVED along the edge of the ballroom that now swam in a sea of brightly colored masks and costumes. There was an air of anticipation mixed in with the orchestra music, the oceanlike roar of voices and the rattle of champagne glasses and silver trays as servants moved among the masses.

All of it turned Devlin's stomach as he watched the opulent extravagance in the name of royalty. He spotted Prince Broderick across the room, talking with Lady Monique and Lord Nicholas. None of the three looked in his direction but he saw Nicholas glance at his watch.

Devlin moved toward the bottom of the staircase and checked his own watch. Only three more minutes before—

He plowed into one of the guests, felt the slosh of icy champagne spill over his arm as he clutched the guest's arm to steady them both as they passed.

Devlin was only vaguely aware that the person he'd collided with was female. His fingers slid over the silken fabric of her sleeve as she slipped past him, both of them moving in opposite directions, neither apparently watching where they were going.

"Sorry," they both said at the same time. At the sound of her voice, his gaze leaped to hers and locked as she slid past, her head turning to look back at him.

Her green eyes wide with surprise.

Devlin felt as if he'd been jabbed with a cattle prod. He stumbled to a stop as the crowd filled in behind her. He would know those eyes anywhere.

In that instant, he'd seen something else in those green eyes. Not only had *he* known *her,* she had recognized him!

Rory! But what was she doing there? His heart began to pound at just the sight of her. It brought to mind the flickering light of the storm, those beautiful unusual green eyes and their lovemaking.

Not to mention the fact that now this woman was here and had recognized him. If he was wrong about her...

Devlin changed directions, fighting the swarm of party-goers, as he started after her. Rory was moving fast, winding her way through the crowd, heading for one of the terrace doors. Once she was through it and out in the night, she would be gone.

He couldn't let her get away. Not again.

HEART POUNDING, RORY BOUND through the open terrace doors, pausing to look back, afraid Devlin would come after her.

She told herself she'd overreacted. That couldn't have been the groom from the night of the storm. The man with the dark blue eyes she'd just collided with had been wearing the colors of royalty. Rory was certain no mere groom would have been invited to this ball.

But then she hadn't been invited either, and she was here. And there was no denying the way those blue eyes had looked at her. Had recognized her.

Her heart drummed, her skin rippling with memory of the man's touch, his voice.

"My fair forest sprite. You have bewitched me."

Words whispered into the hollow of her throat as his warm mouth moved over her skin.

She looked back and felt a shiver as she caught sight of him in the throng. Their gazes locked across the crowded room. His expression alone sent another shiver through her. There was both challenge and promise in his eyes. It left no doubt. He had recognized her.

And he was more than wondering what she was doing here.

She could have asked him the same question, given the way he was dressed.

He gave her a slight nod of his head, his eyes never leaving hers. She felt confusion and fear. What was he doing at the ball dressed as if he were royalty?

She couldn't move, couldn't breathe. Music, voices and laughter rode as one on the night air. Closer, there came a high-pitched *clink* as someone tapped a piece of silverware on one of the champagne glasses, trying to get the crowd's attention.

As the crowd all turned, Rory spotted Deputy Griffin Crowley. He wore his uniform and a thin black mask. He was looking around, frowning, almost as if he'd glimpsed her in the crowd.

Rory found her feet and fled.

DEVLIN HAD GONE AFTER HER but after a few steps had been impeded by the crowd. He saw that he would never be able to catch her without drawing attention to them both.

He swore under his breath, furious that he'd actually had her in his grasp, only to lose her again. He could only watch with frustration as Snow White disappeared through the French doors and into the night.

It took all his control not to say to hell with everything and chase after her.

A sound drew him back to the ballroom.

"May I have your attention please," Lord Nicholas Ashford called out over the crowd as he tapped a piece of fine silverware to his champagne crystal. "Your attention, please."

The crowd began to quiet, heads turning to see why the music had stopped, why one of the royal guests was standing on the bandstand at the end of the great hall and addressing them.

Forcing away thoughts of the green-eyed woman, Devlin quickly turned toward the stairs at the opposite end of the great hall. He should have been closer, but he'd lost valuable time going after Rory even as far as he had.

Now he might miss his chance to get on the royal wing, miss the chance to find the papers Anna had told him about that somehow involved the murder of his mother.

And yet the memory of those green eyes followed him like a sweet, seductive perfume. How he wanted to chase after her. The fact that she was here made him suspicious of her again. After the kiss he'd been so sure she'd been telling him the truth…

He forced her from his thoughts. Tonight was his only chance of getting upstairs. He had only a limited amount of time to get onto the royal wing, get into Evangeline's suite and find the papers.

He continued to move toward the stairs, weaving his way through the guests as everyone's eyes were on the bandstand and the handsome man before them. Someone handed Lord Ashford a microphone.

"If I may have your attention," he said into it. Expectation fell over the crowd as Devlin slipped to the bottom of the stairs.

"If Lady Gray would please join me," Nicholas said. There was a murmur of surprise, then a stirring as the Black Widow made her way to him.

Devlin caught sight of Lady Monique's intrigued expression as she joined Lord Ashford. Devlin started up the stairs, moving as if he knew where he was going, belonged there, had maybe forgotten something from his room.

"Lady Gray and I are going to sing a duet in honor of Princess Evangeline and Prince Broderick on this wonderful occasion," Nicholas announced as he took Monique's hand and smiled at her.

At the top of the stairs, Devlin glanced back. All eyes were on the two on stage as the orchestra struck up a tune and Nicholas moved closer to share his microphone with Lady Monique. Devlin could see Prince Broderick at the edge of the stage. The lord prince didn't look happy. Nor did he look as if he would be going anywhere until the two were off the stage.

Devlin walked with his head down as if his mind were on something else as he headed for the royal wing. Nicholas had given him directions to Lady Evangeline's suite and taken the dangerous risk of getting him a pass key from the laundry servant's quarters.

From out of the corner of his eye, Devlin saw both guards look in his direction. He muttered under his breath, staggered a little as if already drunk and walked past them without a look or a word.

His heart was pounding in his ears so loudly that he feared he wouldn't hear them if they called after him. He didn't dare look back.

At the door to the Princess's suite, he stopped. Out

of the corner of his eye, he could see both guards at their stations down the hall. Neither was looking in this direction.

With shaking fingers he pulled out the key and opened the door to the suite and hurriedly stepped inside.

RORY WAS STILL SHAKEN after seeing the groom at the ball—dressed as a royal—and Griff. Unlike her, the deputy had probably been invited.

Devlin had seen her and started to come after her, but seemed to change his mind. She'd seen the anger and frustration in his expression. He'd wanted to chase after her but something had held him back. The same thing that had kept him from calling to a guard to stop her?

Which made her think that, as she'd suspected, he didn't belong at the ball any more than she did.

Interesting, she thought as she circled around the palace and tried to decide what to do next. She stopped under some shrubbery, chastising herself for being so foolish as to come here tonight in the first place.

Getting into the ball had been easier than she'd hoped. So had mingling among the many guests. But getting upstairs to this massive desk was a much bigger problem than she'd thought it would be. She'd seen herself having a run of the palace simply because she was in costume.

Discouraged, she glanced upward. According to the plans Georgia had gotten her, the princess's suite should be directly—

Rory started at the sight of a strange light flickering in what was one of the rooms in the royal suite.

She moved to get a better look. The drapes were drawn, but through a space between them, she could see movement. It appeared someone dressed identically to her groom was in the room above her just beyond the parted curtains.

What was he doing in the princess's rooms? Or was that Prince Broderick dressed in the same costume? But if it was the prince, why was the man sneaking around with a small flashlight?

It had to be her groom. But what was Devlin doing in the same room Rory herself had hoped to get into? Apparently they had more in common than she'd first thought.

She watched him. He seemed to be looking for something.

Her gaze took in a second set of French doors that led to the wide balcony, the drapes on its doors drawn. She let her gaze fall from the balcony down the lattice trellis to a small stone wall a few yards in front of her.

As a tomboy, she'd climbed her share of trees. It had been awhile, but she hoped now that it was a lot like riding a bike.

Cursing her costume under her breath, she considered taking the time to go back to her horse and change clothes since she had no reason to return to the ball—especially after seeing Griff in there.

Deciding it would take too long, she crossed to the stone wall, hiked up her dress and swung up to grab hold of the trellis, praying it would hold her weight as she began to climb.

DEVLIN COULDN'T HAVE missed the desk—even in the dark. It was huge and took up most of the room just off the balcony.

Using the penlight, he moved to it, noticing a second set of French doors that he assumed also exited to the balcony.

He knew he had to move fast. He was counting on both the prince and princess to remain downstairs at least until Nicholas and Monique finished their songs since Nicholas planned to make the most of it.

The bottom drawer was locked—just as Anna had told him it would be. Taking out the small tool he'd brought, he carefully pried the lock until it broke. Quietly, he opened the drawer.

He had no idea what these so-called papers looked like, not to mention the underlying fear that Anna might have been mistaken. Or that the princess had moved them.

Devlin tried not to think about any of that as he hurriedly went through the drawer. He worried about making too much noise even though the guards were stationed at the other end of the hall and the noise from the party should mask any sounds he made.

Still, he felt exposed being in the princess's quarters. He might be in America, but he was a foreigner. If caught, he would be sent back to his home country. His punishment could be worse than death if he was seen as a traitor, or worse, a terrorist.

He knew that Princess Evangeline could be excessively cruel and, as the only child of the king, was given anything she wanted. She'd want his head if she caught him breaking into what was obviously an antique.

The manila envelope was at the very bottom of the drawer, tucked under some writing stationery. As he pulled it out he saw the government stamp. There was no address. His fingers trembled as he flipped the flap and pulled out the sheets inside.

The papers crinkled in his tense fingers as he saw the royal crest on the familiar document—and his name.

His birth certificate? Why would Princess Evangeline have his birth certificate?

His hands began to shake and he had to put the paper down on the desk to read it, fighting to focus the slight beam of the penlight on the words.

Confusion made the words blur. He'd come up here expecting to find something about his mother's murder.

As the words on the document came into focus, he felt his pulse jump. *What?* That wasn't right. He dropped the penlight.

His heart drummed in his ears and he felt his blood rush from his head. He slumped into the chair, as he snatched up the penlight to read the document again. It had to be a lie. These documents had to have been forged. But why?

Otherwise... Otherwise, he realized with a shock he held the reason for his mother's death in his hands.

His mother. If this was true, then she had lied to him. His father hadn't died before Devlin was born. His father was *alive.*

He heard a sound behind him and instinctively turned off the penlight. The chair under him creaked as he turned his head to look toward the French doors from the balcony, half expecting to find a royal guard with a weapon coming through them.

For the first time, he saw that the thick dark drapes weren't closed all the way. Through the narrow strip between them, he could make out the balcony and past that the twinkling lights of the grounds in the distance.

Nothing moved. For a moment he thought he'd only imagined the sound as he quietly tucked the documents back into the envelope as he rose from the chair.

The second set of French doors slowly opened, the breeze catching the drapes and billowing them out into the dark room.

CHAPTER NINE

A GUST OF cold night air stirred the papers on the desk. Even if he could reach the French doors behind him, Devlin knew he wouldn't be able to get out them without being caught. Hurriedly he stuffed the manila envelope beneath his costume jacket.

With no time to spare, he leaped behind the long thick velvet drapes as someone entered the room. He heard the doors close, felt the night breeze still.

Devlin held his breath, afraid to move a muscle for fear he would be discovered. He heard someone move to the desk, brush some of the papers on the edge. A moment later, a drawer opened, then another. Whoever it was seemed to be searching for something. His birth certificate?

He took a shallow breath, still shaken and confused by what he'd found as he listened to the intruder searching the drawers much as he had done.

He wished he had a weapon. He'd become an expert marksman thanks to Nicholas, who'd taught him to shoot. He could also fence. Neither helped at the moment, though.

Carefully, he inched to an opening between the drapes as his curiosity got the better of him. Who was searching the desk—and why? He feared what they would do when they didn't find the documents he'd taken.

In the glow of the lamp light, he saw the figure bent over one of the drawers, her black wig askew, her Snow White costume torn at the hem and a piece of what appeared to be a twig caught in the fabric.

Rory? What was *she* searching for? He willed himself to stay hidden until she found whatever she was searching for. Unless she couldn't find it because he'd already taken it.

THE ROOM WAS EERILY QUIET, putting Rory's nerves on edge. Unfortunately, it appeared that her groom had left before she got there. She'd been forced to turn on the desk lamp since she hadn't had the foresight to bring along a flashlight as he had.

What had he been looking for? The same thing she was? But why would he care about offers made on her ranch? Clearly, he wasn't royalty as his costume suggested or why did he need to be sneaking around the princess's suite?

Heart sinking, Rory realized she had no idea what kind of man Devlin Barrow was. Just as he had no idea what kind of woman she was, she thought as she finally found what she was looking for in the last drawer she searched.

The file was marked Buchanan Ranch.

Hurriedly, she pulled it out and leafed through the contents under the glow of the lamp light. Someone had written notations on each copy of the offer that had been sent to her. She tried to read them, but she was too nervous. Especially since she thought she'd just heard a sound out in the hallway.

Just take the file and run!

She realized she should have brought something to carry the contents in. The file was too thick. There was no chance she could hide it under her costume and she had that climb back down—

She jumped at a key snick in the hall door lock.

Rory froze as she watched the doorknob turn, the door begin to open.

A scream caught in her throat as she was grabbed from behind forcing her to drop the file. A hand clamped over her mouth as a strong arm circled her waist tightly and she was dragged back through the dark velvet drapery to slam against the rock-hard body of a man who whispered, "Make a sound and we're both dead."

DEVLIN HELD THE WOMAN tightly in his grasp as the door from the hallway opened. Light spilled across the floor and under the thin space between the floor and the hem of the drapes.

The door closed.

He could see part of the room through the crack in the drapes and feared that he and Rory could be seen as well.

But he didn't dare move to the side for fear that the person who'd entered would hear him.

He caught a glimpse of the princess as she headed to the bed and bathroom area of the suite. Fear made him freeze at just the sight of Evangeline. If the two of them were caught here now...

He breathed a little easier as he heard Evangeline moving around in the adjacent room. This had been one hell of night, all things considered. Not only had he found out that his mother had lied to him his entire life, he'd discovered that his father was alive. And now here he was with this woman; their paths just seemed to continue to cross.

Now why was that?

He hoped to hell the woman wasn't a cat burglar. Or worse.

Devlin could feel Rory getting restless and knew she was thinking the same thing he was—that maybe this was their chance to get out of there before the princess came out.

But before he could make a decision, Princess Evangeline appeared again, only this time in a different costume.

It took him a moment to place the new costume. Wasn't it exactly like the one Lady Monique Gray had been wearing when she'd climbed up on the stage next to Nicholas? Odd that the princess would change into a costume like that of the Black Widow.

Royalty. He didn't even want to speculate as the princess left again.

Breathing a sigh of relief, he waited a few moments before he loosened his grip on the woman in his arms.

"Wait," he whispered next to her ear. He caught the clean scent of her and was transported back to that damned shack where they'd first met. He wished he didn't know this woman—know her intimately. Being this close to her made him feel things he didn't want to feel. Especially now.

What he'd found in Evangeline's desk drawer made him feel as vulnerable as the information made him. This woman, on top of that, knocked him off kilter.

He was more than confused. He was running scared and that made him all the more anxious to get Rory away from there so he could find out who the hell she really was and how she fit in to all this.

The problem was, how the devil were they going to get out of there *together?* Because there was no way he was letting this woman get away again.

PRINCESS EVANGELINE TOOK the back way to Stanwood's
guest wing. In one hand, she gripped the master key that
would open Lady Monique Gray's suite. In the other she
carried the bag she'd retrieved from the pantry.

Her heart was pounding hard, expectation making
her limbs weak. Everything had to be just perfect for
this to work. If Broderick suspected for a moment...

She pushed the negative thoughts away as she
stopped partway down the hall, looked around and,
seeing no one, slipped the master key into the lock of
Monique's room and stepped in, feeling like a thief in
her own home.

Evangeline stood for a moment, hit with the scent
of Monique's perfume. The smell made her nauseous.
She tried not to think about her husband and Monique
together or recall other times she'd caught this particular scent on her husband.

The silence assured her that Laurencia had been
successful in detaining Lady Monique. Evangeline
flipped the light switch and blinked at the cluttered
suite. Clothes were strewn everywhere. If the woman
was planning to seduce the prince tonight, her seduction
clearly didn't include a romantic atmosphere.

After quickly cleaning up the room, lighting the candles she'd brought, setting out the drugged bottle of
bourbon—Broderick's favorite—and putting the note
next to it in a Monique-like scrawl, Evangeline waited.

She was suddenly very calm as she looked around
the dim room. She'd seen to everything, including un-
plugging the lamps, leaving the area around the bed
purposely dark.

She was ready. Slowly, she began to take off the costume a piece at a time, dropping each to leave a trail to
the bedroom that any fool could follow.

Even Broderick.

By the time she reached the bed, she was naked.

Except for the mask.

RORY COULDN'T HAVE made a sound or taken a breath if she'd wanted to. Even if she hadn't recognized the man's voice, there was no mistaking the scent of him or the solid feel of his body. The sound of footfalls had long ago died off, and yet Devlin still held her tightly against him.

His breath tickled her ear. His body, so close she could feel way too much of him. She shivered and he drew her even tighter against him as if to keep her warm. The gesture touched her. Until she reminded herself that the man was holding her captive behind the drapes of the princess's quarters—and like her, he apparently had no business here.

So what *was* he doing here? Robbing the place? The thought turned her blood to sludge. If caught, the princess would think they were both burglars, Rory thought indignantly. Not that she hadn't planned to take the contents of her file. But it was a file on *her*...

"We have to get out of here," her groom whispered finally.

She couldn't have agreed more. She just wondered where he thought they were going.

DEVLIN WAITED UNTIL he believed the coast to be clear before he moved aside the heavy drape and drew the woman out the French doors to the balcony.

The balcony was large with huge planters. He pulled her into a shadowed dark corner. From here all he could see was darkness and pine trees. Nor did he think she could be heard should she decide to start screaming.

Grabbing her arm, he spun her around to face him. "What are *you* doing here?" he whispered hoarsely.

"What are *you* doing here?"

He tightened his grip on her arm. "You first."

"I'm here because your boss is trying to force me to sell my ranch. I'd thrown the offers away. I needed copies but because of you, I had to leave them in there."

"Wouldn't it have been easier just to ask for copies?"

"You really think the princess would have given them to me?" she demanded, pulling away.

She had a point. But breaking into the princess's suite... Was the woman crazy? No crazier than he was, he realized.

Just being this close to her and not being able to touch her was pure torture. The memory of their night together haunted him. He would gladly have thrown caution to the wind and taken her in his arms again had she let him.

But there was little chance of that as she leaned against the balcony railing, glaring at him. "Your turn," she said, her hands going to her slim hips. She looked adorable as Snow White. And a little ridiculous, under the circumstances.

"If I told you, I'd have to kill you," he joked.

"Funny."

"You have no idea."

She started to step past him.

"Where do you think you're going?"

"Back inside. I have to get those copies. I'm not leaving here without them."

"You go back in there and you're risking more than your neck. You're risking *mine*."

She slipped past him so quickly Devlin didn't catch her until they were inside the suite door.

Two loud pops reverberated through the room.

"What was that?" Rory whispered.

Devlin shook his head. "Either someone is opening champagne out in the hall," he whispered, "or there were gunshots in the room next door. Either way, we're out of here."

This time she didn't argue as they hightailed it out of the suite and back to their spot on the balcony. The moon had risen higher in the night sky, filling even the shadows of the balcony, exposing their hiding place.

Devlin saw something move below them in the darkness. A man watching them. He grabbed Rory and pulled her into a kiss, turning her so the man below them could only see someone dressed in the same costume as Prince Broderick kissing some strange woman. Nothing new there.

At first Rory struggled against the kiss, but after a moment gave into it, her arms coming up to circle around his neck. He loosened his grip on her as she deepened the kiss.

His mistake. She slipped from his arms and dropped over the side of the balcony railing. All he got was a handful of fake hair as the black wig came off in his hand.

Devlin lurched to the edge of the balcony, fearful that she'd fallen to her death. In the darkness, he caught sight of his green-eyed forest sprite clambering down the trellis.

His first instinct was to leap over the edge after her, but she was almost to the ground and heading for the trees. He thought about her damned copies, which she'd risked her neck for.

"Damned woman," he muttered under his breath.

But as he started to turn to go back into the suite, he

remembered the man he'd seen watching them along the edge of the building. The man was looking after Rory.

The figure bled back into the shadows and a moment later rounded the edge of the building, heading back as if toward the ball.

With relief, Devlin saw that it was a sheriff's deputy, dressed in uniform and wearing a thin black mask.

Devlin waited until the deputy disappeared back inside. He could hear music and laughter floating up from the ballroom. Devlin had to finish what he started and yet he couldn't help but worry about Rory as he rushed back inside the suite and turned on his penlight.

The Buchanan Ranch file was on top of the desk. He scooped it up, stuffing it along with his own papers under his costume jacket.

Now how the hell was he going to get out of there?

FROM THE DARKNESS another man watched the deputy go back into the ball as what appeared to be Prince Broderick slipped back into the royal suite from the balcony.

It wasn't the first time Jules Armitage had seen the two in the same vicinity.

As he saw a strange light come on in the princess's suite, Jules debated what to do. Prince Broderick had left the ballroom earlier—not long after the princess. As far as Jules knew, neither had returned.

So if that was Prince Broderick in the royal suite, then why was he using a small flashlight?

Just as Jules's curiosity was peaked and he started to step from the shadows to alert the guards to check the suite, the light went out. The French doors opened and the man slipped out, closing the doors behind him.

To Jules's amazement, the man came to the edge of

the railing, looked down for a moment, then swung over
the rail and began to climb down the lattice.

The head of security reached for his weapon as the
man reached the ground. He'd lost his mask on the climb
down. As he turned, Jules saw that it wasn't Prince
Broderick.

It was Devlin Barrow.

Jules stayed in the dark shadows as the groom passed
by him. Finally, he would have the royal groom right
where he wanted him.

CHAPTER TEN

EVANGELINE HEARD THE snick of a key in the lock. Her heart was pounding, each breath a labor. So much was riding on her being able to pull this off tonight.

The door swung open on a soft *whoosh*. She waited, lay on the big bed, only dim candlelight flickering around her. She'd made sure he wouldn't be able to turn on a lamp. Around her, Monique's perfume scented the air, making Evangeline nauseous.

She could do this. She had no choice.

She heard the door close softly. She held her breath. If it was Broderick, he would do as the note in the hallway had instructed. When it came to other women, Broderick was accommodating.

The soft clink of crystal assured her he was now having the drink she'd left for him. The pills would take only a matter of minutes to work.

If he did as instructed… She heard the sound of him shedding his costume, and she tried to relax. He was following her orders. Only because he thought they'd come from Monique.

Evangeline tamped down her anger. She could be angry later. If the pills worked their wonder, he would be so out of it by the time he reached the bedroom, he wouldn't know she wasn't Monique until it was too late—if ever.

From behind her mask, Evangeline watched the doorway. She'd never had any interest in sex. Just as she'd never liked alcohol except for an occasional glass of wine.

For her, losing control was her greatest fear. Sex with the right man, she'd heard, could make a woman lose all control. The thought of a man having that kind of power over her terrified her—although she'd had nothing to fear with Broderick.

While Broderick's good looks had appealed to her for propagation reasons, his suave man-about-town charm had always left her cold.

But tonight she must be Monique, a tramp in heat. It would be her best acting role yet.

The doorway filled with the dark shadow of a naked man, relieving her mind that her plan was working as he stumbled and had to lean against the door jamb.

His face, like the room, was in shadow but she could imagine his smile, anticipation and excitement in his eyes. She would have liked to have seen it since she'd never had that opportunity as his wife.

Broderick had never even pretended to be madly in love with her. They both had known why he'd married her. She just hadn't realized he had never meant to impregnate her with an heir.

But after tonight, if the Fates were with her...

He staggered toward the bed, the drug giving him the appearance of being drunk. With luck he wouldn't remember anything.

As he neared the bed, she couldn't see *him* any more than he could see *her* clearly in the near darkness—just as she'd planned it. Now, if he just followed the rest of her directions and didn't speak.

He chuckled, though, as he slipped into bed wearing nothing but his mask.

RORY HAD LOOKED BACK only once, afraid Devlin was in
hot pursuit. Nothing moved in the darkness. Stanwood
cast a long black shadow over the landscape. Along the
edge of the building, she spotted a figure.

Not Devlin. But someone else. And she had the distinct impression the person was watching her.

She ran deeper into the woods, disoriented in the
darkness and the dense pine forest. Her chest ached
from running and she couldn't wait to get out of her
ridiculous costume. As she stopped and caught her
breath, she heard movement nearby. The soft rustle of
dried pine needles, the blow of her horse as the mare
snuffled some grass.

With relief, she moved toward the welcoming sound,
anxious to end this horrible night. It hadn't all been horrible, she had to admit, remembering being behind the
curtain with Devlin and kissing him.

But she hadn't gotten the copies of the offers she'd
gone to all this trouble to get. And Devlin had proved
to be less than a hero. She had no idea what he'd been
doing breaking into the princess's desk. Not only that,
he seemed to think she was again part of some conspiracy against him.

Men. No wonder she'd never found her Prince
Charming.

Through the trees, she spotted her horse and rushed
to the mare, grabbing the reins and swinging up into
the saddle. From the time she was young, she'd preferred to be in the saddle more than anywhere else. Not
much about that had changed. She felt safe, finally in
her comfort zone, as she reined the mare around and
headed for home, praying she wouldn't run into any of
the royal guards.

Rory thought that once she left the princess's property, she would put this night and Devlin Barrow behind her. But even when she reached home, had stabled the mare for the night and gone inside, locking the doors behind her, all Rory could think about was the groom.

He was probably a thief. Or worse.

And yet she couldn't believe that a man who could kiss with genuine conviction—could be a criminal.

As much as she hated it, Rory found herself charmed by her mysterious groom as she shed her Snow White costume.

DEVLIN HAD PRAYED the trellis would hold his weight. It had. He knew he wasn't thinking clearly as he headed for his cottage to change. After that, he planned to go to the stables, saddle a horse and take the copies to Rory. Something told him there was a lot more to this woman.

It concerned him that the deputy had been watching them from the shadows. Devlin could only assume the law officer had been part of ball security. He couldn't have known whom he was watching. At least Devlin hoped not. Otherwise, wouldn't the deputy have stopped Rory as she'd left? And called the guard to arrest Devlin?

Devlin felt fear snake up his spine at the thought that Rory might have been seen with him. After what Devlin had learned tonight, that information could put her in danger. It was why he had to sneak over to her ranch tonight, drop off the papers and then keep his distance until he had this mess sorted out.

His mother had been murdered. Devlin had every reason to believe he would be next—especially when Princess Evangeline found her antique desk broken into and the documents gone.

At his cottage, he changed quickly into riding

clothes. From the Buchanan Ranch file, he found the location of her ranch. No surprise, her property wasn't far from the line shack where they'd met. With the full moon, he should be able to find her.

He opened the manila folder and took out what appeared to be copies and the original documents. He knew a place he could hide the copies in the stables where they wouldn't be discovered.

The originals he would take with him. He had to get them off the Stanwood estate. It was his insurance policy—if he lived long enough to use it.

Just the thought that he was the reason his mother had been murdered filled him with fury.

At a soft tap at the door, he jumped. *Rory?* Crazy as it was, he hoped to find her when he opened the door. The woman hadn't just stolen his dreams. She'd captured his every waking thought as well as his desires.

He tried to hide his disappointment as he saw that the person huddled on his doorstep looking terrified wasn't Rory. "Anna?"

He quickly ushered her into his cottage, checking to see if she'd been followed. He saw no one in the darkness, but he knew that didn't necessarily mean anything.

"What's wrong?" he asked, seeing that she'd been crying and was now wringing her hands. She'd aged in the months since his mother's death, and he knew how it weighed on her.

"The guards are looking for me," Anna whispered. "I saw them waiting by my door and came right here."

"Guards? Why—"

She clutched his forearm. "I saw who killed your mother. I thought if I kept quiet…" She began to cry softly. "He came to your mother's house himself, dressed as a royal guard, but I recognized him. It was

Prince Broderick. He took the papers and killed your mother. I thought he didn't know I was there, that I saw. I knew no one would believe me."

"I believe you." Prince Broderick had killed his mother. But on whose orders? "You can't stay on the grounds."

But where could he take her where she would be safe? He didn't know Montana and had little resources. But there was one person. His heart told him he could trust Rory. So had her kisses.

"You will come with me. I know a place you will be safe," he told Anna. "Stay here. I will return with horses. You must trust me." For his mother's memory, he couldn't let anything happen to Anna.

When the deed was over, Evangeline freed herself of the weight of Broderick's body, shoving him aside to climb out of the bed.

She sat for a moment on the side of the bed, praying she now carried the heir she so desperately needed. The timing had been perfect, just as she'd planned it.

Now all she could do was wait. She rose, feeling exhausted, disgusted and furious with Broderick.

For a moment she considered taking the lamp base beside the table and crushing his skull with it.

Instead, she quickly dressed in the extra clothing she'd brought herself, stuffing the Monique costume under the bed for the maid to dispense with in the morning.

As she started out of the room, she made the mistake of looking back at Broderick passed out on the bed, the sheet thrown over his head, where she'd tossed it.

She took a couple of steps toward the bed, afraid

of what she would do if she didn't leave at once. If she
didn't get out of there now...

Quickly, she turned and headed for the door, surprised how late it was. The last thing she wanted to do
was get caught by Monique. This had been humiliat-
ing enough as it was.

But as she neared the door, she saw something that
made her stagger to stop. The floor was littered with
each piece of his costume. Evangeline stared down at
it, her blood thundering in her ears.

Nooooooo.

She spun and stumbled back to the bedroom doorway, all her fears hitting her in a rush. This couldn't
be happening.

She charged the bed, jerking back the sheet. Too
dark. Dropping to the floor, she found the cord for the
lamp beside the bed. The lamp flashed on, blinding her.

Getting to her feet, she finally looked at the man
lying passed out on the soiled sheets.

She had to cover her mouth to keep from screaming.
The man on the bed wasn't Broderick. The man she'd
just possibly conceived an heir with was Lord Charles
Langston, the family attorney.

Had she been the kind of woman to faint, Evangeline would have. She stumbled back under the weight
of what she'd just done, trying to make sense of what
had happened. How could her plan have gone so awry?

Where the hell was Broderick?

RORY WAS DRESSED FOR BED even though she knew she
wouldn't be able to sleep, when she heard the sound of
horses approaching. She jumped up and pulled on her
robe and, taking the shotgun from by the back door,
moved swiftly through the dark house. Since finding

out about the Peeping Tom at her bedroom window, she'd taken to locking her doors and keeping the shotgun loaded and ready.

Moonlight bathed the yard in silver. From out of the pines, two horses emerged. She recognized the horses first. The beautiful Knabstrups. She expected to see two royal soldiers astride the horses and shifted the shotgun, ready to defend herself and her property.

To her shock, Devlin Barrow swung down from the first horse, then went to help the other rider down. An older woman. He led her toward the darkened house cautiously.

Rory snapped on the porch light. Wondering what he was doing here and who the woman was, she opened the front door, still holding the shotgun.

"We need your help," Devlin said, the desperation she heard in his tone cutting straight to her heart. Maybe it was foolish to believe anyone could tell the truth from a few kisses, but she trusted him. Whatever he was hiding, he would tell her when he was ready.

At least that's what she assured herself as she put down the shotgun. "Please, come in." The woman appeared to be shivering, her face taut with fear. "Come back to the kitchen. I'll make some coffee. Or do you prefer tea?"

"Tea, please," the woman said as Rory led them to the back of the house and offered them seats at the table.

She set water to boil on the stove before turning to face the two.

"Thank you," Devlin said, his gaze locking with hers.

Rory felt the full impact of that gaze. She'd run out on him back at Stanwood. And yet he'd brought this woman here because he believed Rory would help.

"This is Anna Pickering. She was a friend of my mother's," Devlin said. "She has reason to fear for her safety at Stanwood. I didn't know where else to bring her."

Rory could see that Anna had been crying and still looked terrified. "You are safe here," Rory said, taking the older woman's hand. Anna's fear seemed to subside a little.

Devlin gave her a grateful smile. "Anna witnessed my mother's murder back in our homeland. She fears the killer knows she saw him—and can identify him."

Rory felt the jolt at heart level. She'd lost her baby sister and both of her parents so she knew the pain he must be feeling. What must it be like to have your mother murdered—and know who had done it?

"You must go to the authorities," Rory said.

"That's not possible." Devlin seemed to hesitate. "The person who Anna saw is Prince Broderick Windham, the princess's husband. Anna would never live long enough to testify against him."

Rory dropped into a chair at the table, too shocked to speak for a moment. "What can you do?"

Devlin shook his head and she saw the fury just below the surface. "While Broderick killed her, we don't know who ordered the murder. That order could have come from the king himself. Until we know…"

Rory feared what he planned to do even before he said it.

"I must go back to Stanwood," Devlin said. "Are you sure about Anna staying here? I promise I will resolve this quickly and come back. But first I have something for you."

He reached inside his jacket and withdrew a thick

file. As he handed it to her, she saw the neat lettering on the tab: Buchanan File.

Her gaze flashed to his. "You went back for this for me?" She could not have been more touched if he'd fought a dragon. "Thank you."

"I hope you won't have to use it. I will do my best to keep the prince from bothering you again, but I didn't want you coming away from the ball tonight without what you'd come there for."

She'd gotten more than she'd hoped out of the ball, as it had turned out. Her only regret was that she hadn't gotten to dance with Devlin, she realized.

"I'll put these away," Rory said, needing a minute. Getting up, she walked down the hallway to her bedroom. She was still touched that he'd done this for her, but concerned how he planned to keep the prince from bothering her again.

She laid the papers on the top of her bureau and turned, surprised to find he'd followed her. The next thing she knew, she was in his arms. It seemed so natural she couldn't have said whose idea it had been.

The kiss, though, had been his. Of all his kisses, she thought she liked this one the best. She found herself melting into his arms, never wanting this to end or his arms to let her go. Who said there were no heroes anymore?

She wanted to cry out when the kiss ended. "You're in danger, aren't you?"

"I have managed to put us all at risk," he said with remorse. "I should never have brought Anna here, but I had nowhere else to go."

"You did right. I will make sure she is safe."

His gaze caressed her face. "You are an amazing woman. I feel as if..."

"You don't know how you've lived this long without me."

He laughed. "I do feel like I know you."

She felt her face heat. He knew her *intimately*.

His gaze held hers for the longest time. "I have to go. Are you sure—"

"Anna will be fine."

He smiled at that. "It's you I was concerned about. I saw someone watching you from the shadows as you left Stanwood tonight. While I don't think he recognized us, he saw the two of us together. He saw me kiss you."

Rory thought of the tracks around her house, the wire cutters in the shrubs outside her bedroom window and shuddered. "Did you get a look at him?"

"It was a sheriff's deputy."

Rory swallowed a curse. "Don't worry about Deputy Griffin Crowley," she said calmly, although she was furious. How dare Griff spy on her and Devlin. "The deputy and I are old friends. I'm sure he was just concerned about my safety. I saw him in the ballroom. I think he saw me, too." He must have followed her outside.

Devlin didn't look reassured. "If you need me, call Stanwood and ask for Lord Nicholas. He is a friend. He will see that I get the message. In the meantime, I think it best if no one knows Anna is here."

Rory couldn't have agreed more. Devlin said goodbye to Anna, and Rory walked him to the door. She was still fuming about Griff's spying on her—and she was worried about Devlin.

"Are you sure it's safe for you to return to Stanwood?" she asked, once they were outside on the porch.

"I have no choice." He cupped her cheek and kissed her softly on the mouth, making her ache for more. "Be careful. I will come back as soon as I can."

She watched him swing up into the saddle. He seemed to hesitate, as if there was something more he wanted to say. But he didn't. He reined his horse around and, leading the other horse behind him, rode off toward Stanwood.

Rory had the strongest feeling that she should warn him not to go. She started to call after him, but felt Anna's hand on her arm.

"We will pray for his safety," Anna said, joining her.

"He *is* in danger, isn't he?"

"Devlin is like his mother, strong, determined."

"I shouldn't have let him go."

Anna chuckled. "Nothing could have stopped him. Not even you." As they stepped back into the house, the woman seemed to study her openly. "You should rest. When was the last time you ate something?"

Rory couldn't recall. She felt as if she was fighting the flu. "I'm really not hungry and I don't want you waiting on me. Please, you are my guest."

Anna patted her arm. "You must eat and I must keep busy."

JULES ARMITAGE FELT his cell phone vibrate and checked the display. Adele Brown. For a moment, the name didn't register. He'd gone back to the ballroom, hoping to see Princess Evangeline and have a word with her.

The phone vibrated again. Stepping out of the ballroom, away from the music and noise, he snapped open his phone. "Hello?"

"I know it's late, but I'm a night owl and you said to call the moment I remembered. Rory Buchanan."

"What?"

"Rory Buchanan. That's the woman who won All-around Best Cowgirl that year, the one you asked me about. I knew I'd remember."

Jules couldn't help being surprised since he'd heard that name mentioned before. Wasn't that the person who was refusing to sell to the princess? But he'd just assumed Rory was a man's name.

As he disconnected, Jules wondered what the groom had been doing with the ranch owner. Was it possible the two of them were conspiring against the princess, the landowner holding out for more money and the groom cutting himself in for some of the money?

The evidence was stacking up against Devlin Barrow, Jules thought with satisfaction. He suspected the princess would appreciate knowing all about this. At the very least, she would send the groom back to the homeland. It would serve him right. Jules didn't like how Devlin acted as if he were a noble.

As the head of security stepped back into the ballroom, he noticed that it was almost midnight. Time for the unmasking and the ball would wind down.

He just had to make sure no one got away with any of the royal silver. No small chore.

Jules looked around for the princess. At the stroke of midnight, Princess Evangeline planned to lead the unmasking. So where was she?

The blare of trumpets announced the approaching midnight hour. Still no sign of the princess. Or the prince.

The crowd stilled as the band began the countdown.

Ten.

Nine.

Eight.

The *pop, pop* could have been champagne bottles opening. No one else seemed to notice it.

Seven.

Six.

Jules moved toward the stairs, toward the direction
the sound had come from, worried that something had
happened to the princess.

Five.

Four.

The princess suddenly appeared at the top of the
stairs. A rush of expectation filled the huge room. Jules
stopped, relieved. As long as she was all right...

Three.

Two.

One.

Confetti fell from overhead like falling snow. Champagne corks popped around the room as masks came
off and the music started up again for the last dance
of the night.

The princess descended the stairs looking elegant,
her mask in her hand. As she passed him, Jules noted
that she looked paler than usual.

He wondered where the prince was and could only
imagine what had kept him from the unmasking. Not
just some woman, he thought as he glanced around the
room and noticed who else seemed to be missing.

When the princess found out who'd been sleeping
with her husband, there would be more than hell to pay.

EVANGELINE HAD BEEN to enough masked balls that she
could have sleepwalked through this part of the night.
She smiled and shook hands with guests and moved
through the crowd as if she just hadn't made love with
the royal family's barrister instead of her cheating, lying
husband.

Trying not to be too obvious, she searched the crowd

for Laurencia. Not that her companion could be held completely accountable for this fiasco, since Evangeline had orchestrated it. But something had gone wrong and Evangeline planned to know why.

She spotted Lord Nicholas. No sign of Lord Alexis. Or Lady Monique. Laurencia had been ordered to release the Black Widow from the steam room before the midnight hour. No sign of either woman. Evangeline hoped nothing had gone wrong.

What would happen when Lady Monique returned to her room to find Lord Charles passed out in her bed? Evangeline couldn't bother herself with that. The fool would no doubt think he'd slept with Monique. Clearly, that had been his intent—and Monique's—was Monique trying to make Alexis jealous? Or the prince? And where was Broderick?

Evangeline wasn't fool enough to think that her husband had disappeared from the ball without a woman being involved. But what woman?

She was shaking inside, furious and scared, a deadly mix, as she made her departure and the ball wound down. She couldn't wait to get to her suite. The guards bowed as she passed. Fumbling her key from her pocket, she managed to get the suite door open, desperately needing peace and solitude for a few moments.

The night was far from over. She had to get herself composed or—

A cool breeze skittered across the floor of the suite as the door swung open. Evangeline frowned as she stepped in, closing the door behind her. Montana was too cold this time of year for her. She missed lying on a white sand beach in some sunny clime with the rest of the aristocrats.

But her suite was never *this* cold. She glanced toward

the French doors and saw that one of them was open although she was positive she'd closed it when she'd left. Just as she was sure Broderick hadn't been back up to the suite since he'd left earlier.

Slowly, she moved toward the balcony, debating if she should call for a guard. To her relief she saw in the blinding moonlight that the balcony was empty.

Stars sparkled in the clear, cold sky. Below, guests were leaving, horses clip-clopping away as they drew carriages to where the guests could pick up their vehicles. The bright colors of the costumes and the sprinkling of lights around the grounds reminded her of all her hopes for tonight.

Evangeline turned in disgust, closing the balcony doors behind her as she stood just inside, studying the room. Someone had been here. A burglar?

The expensive artwork was where it had been when she'd left the room earlier. Her husband's expensive watch was where he'd dropped it on the side table.

Her gaze went to her desk. She'd had the antique desk brought over from the palace at home at no small expense. It was her favorite since it had belonged to more generations of Wycliffe women than she could count.

She let out a cry of horror as she saw that the bottom drawer had been pried open, the lock broken. Rage washed over her as she grabbed the drawer handle and pulled it open, already knowing what had been taken.

Her anger and horror over the marred desk turned to fear. Those papers in the wrong hands…

She slumped into her desk chair and tried to calm herself. Who had taken the documents? And what was she going to do now?

This deadly game she'd been playing was about to end. And badly, she feared.

The knock at the door startled her. "Yes?"

Jules stuck his head in. "Your Royal Highness."

"What is it, Jules?" she demanded irritably.

The head of security seemed to hesitate.

"What?" she demanded.

"It's the prince," he said, stepping in with a bow. "He's been shot. He's...dead. The deputy is demanding to see everyone downstairs."

CHAPTER ELEVEN

THE VOICES IN the dining room carried along the hallway to where Princess Evangeline had stopped.

"I was locked in the steam room!" Evangeline would recognize that whine anywhere. Lady Monique. "I could have been *killed.*"

"Don't look at me," Lord Alexis said, clearly disgruntled. "I spent the night looking for you."

Evangeline heard the suspicion in Alexis's voice. While he didn't mind betraying his mistresses, he apparently didn't like it happening to him, she thought with a smile as she continued on down the hallway.

Everyone turned as the princess entered the room and rose to curtsy or bow. Evangeline motioned them back into their seats with a dismissive wave.

"Someone locked me in the steam room tonight," Monique complained, clearly suspicious of everyone at the table.

Evangeline raised an eyebrow. "I'm so sorry. I'm sure the door must have just stuck. I'll see that it's checked at once."

"Is everyone who had access to the second floor here now?" asked a man in uniform. Evangeline vaguely remembered meeting him during the ball. She'd made a point of inviting the local law, Deputy Griffin Crowley who was apparently filling in for the Sheriff.

She glanced around the room but before she could speak, Monique said, "Where's Charles?"

"Charles?" the deputy echoed.

"Lord Charles Langston, the royal family solicitor," Evangeline said.

"Someone find him, please, and get him down here," the deputy said. "You're sure he hasn't left the property?"

"No one has come in or out the front gate since you instructed us to close it," Jules said.

"And you are?" the deputy asked.

"Jules Armitage, head of security."

The deputy nodded, then quickly dismissed Jules. "Your Royal Highness, I assume you've been told about your husband?"

"That he's dead." Evangeline didn't have to fake the trembling in her fingers as she dabbed at her eyes. "There must be some mistake."

"I'm afraid not. Your husband was found shot to death."

Evangeline raised her gaze to the deputy. "Who found him?"

"I did," Lord Alexis said. "When I was looking for Lady Gray, I stumbled across his body in the extra suite across from yours."

Evangeline couldn't hide her surprise.

"Any idea what he was doing there?" Deputy Crowley asked, no doubt seeing her surprise.

"Apparently, he had planned to meet someone there," Alexis said and shot a look at Lady Monique Gray.

"You know anything about this?" the deputy asked Monique.

"No, I told you. I was locked in the steam room the entire time. If Lady Laurencia hadn't found me and let me out…" She wiped at her own tears as she gave a trembling smile to Laurencia, who sat across from her. "Why don't you find out who locked me in there," she demanded, glaring at the people around the table.

A few moments later, Lord Charles Langston stumbled into the room. He looked hung over and appeared still half-drunk. He dropped into a chair and said, "What's this about Broderick being murdered?"

"*Now* is everyone here?" the deputy asked.

Evangeline glanced around the room. "Not quite." She'd never thought there would be an ideal time to say this, but she'd been wrong, she realized.

"Yes?" the deputy prompted.

"Prince Devlin Barrow Wycliffe isn't here."

A murmur circled the table. Evangeline gauged the surprised faces. No one looked more shocked than Lord Nicholas, the man who'd sponsored Devlin as a groom for Stanwood. Was it possible he hadn't known? That no one had known except her father and Clare Barrow? Until recently, that was.

The deputy was frowning at her. "There's another *prince* here?"

Evangeline nodded gravely. "Indeed there is. Only this one is a *royal* prince by birth."

DEVLIN HAD TIME TO THINK on the way back from Rory Buchanan's ranch. He saw everything much clearer now that he knew about his lineage.

It was no coincidence that he'd been allowed to come to the States to work as a groom on the princess's Montana estate.

Evangeline had known who he was. Which meant that when Lord Nicholas had come to her on Devlin's behalf, she had seen through the ruse at once. How she must have enjoyed letting the two men think they were deceiving her when all the time Devlin had played right into her hands.

It was Evangeline who had secreted Anna Pickering away to Montana. Devlin saw now that Anna had been the bait to get him to the States. To get him to Montana.

Her purpose, though, was still a mystery. Had she planned to get rid of him as she had his mother? While Broderick may have been the one to perform the deed, Devlin was sure the order to kill his mother had come from Princess Evangeline. Or the King, his own father.

So why was he still alive? Or had Evangeline tried to kill him that night in the meadow when Rory Buchanan had saved him?

Once Evangeline discovered the drawer broken on her desk and the papers missing, she would have to move forward whatever plan she'd concocted.

Devlin knew returning to Stanwood could be suicide. But it was the only way he could protect Anna—and now Rory. The deputy had seen both him and Rory on the second floor. Devlin was certain now that it was him Evangeline wanted. He would face her and end this.

With all his heart, he wished it a lie. If only he could convince himself that the birth certificate was a forgery. But had it been, his mother would still be alive. All these years she had protected him from the truth. So what had changed to bring this to light?

There'd been a rumor that the king wasn't well. Devlin had heard talk that Prince Broderick, while he couldn't take the throne, was next in line to rule the country.

That was reason enough for the prince and princess to want all evidence of a true prince in line for the throne to be destroyed.

And yet Devlin had found both a copy and the original of his birth certificate. The copy was now hidden in the stables. The original at Rory's ranch. What had Evangeline planned to do with them?

What hurt the most was that none of this had been necessary—his mother's murder, the deception to get him to Montana. He had no aspirations to be prince, let alone king of his country. His love was of horses, the outdoors, not politics.

He had to find a way out of this.

But first he had to know who had ordered his mother killed. Princess Evangeline? Or her father, the king?

Lost in his thoughts, at first he didn't see the soldiers. They came out of the pines, the moonlight making them ghostlike as they rode toward him.

It wasn't until they surrounded him that he saw they had their weapons drawn.

EVANGELINE STUDIED DEVLIN'S face as he came through the door and into the dining hall. He expected the worst, she thought with amusement. But even so, he looked determined to face it, reminding her of her father. *Their* father.

Devlin Barrow had their father's blue eyes and handsome features, but he'd gotten his dark hair from his mother. The combination was very pleasing. An acid drip of jealousy made her stomach queasy. How she would have liked it if Devlin Barrow had never been born.

Or that, like his mother, he was dead and buried.

But her father already suspected her of having something to do with Clare Barrow's death. If anything happened to Devlin...

She motioned the soldiers away, then rose to her feet

and curtsied to her brother. Half brother. Hating that he'd gotten the better half in both looks and gender.

"I present His Royal Highness Prince Devlin Barrow Wycliffe, son of our king," Evangeline announced.

Devlin's shocked expression alone was worth this moment, she thought. Not to mention the shocked expressions of the others around the table, including the deputy.

"Are you saying…" the deputy began.

"Devlin is my half brother. I brought him here for his protection." Evangeline held out her hand, inviting Devlin to join them. "As you might have heard, there is unrest in our homeland. Devlin's mother was murdered. My father felt it best that his only son come to live in the States, where I could make sure he was safe."

The deputy looked skeptical, but nothing like Devlin himself.

"I'm afraid this is all news to me," Devlin said. "A word, Your Royal Highness?"

"Could you give me a few moments with my… brother?" Evangeline asked. "I feared this news would come as a shock to him. I'm sure he has questions."

"*I* have questions," the deputy snapped. Just then the state police and coroner came through the door. "I want each of these people questioned separately," he said to the officers. The deputy shot a look at Evangeline. "Both of you are next. You have five minutes."

Evangeline gave Devlin a nod, then turned and headed for a private room down the hall. She knew he would follow.

DEVLIN CLOSED THE DOOR behind them. "What the hell is going on?"

The princess seemed taken aback. "How quickly you become the royal prince of the manor."

If what she'd said was true and the papers authentic, then he didn't need to be careful around her any longer and she knew it.

"Why don't we sit down," she suggested.

"Why don't you tell me what's going on?"

She waited a moment for him to sit as ordered. He didn't.

"I thought I made myself perfectly clear out there," Evangeline said finally. "But I suspect it didn't come as a complete surprise. You were the one who broke into my desk tonight, weren't you?"

All of this was coming at him too fast. "What is this about Prince Broderick being murdered?"

The princess shrugged. "I'm told he was shot and killed." She seemed to be taking her husband's death very well.

Devlin knew how the princess operated. For her to announce his lineage, she would have a very good reason. But right now, he was more interested in his mother's killer. "I want to know who killed my mother."

"Don't you already know that as well? I understand one of our housemaids is missing. Anna Pickering? Didn't she tell you that Prince Broderick killed your mother?" Evangeline smiled. "I see that she did."

Now it was finally starting to make sense. Devlin let out a humorless laugh. "You're hoping to pin Prince Broderick's murder on *me?*"

She raised an eyebrow. "You have to admit, you do have the most to gain. Everyone knows Broderick hoped to one day take the throne in my stead. He was ambitious to a fault and clearly acted on his own. It would be understandable that you would want to revenge your mother's death once Anna Pickering told you Broderick killed your mother. And with him gone, you have paved the way straight to the throne on my father's death."

Devlin shook his head. This was just as he'd feared. Just as Evangeline had feared as well. If the king recognized him as his son, then Devlin would be in direct line for throne. His mother had some noble blood. At least as much as Prince Broderick. That meant Devlin was nobility. His father hadn't been a commoner as he'd always believed.

But Evangeline would never allow him to take the throne and they both knew it. "A murderer could never take the throne."

The princess smiled. "That is true. If you killed Broderick—"

"You know I didn't kill anyone, but that's not going to stop you from trying to frame me for his murder."

"You give me more credit than I deserve," Evangeline said.

Heart sinking, Devlin remembered that he hadn't had time to get rid of the copy of the prince's costume he'd hidden in his cottage. He'd played right into the princess's hands.

"I'll swear the documents are forgeries. My mother wouldn't lie to me. What about my other birth certificate that has me the son of a commoner?"

"Destroyed, unfortunately," Evangeline said.

"My mother wouldn't have lied to me. I will swear to that."

"As if your word would carry any weight," she said, disgusted. "Your mother had no choice. She did it to protect you."

"And the king? Did he also keep it a secret to protect *me*?"

Evangeline frowned at his sarcasm. "You would have

to ask him." Her gaze seemed to soften. "I am told your mother was the love of my father's life. His father, King Roland the First, forbade it. I do believe allowing his father to force him into marrying my mother was our father's greatest regret."

Was what she was saying possible? When he'd seen his mother with that sad, faraway look in her eyes, he'd always thought it was because she missed the man she'd married and lost. Now he knew no such man had existed. And since there had been no one else in his mother's life, that could only mean that the pain he'd seen in her had been for Devlin's father, the man who had spurned her for another—and forced her to lie about her own son.

"It does not matter what happened in the past," Evangeline was saying. "You have now been acknowledged as the son of a king, a prince."

"Sorry, but I'll pass."

She laughed at that. "I would think you would be pleased to learn that you are of royal blood. The title comes with both wealth and privilege, which you have had little of in your past."

He could argue that. He'd loved growing up at the stables with freedom, the love of his mother and security—even if false. "The timing of this title you have bestowed on me is a little questionable, don't you think? Trying to kill me failed so you decided to kill two birds with one stone—so to speak—and frame me for Prince Broderick's death."

The princess looked puzzled. "Did you say someone tried to kill you?"

"As if you didn't order it."

"When was this?"

"The first night I arrived. Remember the drink I had

in your main parlor? It was drugged and I was lured into the woods where someone took a potshot at my horse."

The princess rose from her chair and rang for a drink, her expression one of fury. "This drug? It made you feel as if you were hung over? Lack of memory? Confusion? And yet full of desire?"

"So you're familiar with it," Devlin said, not bothering to hide his sarcasm.

"You remind me so much of our father."

He doubted she meant that as a compliment. A servant arrived with her drink and quickly left.

Evangeline turned with glass in hand to look at him.

"I'm familiar with the drug because of my husband," she said. "I believe he used it on women."

Devlin stared at her, hating that he felt sympathy for a woman he knew had done much worse than Broderick in her life.

"What happens now?" he asked.

"I guess that will be up to the deputy." She took a sip of the drink. He noted that her hand shook. "Unless you can produce an alibi for the time of the murder…"

Devlin had two alibis—Anna and Rory. But he could use neither. If he did, he would be risking both of their lives.

RORY WAITED FOR WORD from Devlin. News of Prince Broderick's murder swept across the county like a range fire.

"You don't think Devlin…"

Anna shook her head, but Rory wasn't convinced. She recalled how upset he'd been when he'd left. She'd waited anxiously for word. All Georgia knew was that the state police had been called in and that Deputy Crowley was busy with the investigation.

"There are lots of rumors circulating," Georgia told her. "I was scared to death you'd done the prince in."

"I never saw the man," Rory told her, but then remembered she *had* seen him in the ballroom. Worse, she'd been seen herself on the second floor balcony with a man wearing the same costume as Lord Broderick.

As the days passed and still no word from Devlin— or a visit from the deputy—Rory thought maybe Griff hadn't recognized her the night of the ball.

Apparently, from what she'd heard, he was restricting his questioning to the guests and princess since no one else had been allowed on that floor the night of the ball. Not even servants.

But the biggest news by far was that a *second* prince had been on the grounds the night of the ball. The prince was being questioned in Prince Broderick's death.

Rory waited for word from Devlin as to what was happening next door. She grew more antsy as the weather turned as it so often did this time of year. It began with rain, long dark dreary days.

As the temperature dropped, the rain turned to sleet, leaving the yard and Rory's pickup coated in ice. Finally, it began to snow with a vengeance, blanketing the ranch with a foot of the cold white stuff.

Rory had always liked snow. It signaled the end of one season and the beginning of a new one. She didn't even mind the cold mornings, taking the wagon out to feed the cattle.

But she'd sold off the cattle, and between the flu bug she couldn't get rid of, making sure Anna was safe and worrying about Devlin and what was happening with the murder investigation, she didn't have the energy to leave the house anyway. Fortunately, there wasn't much to running the ranch this time of year other than keeping the horses fed and watered.

With Prince Broderick's murder, the offers on her ranch had stopped as abruptly as they'd started. She knew she should feel relieved since Devlin had said he would take care of it. No wonder she found herself waiting for the other shoe to drop.

Had she felt better, she might have at least checked to see if any more of her fence had been cut. But she really wasn't up to that, either.

She wondered if this was delayed grief over her parents' deaths. She'd been so busy trying to save the ranch, she hadn't had time to grieve.

The weather and worry left her with a strange melancholy. If it wasn't for Anna, Rory feared she would have fallen into a deep depression. Anna had insisted on doing all the cooking. Probably after having one of Rory's meals. Now Rory was eating too much and still didn't feel all that well. Although she ached to see Devlin.

A few times over those dark and depressing weeks, she noticed tracks in her yard again. She kept the doors locked now and the curtains drawn even in daylight with Anna there. But some nights, Rory swore she could sense someone just outside. If she let her imagination run away with her, she could hear him breathing against her window pane.

Sometimes she pretended it was Devlin. That he stood out there wanting to knock, but wouldn't allow himself to.

Rory had no knowledge of the strange world he lived in. For all she knew his visa had come due and he'd been forced to return to his birth country.

And yet she sensed that he was still just miles from her. Within reach if only she could reach out to him.

"I'm worried about you," Georgia said the last time she was out to the ranch house. "Are you sure you're feeling better?" Georgia was the only person who knew about Anna. And Devlin.

"I'm fine. It's just this time of year." Winter, once it started, lasted for months in this part of Montana. This year, Rory didn't feel up to it.

"You should come in for my knitted stocking class next month," Georgia suggested. "It's a really easy pattern."

In the past, Rory would have laughed at the suggestion. It was odd. The thought of knitting suddenly had a strange appeal.

That was when Rory knew she probably needed help. Maybe she'd schedule an appointment with her doctor. Her stomach roiled. When was this flu ever going to run its course? Maybe she had an ulcer. She blamed it on nerves.

Rory only half listened as Georgia filled her in on all the Whitehorse gossip. A Texas family named Corbett had bought the old Trails West Ranch, Arlene Evans was now a grandmother—and was dating of all things, and their mutual friends Maddie Cavanaugh and Faith Bailey might both be coming back to town, possibly to stay.

"Are you sure you're all right?" Georgia asked.

She pushed away her coffee, the smell making her ill. "I'm fine."

"Maybe you should see a doctor," Georgia said before she left.

"I'm *fine,*" she'd protested and walked her friend to the door. She barely made it back inside to the bathroom before she threw up—and finally admitted that she didn't have the flu.

THE NEXT DAY, Rory called Georgia and asked her to come out. "Would you mind staying here with Anna while I go into town?"

Her friend had been happy to agree. Rory knew she could have asked Georgia to pick up what she needed as Georgia had done over the past few weeks.

But this was something Rory wanted to handle on her own. Also, she hadn't been out of the house in days and thought it might make her feel better to get out.

She knew she was being paranoid, but she had the strangest feeling she was being followed even though every time she looked back, she didn't see anyone.

At the drugstore, she purchased several pregnancy tests, again feeling as if someone was watching her. It was embarrassing enough checking out, especially in a small town where everyone knew everyone's business.

It was also the reason Rory hadn't asked Georgia to buy the tests for her.

Back at the ranch house, Anna was doing what she was always doing, cooking or cleaning, keeping busy.

Rory showed the tests to Georgia, then quickly went into the bathroom to confirm what she already had accepted.

"Oh, Rory," Georgia said as she saw Rory's face when she came out of the bathroom. "It's definite?" she whispered even though Anna was in the kitchen with the radio on and couldn't hear them.

Rory could only nod.

"I suppose I don't need to ask—"

"It's the groom's." Devlin Barrow's baby.

Georgia hugged her friend. "Oh, sweetie. You've fallen in love with your groom?"

All Rory could do was nod numbly.

"You have to tell him," she said as they sat down in the living room.

Anna had built a fire earlier when she'd gotten up. The woman seemed to feel the need to be busy, rising early each morning. The flames licked at the logs, a soft popping sound filling the room.

Rory had thought about nothing else since she'd realized she was pregnant. She hadn't needed the test. She'd known, the way women had always known.

"You have time to decide what to do," Georgia said.

Rory smiled at her friend. The decision had been made the moment she'd finally admitted she was pregnant. "I'm having this baby."

"Shouldn't you discuss this with the father first?"

"He isn't a factor in my decision," Rory said. "He can't be. He's not even a U.S. citizen. For all I know he's been sent back to his country."

"Rory—"

"I know what you're going to say."

Her friend had tears in her eyes. "It's just that I know you. I've seen you struggle the past four years trying to hold on to the ranch. Once you make your mind up about something…"

"I know it's been a losing battle," Rory said, hating that everyone had been right. Especially Griff. "It's been impossible to let go, though."

"And now with a baby…"

Her hand went to her stomach. She thought of the life growing inside her. "I'm going to sell the ranch." As hard as the words were to say, Rory knew it was the only thing she could do now.

"Are you sure?"

Rory couldn't help but laugh at her friend's expression. "All this time, you've encouraged me to consider selling and now you're worried that I'm making a mistake?"

"Not a mistake. It's just that I know what this place means to you. Won't you resent that you had to sell?"

"I want this baby," Rory said with a rueful smile. "Part of the reason I clung to the ranch was that it was all I had left of my family."

"You are going to tell him, aren't you?"

Rory nodded. "But only because he has the right to know."

"Good." Georgia sounded relieved.

"There isn't going to be a happy ending here, you know."

Georgia shrugged with a wry grin. "I can hope, can't I?" Her expression changed to one of horror. "Oh, God, what happens when Griff finds out about this?"

"Griff is the least of my problems." Rory was worried about what would happen when Devlin found out about the baby.

Anna came in with warm peanut butter cookies from the oven and a pitcher of milk.

"At least Anna will see that you eat like you're supposed to," Georgia said after Anna had left the room. "You don't think she knows, do you?"

DEVLIN HAD BECOME A PRISONER at Stanwood. He was never without guards.

"It's for your own protection," the princess had told him.

He was also not allowed to leave the country because of the murder investigation. He had little doubt that he would be arrested soon. Unless he produced an alibi for the night of the ball. He had to make sure both Rory and Anna were safe from any repercussions before he could do that.

So far the deputy had told him not to leave Montana.

So he waited for the chance to escape and return to Rory's ranch. He'd dreamed about her every night and worried about her safety and Anna's. To keep himself sane, he'd thought about Rory's ranch house with its rock fireplace, its warm rugs on the hardwood floors, its history.

When Rory had talked about her ranch, he'd heard her love for her home. He missed his home although he'd known he'd never return to Barrow Stables, but he'd thought he would return to his country. Now he knew that wouldn't be possible.

Even *with* alibis, Devlin worried the evidence was stacked against him—and his alibis were both questionable anyway, since one had been his lover—and the other was now his mother's friend, a woman presumed missing.

He no longer wanted to return to his homeland. That had become the past, one of cherished memories of his mother and nothing more. He wasn't fool enough not to realize the danger he would be in the rest of his life as the royal prince in line for the throne in his country.

Devlin had hoped to talk to Lord Nicholas. They'd had only a few words together without being interrupted. He suspected that was the princess's doing. But yesterday Nicholas had managed to get him a quick message.

"Be ready in case there is a fire on the estate," Nicholas had said.

Devlin hadn't understood his friend's meaning. But

tonight as he heard the commotion, he saw the blaze in
one of the cottages closest to the palace and knew. As
the alarm went out, Devlin saw that his guards seemed
confused as to what to do. When they finally realized
they had no choice but to leave their posts and fight the
fire, Devlin slipped out.

When he reached the stables he was none too surprised to find a horse already saddled, waiting for him.
He swung up onto the mount, thoughts of Rory driving him forward.

He rode hard, snow blowing up as his horse's hooves
churned across the frozen expanse. He breathed in the
fresh air, feeling free for the first time in weeks.

As he glanced back to make sure he hadn't been
followed, Stanwood rose out of the pines, illuminated
by the blaze of the groom's cottage. He half hoped the
whole place would go up in flames and put an end to
Stanwood.

But he knew the princess would rebuild something
even more ostentatious, cold and impersonal.

By the time Devlin reached the Buchanan Ranch it
was late. No lights burned from behind the curtains.

He hid his horse in the barn and started toward the
house, willing himself not to run although his heart
urged him to. He couldn't wait to see Rory and now he
was so close...

Through the pines, he could see the snowcapped
Bear Paw Mountains and Little Rockies rising from
the prairie floor to pierce the huge dark sky.

He suddenly missed his homeland, missed the familiar smells and foods and people. Missed his mother.
They'd worked together for years, been best friends.

Devlin had hoped to one day give her a daughter-in-
law to love as a daughter. Had hoped to give her grand-

children. That made him clench his jaw as he recalled one of his last discussions with his mother. Had she been trying to warn him?

She had encouraged him to wait for the right woman. "There is no hurry. The right one is out there. Wait for her."

Now, knowing what he did about his birth father, he knew she feared he would marry and produce an heir to the throne. She had protected him for more than thirty years. He'd been safe. As long as he didn't produce an heir before Princess Evangeline did.

He closed his eyes and cursed the king under his breath. His father. The king would have been only a prince when Devlin had been born. Was it possible his mother had been in love with Prince Roland Wycliffe? Or had the man forced himself on her?

Devlin blew out a breath, thinking of his own one-night stand with Rory. He wanted her just as desperately tonight. More so.

He warned himself that the timing was all wrong. Would always be all wrong. Now that he knew who he was.

As he neared the house, he ached at the thought of what he must do. He had to tell her the truth.

Devlin started as the door flew open. Rory ran out, barefoot, the ends of her robe flapping in the breeze. He caught her, picking her up, laughing in spite of himself, their breaths coming out in icy white puffs.

"I knew you would come," she whispered against his ear as he carried her inside and set her down.

"I would have come sooner if I could have." He touched her flushed cheek, warning himself not to kiss her. This was hard enough. "So much has happened. There's so much I need to tell you."

She pressed a finger to his lips and shook her head, then kissed him softly before she took his hand and led him through the dark house.

RORY HAD AWAKENED TO A SOUND. Instantly, she'd been afraid it was her Peeping Tom outside. But her heart had begun to pound, and she'd found herself flying out of the bed, grabbing her robe as she'd hurried to the door, knowing even before she'd opened it that it was Devlin.

They moved quietly past Anna's bedroom, the older woman snoring loudly enough to be heard even through the closed door.

Rory led him to her bedroom at the back, closing the door behind him.

"We have to talk, Rory," he said. "There is something I must tell you."

Something she must tell him, too. But not now.

Just the sight of him standing there after these many days of worrying, all she wanted was to be held in his arms.

"Please," she whispered, her gaze locking with his. She saw his eyes fill with something akin to love. Or lust. Right now it didn't matter.

He swept her up, kissing her, burying his hands in her hair as he drew her against him as if she was the first breath he'd taken in days.

He peppered her with kisses as his hands moved along her curves, a soft groan escaping his lips before he found her mouth again.

In a flurry, they kissed, tugging at clothing as if in silent assent that they wanted nothing between them tonight.

Naked, they stood clutching each other, movements slowing as their gazes touched. Rory looked into his eyes and saw the emotional war raging there. The one thing she knew for certain is that she didn't want to hear what he had to tell her. Any more than she wanted to tell him her news.

Tonight, she just wanted him. Nothing more. She kissed him, brushing her lips across his. He caught her up in his arms again and gently laid her on the bed, lowering himself beside her.

"Rory." He breathed her name like a promise. Or a curse.

She raised up on an elbow to brush his dark hair back from his forehead, just as she had done that first night.

His dark blue eyes flashed with a need as strong as breathing. He cupped her head with his hands and drew her down, his mouth capturing hers, their bodies melding in the heat of passion and this all-consuming need for each other.

CHAPTER TWELVE

AS THE SKY began to lighten, Devlin lay spent; Rory snuggled into the curve of his shoulder. He knew she wasn't asleep and hadn't been for some time.

Devlin didn't want to be the one to break the sated silence between them. He wanted to stay right there, in the big old iron bed, photos of cowboys and favorite horses on the rough walls of the old ranch house.

For weeks he'd been living in the palace, been treated like a prince. He'd hated every moment of it.

He knew what he wanted. But because of the blood that coursed through his veins, he thought it would always be denied him.

He had to tell Rory the truth. The sun would be rising soon. He had to return before he was missed. If he hadn't already been missed.

"There's something I need to tell you," she said.

"Please, let me go first." Whatever she had to say to him, he couldn't hear it. Not until she knew the truth about him.

He drew away from her, getting out of bed and pulling on his britches.

Rory sat up in the bed, looking worried. At a sound at the window, she turned quickly. He saw her expression.

"What is it?"

She shook her head. "Nothing. It's just that I had a Peeping Tom. I'm sure it's just the wind."

He glanced toward the window, thinking if anyone was out there, it would more than likely be royal soldiers come for him. But he didn't like the idea that someone had been hanging around the ranch. At least Anna was here with Rory now, although that didn't relieve his worries about either woman's safety.

"I'm sorry," Rory said. "There was something you needed to tell me."

Devlin nodded solemnly. "The night of the ball, you asked me what I was doing in the princess's desk…"

"And you said you'd have to kill me if you told me."

"What I should have said was that telling you would put your life in danger," he said. "Now your life is in danger because of me anyway and I have no choice but to tell you for your own safety." He hurried on before she could stop him. "I found a document in the bottom drawer of that desk. It was my birth certificate. My *real* birth certificate—and the reason my mother was murdered."

He expelled a breath. "I'm the son of the king, a prince, the prince in line for the throne of my country."

It took a moment for the words to register. "You're a *prince?*" Hadn't Georgia told her that there had been a *second* prince at the ball that night? Someone who was being questioned for the murder of Prince Broderick?

"I had no idea," Devlin was saying. "Even when I saw the birth certificate…" He sat down on the edge of the bed beside her. "You have to understand. I hate this."

"You're saying you have to go back and rule your country?"

"No. It's not that simple," Devlin said.

No, it wasn't simple at all. Rory thought about what she had to tell him. The words froze in her throat. If

Devlin was a prince, heir to the throne, then what did that make the baby she was carrying?

The light tap on the door made them both start.

"Yes?" Rory's voice broke as she swung out of bed and away from Devlin. She'd thought she was getting a groom, but he'd turned out to be a prince—and she was devastated by the news. Something was definitely wrong with this fairy tale.

"I have made breakfast," Anna said. "It is almost light. Devlin must return as soon as he has eaten. I have made his favorite."

Rory reached for her clothes, not surprised Anna had also heard Devlin's arrival last night. Apparently Anna also knew more about Devlin Barrow than Rory did.

"Wait, I can't leave you like this," he pleaded.

"There isn't anything else to say. You're a prince and you will be returning to your country." The irony was that she'd fallen in love with a groom and been completely content with that.

The sky was lightening. Shafts of silver filtered through the curtains. Rory dressed quickly and hurried out to the kitchen, avoiding Devlin's gaze as well as his grasp.

Anna glanced back at her; her gaze shifted to something over Rory's shoulder as Devlin followed her into the room. The older woman seemed to study the two of them. She didn't look happy.

"I need to talk to Devlin," Anna said as she slid a plate onto the table.

"I'll go check his horse," Rory said and grabbed her coat from the hook, disappearing out the back door before Devlin could stop her. Before she let the painful tears reach her eyes.

But not before she'd smelled the sausage Anna had

cooked Devlin for breakfast. She hadn't gone two feet out the back door before she was sick to her stomach.

THE THIRD TEST was also negative. Evangeline dropped the testing equipment into the trash can with a curse and gripped the sink, her fingers aching from the pressure. She had failed miserably. Her dreams of returning to her homeland with the next king were shattered.

She was alone, childless, banished to this alien country. For the first time, she let herself break down. It was early, the servants wouldn't be coming up for another hour. And she was alone, able to finally let it all come out.

Huge shuddering sobs racked her body. The pain poured out of her, years of it, until the sobs slowed and she realized she was crying for Broderick. For what could have been between a husband and wife.

Evangeline wiped her tears, pulling herself together. Broderick was a bastard. Now a dead bastard. All she had to concern herself with at present was the arrest of Devlin Barrow Wycliffe for Broderick's murder. Two birds, one stone, she thought.

She had taken care of the threat, but she had failed to produce an heir. Without an heir, all was lost. Her father would never let her return home.

The thought paralyzed her. She'd never taken her fate lying down. She'd always fought back, going after all she wanted. How could she give up now?

At thirty-six, there was little chance of remarrying now that word of Broderick's murder was out. Even with Devlin convicted of the crime, there would be those who would never believe she hadn't done it. She would be seen as a woman as despicable as Lady Monique. A Black Widow.

No noble worthy of producing an heir to the throne would want anything to do with her. Few ever had. At her age there was little chance she could produce an heir even if there had been a man willing to chance suffering the same fate as Broderick.

The husband of a princess was little more than window dressing. Evangeline suspected Broderick hadn't realized that—until he'd married her. He'd wanted more. Most men would.

The princess ignored the knock at her door. She didn't want to see anyone. Especially Laurencia. She'd made a point of avoiding the woman since she'd heard Laurencia had taken to her bed as soon as the deputy had questioned her. Apparently she felt some guilt for the prince's demise. Probably because she hadn't gotten Broderick to the right bedroom the night of the ball.

Had Broderick come to Lady Monique's room, been tricked into bedding Evangeline...

The princess pushed the thought away. Broderick was dead and she wasn't pregnant. Evangeline no longer had any interest in how she'd ended up in bed with the wrong man.

The knocking became more insistent.

Evangeline checked herself in the mirror and went to the door, looking forward to the tongue-lashing she intended to give whoever was standing there.

"Your Royal Highness." Jules Armitage quickly bowed. "I must speak with you. It is a matter of utmost urgency."

"Whatever it is—"

"You will want to hear this, Your Highness." He lowered his voice so the guards at the end of the hall didn't hear. "It concerns Devlin—*Prince* Devlin."

"You wouldn't dare speak evil of the son of the king, would you?" she demanded.

Jules met her gaze. "I serve you, Your Highness. The true heir to the throne."

Evangeline studied the little man for a moment before she stepped back and motioned him into the suite, closing the door firmly behind him.

DEVLIN STARTED AFTER RORY, but Anna stopped him. "I have to go to her. Can't you see? She's ill."

"Do you not see what is wrong with her?" Anna demanded in a hushed tone as she drew him away from the door.

"I told her about the birth certificate I found in the princess's bottom desk drawer. She is sick because of who she thinks I will become."

Anna frowned impatiently at him. "Rory carries a child. It is morning sickness that makes her ill. Trust me, I know such things."

Devlin looked toward the back door, feeling as if she'd stuck a fork in his throat. "Who is the father?" When Anna didn't answer, he glanced back at her and saw her expression. *"Me?"*

"Can you not tell by how angry she is with you?" Anna demanded.

His mind raced. Was this the news she had meant to tell him? And had changed her mind when he'd told her his news. The impact of that revelation finally hit him.

Rory was carrying his child. He thought *he'd* be sick. "Anna, she can't be pregnant. Not with *my* child. If Evangeline should find out…"

Anna shuddered, wrapping her dimpled arms around herself as if to chase off the chill. "She wants this baby."

"She can't have this baby," Devlin said and heard his

pain registered in his voice. *His* child. His child with a woman he'd fallen in love with. And yet, this baby couldn't be born. Not now that he knew whose blood ran through his veins.

"She thinks because I am the bastard prince I must return to our homeland to take the throne. She will change her mind about keeping the baby."

Anna shook her head. "She is strong and determined and in love with you. She will not give up this baby— not at any cost."

Devlin cursed under his breath. "Princess Evangeline is trying to frame me for her husband's murder." The older woman didn't seem surprised. "You and Rory are my alibi, but I can't tell the deputy about either of you—especially now. You must make her understand. If Evangeline finds out Rory is pregnant with a possible heir…"

The back door opened on a gust of cold snowy air. Rory stood silhouetted against the dawn. "Your horse is ready and I just saw the deputy's patrol car headed this way. Also I found fresh footprints outside my bedroom window."

"HAVE YOU TOLD THE DEPUTY about this?" Evangeline asked when Jules Armitage had finished.

"No, Your Highness. I wanted to speak with you first."

"And you are sure you saw both Prince Devlin and this Rory Buchanan on the second floor outside my suite?"

"Yes. I will swear to that."

She thought about the trouble Broderick had had purchasing the Buchanan Ranch. "You say they met before that night?"

"In an old line shack on your property. They were intimate, Your Highness," he said, clearly reading that was what she most wanted to know.

"Lovers?"

He nodded.

She remained still even though her insides were in turmoil. If Devlin and this ranchwoman were lovers on his first night in Montana… "Is there more?"

Jules nodded. "I believe Rory Buchanan is harboring your missing servant, Anna Pickering." He took a breath, no doubt knowing how the next news would affect the princess. "I also have reason to believe that Rory Buchanan is with child. Prince Devlin's child."

RORY WAITED BACK in the kitchen, fighting not to breathe in the sickening smell of sausage. Anna was now hidden upstairs in the attic.

"You must trust Devlin," Anna had said before going up. "He is a good man. He will make the right decision about the future."

"He's a real prince."

"Yes," Anna agreed, missing Rory's sarcasm.

Now Rory heard the slamming of a car door in front of the house. She braced herself for the worst. Footfalls on the porch, then pounding on her front door.

Let this not be about Devlin.

She stood and went to open the door to the deputy.

"You're up early," Griff said the moment he saw her dressed and wide-awake at the door.

"Griff." She glanced at her watch. "Is something—"

"Are you alone?"

She blinked as his question sunk in. "What?"

He pushed past her. "I asked if you're alone."

"Yes," she snapped. "Why would you ask?"

He was standing in the middle of her living room. The county deputy sheriff. And yet she felt an odd sense of unease.

He turned to look at her, anger in his expression. "The last time I saw you, you *weren't* alone."

She frowned. Had he seen her with Devlin earlier?

"The night of the ball," he supplied. "I saw you on the second floor balcony with a man."

"You were *spying* on me?" she demanded, going on the offense.

He wasn't fazed. "I checked. You didn't have an invitation to the party."

The smell of fried sausage unfortunately still wafted in the air. Rory tried to hold down the nausea as she faced the deputy. "Why would you care whether or not—"

"Surely you've heard. Prince Broderick Windham was murdered the night of the ball."

"What does that have to do with me?"

Griff was looking toward the kitchen. "You've already had breakfast?"

"Why? Are you hungry? I think there's some sausage left."

"I didn't come out here for breakfast," he snapped.

"Well, then, I don't understand what you're doing here." She feared she understood only too well. Devlin had gone back to Stanwood after learning that Prince Broderick Windham had killed his mother. Devlin would have told the deputy where he'd been at the time of the murder when he gave his statement, wouldn't he have? So why was Griff asking her about this?

"What were you doing at the ball?"

She stared at him. "You don't think I killed the prince, do you?"

"You said you were going to take care of your problem with your neighbors yourself."

"Not by killing some stupid prince."

"You were *there*."

Rory couldn't believe this. She didn't feel well and had to sit down. "I went to get copies of the offers made on my ranch so I could prove harassment just like you suggested."

Griff took off his Western hat to rake his fingers through his hair in obvious agitation. "I didn't think you would *break* in to get them."

"I didn't break in. I crashed a masked ball. I don't believe that's a criminal offense."

He slapped his hat back on his head. "I know what a hothead you are. You threatened me with that shotgun you keep by your back door just the other day."

"I said I was going to get my shotgun. That's not the same as threatening you with it."

"You were on the second floor where the prince was killed," Griff shouted at her.

She cringed and he lowered his voice.

"What were you doing with that man? How is it you even know him?"

So he had seen her and Devlin together. Or Devlin had told him. "I'm sure Devlin told you how it happened. As I said, I was there for the offers on my property."

"I asked how it is you knew him?"

"I don't really know him." It was her first lie. "We just crossed paths." That at least was true. And if you were a person who believed in fate...

"And the night of the ball was the first time you'd met him?"

"What does this have to do with the murder?"

"Prince Devlin Wycliffe Barrow is the number one suspect in my murder case."

Rory took the news badly. "He didn't kill anyone."

"And you know this how, since you barely know the man?"

She shook her head. All this was coming at her too fast and the smell of sausage was making her sick. "I was with him. I'm his alibi."

The moment she said it, she saw Griff's expression and knew Devlin hadn't told him. Why wouldn't Devlin have told him that he was with her and couldn't have killed Broderick?

"Why wouldn't he have mentioned that he was with you?"

"I don't know. Maybe to protect me."

"A woman he barely knows?" the deputy asked sarcastically.

"I'm telling you the truth."

"All I have is your word that you were with Prince Devlin at the time of the murder."

"My word has always been good enough before," Rory said, her anger growing. Griff had been spying on her at the ball. He knew damned well she hadn't killed anyone. He also knew she hadn't been alone on that balcony.

"You have any other guns in the house besides the shotgun?" he asked, all business now.

"You know I have my father's guns, but I keep them locked up."

"Let's see 'em."

She couldn't believe this was happening. Getting to her feet, she led him to her father's den. His gun cabinet was against the wall. She reached on top of it to take down the key. Opening the old-fashioned pine gun cabinet, she stepped back so Griff could get to the contents.

The deputy had pulled on latex gloves, she saw. Fear made her weak as she watched him rummage in the cabinet, pulling out several of her father's pistols.

He sniffed the barrel end of the .45. "When was the last time this was fired?"

She shook her head.

"I'm going to have to take this to the lab."

Rory could only stare at him. He didn't really believe she would shoot someone. This was about her turning down his marriage proposal. That and Devlin. He'd seen her with Devlin. Had he also witnessed the kiss?

She thought of Anna in the attic and prayed Griff wouldn't do something crazy like insist on searching the house. Rory was all set to demand a search warrant.

"I'm going to need you to make a statement as to your whereabouts the night of the murder."

"I can come down to the station as soon as I change."

His gaze took her in.

She was feeling a little green around the gills.

"No need. We can do it here."

She would have much preferred meeting him at the station away from the house—and Anna. But she also didn't want to make him suspicious by insisting on going into town to the sheriff's department.

She watched him bag her father's .45, then had her sign that she'd allowed him to take it. The whole thing seemed ridiculous, but she said nothing as he pulled a small tape recorder from his pocket and set it on the coffee table in front of her.

"You look pale."

"I'm fine," she said noticing the way he was looking at her. "I don't think my early breakfast agreed with me."

He looked at her as if he knew she was lying.

But there was nothing he could do about it. And she wasn't about to tell him what was really going on with her.

"Tell me everything," Griff ordered, officious again and clearly angry as he snapped on the tape recorder. His gaze locked with hers. "And I mean *everything*."

Rory had the horrible feeling that Griff knew everything already. Or at least a lot of it. Devlin had told her that the deputy appeared to have been following her the night of the ball. Did he just want to hear it from her? Then what?

Griff's cell phone rang. He cursed, checked the screen, then cursed again. "I have to take this." He shut off the tape recorder, rose and stepped out onto the porch.

Rory watched him from the window. Whatever news he was getting, Griff seemed to be upset by it. When he finished the call, he placed one.

She'd expected him to come back in when he finished. Instead, he walked to the porch railing. She saw that he was gripping the top rail, his knuckles white from the pressure.

Rory glanced toward the stairs, all her instincts telling her to get Anna out of there, and fast. But the older woman wouldn't be able to go far in the snow on foot even if she knew which way to go.

Maybe if she hid in the barn—

The front door opened and Griff came back in. She noted his face was flushed, his eyes appearing red-rimmed.

"I have backup on the way," he said in a calm voice

that belied the look in his eyes. "I know you have been harboring a criminal." He glanced toward the stairs. "Anna Pickering is wanted as an accomplice in the murder of Prince Broderick Windham. Along with providing Devlin Barrow with inflammatory information about his mother's death, she also gave him detailed information about the palace."

"Anna had nothing to do with Broderick's death and neither did Devlin," Rory snapped. "Someone is trying to frame her."

"Frame her?" The deputy snorted. "Just like someone is trying to frame Devlin Barrow? Excuse me. *Prince* Devlin Barrow Wycliffe." He must have seen her expression. "Proof has been found that implicates him as well as Anna Pickering."

Griff stepped toward the stairs and Rory instinctively moved in front of him to block his way.

He glared at her, his eyes as hard and cold as obsidian. "Either get her down here or I'll go up and drag her down and arrest you for aiding and abetting. Your choice, Ms. Buchanan."

CHAPTER THIRTEEN

AT THE SOUND of sirens, Rory went upstairs to get Anna. She knew Griff would make good his threat although Rory wasn't worried about herself, but Anna. She'd seen something in the deputy's eyes that had warned her he could be cruel to Anna to get back at Rory.

Anna and Rory waited downstairs with one of the state investigators as Griff and the others searched the house and the grounds. Rory couldn't imagine what they were looking for. Devlin? Or proof that he'd been there?

When they returned to the living room, though, Rory could tell from the deputy's displeased expression that he hadn't found what he'd hoped for.

"We're taking Anna Pickering in now," Griff said and ordered the investigators to cuff her.

"Is that really necessary?" Rory demanded. "I doubt she is capable of overpowering you since she isn't half your size."

Griff shot her a warning look, but told the man to forget the handcuffs. "I'm not through with you," he said when the others had gone out to the patrol cars. "Don't leave. I'll be back. I still need a statement from you."

Rory said nothing as she watched him go. All she could think about was that, according to Griff, Devlin would be arrested for the murder of Prince Broderick Windham. She remembered what Devlin had told her about who to call if she was in trouble.

She hurried to the phone and dialed Lord Nicholas Ashford's cell number. It rang only twice before he picked up.

"Nicholas," he answered.

Rory could hear a racket in the background. "It's Rory Buchanan. I'm—"

"I know who you are."

"They've arrested Anna Pickering as an accomplice to the prince's murder," she said quickly. "The deputy sheriff said they were going to arrest Devlin—"

"They already have," he said. "The royal guards are holding him until the deputy sheriff gets here."

She choked back a sob. "He didn't kill anyone. He was with me the whole time or Anna when Prince Broderick was killed. Surely once he tells—"

"I'm afraid that information would only put both you and Anna in more danger," Nicholas said. "You must trust me. I'm doing everything I can to help Dev. Right now he is only worried about you."

"I'm fine." She didn't take Griff's threat seriously. Even if he did arrest her for aiding and abetting alleged criminals, Rory knew once she told Judge Randall her side, he would throw the case out.

Unfortunately, the judge couldn't help Anna or Devlin, not with them both facing murder charges.

"I have to go," Nicholas said. "I'll tell Devlin you called and that you're safe."

"Tell him I…" Fortunately, Nicholas had already hung up before she had the chance to make a fool of herself.

"Your sister sent me," Charles Langston said as he glanced into Devlin's small cell block, nose wrinkled.

"The last person I need help from is my…sister or her

father's barrister," Devlin said, not bothering to get up from the cot where he sat. He was more worried about Rory and Anna than himself even though Nicholas had assured him that Anna had been taken into custody and Rory had said to tell him she was fine.

"Princess Evangeline insists," Charles said as he looked around for a place to put down his briefcase. "I'm sure you'll want to know about the evidence against you at this point."

The barrister found a stool and dragged it to the front of Devlin's cell. "Now, let's see. Motive. According to the princess's statement to the deputy sheriff, Anna Pickering had informed you before the ball that Prince Broderick had murdered your mother and had made an attempt on your life as well."

The royal attorney took a breath and continued. "Opportunity. You were seen on the second floor wearing a costume like the one Prince Broderick had worn the night of the ball. The head of security has testified as much and the costume you wore was found in your cottage. Apparently the seamstress had made copies of the original design as per the princess's request in case of any accident prior to or during the ball."

Evangeline had thought of everything, Devlin realized.

Charles looked up at him. "All that seems to be missing is the weapon. Deputies are searching the grounds as we speak. The princess is sure the gun will be found."

"I'm sure she is." Devlin got up from the cot to move to the bars, wishing he could reach through them and get his hands around the attorney's neck. "I'm sorry, other than to let me know that the princess has me right where she wants me, what is your purpose for coming here? I know it isn't to help me."

"You're wrong," Charles said indignantly. "The princess says she will ask for leniency for you to keep you from the death penalty. She also," he rushed on before Devlin could comment on that, "asked me to tell you that the head of security is in possession of evidence that you met one—" he checked his notes "—Rory Buchanan at a small cabin on your first night at Stanwood and again the night of the ball, if not on several other occasions, for the purpose of driving up the selling price of her ranch and thwarting Prince Broderick's attempts to buy said ranch."

Devlin gripped the bars. "That's a damned lie."

Charles didn't even blink. "The princess wanted me to inform you that she would be willing not to take action against said Rory Buchanan. She also would consider helping clear Anna Pickering so that she might be sent back to her homeland to be with her family."

Devlin stared at the man. "In exchange for what?"

RORY CALLED GEORGIA CRYING. "He's a prince," she blurted out the moment she heard her friend's voice.

"Rory?"

"Devlin. He's the prince. The other one. The one who's not dead."

"Sweetie, what are you talking about?"

"Devlin told me. He's going to be king. He's…" She couldn't stop crying.

"I'm coming out to the ranch. Don't move. I'll be right there."

True to her word, Georgia arrived only minutes later. By then Rory had gotten control of herself.

"Hormones," she said as she opened the door and felt herself tear up again at just the sight of her friend.

Georgia hugged her and led her over to the couch. "Now what is this about Devlin?"

"He's a prince. He found his real birth certificate. He's the son of the king and in line to the throne."

"He's that *other* prince we heard about?"

Rory nodded.

Georgia's eyes lit up. "You're in love with a prince? You're having a baby with a prince? Why are you crying?"

"I don't want to be in love with a prince. I don't want to have a prince's baby. I wanted a groom who would stay here on the ranch with me and our baby."

She'd said it. Her fairy-tale fantasy. And Devlin had gone and ruined it all by being a prince who would be a king. "He has to go back to his own country to become the king. I really don't want to be married to a king." She teared up again. "Why couldn't he just be a groom?"

Georgia laughed and took her hand. "Do you realize how many women would love to find out the man they love is a prince? I'm sure the two of you can work something out. You told him about the baby, right? Oh, Rory, you didn't. Why not?"

"I couldn't and now he's been arrested for Prince Broderick's murder. Griff saw the two of us together. I told him that Devlin couldn't have done it. That he was with me at the time of the shooting."

"He thinks you're covering for Devlin."

Rory nodded. "Anna's been taken into custody as well and charged with aiding and abetting Devlin."

"Oh, no." Georgia seemed to hesitate. "Griff doesn't know that you're pregnant yet, right?"

Rory shook her head.

"I think that's good. Sweetie, Griff seems a little too obsessed with you."

"He'll just have to accept it."

Georgia didn't look convinced. "I hope so."

"He's just jealous, but I'm afraid he'll use it against Devlin and Anna."

Georgia nodded. "I'm more afraid he'll use it against you."

"I can handle Griff."

"I hope so. Rory, you have to tell Devlin. He needs to know everything if he hopes to defend himself against these charges."

"WHAT DID PRINCE DEVLIN SAY?" Evangeline asked when Lord Charles arrived at Stanwood after coming straight from the local jail.

"He denied everything."

She smiled. "I'm not surprised."

"He asked what assurance you could give that you wouldn't go back on your word."

Evangeline laughed. Her bastard brother was no fool. He clearly had taken after their father.

"I believe he suspects you plan to use Broderick's murder as a way to get the Buchanan ranch and get rid of him and Rory Buchanan," Charles said. "He says he wants no title nor does he aspire to the throne."

"Everyone wants to be king and have all that that entails," she snapped angrily. "He will change his mind when my father dies."

Charles shrugged. "How shall I proceed?"

"Hire him a lawyer. A good one, but not too good." She waved her hand through the air. "That's all."

Evangeline waited until Charles left before she rose to pour herself a drink. She needed to take the edge off, but she never drank to excess. Control was as essential as breathing for her.

For the first time in weeks, she felt as if she finally had the situation in hand.

Turning at a sound behind her, she was shocked to find Lady Laurencia standing in the middle of the room. Had she not heard the knock? Or had the woman simply walked in without being acknowledged?

"What are you—"

"I came in as Charles left," Laurencia said.

Evangeline was taken aback by the impatience she heard in her friend and companion's tone. Nor had Lady Laurencia curtsied or greeted her as was custom.

The woman looked awful, her face puffy, eyes red.

The princess said as much, assuming this explained her friend's rude behavior.

"I just came from the doctor."

"You're ill?" This, Evangeline thought, would give her the perfect excuse to send Lady Laurencia back to their homeland— and out of her sight.

Laurencia straightened, her gaze locking with the princess's. Evangeline had only an instant to realize that something had changed in her companion.

"I'm pregnant."

Evangeline stared at her, wondering why she hadn't seen it. The weight gain, the times Laurencia had seemed weak and ill. Evangeline had thought her a malingerer.

"Pregnant?" This silly nit was having a baby out of wedlock when Evangeline had to go to extraordinary levels to attempt to get pregnant? And when had Laurencia found time to propagate as busy as the princess had kept her?

"Yes, pregnant," her companion said, her look almost challenging.

"Who is the father?" Evangeline couldn't imagine. Someone back in their homeland because, on closer observation, Laurencia appeared to be fairly far along.

"Don't you know?"

Evangeline was tired of whatever game Laurencia was playing. "Just tell me," she said with an irritated, bored sigh. "Or don't. I suppose this means you'll want to return home."

Laurencia didn't answer but walked to the window, her back to the princess. "That's up to you."

"I'll make the necessary arrangements for you to return," Evangeline said, glad to have it settled. She didn't like this Laurencia and thought it must be hormones. Otherwise the woman would have known better than to disrespect the princess, let alone to flaunt her pregnancy.

Laurencia would be useless pregnant anyway. Evangeline would find herself taking care of her companion instead of the other way around.

"You might want to reconsider," Laurencia said, smiling as she turned to face her again. "I'm carrying the next heir to the throne."

For a moment, Evangeline thought she had to have heard wrong. "You're carrying Devlin's child?"

Laurencia laughed. "Devlin? The bastard prince?" She shook her head. "No, I'm pregnant with Broderick's baby."

The floor seemed to collapse under Evangeline. She grabbed the back of a nearby chair. "You're lying."

"This from the woman who threw me at her husband?"

Evangeline would have gone for Laurencia's throat had she not felt so ill herself. "How dare you speak to me—"

"Why don't you call a guard? Or shoot me like you did Broderick. Or…we can make a deal."

Evangeline stared at her. She'd rather rip the woman's head off than make a deal with her. How long had she been playing her? Obviously for months and all the while sleeping with Evangeline's husband.

"A deal?" the princess repeated.

"You need this baby I'm carrying. The doctor confirmed it today. I'm carrying a boy."

A male heir. Isn't this what Evangeline had prayed for—for herself? And most feared that her husband would conceive some bastard with one of his whores? She just hadn't thought it would hit so close to home.

"My blood isn't quite as royal as yours, but it's noble enough on both sides of the family and Broderick's. You should be able to pass the baby off as yours."

Evangeline battled through her confusion and anger. "Are you telling me you're willing to sell me an heir to the throne?"

"You can afford it and you really can't afford to pass on my offer," Laurencia said with a chuckle. "I know too well, and just in case you're thinking what I know you are, I took out an insurance policy. If anything should happen to me or this baby… Well, I don't have to tell you how this works. You wrote the book on deception."

"Whatever made me think you were stupid? Or meek? Or loyal?"

"I *am* loyal. I'm the best friend you've ever had although you always treated me more like a servant," Lady Laurencia said as she placed her hand over her bulging belly. "I'm giving you what you always wanted. An heir to the throne."

"And what am I giving you, Lady Laurencia?"

"I WANT TO SEE THE PRISONER," Rory demanded of the dispatcher when she reached the sheriff's department.

"Neither prisoner is allowed visitors," she said. "Deputy Sheriff Griffin Crowley's orders."

"You tell Griff that I'm going to see what Judge Randall has to say about this if he doesn't—"

"Rory." Griff stuck his head out the doorway from the back of the department. "Send Ms. Buchanan back."

Rory pushed through the swinging gate and down the hallway to where Griff stood waiting for her. His glare didn't faze her. Nor did his threats. She was running on high-grade fury.

"Step into my office," he ordered, opening the door and practically shoving her inside. "I could have you arrested for coming down here, causing a disturbance and threatening me."

"Who's threatening who? If you were going to put me in jail, you would have already done it. You know the princess is behind this. Just like she was behind trying to buy me off my ranch. If you'd let me see Devlin—"

"His lawyer's in with him."

"I'll wait," Rory said, hugging her purse to her as she took a chair across the desk from Griff. "Devlin didn't kill anyone and Anna certainly had nothing at all to do with this."

"So you've said," Griff said, leaning back in his chair, his gaze intent on her.

"Had you let me give my statement, I would have told you about Devlin's alibi." No matter how she felt about Griff at the moment, she'd known him her entire life.

He would do the right thing once he understood what was going on. "I was with Devlin at the time Prince Broderick was murdered."

Griff raised an eyebrow. "You'd better tell me everything. How again do you even know Devlin Barrow?"

She told him about the night of the thunderstorm and being trapped in the line shack with Devlin.

"That was the morning I asked you to marry me," Griff said. "I thought you said you were alone?"

Rory couldn't help but look shamefaced. "It wasn't something I was proud of. I—"

"You slept with him?" Griff was on his feet, his voice raised. "You..slept...with...him?"

Rory felt all the air rush from her. "I—"

"Get out."

She stumbled to her feet. "Griff—"

"Get out."

"Let me see Devlin. Let me talk to him."

"Go home, Rory. Haven't you heard? There's a winter storm warning out. You'll be lucky to get home before the blizzard hits."

She'd heard about the storm on the radio coming into town. "Please, Griff. This isn't about you and me. Let me see him."

"No visitors are allowed."

"Don't you mean just me?" Rory demanded.

Griff looked her in the eye. "Especially *you.* At his request. He doesn't want to see you, Rory. Now go home. I'll call later to make sure you made it."

"Don't bother." She turned and left, fighting tears as she stepped out of the sheriff's department into a blizzard. The winter storm had already begun.

CHAPTER FOURTEEN

DEVLIN HEARD THE *whoosh* of the cell block door opening, followed by footfalls as the door clanged shut. If it was that royal attorney coming back with another deal...

Deputy Sheriff Griffin Crowley came to a stop in front of Devlin's cell. "I hope your accommodations are satisfactory. I know you've grown accustomed to living in a palace now that you're a prince."

Devlin ignored the man's sarcasm.

"I just spoke with Rory Buchanan," the deputy said after a moment. "She tells me she was with you at the time of the shooting."

Devlin recalled what Rory had said about Deputy Griffin Crowley being her friend, the two of them having grown up together. "It's true. We were together. We heard what I believe were two shots being fired. The sound seemed to be coming from the next room."

The deputy looked surprised. "Why didn't you tell me that when I took your statement right after the ball?"

"I was fearful for Rory's safety."

The deputy pushed back his hat. "Why is that?"

"I didn't want her involved."

"In Prince Broderick's murder?"

Devlin swore. "I told you. I didn't kill him. Deputy, I have to make bail and get out of here."

"That's not likely since you're a flight risk."

"You don't understand. I can't protect Rory if I'm locked up in here."

"That's real noble. Still, you're facing murder charges. I would think if you had an alibi…"

"I didn't mention that I was with Rory because I was afraid Princess Evangeline would find out."

"What makes it job to protect Rory from your sister?" the deputy inquired.

Devlin hesitated for only a moment. The deputy was Rory's friend. The man obviously cared about her or he wouldn't have been keeping an eye on her the night of the ball. "Rory's pregnant with my baby."

"What?" The deputy scoffed. "I thought you said the first time you were together was on that balcony at the ball—"

"We were together before that. The night of the big thunderstorm back in September."

The deputy's eyes narrowed. "At that old line shack."

How had he known about that? Rory must have told him.

"You can understand now why I'm worried about Rory and why I need your help. Please, you're Rory's friend."

"Friend? Is that what she told you? That we're just friends? We're a lot more than that." The deputy smiled and Devlin felt his stomach lurch. "I knew something was wrong with her. Pregnant. With your baby?" The deputy let out a curse as he slammed his fist into the cell door.

Blood spewed across the concrete floor as the man cursed and drew his injured hand into his mouth.

"Rory is mine," the deputy spat. "She has always been mine. Even when she was engaged to that dumb jackass Bryce. I knew it wouldn't last. All I did was make sure it ended sooner rather than later. Bryce was a fool. He would believe anything you told him."

The deputy had a faraway look in his eye now that frightened Devlin more than his earlier rage. "I waited it out, telling myself that my day would come. Just give her time. Do you know how many years I've waited? Did she tell you I asked her to marry me? Bet the two of you had a good laugh about that."

Devlin had stepped back, fearing that the deputy would open the cell door.

"And now she's pregnant with some foreigner's baby?" The deputy shook his head as if it was all too much for him. "Friends? I couldn't be friends with a woman like that. No," he said. "Rory isn't having some murdering foreigner's baby. I can tell you right now that isn't going to happen."

"I need to talk to my lawyer," Devlin said as the deputy backed away from the cell door.

If the deputy heard him, he gave no indication as he turned and stalked toward the cell block door.

The door *whooshed* open, clanging shut behind the deputy. Devlin stood, too stunned to move for a few minutes, all his fears paralyzing him to the spot.

From behind his small barred cell window, he heard the rev of an engine. In two strides, he was on the cot and looking out the window as the deputy in his patrol car sped down the street in the direction of Rory Buchanan's ranch.

Devlin jumped back over to the cell door, grabbed the bars and screamed for a guard.

"You keep that up and—"

"I will give you a million dollars if you bring me a phone."

The guard blinked. "Like you have—"

"I am Prince Devlin Barrow Wycliffe, the son of a king. Bring me a phone and I will see that you never have to work another day of your life."

The guard licked his lips and looked around the empty cell block. "I suppose it would be all right for you to make a call."

Devlin called Rory at once, but the connection was terrible. He couldn't be sure she'd heard him before the line went dead.

Panicked, he had no choice but to make the second call. Surprisingly, he had less trouble than calling Rory, who was only a few miles out of town.

"Tell him my name is Devlin Barrow Wycliffe, son of Clare Barrow. It is urgent he take my call. A matter of life and death."

King Roland Wycliffe's voice wavered only slightly as he took the phone. "Who is this?"

For a moment, Devlin was at a loss for words. "Devlin Barrow Wycliffe, son of Clare Barrow and King Roland Wycliffe the Second. I'm calling from jail in Montana. I need your help."

OVER THE WIND, Rory had barely heard the sound of the phone ringing. She'd hurried to the phone before she remembered that Griff had said he would call to make sure she'd made it home safely.

Her hand wavered over the receiver as it rang a second time and a third. Finally, she picked it up. "Hello."

"Rory, get out of there now! He's on his way—" The line popped and crackled too loudly for her to make out the rest of his words.

"Devlin?"

No answer, the interference on the line growing louder and then nothing.

"Devlin? *Devlin?*" He was gone. Worse, she feared the line had gone dead. The blizzard outside. Often the phone went out, snow taking down the lines. The power often failed as well in a storm of this magnitude.

It had been Devlin. But where had he been calling from? The jail? Or had he gotten released?

She hung up, picked up again, planning to call the jail. No dial tone. The line was dead.

She tried to remember his exact words before they'd been disconnected. *You have to get out of there.*

Out of the house?

He couldn't have meant that. Not in the middle of the worst blizzard of the year. What kind of sense did that make?

He's on his way...

The urgency she remembered in Devlin's tone more than the words had her glancing toward the front of the house.

He's on his way...

A chill rippled over her skin. She reached for her coat and truck keys, going on nothing more than faith. It had been Devlin. He'd been trying to warn her. But warn her about whom?

The wind whirled snow around her in a blinding funnel of cold white as she stepped out onto the porch. She could barely see her pickup parked only yards away. A snowdrift had formed around it. She'd pay hell getting out her road and when she reached the county road, the drifts could be even worse.

For a moment, she hesitated, the warmth of the house calling her back along with her common sense.

The urgency and fear she'd heard in the voice on the phone forced her down the steps. The snow was deep and getting deeper by the moment. She plowed through it to the pickup and jerked open the door, slipping a little on the running board as she climbed in.

Once behind the wheel, she dug her keys from her coat pocket. Her fingers trembled from the cold inside the pickup as she found the right key and stuck it into the ignition. The temperature had dropped drastically.

She thought of her parents. They'd gone off the road in a blizzard only four years before. Because of the lack of traffic on roads in this part of Montana, they'd been trapped in their car until a snowplow had discovered them.

Even with extra clothing, some food and water her mother had always carried in the winter, they'd died. Frozen to death when the temperature had plummeted, their car running out of gas after hours trapped in a snowdrift.

Going out in this weather could be suicide. But staying...

Rory turned the key in the ignition. Over the howling wind she heard a click. She tried again. The pickup had always started, even in the dead of winter. Had to be one of the battery cables again. She tried once more, then picking up the wrench she used for this particular problem, she popped the hood release and climbed out into the storm again.

Breaking through the drifts to the front of the pickup, she raised the hood, her breath coming out in white puffs, her fingers and toes already cold and aching. She couldn't wait to get the pickup going, turn on the heater and—

As she reached in with the wrench to tap the battery cable connection, she froze. The battery was gone.

DEVLIN COULDN'T BELIEVE IT when the guard came back into the cell block, this time carrying the keys.

"You have some mighty powerful friends," the guard said. "The governor himself called to say we had to let you go. I told him the deputy sheriff in charge wasn't here right now and he said I was to get my ass down here and let you out right away. So…"

Devlin waited anxiously as the guard put the key in the lock. There was a clank and the door groaned open. Devlin was out in an instant.

"I'm going to need a car. Any car. I'll pay," he said to the guard.

"Pay how much?" the guard asked warily.

"Give me the keys to whatever you've got. I'll pay you twice what it's worth. Three times as much. Just give me the damned keys and your gun."

"My gun?"

"Come on."

The guard dug out his keys and handed over his weapon, looking dazed. "The governor didn't say anything about giving you my keys or my gun."

"Where's your car parked?" Devlin asked as he tucked the pistol into his jail-issue pants and covered it with his shirttail.

"It's that old blue pickup outside the front door. It ain't worth much, but it's got four-wheel-drive and you're going to need it if you're planning to go anywhere in this storm."

The last of the guard's words were lost to Devlin as he borrowed a coat and ran out of the sheriff's department and into the storm.

The pickup was right where the guard had said it would be. The engine turned over on the first try. Devlin shifted the truck into Reverse and backed out.

He knew which way to go since he'd seen the sign to the Buchanan Ranch when he was taken from Stanwood in the patrol car.

The deputy had a head start. Worse, Devlin couldn't be sure that Rory had gotten his message. If she hadn't, she would open the door to the deputy, still believing she had nothing to fear from him.

Devlin drove through the blowing and drifting snow toward the ranch, praying he'd get there in time to save Rory. And their baby.

RORY SLAMMED THE HOOD and glanced down. The snow had drifted, obliterating all tracks. Was whoever had taken her battery still here on the property?

She had to assume so. Someone didn't want her leaving.

She moved around the side of the pickup, gauging the distance between her and the house. Her tracks had already filled in from where she'd tromped through the snow to reach the truck.

The wind swirled the snow around her in a cold, blinding whiteout. She could barely see the house let alone tell if someone was waiting for her on the porch.

Her shotgun was hanging by the back door. Her only hope was reaching the house, getting the gun—

She took an exhausting step toward the house, then another, plowing through the blowing snow. The cold seeped into her bones. Fear already had her chilled. She sought anger, hoping to fuel her for what she had to face.

She was almost to the house when she was struck by a feeling so intense she stopped to spin around, knowing she was about to come face-to-face with—

There was no one there. Just snow and cold and wind howling eerily off the eaves of the house. But the feeling that she wasn't alone was still with her, so strong it made her skin dimple with goose flesh. She stumbled as she turned and practically ran the rest of the way to the house.

The porch appeared empty as she darted up the steps, across the worn wood and grabbed open the door. The wind caught the storm door, ripped it out of her hand and slammed it against the house.

The glass shattered, tinkling into a million pieces onto the cold porch floor.

Rory had her hand on the knob of the large wooden door behind it and was shoving the front door open, stumbling in as she hurried to get the door closed and locked behind her.

She knew he was probably in the house waiting for her but she had to try to get to her shotgun. Even with the gun, she didn't have great odds since she had no idea what she was up against.

The shotgun held two shells. That meant she would have two chances. But without the weapon, she'd have no chance.

Running on adrenaline and fright, she looked down the dark hallway toward the kitchen and the back door. Even as she reached for the light switch, she knew her power line was out. Either down because of the storm or cut like her phone line.

The suffused white light from the storm bled in through the windows, ghostlike.

Rory could see the kitchen wall and the shape of the shotgun on its rack by the back door. Between her and the shotgun were the doors along the hallway.

If he was in the house, he was probably hiding in one of the rooms off the hall. Waiting to grab her as she passed. She couldn't shake the feeling that he'd been watching her for weeks. Maybe even longer. Waiting for this day.

Every fiber in her wanted to run down that hallway to the shotgun, but the wood floor was slick under the snow-coated soles of her boots, forcing her to walk.

She kept her gaze on the shotgun, all her hopes pinned on it as she walked. The only sound was the squeak of the snow beneath her boots and the blood rushing to her head. Just a few more feet.

Rory passed the first door, then the next, her nerves on edge. At the sound of a gust of wind blowing snow against the kitchen window, she jumped and had to get control of herself again.

She couldn't panic. Not yet, anyway. As she stepped into the large ranch kitchen, she couldn't hold herself in check any longer. She sprinted to the back wall, grabbed the shotgun and spun around, knowing he was there. Had been there all along.

He was.

CHAPTER FIFTEEN

DEPUTY GRIFFIN CROWLEY stood in the kitchen doorway, silhouetted against the light of the storm. "Easy, it's just me."

Rory swallowed back a scream, relief making her weak, the shotgun in her hands suddenly too heavy. She let it slump down against her thighs as she took a shaky breath.

"You scared me. I thought…" She shook her head. What had she thought? She was just so relieved that it was only Griff.

"Someone took my battery out of my pickup," she said. "My phone went dead and the power is out. I think the lines have been cut."

"Who would do that?" Griff asked.

"The Peeping Tom."

"I thought you were so sure it was one of your royal neighbors?"

Griff hadn't moved and while she couldn't see his features in the dim light of the storm, she felt a pang of disquiet. His body language seemed all wrong. So did his tone of voice.

She'd just told him that someone had taken the battery from her truck, possibly cut her phone and power lines, and it was as if he hadn't heard her. The same lack of real concern he'd shown when she'd told him about someone sneaking around her place, cutting her barbed-wire fence.

"What are you doing here, Griff?" Her voice broke.

"Don't you need me, Rory?"

"Yes, but…"

"You only need me on *your* terms, isn't that right? But I've always been here for you, Rory. When Bryce left town, I was here. I tried to help you then, but you weren't having any of it, were you, Rory?"

Her fingers tightened on the shotgun, but she tried not to make any quick movements. Devlin's urgent words on the phone. "You have to get out of there. He's on his way—"

Griff? Is that who Devlin had tried to warn her about?

"I did everything I could," Griff was saying. "I thought once you realized that you couldn't run this place without me… I figured once you knew someone had been around the place, cutting your fence—"

"You cut my fence?" Her heart slammed against her chest. She swallowed back the bile rising in her throat and tried to breathe.

Griff took a step toward her. "I just wanted you to see that you needed me."

All this time it had been Griff. The wire cutters in the shrubs outside her bedroom window—they'd been his? She had a flash of a memory of his pocketing the tool. He'd said he hadn't wanted her to see it, to protect her, but he'd been protecting himself.

A mixture of fear and revulsion threatened to drown her. She took a step back, remembering the broken shrubbery where someone had stood and looked in her bedroom window. Deputy Griffin Crowley.

She was going to be sick. Why hadn't she seen it before? Rory willed back the wave of nausea and lifted the shotgun, pointing it at him.

"What are you going to do? Shoot me?" Griffin asked. He sounded more hurt than worried.

"You've been stalking me?" Her voice cracked.

"You had to have known how I felt about you."

She shook her head.

"I asked you out after you and Bryce split up. I thought you just needed time. But it turns out you just needed a prince instead of a deputy."

"I want you to leave," she said motioning with the shotgun. "I mean it, Griff. I don't want to shoot you, but I will."

He took a step toward her. "I'm not going *anywhere*. I've waited for you and waited for you. Now I'm going to take what I should have had a long time ago."

She felt her blood turn to ice as she flipped off the safety on the shotgun and pulled the trigger.

A loud click filled the kitchen. Alarm rocketed through her. Griff had removed the shells.

He snatched the shotgun from her hands and threw it across the kitchen. The gun crashed into the cabinet, wood splintering. His palm smacked the side of her face with a stinging blow, the sound of the slap filling the silence.

She ducked as he tried to hit her again and he knocked her to her knees. His hand threaded through her long hair. She let out a scream as he dragged her across the kitchen floor and down the hallway toward her bedroom.

"Griff, no! Please!"

He stopped and spun on her. She cowered on the floor, afraid he would hit her again. Instead, he knelt next to her, jerking her head up by her hair so that their faces were only inches apart.

"I told myself you couldn't shoot me," he said, spittle and stinking breath hitting her in the face. "Rory couldn't kill me. Not the man who has loved her all these years, the man who has been here for her whenever she needed help. But I thought just to be safe, I'd take the shells out anyway. You disappointed me, Rory. And now you're going to make it up to me."

He tightened his hold on her hair and jerked her off balance. She was sliding on her back now as he dragged her down the hall to her bedroom doorway.

Rory fought to get her feet under her. Her hands clutched at the walls, the edge of the bedroom door frame, anything to keep this from happening. She had no illusions about what he planned to do to her.

Hurt her. Hurt her in the worst possible way.

"Griff, for God's sake, please. Don't do this. I'm sorry if I hurt you. I had no idea how you felt."

They had reached her bedroom. He let go of her hair to kick the door closed. The only light in the room was that coming in through the curtains from the storm.

Rory scrambled to her feet, frantically looking for something in the room that she could use as a weapon.

But Griff was on her before she could take a step. He closed one large hand around her neck and forced her down on the bed. She dug her fingers into his forearms, fighting to take the pressure off her throat as he held her down.

"Your life is in my hands," he said. "I could kill you right now."

She said nothing. Couldn't have gotten a word out with his fingers digging into her throat. She clamped her hands around his wrist and pushed as hard as she could, relieving a little of the pressure.

Her gaze locked with his. Tears filled her eyes from the pain, the horror and the realization that she'd never known this man. Or what he was capable of.

His expression changed. He loosened his hold. "Rory," he said, his voice thick with emotion. "I didn't want it to be like this. Why couldn't I have been the one you loved?"

His head jerked up as if he'd heard something. She could see him listening. She did the same, praying someone was coming. But all she heard was the wind and the sound of ice crystals pelting her bedroom window. No one would be out in this weather. By now the road was probably closed.

Griff let her go, stepping back to her closet, all the time keeping her in view as he reached in and dug around.

She glanced behind her, desperate for something she could use as a weapon. Her letter opener was on the desk on the other side of the bed.

She knew she'd never be able to get to it before Griff caught her. Even as he dug around in the closet, he was watching her, expecting her to do something. Maybe even hoping she would so he could hurt her some more.

He moved away from the closet with one of the large, worn T-shirts that she slept in. "Here, put this on. Nothing else."

She noticed his other hand was behind him as he tossed her the T-shirt. She was shaking so hard, the T-shirt slipped from her fingers.

"If you can't do it…" He took a threatening step toward her. Oh, God, what was he holding behind him?

"I can do it," she said quickly. She hadn't realized she was crying until then.

Griff reached toward her with the hand that she could see. She flinched. He swore under his breath. "Stop acting like you're afraid of me," he said as he tenderly brushed a tear from her cheek.

Rory swallowed and tried to stem the tears, but the heaving sobs boiled up from deep within her.

"Don't cry," Griff said softly. "I'm here to help you now. I'll take care of you. I can make this all go away."

His tone was so gentle, she looked up at him. Was there a chance he wasn't going to rape her? She told herself she would agree to whatever he wanted, anything, just to buy time and delay whatever he had planned for her.

She stripped out of her clothing, feeling his eyes greedily on her. Her stomach roiled with fear and repulsion as she slipped the T-shirt over her head, tucking it around her.

Griff smiled at her modesty. "Well, Rory?" he asked as he wiped at her tears, his thumb pad rough against her cheek. But it was the other hand, the one he still held behind him, that sent her terror spiraling. "What's it going to be?"

Rory tried to breathe, the weight against her heart making it next to impossible. She thought of the baby she carried and knew she would do anything to protect it.

"What do I have to do?" she asked meekly, thinking of the letter opener on her desk behind her.

"All you have to do is get rid of that foreign bastard's baby," he said, to her horror. "Don't worry. I'm going to help you."

He pulled his hand from behind him and she saw
that he held one of the wire hangers from her closet.

DEVLIN ALMOST MISSED the turnoff to the Buchanan
Ranch. Visibility in the blizzard was only a few feet
in front of the pickup and the ranch road had blown in.

He'd been busting through drifts all the way down
the county road. Now he touched his brakes as he realized he'd missed the turn. The pavement had been
warmer than the air when the storm had begun.

Now it was black ice, shiny in the old pickup's headlights. He felt the tires lose traction and begin to slide.

Fighting the wheel, he pulled it out of the slide only
to crash into a drift. The pickup spun like a top, careen-
ing off the road and into the ditch. Snow flew up over
the windshield as the pickup kept going.

When it finally came to a stop, Devlin tried to drive
it out, but the snow was too deep, the pickup bogged
down, the drift so deep the pickup would probably be
there until spring.

He had to put all his weight against the driver's side
door to push it open and then fight the snow to reach
the road.

Not much time had passed and yet he felt as if he
was moving in slow motion as he started down the
road at a run.

The deputy had a head start. He would already be
at the house. Already be with Rory. *God, don't let me
be too late.*

The wind blew the snow horizontally across the road.
If it hadn't been for the tops of the fence posts sticking
out of the drifts, Devlin wouldn't have known he was
even on a road.

He hadn't gone far when he saw the patrol car in the

ditch. Only faint indentations could be seen in the snow where the deputy had climbed out and made his way down the drifted-in road.

Through the pelting snow, Devlin caught sight of the ranch house ahead. No lights burned behind the curtains. Maybe Rory had understood his phone call before they'd been cut off. Maybe she'd gotten out in time.

All hope of that died, though, when he saw her pickup nearly buried by a drift in her front yard.

"Rory." Her name blew out in a puff of frosty air. A cry of pain and prayer.

He pulled the weapon he'd taken from the guard and slowed his pace as he neared the house. The front stairs had disappeared in the snow. He stumbled and almost fell as stepped into the deep snow only to hit his boot toe on one of the stairs beneath the snow.

Grabbing the railing, he climbed up to the porch, trying to be as quiet as possible even though the wind howled around him like a wounded animal.

No sound came from within the house as he tried the front door. Locked.

Backtracking, he made his way around to the rear, telling himself if it was locked as well, he would break in through a window, do whatever it took to get inside that house.

The back door was unlocked. He let it swing into the kitchen, his pistol ready.

An eerie silence filled the kitchen as he stepped in and closed the door behind him. He was breathing hard. He steadied his breath and his hand holding the gun as he listened.

Voices. He took a step toward the sound of Rory crying, with murder in his heart.

"Griff. No." Rory scrambled back on the bed. "You'll kill me." The desk was behind her. Just a few more inches and she would be able to reach the letter opener.

But she knew the letter opener would be useless unless Griff was within striking range. She would get only one chance. She had to make the blow count or she was dead. Griff was too close to the edge of sanity, wavering like a tightrope walker on that thin line.

Once she went for the letter opener, it would push him over, she had no doubt of that. She could only imagine what he would do to her. If she failed, she prayed he would kill her quickly.

Just the thought of the baby she carried almost killed her courage. Maybe she could talk Griff out of this. There had to be another way that she could save her baby. Firing the shotgun at him was different from stabbing the man with a letter opener. What if she froze?

Griff began to unwind the coat hanger, straightened it to a horrible point, all the time watching her. She didn't dare move, barely breathed.

His hand grabbed her ankle to pull her toward him.

Rory flung herself backward. Her hand came down on the surface of the desk. She'd underestimated where the letter opener had been. Her fingers brushed it. The cold metal skittered away.

She reared back further, her fingers closing around the blade as Griff's fingers locked on her ankle and jerked her toward him and the edge of the bed.

He was so much stronger than she was. She slid across the bed, banging her head on the edge of the desk as she was jerked toward him.

He laughed as if he'd thought she'd been clutching at the desk, reaching for something to hold on to. His attention was on her naked thighs as he parted her legs, the coat hanger scraping her inner thigh.

She sat up, letting the momentum as he dragged her toward him carry her forward. With the letter opener clutched in her fist, she barely noticed the bedroom door open.

Her arm shot out in a roundhouse swing, the blade of the letter opener catching the light from the storm, as she drove the point into the side of Deputy Griffin Crowley's neck.

Griff looked up. His fingers dug into her thigh. "You ungrateful bitch!"

A scream broke from her throat, filling the air with a high-pitched terrified cry as she felt the clothes hanger pierce her skin.

Even the sight of Devlin coming through the door seemed surreal as if she'd conjured him up out of nothing but air. She watched as if no longer part of the scene as Griff was dragged backward, the tip of the clothes hanger scraping the length of her leg as she screamed in pain and horror.

At the sound of a struggle, she scrambled wildly back on the bed, landing on the floor on the other side, pressing herself against the wall, unable to stop as if the scream had a life of its own.

The boom of the gunshot finally silenced it.

Rory clung to the wall. She could feel blood running down her legs. *The baby. Oh, God, not the baby.*

When a large, dark figure came around the end of the bed, Rory recoiled.

Not until Devlin spoke her name and knelt next to her, taking her trembling body to him, did she finally let the tears come.

CHAPTER SIXTEEN

DEVLIN RODE IN the front of the snowplow, holding Rory wrapped in a quilt. She'd stopped crying but still trembled, her eyes glazed over as if she'd seen something so terrifying it had blinded her.

He could only imagine what had happened before he'd gotten to the ranch house. Her face was bruised, her lip cut, one eye swollen shut.

As he'd wrapped her in the quilt, he'd seen the blood that had run down her leg and the bright red cut that trailed from her inner thigh to her ankle.

It had been all he could do not to put another bullet into that crazy son of a bitch lying dead on the floor.

As the hospital came into view, Devlin saw the state patrol cars waiting for them, light bars flashing.

The moment the snowplow came to a stop, one of the state troopers opened the passenger side door. From inside the emergency room, medical personnel rolled out a gurney. Within minutes, Rory was taken inside.

"I don't want to leave her," Devlin said to the state investigator.

"I'm sorry, but you have a lot of explaining to do," the trooper said.

"Just let me make sure she's going to be all right first, then I'll tell you everything."

Several of the troopers exchanged looks. "We'll go in with you."

It wasn't until Devlin was assured by the emergency room doctor that Rory's injuries were superficial that he finally let himself take a real breath.

"What about the baby?" he asked.

"She didn't lose it. But after what she's been through..."

Devlin knew it was too early to know what the emotional damage would be. Or if she still might not miscarry.

"We're going to keep her here for a few days," the doctor said.

"Can I see her?"

The doctor shook his head. "We have her lightly sedated."

"Would you tell her when she wakes up that I'll be back as soon as I can?"

The doctor nodded and glanced toward the waiting troopers. "I know Rory Buchanan. She's a strong woman. Little can keep her down."

Devlin hoped the doctor was right about that as he left the hospital with the state troopers.

IT WAS SEVERAL DAYS before Devlin was released and cleared of the two killings—one he had actually committed but only to save Rory's life and that of his child's.

His statement about Deputy Griffin Crowley was supported by what Rory had told the state investigator—and what they found in Crowley's house.

In one room, a large bulletin board was covered with surveillance-type shots of Rory. The photos had been taken from various vantage points around her ranch with a telephoto lens. All of the shots had been candid ones taken without her knowledge.

In a drawer at the deputy's house, they'd found evidence that he had spied on other residents—just not to the extent he had Rory Buchanan.

During that time, the murder investigation of Prince Broderick had also taken an unexpected turn. Lady Monique Gray had been arrested.

She had been apprehended trying to leave the country. Trace evidence of gunpowder residue had been discovered on one sleeve of her masquerade ball costume. She swore that she hadn't killed Prince Broderick, that there was a second costume like hers, but no such costume was found.

In the Black Widow's luggage, a .45 pistol had been discovered, the same one used to kill Prince Broderick. Apparently she'd shot him with his own gun. Lady Monique continued to argue her innocence, saying she'd never fired a weapon in her life and that she'd been framed.

But upon her arrest, investigations were underway in the deaths of not only her former husbands, but also some of her now-deceased lovers. Further charges were expected to be filed in other countries.

Anna Pickering had been released and allowed to return home to her country. Princess Evangeline Wycliffe Windham had no comment on Lady Monique's arrest or Anna Pickering's release. The princess was reportedly holed up in the palace, sending everyone except her best friend and companion Lady Laurencia back to their homeland. Word spread that the princess was with child.

The day Devlin was released, a free man, all he could think about was getting to Rory. That's why he hardly noticed the large black car waiting for him outside the sheriff's department until the back door opened and he saw King Roland Wycliffe waiting for him.

"A moment of your time," the king said and Devlin climbed into the back of the car next to his father.

RORY HAD BEEN HOME TWO DAYS when she heard a vehicle coming up the road. She was still jumpy, every little sound making her nervous. She hated feeling afraid. She kept the doors locked all the time and found herself always looking outside as if she feared she'd see Griffin Crowley peering in through the frosted window at her.

She no longer felt safe in her home. She feared she'd be putting bars on the window and doors just like homes in big cities and cursed Griffin Crowley to hell for making her feel this way.

At the sound of a vehicle coming up the drive, she looked out. The snowplow had been in earlier to clear the road again since the snow had continued for days now. The driver had told her that the deputy's patrol car had been removed from the ditch back up her road, that reminder at least now gone.

He'd said he just wanted to make sure she was all right and see if she needed anything. Rory thanked him and sent him on his way before going back into the house. She no longer trusted anyone who said they wanted to make sure she was all right out here alone.

The door to her bedroom was closed. She wasn't sure she could ever go in there again even though Georgia had come in with Faith Bailey and some friends and cleaned the room after the state investigators had finished.

Rory thought it might be Georgia who'd pulled up in the yard. Her friend had practically moved in over the past few days she was there so much.

But it wasn't Georgia. Rory saw Devlin climb out of the back of a large black car. She caught sight of an older man in the rear and what appeared to be armed guards in the front.

As Devlin got out and closed the door, the car pulled away, leaving him standing out front.

Rory stepped to the front door, unlocked it and, opening the door, walked out onto the porch, hugging herself against the cold and the inevitability of Devlin's visit.

She'd been expecting him to come by and tell her he would be returning to his country. That's what princes who were destined to one day be kings did. She'd warned herself of this day, dreading it and aching to see him one more time.

At just the sight of him her heart took wing. She felt tears blur her eyes and quickly brushed them away. This was the man who'd stolen her heart, given her something so precious and saved her life. If he hadn't braved the storm to get to her…

He smiled as he climbed up the steps to the porch where she stood. She was a sucker for that smile. "You look so good."

She laughed. She knew she looked pretty bad, her bruised face discolored, her black eye still swollen.

His touch had the exact effect she'd sworn she wouldn't let it have. When he reached for her, she stepped into his arms as if she was coming home instead of saying goodbye. When he kissed her, Rory told herself she was only making things worse by kissing him back.

"You're freezing," he said and led her into the house.

Once inside, they stood facing each other in the living room, suddenly both seemingly shy and tongue-tied.

"You can't stay here," he said. "At least not for a while."

"I'm not staying." Her throat tightened around the words in a stranglehold. "I'm selling the ranch."

His look brought fresh tears to her eyes. "You can't sell this place. You can't let what happened erase everything that came before it. I know how much you love this ranch, what staying on it means to you."

Rory said nothing. Even if she could have spoken without crying, she wasn't sure what she would have said.

"I want to take care of you," he said quietly. "I want to marry you and give our child a name."

"What name would that be? Barrow? Or Wycliffe?" She shook her head. "You're a prince. I'm just a cowgirl. You belong in your country. I belong in mine."

He smiled ruefully. "I'm no prince. You can attest to the fact that I'm not even a gentleman." His hand dropped to her stomach, his palm warm.

She returned his smile. "You saved my life."

"You saved mine. If I hadn't met you…" She watched as Devlin stepped to the fireplace, reached behind one of the stones and pulled out some folded light green papers.

"What are those?" she asked, stepping over to join him in front of the blazing fire. She'd built the fire hoping it would scare off her chill. It hadn't.

"It's my original birth certificate. Evangeline had it stolen from my country's archives office."

Rory gasped as he tossed the papers into the fire. The flames licked over them an instant before the paper burst into flame and disintegrated before their eyes.

"Devlin, what have you done?"

"I've burned up any proof that I am the son of King Roland Wycliffe the Second."

"But you're the *prince.* You're to be the next king of your country."

Devlin chuckled as he pulled her to him. "I never wanted to be a prince, let alone a king. I'm a groom. All I know is horses."

"But your father—"

"He and I have spoken. We are in agreement about the future. It turns out that my father is a romantic at heart. He once loved a woman with a mind of her own—"

"Your mother."

Devlin nodded. "She was pregnant with his child, but unlike me, he made the mistake of letting that woman get away from him. He's regretted it to this day. I refuse to have that kind of regret."

She shook her head. "You would give up all of that—"

"To stay here and raise our child together? I already have, Rory. The only question is whether you will have me."

Devlin took Rory in his arms. "I love you. I love our baby. Rory Buchanan, marry me."

He looked into Rory's eyes. The most beautiful green eyes he had ever seen. Like priceless jewels. Rare as the woman.

He wished his mother was still alive so she could have known Rory. He knew she would understand the power of love. All she'd ever wanted for him was to be happy.

"You would give up being a prince? Give up your homeland?"

"My home is where you are," he said as he kissed her until she finally gave him what he wanted—a breathless yes.

EPILOGUE

MOST THINGS IN that wintry part of Montana got back
to normal after that.

Rory Buchanan and Devlin Barrow were married
by the Justice of the Peace in Whitehorse. They hon-
eymooned in Hawaii, where Devlin studied to become
a U.S. citizen.

Back in Montana, there were only a few reminders
of what had happened. A former sheriff's department
guard was now driving a brand new four-wheel-drive
pickup and throwing money around like he had it.

Just before winter really set in, a son was born to
the princess in a home birth at Stanwood. Lady Laurencia was in attendance for the birth of Prince Roland
Wycliffe the Third and received a king's ransom for it.

Within weeks, Evangeline and her son had returned
to their homeland. Stanwood estate was put up for sale.
The horses had already been purchased, and were being
boarded at the Buchanan Ranch.

The palace sold much faster than anyone in town had
expected. There was speculation on who'd bought the
place and what he planned to do with it.

A huge garage sale was held that brought people
from all over the world. The furnishings were sold at
pennies on the dollar.

The biggest shock came that spring when one day

the guard house was gone—and so was the palace as if it had been carried off stone by stone.

Wasn't long after that that the rumors were proven true. The whole place, horses, acreage and all, had been given to Devlin and Rory as a wedding present by King Roland Stanwood Wycliffe the Second.

"Do you think Lady Monique really killed Prince Broderick?" Rory asked her husband one winter night when they were curled up in bed together.

"Maybe. She was capable. But I think more than likely it was Princess Evangeline."

"She got away with murder?"

Devlin pulled Rory close. "No, I'm sure the king is familiar with the way Evangeline operates. She won't be beheaded or thrown in prison. After all, she is the princess."

"But surely she won't be allowed to get away with murdering your mother or her husband."

He shook his head. "She will be a prisoner at the palace, not allowed out of her chambers except to make the appearance of being a mother to her son, the next heir to the throne." Devlin kissed the top of her head. "Don't worry. Our child is safe."

He'd known from the moment his mother had been murdered and he'd sworn he'd get justice for her that he'd never be able to return to his homeland. His heart had ached at the thought.

But that was before he'd met Rory Buchanan. Her love for this land—and him—had healed that ache. He belonged there, with Rory and their unborn child. There was no place on this earth he wanted to be other than right here in Rory's arms.

"Any regrets? You could have been married to a prince," he whispered against her hair.

She laughed softly. "I am."

* * * * *

We hope you enjoyed reading
SIERRA'S HOMECOMING
by #1 *New York Times* bestselling author
LINDA LAEL MILLER
and
MONTANA ROYALTY
by *New York Times* bestselling author
B.J. DANIELS

Both were originally **Harlequin® Series** stories!

You crave excitement!
Harlequin® Intrigue stories deal in serious
romantic suspense, keeping you on the edge
of your seat as resourceful, true-to-life women
and strong, fearless men fight for survival.

INTRIGUE

EDGE-OF-YOUR-SEAT INTRIGUE,
FEARLESS ROMANCE.

Look for six *new* romances every month from
Harlequin Intrigue!

Available wherever books and ebooks are sold.

⊕ HARLEQUIN®

I N T R I G U E

*Ranching was Angus Ketchum's first love—until
his last tour of duty shattered that dream. The wounded
ex-soldier gets his second chance when he's recruited
to go undercover to protect widowed ranch owner
Reggie Davis.*

Angus slipped through the wooden rails and waded through the cattle milling around, waiting for the gate to open with the promise of being fed on the other side.

The rider nudged his horse toward the gate and leaned down to open it. Apparently the latch stuck and refused to open. Still too far back to reach the gate first, Angus continued forward, frustrated at his slow pace.

As the horseman swung his leg over to dismount, the gelding screamed, reared and backed away so fast the rider lost his balance and fell backward into the herd of cattle.

Spooked by the horse's distress, the cattle bellowed and churned in place, too tightly packed to figure a way out of the corner they were in.

The horse reared again. Its front hooves pawed at the air then crashed to the ground.

Unable to see the downed cowboy, Angus pushed forward, slapping at the cattle, shoving them apart to make a path through their warm bodies.

Afraid the rider would be trampled by the horse or the cattle, Angus doubled his efforts. By the time he reached him, the cowboy had pushed to his feet.

The horse chose that moment to rear again, his hooves directly over the rider.

Angus broke through the herd and threw himself into the cowboy, sending them both flying toward the fence, out of striking distance of the horse's hooves and the panicking cattle.

Thankfully the ground was a soft layer of mud to cushion their landing, but the cowboy beneath Angus definitely took the full force of the fall, crushed beneath Angus's six-foot-three frame.

Immediately he rolled off the horseman. "Are you okay?" Dusk had settled in, making it hard to see.

Angus grabbed the man's shoulder and rolled him over, his fingers brushing against the soft swell of flesh beneath the jacket he wore. His hat fell off and a cascade of sandy-blond hair spilled from beneath. Blue eyes glared up at him.

The cowboy was no boy, but a woman, with curves in all the right places and an angry scowl adding to the mess of her muddy but beautiful face. "Who the hell are you, and what are you doing on my ranch?"

Don't miss HIGH COUNTRY HIDEOUT
by New York Times *bestselling author Elle James,*
available October 2015 wherever
Harlequin Intrigue® books and ebooks are sold.

www.Harlequin.com

INTRIGUE

EDGE-OF-YOUR-SEAT INTRIGUE, FEARLESS ROMANCE.

Save $1.00

on the purchase of

HIGH COUNTRY HIDEOUT

by Elle James, available September 15, 2015, or on any other Harlequin® Intrigue book.

Available wherever books are sold, including most bookstores, supermarkets, drugstores and discount stores.

Save $1.00

on the purchase of any Harlequin® Intrigue book.

Coupon valid until November 25, 2015. Redeemable at participating outlets in the U.S.A. and Canada only. Not redeemable at Barnes & Noble stores.
Limit one coupon per customer.

52613034

5 65373 00076 2   (8100)0 12094

NYTCOUP0915